THE FIFTH FORCE

QUANTUM GHOSTS TRILOGY

BOOK TWO

Libby McGugan

To Life, for living us.

Impressions of *The Eidolon,*
Quantum Ghosts Trilogy, Book 1

'This is an intriguing, opportune 'day after tomorrow' thriller…absolutely fascinating, thought-provoking and thoroughly engrossing read which, while in no hurry to shock, holds your attention right to the end.'
– Paul F. Cockburn, *The Skinny*

'Libby McGugan's first novel, *The Eidolon* is ambitious on a number of counts… Not only does McGugan successfully navigate between the occult and the scientific, but she tells a taut, tense, fast-paced thriller with a neat denouement.'
– Eric Brown, *The Guardian*

'With her debut Libby McGugan neatly manages to create a fresh new introduction in the already established science fiction genre. Blending hard science, myths and espionage into one story makes up for a series that knows no stops and you will be wanting to finish this book as soon as possible. I at least, will be hoping that this first book will be the start of an exciting new and fresh science fiction series.'
– Jasper de Joode, *the Bookplank*

'This is no run-of-the-mill thriller. The prose is riveting…each character is real and vivid. The novel is well-crafted, tautly constructed, strong and intelligent.'
– Carol Kean, *Perihelion Science Fiction*

Impressions of The Fifth Force,
Quantum Ghosts Trilogy, Book 2

'This book helped me see that truth is more than the three-sided paradigm of subject, object and abject that I had always thought. Quantum mechanics has never been so exciting and accessible to the modern mainstream reader. Suspend yourself in a world where reality is at the very core of your being. One word sums up this masterpiece: mind altering.'
– Dr Joe Willoughby, Doctor of English Literature and Para-Alpine Athlete

APPRECIATION

To those who are curious about the concepts that this world points towards – thank you for your willingness to explore; to those who asked, some many times, about when this book would be published – thank you for your patience! To Studio Roosegaarde – thank you for the inspiring cover art. To Dr Joe Willoughby for your editing and incredibly inspiring spirit; to Carol Kean for your editing, questioning and encouragement. To Yanina Goldenberg and the team at Gold Wind Publishing for your wisdom and expertise in publishing this book. And to my family for being them.

CONTENTS

PROLOGUE

A wind blew across the barren landscape, but it did not move the mist that hung above the cracked earth, nor bend the skeletons of trees that reached for something they could not remember. The frayed ends of phantom ropes lay blackened beside the trunks, obsolete. Some, at least. Others still had things to bind, but these were sheltered by the dark. Only in the pools of light that punched holes in the sky, would you find the severed ropes. That light, too fierce to face directly, scorched whatever lay beneath.

But holes can be repaired.

CHAPTER ONE

T he station bustled. Commuters moved between the shops and the platforms; blank faces, locked in their own worlds by their thoughts or their mobile phones. Light filtered in from the latticed glass roof above, spilling small squares of yellow onto the industrial dimness below. A woman's voice echoed in French, announcing the next train to arrive at Geneva, and the sound bounced between the brick arches and walls in a harsh mechanical garble.

No one noticed the unshaven, sandy-haired man who stood in the shadows next to the coffee shop, or the redheaded woman who rested against his body, her back to the crowd. She could not look at them. Like those other people, Cora Martin was shackled inside her own world, not by the irritations and frettings of everyday life but by memories that blistered her mind. The man, Robert Strong, felt the rapid rise and fall of her chest as he scanned the passers-by, and glanced down to see her eyes blank, unreachable. He didn't have to imagine what she was thinking – he already knew. He had witnessed it himself when he trespassed into Mindscape.

Mindscape. They called it a 'Mind Management Program', like some self-improvement regime. The truth was far darker. He squeezed Cora's waist, sickened as he recalled her ordeal. She now knew how it felt to be mentally raped.

And there was the other anxiety. He blindsided it as his gaze returned to the crowd, but it sat there at the edge of his mind, watching. Sooner or later he would have to look, but right now, he didn't have the stomach. He scanned the commuters. His father should have been here by now. Where was he?

He caught sight of him entering the station. Elliot Strong walked with an unremarkable gait. His whole appearance was forgettable, not so much the details – grey hair that fell to his slightly hunched shoulders, small round glasses – but rather the overall impression. It was something practised out of necessity, Robert realised, as he watched this grey man blend with the crowd. With no choice but to reinvent himself when circumstances forced him to cut ties with the people he loved in order to protect them, he had lived a shadow life, dedicating himself to physics to help him forget. As he watched the man who had been his absent father cross the station, Robert glimpsed his pain. He had dismissed it before, blinded by the blame and bitterness of abandonment. Sometimes courage goes unnoticed, but he saw it now. His father was a brave man.

Elliot's glasses masked the haunted look Robert saw in Cora, and he wondered how much of it was Mindscape and how much of it was just life. The past was gone, but it still lived in their eyes; a hollow parasite. Those eyes met Robert's for a brief moment, before Elliot walked into the bank beside the coffee shop. He emerged a few moments later, stopping at the newsagents to buy something, then headed for the ticket office, a plastic bag in his hand. Robert watched through the glass partition as he reached the front of the queue. He saw him insert his credit card into the reader, like they had discussed. Three tickets to Barcelona. Except none of them intended to go there.

"Time to go," whispered Robert as he squeezed Cora's hand, and she nodded, her eyes to the floor. They followed Elliot as he weaved through the crowd. Robert dropped a padded envelope into the mailbox containing a set of keys and a brief note to Rene Valmont, whose motorbike now sat outside Geneva station. He hoped Rene would understand, but could do nothing if he didn't.

When they reached platform eleven, the train was boarding. Cora's eyes flitted to the other passengers and Robert felt her tense as they stepped on board. "Relax," he breathed in her ear, his arm at her back. "It's okay."

She dropped her gaze as they walked between the rows of double seats, towards the back of the carriage. The rear seats were taken, but they found some not far from the connecting door, *Near an exit*, Robert found himself thinking. He scanned the other passengers – a woman with white hair and a wrinkled face, a spotty teenager secluded under a woollen beanie that bobbed in time to the tinny sound of music escaping from his headphones, a young couple in the rear seat huddled together. No one took much notice as they entered.

Cora took a seat next to the window and Elliot sat across the aisle a few seats further down, his back to Robert. He took out a writing pad and pen from the plastic bag, flipped down the small tray table from the seat in front, and began scribbling. *Maybe he's downloading his ordeal,* thought Robert. *Venting the shit-storm of a lifetime.* He glanced at the disinterested passengers, wondering if they could ever begin to guess what the grey-haired man had seen and suffered in his life, his mind; his silence. *How can realities be so wildly different when you live on the same planet?*

A balding businessman stepped onto the train, sat down beyond the partition on the other half of the carriage and turned to look out of the window. Absentmindedly his fingers reached for the curved tram-mark that ran just above his left temple, the signature of a neurosurgeon who had opened his skull at some point in the past. A beeping announced their imminent departure and the doors slid together.

The train lurched and groaned as it picked up speed, and sunlight splintered the dimness as they broke from the station. They were on their way. Robert watched his father hunched over on his writing pad, his pen poised above the paper.

"What's he writing?" whispered Cora, peering past Robert.

"I don't know," said Robert.

The city petered out into countryside and Cora leaned her head on Robert's shoulder. She closed her eyes, the circles beneath them greyer than he had seen before, even after Sarah died. She was haunted then, but now she looked like a shell. He recalled a book she read a lot when they lived together, about how to clear your mind to emptiness, but not all shades of empty are the same. The space inside her now was dark nothingness. He put his arm around her and felt the warmth of her body next to his, the feel of her breath on his chest. She was right next to him, but the void between them was a chasm. She may as well have been in another universe, given what she had lived through and what he had become. Perhaps she was. Sattva's words echoed in his mind when he had asked what he should tell her. *Nothing*, the Eidolon had said, *if you want to stay focused.*

The Eidolon. The word hung in his mind like an enigma. A name some anthropologist could have come up with to describe a form of human that had evolved beyond death, remembering those things that most people forget, each time they die. A curiosity. It was the word that now defined him.

A tingling sensation drew his eyes down. He drew breath as the substance of his left arm began fading and the fuzzy blue chequered pattern of the seat emerged where his forearm should have obscured it. His gaze darted to Cora, her eyes still closed, then to his father, still pondering his letter. He shot a glance back – the couple were still huddled together, only the tops of their heads visible over the seats. The dissolution was creeping slowly up his arm, erasing the matter that marked his existence. Panic flashed in him. Cautiously, he disentangled himself from Cora then froze as she shifted in the seat and leaned her head against the window. She frowned, but didn't open her eyes.

Hardly daring to breathe, he wrapped the right side of his jacket around his fading limb, but the material too was beginning to show hints of transparency. He got up, eyeing the other passengers who took no notice as he headed for the privacy of the connecting corridor that housed the toilet and an exit. Somewhere out of sight. He paced the small space where the train tracks flashed past beneath the gap in the floor in time to the rhythmical rattle of high-speed metal. With everything he was, which was rapidly diminishing, he tried to remember what it felt like to have a left arm. How hard could it be? He had had it his whole life. But he could not remember. All he could feel was the tingling, like a thousand tiny insects needling his flesh, and the rising panic. It squeezed at his throat as the wall became visible through his shoulder. He pushed into the toilet. The space was cramped and he caught his breath – a mixture of the stench of urine and what he saw in the mirror. His upper left chest was missing and the nothingness was encroaching on his neck, creeping like some rampant flesh-eating bug that moved too fast for pus to form. His heart was hammering against the invisible vice round his chest and he was becoming dizzy from the over-breathing. Tiny flashes appeared across his vision, and through them he saw his face shrouded in sweat. It was taking him and there was nothing he could do.

FOCUS!

The word came from somewhere. From inside his head or somewhere else, he couldn't be sure, but it felt like his mind had been slapped. It was a command. Shutting out the mirror's truth, he closed his eyes and tuned to his breath, the only thing left he could control. He let the air trickle from his mouth, slowly, evenly. He inhaled, deeper, longer this time, fighting the urge to hyperventilate and the urge to vomit from the stink in the air. Another exhalation; calmer, smoother. He felt his body begin to listen.

Hope threw a thin lifeline into the blizzard in his mind and he seized it. With each breath, he tried to surrender to the tingling, to accept it and use it. The sensation took on a new meaning – reforming instead of destroying – building him up cell by cell into the tissues and systems and muscles and vessels that allowed him to exist. His thoughts – were they his? – he couldn't tell anymore – yelled at him through the storm, *But what if you can't? What if this is it? What if...?*

He closed his eyes to the world and his mind to the fear. There was only his breathing and his imagery and the thin line of hope. Nothing else mattered.

It was only by a fraction, but the vice eased, enough to feel relief. The tingling remained but the panic was fading. Sometime after that, he didn't know how long, the stabs in his flesh ebbed away to stillness. He stood for a moment then, steeling himself, opened his eyes. The man in the mirror was unremarkable apart from the pallor of his cheeks and the beads of sweat on his brow. He looked down and saw the muscles and tendons flex as he squeezed his left fist.

Cora was awake when he sat down.

"What's wrong?" she said.

"Nothing," he replied. "I'm fine."

She frowned.

"Really," he said. "I'm okay." He glanced up as the refreshments trolley trundled towards them, pushed by a stout woman with a round face who smiled at the passengers, despite their indifference. Cora's eyes stayed on Robert.

"You hungry?" he asked. She shook her head. "Me neither," he said.

*

They disembarked at Lyon and made their way through the backstreets, stopping at a second-hand shop to pick up some clothes – a dark hooded jacket for Cora; a hooded top and a navy-blue beanie hat for Robert. They found a bedsit in Part-Dieu near the station, and booked in.

Their rooms were on the fourth floor. The wallpaper, once a yellow leaf pattern, was peeling and stained under the flickering wall light. A bass rhythm thumped from behind a closed door as they walked along the corridor.

"I need to get some rest," said Elliot as he turned the key to his room. "I'll see you in a while."

Robert opened the door to their room and held it as Cora walked inside, bolting it behind her. He crossed to the window and eased back the curtain. Yellow cranes crawled around the muddy building site below. Beyond them, train tracks ran like rusty veins to the next town. He became aware of Cora watching him and, now alone together in the stillness of the room, he felt his vulnerability surface. She moved towards him, her eyes on his as she slid the curtain closed. Standing in silence, still she did not look away. He felt the space between them change, charged with a feeling he had almost forgotten. Part of him was afraid of giving in to it, because what would happen if he did? Her fingers touched his arm softly. Still she was looking at him in silence, closer now, close enough to kiss. The air between them, laced with anticipation, mingled their breath. He couldn't remember the last time he felt like this...

In the dimness of the creeping dusk, in those moments of surrender and connection, passion and vulnerability, as though for the first time, Robert forgot what he had become.

*

The last of the day light had leaked from their window and darkness had settled in when they knocked on Elliot's door. As they stood waiting, Cora glanced at Robert and he touched her cheek with the back of his hand. He felt a connection with her he had never felt before, like a wormhole had opened up between them and only them, channelling something no one else could access or experience. It was like she knew him, she *was* him, that every part of them aligned as the one thing. His mind wandered to their intimacy, moments before. *Christ,* he thought, *who'd have thought you can get a hard-on even after you die?* He snorted. *A stiff with a stiffy.*

Cora frowned. "What?"

"Nothing," he said.

The door opened, disrupting his thoughts. They followed Elliot inside. The single bed lay undisturbed and the only light in the room came from the small desk-lamp which poured over his writing paper, pen and a passport photo. He didn't look like he had had much rest.

"We should get something to eat," said Elliot as he put on his jacket, then folded the letter and placed it inside an envelope.

"What are you writing?" asked Cora.

Elliot looked down at the letter in his hands. "It's to my wife," he said. "I don't know if she'll ever understand, but…" His voice tailed off into silence.

How could she? thought Robert.

Elliot handed her the photo. "We were a lot younger then," he said.

Robert stared at the faded image. His father's arms were wrapped around his mother's shoulders, their silent laughter frozen in time. What do you say to the person whose life went into free-fall the night you didn't come home?

Elliot let out a quiet breath. "I can barely believe that I might actually see her again." Robert handed back the photo and watched the lines round his father's eyes soften as he looked at his wife. He swallowed. "I've not allowed myself to think that thought for a very long time."

Cora placed a hand on his arm. "Let's get some food," she said.

*

They found a small café on the edge of the town. It was poorly lit and dingy, with a faint smell of stale smoke. Tables lined one side opposite the glass counter, which displayed an assortment of limp-looking sandwiches and unappetising cakes, but it was quiet. Its only customers, they took the table in the back corner, next to the toilets. Robert sat so that he could see the door, Cora with her back to it, while Elliot ordered some coffee and food at the counter.

A few moments later, the door from the kitchen swung open, wafting in a faint smell of grease, as the grey-haired waiter balanced a tray of food and coffees and set them down before them. He shuffled to his place behind the counter and began slicing a large loaf.

Elliot leaned on the table. "How long do we have?" he asked quietly.

"A few days," said Robert. "A week maybe. It should buy us some time, but you know how ORB works. They'll be operational again and stronger for it." He swigged some coffee, which tasted bitter on his tongue.

The hollow, haunted look had returned to Cora's eyes. "What about Mindscape?" she whispered.

"I don't know." Robert reached for her hand. "But you're here now. You're safe."

Elliot glanced at him but said nothing.

Staring at the food on her plate, Cora pushed it away. A sweat had broken out on her brow. "I feel sick," she said as she stood up.

"Cora?" said Robert, getting up after her.

She shook her head. "Just give me a minute." She pushed open the door into the toilet and disappeared.

Elliot leaned towards Robert as he sat down again. "Safe?" he whispered.

"It's all relative," said Robert.

"It took them years to develop Mindscape and we broke out of it. You crippled ORB with its own virus. Amos will be on the hunt. If anything, he's more dangerous now than ever."

Robert stirred some sugar into his coffee without meeting his eye.

"And as long as Cora stays with you, she's not safe."

The comment stung and Robert flashed. "You think I haven't

thought of that?"

"We need to lay low for a while," said Elliot. "Stay under the radar."

Robert shook his head. "No. We have a window of opportunity now. You said it yourself – ORB is crippled. This is our chance to move."

"Where to?" asked Elliot.

The door to the street opened and a man in a boiler suit walked in, adjusting his cap as he approached the counter.

"Look, I've been thinking…" began Elliot, but he paused, his eyes on Robert. His voice dropped to a whisper. "What's wrong?"

Robert was watching the counter. The man reached into his boiler-suit pocket and slid some notes across the counter, too many for the coffee in front of him. The waiter shot a glance at their table then shuffled into the kitchen, the door swinging shut behind him. Taking a gulp of coffee, the man removed his cap and ran his fingers over his balding head, over the curved scar that ran just above his left temple. He walked towards the toilets, his gaze fixed ahead. Robert caught the glint of something slender and silver as it slipped from the edge of his sleeve.

A needle?

The man's gaze slid to Robert as he approached. Cold, empty eyes. His fist tensed. Robert launched himself towards him as the man swiped the needle at his arm, only just missing it. Elliot was on his feet as they tumbled to the floor and the man swiped again, his emptiness turned savage. Robert's fist caught the underside of his chin and in the second it slowed him, he pinned his arms to the floor and knelt on his chest. Elliot kicked at the man's fist then stood on it, crushing it under his boot, as the syringe with its unquantified threat spun from his grip.

"Who sent you?" Fury welled inside Robert as a faint smile rose on the man's lips. Robert lunged for the syringe and held it to the man's neck, watching his smugness dissolve.

"*Who sent you?*" The point of the needle was tenting the skin in the man's neck, the blue rope of a large vein just millimetres beneath it. Beads of sweat appeared on the man's forehead as his face drained to the colour of wet clay.

"Please…" stuttered the man. "No…"

"Was it Amos?" hissed Robert. "ORB?"

The man was shaking, his wide eyes fixed on the needle pressing on his neck.

Robert's grip on the syringe tightened. He stared at the man whose fate he now held in his right hand, feeling him tremble like an animal waiting for slaughter. It would be so easy… So easy to plunge the needle into his vein and watch its liquid trickle its poison into his cells, arresting their cycles, switching him off…

But what would that make him?

"Get up," he said.

Gingerly, the man got to his feet, the needle still poised above his jugular.

"Put your hands on the counter," said Robert, grasping the back of his suit.

The man obeyed.

"Tell me who sent you."

Struggling, torn between duty and survival, the man opened his mouth to speak but nothing came out. Robert tightened his grip.

"Robert?" Cora emerged from the toilet and froze as she took in the scene. Her voice fractured his attention for only a second but enough for the man to act. He lunged along the counter, his fingers closing around the large knife beside the half-sliced loaf. In one slick spin, he hurled the blade, as Elliot pushed Robert aside and stepped into its path. Cora screamed. The man burst through the doors into the street and disappeared as Robert turned to see Elliot crumple to his knees against the counter as the knife dislodged, a dark stain oozing from his shirt.

"No, no, no…" Robert caught him as he slumped to the floor.

"Elliot!" Cora's voice cut through the fog inside Robert's head. "Oh Jesus…"

"Call an ambulance!" said Robert.

"No," said Elliot. "No ambulance. He'll only find us again. You have to go."

"We're not leaving you here," said Robert as he cradled his father's head, pushing a hand against his chest, the dark red mark creeping between his fingers.

"Robert, you have to. You have a chance – take it..." Elliot winced, pain etching his face, his skin now pasty and beaded with sweat, his breaths becoming shallower, faster, as he reached into his pocket. He pulled out the letter, staining it with his own blood. "Give this to her, if you can. Tell her... *I'm sorry*..." He blinked away tears as he struggled to focus. "I wish..."

He gasped and fell silent. Then, as though washed with a wave of peace, a lifetime of lines scored by pain and stress and fear and fighting dissolved from Elliot's face and his skin softened to the smoothness of a shroud. Mist clouded the eyes that could no longer see as Robert felt Elliot's body sag in his arms. Hot tears fell from Robert's face and a shard drove itself into his heart as Cora knelt beside them. He felt her arm round him and her lips on his forehead as he lowered his father's limp body to the floor. She reached forwards and gently closed Elliot's eyes.

Robert turned to her, clinging to her like a child, his face buried in her neck. Was this real? The shard twisting inside his chest told him it was. All that he had learned made no difference to the pain. He stayed there, afraid to let her go, trembling as he tried to process the shift in his world.

Through waves of immeasurable grief, he became aware of a sound. It began as a single chime, softly at first, growing in purity and intensity, and whether it was real or inside his head, he couldn't say, but he felt it in his heart. It was as though he could point to it with one fingertip. The light changed and he opened his eyes, peering into the space over Cora's shoulder.

A few feet away was the faint silhouette of a man who looked like his father, his features bleached by the arch-shaped swell of light behind him. He paused, glancing back at Robert, and Robert felt the pull inside him as he had done once before. His father turned to the Arch and Robert knew he felt it too, but as he moved towards it, he hesitated. The sound was changing. Another noise crept in. Discord; distorting the purity, staining the chime. Something else was forming.

An undefined fog the colour of lead, its shape only vaguely human, condensed on the air. The room was suddenly cold.

Go! Robert screamed silently but his father stood transfixed as the shadow seethed and swelled and took hold. With a sudden violence, the ghost of his father's chest arced as his head fell back. A dark tendril snaked towards him, the filament drawing the light from inside him towards itself, as though sucking the essence from his core. Whispers rose on the air, unintelligible sounds. When only the shell of his ghost remained, the whispers echoed to silence and the chime re-emerged as the fog faded to nothing.

The Arch stood alone. Its glow ebbed as the chime died away, until the light faded and went out. Then, as if it had never been, the image vanished and the tables and smoke-stained wallpaper of the ordinary café were all that there was.

Robert stared at the space, his breathing rapid and splintered from the vision.

"Robert?" Cora was holding his face, trying to reach him.

He found his focus on her, coming back to his surroundings. A faint smell of copper rose on the air, the smell of blood. His gaze fell to the corpse that had, until moments ago, been his father. Blinking through wet eyes, he took the letter and the photograph of his parents from his father's wallet then stood up. Taking Cora's hand, he made for the door, feeling the ache in his heart crystallise into ice.

*

Cora glanced back at the café, as Robert held a tight grip on her hand. His gaze was fixed on the street ahead and she almost had to run to keep up with his stride. "It feels so wrong…" she whispered. "Leaving him there…"

He squeezed her hand, his mouth a tight line. Sirens struck up their shrill clashing cries in the distance, closing in. Robert glanced back then paused as they passed a late-night pharmacy.

"Get some dark hair dye and scissors," he said as he pulled some euros from his pocket and handed them to Cora. "I can't go in like this."

She looked down at his blood-stained hands and took the money then disappeared inside.

The dark street lit up in blue flashes as the emergency vehicles raced towards them, their sirens warping as they passed. Robert turned away to face the window of the shop, pulling his beanie lower onto his forehead and stood, hands in pockets until Cora came out. He took her by the arm and steered her down a narrow side street, where the buildings rose windowless and dank on either side.

Cora pulled against him. "The station's this way," she said.

"No trains," said Robert. "It's the first place Amos will look."

"You think he sent him?"

"I know he did."

"Then we should get away from here—"

"No." He stopped, turning towards her. "We can't live like this, Cora, always looking over our shoulders. I have to end this." He smoothed away some hair that had blown across her face. "Listen, I can't risk you—"

"That's not your choice to make," she said. "It's mine." Life blazed in her eyes, the first he had seen since all this began. "I'm with you," she said.

He hesitated, uncertain of whether he could trust himself, then nodded. "Then we have to go home."

*

They did not return to the bedsit but rented a room at the edge of town for a small fee. Cora washed her hair in the bathroom sink, rubbing the black dye into her scalp. When she was done, she stood watching her reflection under the single limp light bulb as Robert snipped away her dark locks. Her eyes followed them as they fell to the floor, tokens of someone else's life, leaving her looking smaller and more vulnerable. Robert stared at the strangers in the mirror – the man with the sandy beard and the woman with the cropped dark hair. And their eyes... hers, the vividness and fragility of an orchid leaf and his, the timeless blue of a troubled ocean. Who had they become?

*

They hitched through the back roads that cut north into the countryside, in a truck carrying animal feed. The driver, whose face was weathered with sun and hard living, did not speak English, and

Robert and Cora's French was not good enough to converse, so they sat in silence as the headlights sliced the darkness of the long straight road. Moonlight blanched the petals in the flat fields on either side, and the monotonous hum of the engine masked the fog in Robert's head and the ache in his chest. He closed his eyes, numbed to his feelings. A sudden *bang!* jolted him awake as the truck swerved. The brakes screeched and whined as the driver swore in French and wrestled with the wheel to regain control. The truck chugged to a stop and Robert followed, warily, as the driver jumped out.

"Merde," said the trucker, kicking the flat tyre. He lit a cigarette and shook his head, as he followed up with a barrage of gravelly French which Robert did not understand. Then he broke into a smile, his eyes warm under his cap and wiry black hair and shrugged, as though saying, *Life. What can you do?*

They bantered as Robert worked with him to replace the tyre, neither understanding the other's words, but neither needing to. When it was done, the driver lit the stump of his cigarette and appraised Robert. He gestured a question, *where are you staying tonight?*

Robert shrugged. "I don't know."

The driver nodded then ground out his cigarette with his boot.

*

The truck drew to a stop at a farm in the middle of nowhere, where the driver led them to a large dusty barn and gave them a hunk of bread and cheese wrapped in a piece of cloth. They shook hands, Robert moved by the connection that transcends language and culture. Being human was enough.

The bales of straw piled up against the walls kept out the breeze and provided a comfortable mattress. Cora curled up beside him and drifted off to sleep, while Robert sat awake in the darkness. He reached into his pocket and pulled out the envelope smeared with dark red that contained the letter his father would never give to his mother.

Agitated, he got up. He opened the barn door where moonlight spilled onto the weeds on the track and crossed to the small woodland opposite. He looked up in the gaps between the trees, their canopies dark blots on the star-studded sky above. Gripping the letter in his fist, he felt the swell of injustice in his gut that threatened to consume him.

"What happened?"

He jumped. Standing a few feet away in the shadows, was Michael Casimir. A companion to Robert through life and now death, he had helped Robert sculpt the details of his own existence. It would be impossible to age him. His face carried the wisdom of several lifetimes in the youthfulness of his expression. Robert had missed him when he died, and he had been wary of him when they shook hands, just days after Robert had lowered his cold, still body into the ground. It had been Casimir who reminded him of the trust they once shared, Casimir who persuaded him to listen to what Sattva had to tell him, to the words that would rock Robert's world and reset everything. It seemed that they were entangled in their journeys through life and death, first in their passion for science and now in their existence as Eidolon.

"Elliot's dead," said Robert. "Amos sent someone…" The words caught in his throat.

"Robert… I'm so sorry." Casimir paused, watching him. "Although, there is no death. You know that now."

Robert let out a harsh breath. "Don't trivialise it."

Casimir walked towards him. "Your father is not defined by his body, any more than you…" he plucked a hair from Robert's head, "are defined by this hair."

"He had a life, Casimir! This letter?" Robert held up the bloodied envelope in his hand. "He wrote this to my mother just hours before he died to tell her he was alive, that he still loved her…"

Casimir watched him, compassionate, but unyielding to Robert's emotion. The kind of look a parent might give a child whose bad day at school seems to be the end of the world. All it did was piss Robert off.

"Does it mean anything to you? He was murdered! My father was murdered and I couldn't do anything—" He lashed out at the trunk of the nearest tree and felt his hand smart in the darkness.

"You know how it works now…"

"No," said Robert, pacing towards him. "This was wrong. He never made it through the Arch. I felt it call him but then it was like he was pulled away from it, by something… something dark…"

A frown was gathering on Casimir's brow.

"Look, I'm still trying to get to grips with how this whole screwy, fucked up, dead world works, Casimir, but you tell me. Was that meant to happen?"

"No," he breathed.

"It's got to be Amos," said Robert. "He has him in Mindscape, like he took Sarah. I've got to get back in there…"

"How do you plan to do that?" The voice came from his left, deep and measured. Robert turned to see Sattva walking through the trees towards them. Like Casimir, he seemed timeless. Everything about him – his gait, his voice, his presence – was unhurried, steady. He held Robert with an even stare.

Robert stopped. "I don't know, yet," he said.

"If he is in Mindscape," said Sattva, "you'll have to wait for him to reach out to you."

"I got in before," said Robert.

"But your father, Cora and Sarah – *they* connected with *you*, not the other way round."

"Then I'll find Amos," said Robert. "I'll find him and I'll kill him."

"Kill him?" said Casimir. "Did you hear anything Sattva told you about him?"

"He's still a man," said Robert.

"It's a front," said Sattva. "He is the conscious embodiment of eons of negativity bred in our own minds. *We* created *him*. Every attempt on his life only strengthens him. There is no way to kill him."

The words sunk in like acid rain. Robert slumped onto a tree stump, fuming in silent fury. A moment later, he straightened up. "Then we cut off his power," he said.

"How?" said Casimir.

Robert reached into his pocket and pulled out the smooth plastic casing of a flash-drive. He turned it over in his hand, its red coating indistinguishable in the dark. "By understanding what keeps him alive."

CHAPTER TWO

T he herder picked up a stone and threw it like he was skimming it on water, watching as it bounced into the dusty distance. There was no water here though. It would be tomorrow before he saw any. The mountainous plain guarded its liquid, confining it to the snowy peaks and the lakes. He could skim stones on the lakes too and he was good at it, better than most of his friends. This barren land was his practice ground. His goats meandered ahead, bleating and baaing, their hooves at home amongst the rocks and gravel. The soft muted tinkling of their bells was their way of speaking to him, of letting him know where they were. His stones were his way of speaking to them. It gave them direction, and they had learned to make their way towards the puffs of earth where the small rocks landed. Some of them were stragglers, and occasionally a stone in their woolly behind sent them trotting to catch up with the others.

He was lucky. He came this way four times in every year, which meant that four times a year he could cleanse his sins. Drinking the water from the lake washed them away. Sometimes he wondered if knowing this made him want to do some of the things he thought about. He sat on a rock and ate some tsampa. Overhead the black-headed ibis began their journey south.

When he got to the lake the next day, the sun glinted on its mirror surface and beyond, the mountain rose from the dusty earth; a temple to the sky. There were more pilgrims there than he had seen before, even in the height of summer. They were gathered around its shores, some bathing, some in prostration, some sitting in meditation, some talking. They lit candles and burned incense and erected prayer flags. Perhaps he would sell some of his goats here.

He wandered across the plain towards the growing swell of people, amused by how many there were. *There must have been a lot of sins this year*, he thought. His goats began nibbling at tufts of green sprouting from between the rocks, ignoring the people who came and went around them. They were happy enough, so he decided to let them be for a while.

He sat down at the edge of the lake, next to a man with deeply etched lines on his face, who beamed a toothless grin. The herder smiled in return and leaned forwards to drink from the lake. He could feel it trickling down inside, into the dark parts of his body where his sins lived, and he felt them wash away. It always felt good to be cleansed. But as he drank, the chatter of the crowd faded to silence, and it made him look up. Something was changing. People were getting to their feet, one by one, facing the place where the sun would set. The only sound became the whisper of a breeze. It picked up from the west, billowing their prayer flags and their colourful robes as the current billows the coral on the ocean bed. One by one, they closed their eyes as it touched their skin. The herder stood up and turned to face it, feeling it wash through him. Something he had not felt before.

"What is it?" he asked, his voice hushed in reverence.

The lines around the old man's eyes deepened and he grinned with his gums again as his gaze swept upwards. He raised a wrinkled finger and pointed to the sky.

*

There was no mist in orbit. The sun's rays glinted off the panels of the leading GRACE satellite as it continued its path five hundred kilometres above the earth's surface. Affectionately named 'Jerry' by its makers, it was in a perpetual chase with 'Tom', its replica, as the two circled the earth fifteen times each day. Rather than a hostile chase, they were friends, constantly whispering their positions to each other through the microwave ranging link that joined them. Their trajectory round the planet was a subtle dance, the earth setting the tempo with its gravitational moods. Like every good satellite, they would beam their findings back to earth. For GRACE, it was once every thirty days.

Those packets of information found their way onto Sven Amsel's computer, at the Weilheim ground station. Once a month the data would assemble itself into a global map that rotated on his screen, like a multi-coloured meteorite that had been bludgeoned by too many passing space rocks. Unlike the perfect blue sphere that people recognised as Earth-as-seen-from-space, or home, this was lumpy. To the untrained eye, it looked like a mistake but to Sven, it was beautiful. The blue mountains and red dips were the dynamism of the planet, evidence that it lived and breathed and changed. Not through the slumbering landmasses, but through water, its lifeblood, as it circulated from the ice caps to the ocean floors, from underground caverns to waterfalls. It was the fluctuations in gravity from these cycles that tugged at his satellites, coaxing first Jerry then Tom to fall a little faster towards the earth, whenever they passed over an area where the pull was stronger. They weren't his satellites, of course, but he had become so accustomed to them checking in and sharing their month's findings, year after year, that he had come to think of them as friends. Sometimes he would find himself at night, when he pulled into the driveway, before he exchanged the role of scientist for husband and father, staring up through the windscreen, working out where they might be right then and how the earth would seem to them, lumps and all. Sometimes he wished he could see for himself.

He always had a mixed sense of anticipation and dread when the month's map uploaded itself onto his screen – the anticipation from his scientific curiosity and the thrill he still had of talking to something in space; the dread about what it all meant. Ice cap densities were decreasing with depressing predictability. River basins in Australia were drying up at disturbing rates. The gravitational ebbs and flows of the planet made a pretty map but a damning indictment. It was, on the whole, a relatively consistent pattern. What he saw on his screen, early that morning, was not.

He peered closer, adjusting his glasses, as though this might change what he thought he saw. It didn't. He sat back in his chair and stared at the branches of the larch tree on the other side of the ground station window, then closed the screen and repeated the upload. The same image formed and rotated before him.

"Hans?" he said, without taking his eyes from the console. "Can you take a look at this?"

Hans propelled himself across the room in his chair and stared at the unsightly turquoise bulge sticking out on one side of the gravity globe. Younger, fitter and shrewder than Sven, Hans made decisions and stuck to them. He shook his head. "Upload it again."

"I already did that."

Hans scratched his chin. "It was bound to malfunction at some point."

"Maybe it's real."

"Unless the earth grew a new mountain range since last month, that's not real data. Cross-check the baseline positions manually." He whirled his chair across the room again and returned to his console.

Sven turned to his screen, minimised the image and linked into the star cameras, GPS receivers and magnetometers, to begin the checks.

*

The same data that found its way to Sven Amsel's computer did not end its journey there. It took another route along the superconducting highways from his mainframe to the relay station. From there it rode the radio waves to a different satellite drifting above the planet where, for all that those waves carry, there is no sound. This satellite beamed it back to Earth, to the antenna of an underground listening station. From radio wave to infrared light, the information hitched a ride on the fibreoptic cables that took it to Nadine Proust's screen. Conscious of an audience again, it reassembled itself into something meaningful.

"Seth?" Nadine said. "This just came in from the Weilheim ground station."

Seth Winters strode across the room. Tall, lean with sleek blond hair and a clean-shaven face, he studied her screen through pale blue eyes.

"It wasn't there last month. They've begun manual checks," she said, peeking up over thick rimmed glasses perched too low on her nose while she absentmindedly twisted a strand of dark hair. She liked watching his profile.

He leaned closer and peered at the screen, frowning. "What is that?"

She shook her head, as her gaze returned to the anomalous turquoise bulge on the map. "I've no idea."

"Anything from the tests so far?" said Seth.

"The magnetometers concur, the others are still outstanding."

"How long until GRACE does its next download?" asked Seth.

"One month from today."

At first glance, he appeared composed. But the subtle repeated flexing of his cheek muscles betrayed the mask and Nadine knew he was wrestling with the decision. He had spent the best part of two years trying to emulate the leadership qualities of their employer, and it had not gone unnoticed. He had moved up through ORB's ranks, bypassing peers that had ten years on him, much to their irritation. His potential had been marked and he had been handed the chance to shine. He was not about to blow his promotion by pushing every piece of data that crossed his hub until he knew it meant something.

"When's the meeting?" she asked.

Seth glanced at his watch. "Twenty minutes."

There was a pause as he stared at the irregular spinning globe. Finally, he said, "It's too speculative at this stage."

"But if it turns out to be a tagger and we didn't notify him…" Her voice tailed off.

*

A bead of sweat formed on Seth's brow as he paused outside the glass door. He wiped it away, straightened his stance and his suit, and walked in.

The others were already assembled around one side of the large oblong glass table. They glanced up from their tablets as he approached, meeting his eye but withholding pleasantries. With the way things had been here lately, he knew why. He took an empty seat, avoiding the one at the head of the table and eyeing the other. Dana Bishop had not returned since the CERN operation ceased. He missed her. They had connected the first time they saw one another in this very room. He had felt her stare on him and met her eye for only a second, before she turned away, the ghost of a smile on her lips. It was only a matter of days before they found a reason to meet again, and soon after that there had been no need for excuses. But during the CERN operation she withdrew, caught in its unravelling, and then she didn't return his calls. He was left with nothing but the hollow feeling of speculation and the ache that sometimes kept him awake at night.

Her replacement, Leone Harper, had been given a different place at the table, leaving Dana's empty. Seth had a feeling the vacant chair was there to make a point.

He glanced round at his colleagues. It was too strong a word, for although they came together each week, they worked in silos for the most part. It was like a United Nations of the world's advancements, with each person representing a different field and each responsible for scouring the planet for research that potentially conflicted with ORB's manifesto. The meetings had become subdued since the CERN incident. The whole place felt like it was afraid to breathe out. Tensions had been running high as the IT teams sweated to make the systems operational again. There had been no outbursts, no hysteria, but it was as though someone had taken the air inside the underground monitoring facility and tightened it. People had gone home from their shift one day to be replaced by a new face the next. ORB's work was serious, Seth had reasoned, and there was no room for error, or passengers. He didn't fully understand what had happened, nor did he ask. He understood that his job was to know as much as he could about the emerging work in geosciences, and nothing else. Knowing things he shouldn't carried with it burden and risk that, while satisfying his curiosity, could come at too high a price.

He had been at enough meetings now to recognise who did what – Linton for Biological Sciences, Cole for Computer Engineering, Berry for Materials Sciences, Pearson for Agriculture and Environmental Sciences, Harper for Physics, Marshall for Astrophysics and Space Engineering. Kane, the IT lead, was not a sector head as what he did crossed all boundaries. The only man Seth didn't know about sat at the bottom of the table. Elijah Lazaro had been at every meeting Seth had attended, but gave no report and passed no comment. A slight man, with shoulder-length dark hair tucked behind his ears and a long, thin face, he observed the group from behind lidded, slate-coloured eyes.

The door opened and Victor Amos walked in, his raven black hair glinting in the manufactured light. It wasn't his stature that still struck Seth. It was more the silent signal that seemed to emanate from him. Seth found himself transfixed with the ease and certainty of his gait, with the cool regard of his gaze on each participant as he took his seat at the head of the table. One day, Seth would have that presence too.

"Ladies and gentlemen," said Amos. "Thank you for coming. Good morning."

Nervous half-smiles and nods flickered round the table but all eyes remained fixed on him, their attention absolute.

"Mr Kane, would you kindly begin this week's proceedings?"

"Of course." Kane cleared his throat. "Well, we've made a great deal of progress since we last met. As of next week, each Sector will be back to full operational capability." He tapped on his tablet and a pie chart appeared on the white wall before them. "We only have four systems left to reboot in C Sector. But we're confident that our firewalls are sound, inside and out."

When Amos spoke, it was with a silken voice. "Let's not forget it was overconfidence which set us back so severely in the first place. A little humility is worth retaining, Mr Kane."

Kane flushed and his eyes found the table before he continued his report.

When he had finished, Amos' gaze moved to the prim woman next to him. "Ms Harper?"

Leone Harper relayed information about the Canadian research into iron selenium use in superconductivity and the artificial photosynthesis study in Berkley. Then, in turn, the Heads of Sectors gave their updates. Climate change impact on food crops, heritability of environmental factors through methylation of DNA, hydrogen fuel cells development, Galileon scalar field and the expansion of the cosmos, urban policy mobility and global governance – Amos listened to them all with composure. Every so often and, with what seemed to Seth like a sixth sense, Amos would dig deeper. By the follow-up meetings, the responsible Sector Heads were expected to have combed for inconsistencies in the research and found solutions that aligned with company policy. Amos missed nothing. Once he pulled Cole up for contradicting a detail on nanorobotic research which Cole himself had offered, six months before. Seth had gone through the minutes and Amos had been right. His shrewdness was something Seth admired, but it also made him nervous. He barely heard the other reports, trying to decide whether to speak to the morning's findings. He plumped for safety and presented the details of the study into ocean acidification, reassuring the group that there were no conflicts.

"Thank you, Seth," said Amos with his signatory courtesy. He turned to the pale-faced bald man next to Seth, whose head was shiny with perspiration. "Mr Pearson?"

"There's one more thing…" A sudden compulsion to share his findings seized Seth, despite the lack of his grip on them.

The group turned their eyes on him and he felt the heat rise in his neck. He summoned every particle of confidence in his body and faked some new ones as he said, "The GRACE satellites are showing a gravitational surge over Europe and western Asia. We're still verifying it but it's seven times the normal values for these areas. We'll know for sure next month when GRACE compiles its next map."

Amos watched him, motionless, and Seth felt his confidence dissolve.

Rutger Marshall, Sector Head for Astrophysics and Space Engineering, who usually had something to say if topics crossed the stratosphere into his turf, dismissed Seth's comments with the frown on his face and the scorn in his voice. "GRACE is on extended time. A gravitational surge of that magnitude is bound to be a monitoring error. I would suggest—"

Amos silenced Marshall with his stare. He turned to Seth. "What else could cause the surge?"

"We don't know."

As Amos studied him, Seth could not fathom his expression. "GRACE is your main priority as of now. Mr Kane and Mr Marshall will provide any additional resources you may require. I want a briefing by the end of the day."

*

Seth was swelled with a mixture of relief and confidence when he returned to the geosciences hub. His team looked up at him in expectation.

"Change of plan," he announced. "Andy, keep scouting. The rest of us are working on the GRACE findings from now on. Nadine, show the team what you found."

Two lumpy globes spun on Marcus Connor's screen, one of them Nadine's new find and one, for comparison, from the previous month. The mountain of gravity appeared to have accumulated in the space of four weeks. "So how often do the satellites circle the globe?" asked Marcus.

"Fifteen times per day," said Nadine without looking up.

"Can you access that data?" asked Marcus.

"It's only compiled every thirty days, into these maps," said Nadine.

"No, I mean raw data from the satellites," Marcus said. "I'll reassemble it here."

Seth stood behind them. The ingenuity of his team always surprised him, but then he sometimes surprised himself. "Good idea," he said. "It will give us an idea of how quickly that thing sprung up."

"And where it came from," said Marcus.

It took some time, but the information that had been laser light and radio waves from space changed form again, becoming pixels on Marcus Connor's screen. Layered over time, as Marcus had instructed, they showed a very different picture.

*

Seth had not been inside Victor Amos' office before. It took him a moment to register that the ocean, with ribbons of soft clouds and birds drifting past, was a projection on the opposite wall of the large white room, and even longer to control the bag of worms that was his stomach. Being called to present to the Director was not something to which he was accustomed. It was not about him, he reminded himself, it was about the findings. All the same, it felt like

26

an audition. Amos leaned back on his leather chair behind his desk and invited him to sit. Seth did, but the seat was uncomfortable. At that moment in time, everything was uncomfortable. He fumbled with his laptop as he linked it wirelessly to the pillar that stood to one side of Amos' desk, his clammy fingertips slipping on the keys. The pillar, black like shiny granite, stood about waist height. On its flat upper surface, something the size and shape of a black golf ball was propped on a fine frame that allowed it to swivel freely.

Seth cleared his throat. "We came up with a program to collect the data directly from the satellites," he began, as the golf ball hummed on the pod. A large cone of light appeared above it, which became a lumpy holographic globe. Seth adjusted its position from his laptop, swivelling the earth to show the large turquoise bulge, which spread from the mid-Atlantic to the western edge of Mongolia, and from Iceland to Zambia. While the rest of the world dipped and troughed in multicolour, this bulge was consistent – a single gravitational mountain that shrouded a quarter of the planet. He hit the return key.

"We think it's still growing," said Seth. "Gravitational changes come from bodies of water, but this dispersion pattern doesn't make any sense. It's as though huge water reserves have expanded over all of these landmasses, except when we use other geophysical checks, there's no extra water there."

"Have you run it backwards in time?" asked Amos.

"Yes," said Seth, feeling a tinge of smugness and a flood of relief that he had pre-empted one of Amos' requests. "This is what we get."

The furthest edges of the turquoise mountain receded, as though the whole thing was draining into an invisible gravity plug. Seth watched as the last of it disappeared into one singular point over the landmass that was Western Europe. He looked up at Amos. "It came from Switzerland."

Amos was silent. Cracks appeared in Seth's triumph as he waited for a reaction. Instead Amos reached for the intercom. "Have Mr Lazaro join us."

*

Elijah Lazaro watched the gravitational events play out in the holographic projection, forwards this time instead of in reverse.

From this vantage point, it was as though Switzerland had exploded and scattered its gravitational debris across a quarter of the globe. If Elijah had any reaction to what he saw, he did not show it.

Uncomfortable with the silence, Seth filled it in. "We're trying to figure out if we've missed an underground water reserve, but other geophysical tests don't support it. There haven't been any unusual weather patterns to account for freak rainfall in these areas, and anyway the distribution doesn't tie up for rain."

"You're assuming it's water," said Lazaro. It was the first time Seth had heard him speak. His voice, thin and at a pitch slightly higher than that of most men, surprised Seth.

"What else could it be?" asked Seth.

Seth could not interpret the thought that Amos and Lazaro shared in their glance. Amos turned to him. "Have your team intercept any data from the GRACE satellites and give the ground stations readings that makes them think this was a monitoring blip."

"You mean feed them false data?" asked Seth.

"Give them a map they expect to see," said Amos. "We cannot afford any unwanted attention on this. No one outside of ORB should know of these findings. That is as much as I want you to do."

"What about investigating what's causing it?" asked Seth.

"Mr Lazaro will take care of that." Amos kept his eyes on Seth, his expression pleasant but clear. Seth stood up, closed his laptop and, a little deflated by the sudden curtailment of his input, left the room.

Amos turned to Lazaro. "This may explain a great deal. I suspect the fracture in Mindscape is due not only to our technical setbacks." He paused. "Can you deal with it?"

Elijah's eyes glazed slightly as he considered. "I had hoped you called me here to say we had found the perpetrator."

"We have some leads, but that will have to wait."

"Whatever is disrupting Mindscape, the hacker's interference has cost me a lot of time on this project."

"Leave the perpetrator to me." Amos watched the edge of Elijah's lips twitch. "Our priority, for now, is to maintain our trajectory." He repeated his question patiently, like a father to a distracted child.

"Can you deal with it?"

"Not through conventional methods."

Amos turned his gold pen over in his fingers in a slow, deliberate motion. "Then perhaps it is time for a fresh approach. Take the good news to the non-believers, as it were." He watched Elijah as the words sank in. There is a space between words and interruptions that, if given the chance to breathe, becomes fertile ground for ideas to germinate. This space Amos held sacred, a space where suggestion – his suggestion – was enough to plant a new seed of creation. Inception.

"There may be a way…" began Elijah. "But it would take time to cultivate, and time may not be willing to indulge us…"

"That's why we need something to accelerate our progress," said Amos. "Something that will amplify our intentions."

Elijah paused, his thin dark eyebrows rising slightly. "Does it still exist?"

Amos' gaze took him from the openness of the room to the privacy of his inner reflections.

When he found Elijah's face again, his stare was hard. "Find it before they do."

CHAPTER THREE

T he captain counted out the money with fat hands etched with
grime. His cursory nod made it clear that they were tolerated, not
welcome. But it was good enough. Robert led Cora aboard the trawler
as the sun spilled the first photons of the day on the North Sea.

The deck was wide; a folded crane on one side, yellow beneath
blackened oil, huge ropes wound round rusting circular drums, a
funnel churning out the sooty products of partially combusted fuel.
The seagulls followed as the vessel chugged from the harbour,
mewing and swooping overhead. The smell of diesel, salt and grease
came too. They stood at the stern, away from the crew, as the port
diminished behind them, the soft spray of wet air cold on their skin.
Cora closed her eyes and breathed in the scent of the sea. Above
them, the seagulls soared on the thermals, circling in a sky with no
walls. Beneath them, the waves broke on the hull, the surface
turbulence of something deeper and more silent. Robert saw none of
it. All he could see was the memory of his father as his life oozed
away on his shirt and the look he had in his eyes, that it had come to
this. All of Casimir and Sattva's talk of 'knowing' meant nothing. It
made no difference to the ache in his chest.

*

Their cabin was cramped, but it was only for a day. He washed his
face in the tiny bathroom, which was just big enough to turn round

in. Catching sight of himself in the cracked mirror nailed to the wall, he froze. His beard was fuller now, the crease in his brow more prominent. He looked away. *I hate mirrors,* he thought, feeling like he was trespassing into someone else's body, someone he could barely remember, and he might get caught. *Knowing?* he thought. *What the fuck do I know?* He was more adrift now than he could remember.

But a shimmer in the mirror drew his eye back to it. Something was moving behind him – arch-shaped and rippling, like steam rising from a kettle. It hovered just a short distance away, not within the bathroom or the door or the cabin on the other side, but still easily within reach. He felt its pull like a compass to magnetic north. Certainty lay beyond it, and it called to him. He stood there, transfixed, watching its intensity burn brighter.

A tingling sensation gripped his left arm and he looked down to see his hand leaning on the sink losing its texture again, thinning, the edge of the basin below becoming visible where it should not have been. *Maybe I should just let it happen...*

"Robert?" Cora's voice came with a knock on the door. "Are you alright?"

He caught his breath as he reoriented then said, "Fine. Yeah. Just be a minute." *I fucking hope so...* He poured all of his focus onto his arm, trying to force it back to form. When he opened his eyes, the transparency had taken his shoulder.

Fear piped up. *You really believe you've any control over this?*

I've done it before. Belief stood its ground.

Luck, sneered Fear. *Coincidence. Face it, Robert, you're a fake. And Cora's going to find you out.* He felt his chest tighten.

Belief did not answer. In the silence that lingered, a thought came to him. A memory. He was standing on a rooftop looking over the edge to a long drop, Sattva by his side, a large tawny bird on the remnants of his dissolving outstretched arm.

"Let go..." Sattva's words rang in his ears.

Robert closed his eyes, breathed out and surrendered. His fingers gripped the edge of the sink, feeling the relief of their own solidity. He splashed cold water on his face and glanced up at the reflection again. The door with its rusty hook was behind him. The archway was gone.

*

They fell asleep with the engine chugging a lullaby to the lurch of the boat on the rough sea. For a while, it all melted into nothing, but it was not long before Robert woke in the darkness with a feeling. It took him a moment to quantify it. All he knew, at first, was that it was wrong. It wasn't fear exactly, it had no form or shape to begin with, just an unsettling undercurrent. He became aware of a sound, like a discordant drone, but was unsure if it was coming from inside his head or somewhere else. When his mind plugged into his body, and conscious thought kicked in, he recognised it as a memory – the feeling he had when his father turned away from the Arch...

It gave way to hollow helplessness, sitting in his gut like a stone. He disentangled himself from Cora, still sleeping beside him, and got up. Steadying himself on the wall as the boat pitched, he made his way to the deck.

He leaned on the cold metal railing, peering over the edge of the vessel into the dark sea. Above, stars laced the night sky; portholes to the universe. The swoosh of the waves and the hum of the engine were the only sounds. He took out the red flash-drive from his pocket, turning it over in his fingers as his mind turned to its previous owner. To Aiyana Wolfe, it had meant death. *Such a small thing to die for*, he thought. And yet to him, it meant life. It gave him purpose, a place to start.

"So, how are you adjusting?"

Startled, Robert turned. Behind him was the vague shadow of a woman. To the untrained eye, she would have been invisible but not to him. Perhaps it was awareness rather than sight, but he could 'see' her move and read her expressions, something no ordinary person would see. As she approached, however, she reformed into her physical self. Her dark hair billowed round her shoulders in the sea breeze. Even in the glow of the shy moon that came and went behind tatters of clouds, he could see the intensity in her eyes that defined her and made it hard to look away.

"Aiyana? Are you hacking my thoughts?"

"I asked first." She stood beside him and looked out at the black liquid blanket.

32

Robert dropped his gaze. "Adjusting? I'm not sure."

"Does Cora know?"

"What do you think?" He sighed. "I don't know how long I can keep this up. It's a charade. I mean, if she ever saw me like…" He couldn't bring himself to finish the words.

Aiyana grew stern. "She can't. You chose to remain physical, Robert. You've got to keep your focus."

He nodded, and picked at a piece of rust on the railing.

"But don't get *too* grounded," she added. "You don't want to deskill…"

"I thought all those 'skills' were just part of the freak show, as far as you were concerned. Overrated."

She snorted and rolled her eyes. "Well I guess some of them are quite useful."

"Like holding your hand in a candle flame and watching while it doesn't burn?"

Grinning, she looked away. He felt a wall dissolve between them.

"Are you telling me you've made peace with your death, Aiyana Wolfe?" he said.

She turned to him, fleetingly coy before her resolve returned. The wall was back up but he could see through it now. "I've not made peace with anything," she said. "I'm nowhere near finished with all this."

"Me neither," said Robert. He hesitated, then asked, "Have you been through the Arch?"

She turned back to the ocean. Her eyes were on the waves but it was as though she didn't see them. "Yes," said. "Many times."

"Why do you come back?"

"I have to. Like I said, I'm not finished with this. But I need both worlds." She studied him, like she was trying to fathom an impossible puzzle. "How can you not go?"

Robert shook his head. The thought of it scared him. "I can't explain it."

They stood in silence side by side, staring out at the edge of the world. Lights in the distance were lanterns on the black waves or stars in the black sky, it was hard to tell. He became aware of her next to him, a man and a woman dislodged from their realities by events beyond their control. There was something about knowing you weren't the only one.

"Do you ever get lonely?" he asked.

"Yeah," she said. "All the time."

He nodded. "Me too." Turning to her, he found she was already looking at him with an intensity that was beyond words, beyond time, beyond who they thought they were. He didn't want it to stop.

She lowered her eyes, breaking the link, leaving him disorientated and isolated again. "Casimir told me about your dad," she said. "I'm sorry."

"Thanks," he said. The ache returned to his chest with its core of ice. "I'm not letting this go. Not anymore."

She nodded.

His fingers clenched around the flash-drive then he opened his palm to show her. She stared at the innocent red casing that held within it the reason why everything changed.

"What you discovered?" he said. "It's a link to what's driving Amos. I need to find out more…"

"I'll help you as much as I can," she said.

"Thanks."

"You comfortable Tunnelling?" she asked.

The ability to focus on someone or something with such clarity that you go straight to them, regardless of where they are in space, or Tunnelling, as it was known, was something that had eluded Robert so far. The best he could do was use the intermediary of a bird, like using armbands when you learn to swim, as Casimir had once described it. It had been a sore point for Aiyana for some time, Robert recalled.

"Not exactly…" he said. "Why, did Crowley finally teach you?"

"Yeah, he caved."

"Can't say I warmed to him. He never really rated me."

"Don't take it personally," she said. "He doesn't rate anyone. But Tunnelling's something you'll have to get good at for all this."

She took his hand and placed something in it. "This will help you find Liam. You don't need it to Tunnel but it helps to have something to channel your focus when you start out." In his palm he found a necklace, glinting like sapphire stars. "He gave it to me, once…" Her brow furrowed in the privacy of her memory, before she composed herself. "Take the flash-drive to him. He can run the program that should shed some light on Mindscape."

Robert stared at the flash-drive. "You could have done this… Why didn't you?"

He caught the look in her eyes before she dropped her gaze. "I'm not strong enough," she said. "Not with him."

Robert saw through the wall again. When he had first met her, she had been liked a caged animal, kicking off against everything around her. His overriding memory of her, as a fledgling Eidolon, was of her bad temper. This fragility was a side he did not know.

"I wish I could, but…" Her voice tailed away.

"It's alright," said Robert. "I'll find him."

*

It was still dark when the ship pulled in to harbour. A few white lights bobbed on the empty docks, their reflections like liquid jewels on the rippling water. Robert and Cora disembarked and the captain watched them as they took to the shadows, the glow from his cigarette amber in his dark eyes. Tonight, they would be sleeping in Edinburgh.

*

The boy sat on the chair in the café as his mum swept the floor. He liked this time of day when it was her turn to sweep up. The doors were locked and it was just the two of them and whichever cake he chose from whatever ones were left. Today it was a crispy cake. The place seemed bigger too, without people blocking its bright yellow walls and red paintings, colours that were a warm reminder. His legs dangled and kicked above the lino, too short to reach it, and he

35

hummed to himself as he turned the pages of a magazine laid out on the wooden table next to his pencils. Glossy pictures, most of them not very interesting, but one caught his eye.

"Mummy, look!" he said, holding up a picture of a snow-capped mountain.

She stopped sweeping.

"It's just like—"

"Ben?" she said, and the tone in her voice silenced his words. He lowered his eyes.

She sighed. "Why don't you do some drawing? You have your paper and pencils right there." She went back to her sweeping.

He put down the magazine, still staring at the image, although he said nothing more about it. Instead he took out his stone. He couldn't remember where he found it, but he'd had it for long enough to wear a smooth concavity on each side from turning it over in his fingers so many times. His pocket felt empty without it. He turned it gently now, first on one point, then the other, so as not to disturb his mum, and the motion calmed him. It wasn't the real one, nothing like the same shape, but it didn't matter. To him, it was close enough. He stared at the picture again and remembered how snow felt – the chill in his hands as he rolled a snowball, the sound his feet made as they crunched through the icy surface into the softer stuff below. The tingle of an icy breeze in his cheeks as the sun went down behind the mountains and the clouds turned pink. He turned his stone over like a meditation and looked out of the window. A man with a beard wearing a beanie hat, and a woman with short dark hair came out of the mobile phone repair shop opposite. Ben watched them then, drawn by something he could not explain, slid from his chair and pressed his hands and nose against the glass. He craned his neck as they walked away, following until he could no longer see them on the street. Instead he turned to watch a boy about his own age, walking with his parents, sharing a story with them. And his parents listened, it seemed.

There was no snow here, not in the summertime.

*

A fine drizzle hung on the night air, the kind of rain that barely forms a drop but still seeps through the pores of the skin and finds its way into the bones. Their footsteps squelched on the sodden pavement as they stole between the pools of yellow in the darkness that lined the side street. Robert glanced up at the brick building to his left, lined with metal fire escape stairs that zigzagged their way up to its roof. They turned into a narrower lane, where the leaves and branches had squeezed their way through the rusted iron railings that lined one side. Robert glanced back. They were alone.

He pulled his collar snug around his neck and his beanie over his ears and reached for Cora's hand, cool and slender in his. Their pace slowed as they approached. The weeds had won the battle against the slabs, reminding the city that the wilderness is there beneath the concrete, creeping in whenever backs are turned.

"This is his place?" whispered Cora as they stopped. A dark door was at the end of the short path and the lights in the flat were out.

"His sister's. She's away for a year." Robert squinted up and down the road again through the drizzle. Still empty. The gate squeaked as he pushed it open. He pressed the doorbell and a muffled buzz came from inside.

Nothing.

A car swished along the damp tarmac further along the lane, its headlights skewering the fine rain. Robert froze, his breath suspended until it turned into the next street. He pressed the bell again. This time, thuds on wood, a clink of keys and indistinguishable grumblings came from inside. The door swung open. Danny Mitchell stood in a red T-shirt and boxers, frowning through puffy eyes and a crinkled face that had spent too long lying on the creases of a pillow. He stared at them, as though trying to decide if they were really there.

"*Robert?*"

"Danny. Can we come in?"

Danny stepped back, scratching his tangle of fair hair. "Just go through," he said, mid-yawn, letting the door slam behind them. "Second on the left."

He flicked on the lights as they walked into the kitchen, slid a pile of unopened mail from the small wooden table onto one of the four chairs, then shuffled to the worktop. They sat down as he filled the kettle over the pile of unwashed dishes in the sink.

"Danny, I…"

Danny held up a hand, his back to them. "Wait," he mumbled, as he opened a cupboard on the wall. "Coffee."

He flung a teaspoon of instant coffee into three mugs, splashed some boiling water on top, and ferried them across to the table along with a carton of milk, a bag of sugar and a teaspoon.

Slumping into a chair, he scooped three sugars into his mug and lounged back, studying them. "Two o'clock in the fucking morning. This better be good." He took a sip. "So, who died?"

Robert shifted in his seat and he felt Cora squeeze his hand under the table. "My dad."

Danny put down his mug. He opened his mouth and closed it again. Then, frowning, he said, "I thought he died when you were a kid?"

Robert nodded. "So did I. Turns out he'd gotten involved with the wrong kind of company. He had to disappear to protect me and my mum. I just found him again, but so did they. They… they killed him a few days ago."

Danny ran his fingers through his hair and blew air out from his puffed cheeks. "Jesus, that's a lot to deal with. Me and my big mouth," he said. "I'm sorry, man." He shook his head, still processing Robert's words.

"We need a place to stay," said Robert. "Just for a few days."

"Of course," said Danny. "Sure." He picked up a key from the bookshelf behind him, crammed with maps and books, and handed to it Robert. "Stay as long as you like."

*

An hour later Robert and Cora were lying on the floor of the living room, after Danny had retrieved two sleeping bags from his vast collection of camping kit and pulled the cushions from the sofa to make a bed. *Should I have told him more?* thought Robert as he lay awake in the darkness. *No. Too much of the truth makes him vulnerable. You can't risk that. Besides, he wouldn't believe you.* The pay-as-you-go phones were charging in their sockets and pinged as they came to life.

Robert watched Cora, lying on her side, her eyes closed, her hand tucked under her chin. He wasn't going to sleep, not tonight.

He sat up, propping himself against the wall, and reached for the crumpled pile of clothes on the floor beside him. Taking Aiyana's USB drive from his jeans' pocket, he turned it over in his fingers, staring at its smooth red casing. The unease in his gut began to swell again as the same thought came to him every time he touched it. *Such a small thing to die for.*

A dog was barking outside. Robert got up quietly and peered through the gap in the curtains that didn't quite meet in the middle. The street was empty. The moon appeared through the drifting clouds, its light slicing into the room, onto Cora. It made her skin look like marble. If it weren't for the slow rise and fall of her chest, she could be a statue, carved out of pale rock. *Dead. Like me.*

He felt a warmth in his right arm and glanced down. It was happening again. The texture was thinning, dissolving, until it was nothing more than a suggestion. Standing in the silence of the darkened room, it hit him. For all that had come and gone, all that seemed surreal and imagined, this was the proof. *This is what I am.*

Cora mumbled and turned over and Robert's pulse picked up pace. There were no walls to shield him this time. A half-ghost, something that doesn't belong anywhere. The moonlight glinted in the mirror hanging on the wall. He made himself move towards it, to the face staring back at him. The him inside of him stared out through those eyes. At the edge of his vision the faint rippling of light crept towards his shoulder, dissolving what lay beneath. He reached for his amulet, an oval pebble on a leather cord, with the fingers of his solid arm. The hollow where it sat above his sternum was reddened, a recent burn, scorched by Aiyana's memory of her murder. Real flesh, newly scarred. *Proof that I am real.* He closed his eyes, holding that thought in his mind until the flickering light began to subside, restoring the skin, muscles, bones – all the components that made him recognisable – the way he should be. He flexed his fingers, noticing the feeling as the tendons stretched over the back of his hand. If nothing else, death had reminded him how it felt to be alive.

He got dressed with as little noise as possible, placed the flash-drive back in his pocket and kissed Cora on her forehead. He closed the door quietly behind him, and left.

*

The street outside glowed in the moonlight that beamed down from space, illuminating the walls and dark windows of the buildings that backed onto the lane, behind the small leafy enclosure opposite. He could see its reflection on one of the panes higher up, and the tendrils of clouds that inched across the white rock in the sky. He made his way back to the old brick building, past someone lying, sprawled and snoring beneath a pile of cardboard, by a dripping overflow pipe in the wall. Robert looked up. It seemed to have a flat roof with enough height for the drop. Tunnelling would be easier but now was not the time to learn. He climbed the metal staircase, quietly, passing the closed doors on the walls, his heart hammering harder with each step. When he reached the last platform, he scrambled onto the railing and climbed up the remaining few feet of a drainpipe that led to the roof.

It was still. There was nothing up here to mask the thudding of his heart. Moonlight hugged the street, spilling a cool glow on the tarmac. He took some deep breaths. *I can do this.*

Fear was waiting for him, dressed up as Cynicism. *But not like this, not alone. And to another continent? Don't be an idiot.*

He ignored it as best he could, and the sick feeling in his gut. Distance wasn't the issue. It was the fact it could happen at all that was the tricky thing to swallow. He had made it from CERN to Scotland this way before, so logic implied that there was no reason he could not go further. No reason other than rational thinking and common sense. These days, common sense seemed to be common to everyone but him. *Step to the edge.* He took a slow breath in. *Never mind the height.*

He took out the necklace that belonged to Aiyana when she was alive and turned it over in his hand. He felt like he was intruding. Liam Bradbury, a man he'd never met, gave this to her in a moment they once shared. Embedded in its silver links and small sapphire-like crystals was the essence of the bond between them, the remnants of what they felt, that linked them together through time and space and death. The blue crystals glinted in the moonlight in his trembling hand. He closed his eyes and opened up to what was beyond sight.

Black.

Just black.

What fucking use is that? He let out a harsh sigh then gathered his thoughts.

Again.

His hand squeezed the necklace, its catch digging into the pulp of his finger. An image began forming in his mind. Vague at first, like static on a TV. A man in his late thirties, fair hair, smart, irritated. White shirt, cropped hair, blue eyes, shrewd. He was writing something at a desk. He crumpled it up and threw it on the floor and ran his hands over his face.

A beating sound came from above. Robert looked up to see the silhouette of descending talons and large outstretched wings. He lifted his arm, barely dodging a facial tear as the bird settled on his wrist, which dipped with its weight. It turned to him, its feathers a smooth curve on its neck, its eyes silver in the pale light, holding steady. The chime struck up, a tone of purity that he felt more than heard, the sound and feeling of clarity, oneness, blending…

Let go…

His breathing quickened as the tingling dissolution crept up his arm leaving nothing but a vague shimmering. Only this time he let it. He knew this could work, but knowing didn't shut up Fear. It yammered away in his mind, as he swallowed parched gasps of air, watching his arm and now his chest dissolve into the bird in strands of hungry light. It was the fear that he might not come back. But for all of fear's cacophony, he kept returning to the chime; the truth.

Step into the drop.

His toes gripped the insides of his boots. The galloping of his heart and the echoes of his gasps punctuated the chime until the purity of its tone out-sang them and became the only sound.

Let go. Now.

He leaned forward, the necklace still in the grip of his fading hand as the air and the ground rushed at him, forgetting what the man looked like, forgetting the reason for it, forgetting everything. He was weightless, silent, high.

*

He was above a runway, lit by two lines of dotted light. The surrounding area was dark but, beyond, streetlights sprinkled the roads, lighting up the arteries of suburbia. Only the occasional vehicle snaked along them, their headlights like tiny tracker beams piercing the black. He touched down on a road that led to a perimeter fence guarded by a security gate. A black cab drove past, on the wrong side of the road. He didn't know they had black cabs in the States, or Royal Mail Post boxes. He stopped.

"Ten out of ten, Robert," he said out loud. "You're in the wrong fucking country."

"You're not."

His heart lurched in his chest. "Shit, Aiyana, will you stop doing that?" She was standing right next to him with a look of vague amusement.

"Well I can leave you to it, if you'd rather..." She regarded him through eyes lidded with sarcasm.

"No... it's fine. Just... next time, could you not Tunnel so close? You scared the shit out of me."

"Aw, I'm sorry. I didn't know you were so sensitive." She rolled her eyes. "Look, you're in the right country. Liam works here three months of the year. This is Farnborough."

"I thought you couldn't do this?" he said.

"I can't and I'm not. You're doing it. I'm just helping you out." She strode off towards the security entrance without looking back, passing through the barriers like they were holograms. "This way."

It was a technology park. Low-lying buildings spread out around them, most of them in darkness. In the central taller building, reaching ten or so storeys high, light still glowed from a few windows higher up. Aiyana paused as Robert glanced up.

"He's still at work?" he said.

"He doesn't sleep much these days," she replied.

Unseen, they passed though the substance of the door, crossing the large atrium, where the night porter watched snooker on a laptop beside a bank of CCTV screens. Silently they climbed the static escalator to the next level. Aiyana led him to a glass corridor where rooms sat in darkness on either side. Light spilled from the office at the end.

"Wait," said Robert. "What do we tell him?"

"Not we – you. I can't have him see me." She took a deep breath, centring herself. "Tell him as little as possible – I don't want him getting wrapped up in all this. Here's what to say."

*

They walked down the corridor, Robert fully visible, Aiyana a mere shadow beside him, and stopped outside the office. Through the glass wall, Robert saw a man leaning back on his chair, slowly twirling a pen in his hand while he stared at his thoughts. Beside the desk was a wastepaper basket full of crumpled paper. Aiyana watched him and Robert saw memories soften her face. "You okay?" he whispered.

She took a breath, drawing herself taller as she assumed a mask of indifference. "Yes. Let's get this done."

Robert knocked on the door as he opened it a little. "Mr Bradbury?"

The man looked up.

"Do you have a moment?"

Liam seemed to find his focus on his surroundings again. "Eh… it's a little late, but…"

Robert closed the door. Aiyana, unseen, crossed the room behind him, her eyes on Liam.

"I wonder if you could take a look at this." Robert placed the flash-drive on the desk.

"What is it?" asked Liam, picking it up.

"Aiyana Wolfe asked me to give it to you."

Liam stiffened, his eyes fixed on Robert. Suspicion crept in on the lines around them.

"She found something at Geowatch – electromagnetic anomalies."

"You knew Aiyana?" breathed Liam.

"Yes. She wanted you to see this, but she never got the chance."

"How did you know her?"

"We worked on a project together a while back, through Caltech. Please. I need you to take a look."

Liam plugged the flash-drive into his desktop. Images unfolded on the screen – the world map on the left and a set of readings on the right. Shrouding North America and Western Europe was a dark haze – the medium of Mindscape. Eavesdropping on Dana Bishop's conversation at ORB had told Robert and Aiyana that much. Liam peered closer then shifted his gaze to Robert. "Where did you get this?"

"She asked me to give it to you."

Liam's eyes narrowed as they returned to the screen. "This data was captured the night that she..." His voice tailed off and he swallowed the words he couldn't say.

"That's why I'm here," said Robert. "The people who killed her wanted this buried."

"I'm sorry, I didn't get your name," said Liam.

"My name is Robert Strong." He tensed as Liam picked up the phone. "What are you doing?"

"I'm calling security."

"No, wait – just hear me out. Aiyana was murdered for this information. Her killers are beyond your security, beyond the police. Please, I need you to trust me – she did."

Unseen, Aiyana crouched down beside Liam and laid a hand on his cheek. He hesitated, staring at the place where she looked back at him. His eyes searched the space, and maybe they found something or maybe he just felt it, Robert couldn't tell, but he put down the phone. He let out a soft breath. "Funny, I..." His words tailed off. Silently, Aiyana withdrew.

A film of moisture glinted in Liam's eyes and he swallowed. Finding his composure, he looked up at Robert, his voice quieter this time. "Alright," he said. He turned back to the screen, to the dark haze over the cities, his brow creasing as he studied it. "She was monitoring on the wrong frequency interval. The range we're interested in for electromagnetic output is low frequency – four hundred to twenty-seven hundred megahertz. These are ultralow frequencies. But still," he said, peering at the digits, "it's way more

44

than it should be…"

He opened another page on his screen and typed. "I don't remember any disturbances recently…" His eyes scanned the information. "No. Nothing."

Glancing at Robert, he picked up the phone again. "Not security," he said. "Hugh? Hi, it's Liam." There was a pause. "Yeah, the flight was fine thanks. Listen, I need some information. Have you guys had any evidence of significant EMPs over the past three months?"

Another pause. "Nothing? Huh. Okay, thanks."

He stared at the screen again, a crease deepening in his brow. "It doesn't make sense. It looks like what we'd see with an electromagnetic pulse, like a solar flare, but we'd have some evidence of it. There should have been major blackouts, power failures…" He shook his head. "It must be a monitoring error."

"Aiyana already checked that," said Robert. "She said it wasn't the equipment. Double check if you like, but the data's real."

"Then I need to call this in to head office."

"No – please. Aiyana's mistake was to flag this up and she paid the price for it. You have to keep this to yourself, for now. But I need you to run her search again at those frequencies. Can you do that?"

Liam paused. "Okay." He opened a different program and amended the search parameters. Robert and Aiyana moved round behind his desk. They watched as Liam tapped into the monitoring systems, instructing the listening sentinels around the globe to tune their ears to another signal. They relayed their silent findings back to him, feeding into Aiyana's program. Data scrolled onto the screen, lists of numbers that meant nothing to Robert. It reassembled itself into a map of the western world. There was no sign of the dark haze that marred the landmasses of the previous map.

Liam sat back. "Whatever it was, it's not there now."

Robert stared at the screen. "Wait, are you sure?" He swallowed. "Run it again."

Liam eyed him, wary of the edge in Robert's voice. He turned back to the console and tapped on the keys, peering at the data then sat back and shook his head. "Like I said. The signal's back to baseline levels. What do you think it was?"

Robert didn't answer. He scribbled a phone number on a piece of paper. "I appreciate your help Liam. I need you to keep checking this," he said, "but only intermittently. Don't leave the program running."

"Why not?" asked Liam.

"Because you never know who's watching. Call me if anything changes."

*

Robert waited for Aiyana in the hallway. When she joined him, she was subdued. "You okay?" he whispered.

She nodded. "It just hurts."

He took the sapphire necklace from his pocket and placed it in her palm. "I know." Wrapping his arms around her, he held her and they stood in silence.

"It doesn't make any sense," Robert breathed. "If there's no evidence of Mindscape, then where is he?"

*

When Robert returned to Danny's place, he was too preoccupied to sleep. The house was silent and he walked into the kitchen in darkness, unaware of how he got there. It felt like he couldn't breathe inside, so he went out of the back door, closing it behind him, and sat on the step. The moon looked down at him, glowing in white indifference. His heart was heavy and he felt more alone than he had done in a long time.

"You okay?"

He turned to the voice. Michael Casimir appeared a few feet away.

"I'm not sure," said Robert.

"Budge up," said Casimir. Robert shuffled along on the step and Casimir sat down beside him. They sat in silence for a while, watching the heavens, pinpricks of the past burned into the vastness of the cosmos. "See Betelgeuse?" said Casimir, pointing to the orange-reddish blob in the Orion constellation.

"Yeah," said Robert. "Still your favourite?"

"Of course. I like it because it's on borrowed time."

"Wonder where we'll be then," said Robert.

"Who knows?" Casimir turned to him, a faint smile on his lips. "That's part of the adventure, not knowing."

Robert gave him an I-don't-quite-buy-that kind of look. He stared up at the sky again. "Mindscape doesn't exist anymore," he said.

Casimir studied him before looking back at the stars. "I suppose you're wondering where he is then," he said.

Robert nodded.

"You're absolutely sure he didn't go through the Arch?"

"Like I told you," said Robert. "Something took him first."

They sat in silence again. A satellite, like a faint speck of dust, drifted slowly and steadily past the distant suns.

"I keep seeing it, the Arch," said Robert.

Casimir nodded. "Its pull is powerful. I've never met anyone who could resist it. Most who go through do not come back – only our kind have that ability."

Robert thought back to the memory Casimir had once shared – which Robert had experienced as though he were living it himself – of the first time he passed through. He was sitting on a pebbled beach, an iridescent sea spread out before him. The colours of the land and the plants were more vibrant and alive and vital than any colour he had ever experienced, thanks to the two suns that hung in the sky. The fabric of the air itself was peace – not a dead peace, but one that shimmered with perfection and potential. He had the feeling anything was possible, that limitations were a construct of a distant memory and no more real than the fears that had once plagued him. He did not want to come back. And yet he did come back.

"Have you been through again?"

"Yes," said Casimir. "I have to." He sat in the stillness of his own mind, a place out of reach to Robert. "We're not earthbound. When I say earthbound, I mean bound to this world. There is only one earth, but there are billions of worlds within it."

Robert picked up a piece of gravel and turned it over in his hands. "So it's the same for the others?" he asked.

"Yes. It's our nature as Eidolon to move between worlds – but we can only last so long in either. We need both to survive. Without them, we have nothing to give."

"Why is it different for me?"

Casimir stared at him and Robert could not fathom his expression. "We don't know," he said. "For an Eidolon to last so long without returning has never happened before. You chose to be earthbound. Only you can discover why that is."

"I don't know if I'd come back," said Robert, "if I went on."

"Then you made a wise choice," said Casimir. "If you're compelled to do more here."

Robert stared at his gravel lump. "What do I do, Casimir? If Mindscape is gone, how do I find him? I don't know where to start."

Casimir looked up at Betelgeuse again. "Life will show you your next move, if you stay open to it." He turned to Robert and smiled with his eyes, and Robert felt the tenderness in his heart; that if he could have shouldered the burden for him, he would have. "All you can do is follow the trail."

*

Robert came to with cold sunlight on his eyelids. It filtered in, in the crack between the curtains, and coaxed him up from the depths of a dreamless sleep. While he wanted only to remain in that stillness where the stresses of life dissolved into a forgotten myth, an unsettling feeling took seed in his gut and as it grew, it drew him from slumber. It took him a few moments to assemble his memory of where and when he was, and how the feeling fitted into it. It came back to him in waves – *Aiyana, Liam, Mindscape, Elliot...*

He stared at the ceiling listening to the sound of the shower next door, a familiar noise that seemed strange in his abstract world.

*

Danny was poring over something on the kitchen table when Robert walked in.

"You must have been tired," he said.

"God, yeah," said Robert, as the clock reflected how long he'd overslept.

"Help yourself to coffee."

"You want a top up?" he asked as he filled the kettle.

Danny slid his mug sideways on the table, still absorbed with what lay in front of him.

"I'll take that as a yes," said Robert. "What have you got there?" he asked as he spooned the coffee into the mugs.

"Something I found in Tibet," Danny said, without looking up.

Cora walked in, towelling her hair, and Robert handed her a mug of coffee. She kissed him, her lips lingering on his, then frowned. "You alright?" she breathed.

He nodded and she stepped back, eyeing him.

"Sorry, Danny," said Robert. "What were you saying?"

"It's a mandala," Danny said.

Cora sat down, moving Danny's mobile aside, her eyes on the material spread out on the table. Its woven fibres were charred round the edges and although time had faded its fabric into a dirty brown, its markings were still visible in black ink. Her gaze moved over the elaborate circles and squares, tracing the delicacy of the design. Beside it was a hexagonal wooden box, about the size of a small bowl. Its intricately carved lid stood open on its hinges.

"I found it in the mountains. Just after you left," said Danny, nodding at Robert, "when I set up a camp near the lakes. Couldn't handle any more butter tea," he grinned. "It was buried in the ground under a rock."

"How come you dug it up?" asked Cora.

"You've got to shit somewhere," Danny grinned.

"So you smuggled it back here?" said Robert.

"I just borrowed it," said Danny. He winked. "For a while."

"Have we seen this before?" Cora glanced at Robert before her gaze was drawn back to the material.

Robert peered at it and shrugged. "Don't think so."

"I reckon it's worth something," said Danny. "I showed it to a guy in Lhasa who was a bit too keen to take it off my hands. It might even fund my next trip back there, if I'm lucky."

"That's your mum," said Cora, her eyes still on the mandala. When she didn't elaborate, Danny glanced at Robert. *What?*

A moment later, the mobile on the table beeped and Danny picked it up. "Hi, Mum," he said, frowning at Cora, who was turning the mandala towards her, her head cocked to one side as she studied it. Danny got up, mouthing *What the fuck?* to Robert as he left the room.

"How did you know?" Robert was staring at her.

She glanced up. "Hmm?"

"How did you know it was his mum?"

She froze, retracing her thoughts, then shrugged. "I just did."

*

The sun's rays pierced the edge of space as they cleared the blue-white curvature of the earth, shards of gold against the cosmos. The world rolled past, silent and changing beneath the GRACE satellites, as they watched and listened and took notes. The gravity mountain they had found was growing. Whatever caused it was surging like a slow, dense wave across the earth, only this wave had no trough. It seemed like their conversations with Sven Amsel were over, although he would not know it. They had a new audience now, one who listened to their findings every day, and kept them secret.

CHAPTER FOUR

B en's mum hesitated as she walked down the stairs in the
tenement building. Something was wrong. Too much noise
from below, the wrong kind of noise. Not a party or a TV or an
argument, but radios. The sound of the police. Ben looked up from
under his red hood. She swept her short blonde hair behind her ear,
her eyes, deep hazel like his own, looking at the stairs but not really
seeing them, as she strained to pick up what was going on. She
squeezed his hand and continued down the stone staircase, past the
black graffiti sprayed on the chipped green wall, which read: *FUCK
ALL POLITICIANS*. Red tape ran across the open door of the
third-floor flat. Something flashed inside. She glimpsed a dark stain
on the light carpet and a foot in a stiletto protruding from a room
inside, as though someone, a woman, were lying on the floor, face-
down. Voices drifted from inside and people in white paper suits and
masks moved between rooms. One glanced up at her as she passed.

"Hey, Simmonds," came a voice from inside. "Close that door,
would ya?"

The door slammed shut. She dropped her gaze and picked up her
pace, turning the corner to the next set of stairs. It was blocked
further down on the next landing by two men – one in a sweatshirt
and joggers, the other in a suit. She hesitated.

"I said I don't know," said the man in the sweatshirt. "I came up and I found her like this."

"Excuse me, ma'am?" She turned to the woman behind her. She wasn't wearing a uniform but she may as well have been. Everything about her smacked of police. "Can I have a moment?"

"Eh… I have to get to work."

"It won't take long. I'm DC Rowan. Can I take your name, please?" She opened a notebook and began scribbling.

"Zoe Phillips."

"Did you know Lisa Fernley?"

"No. I only moved in a month ago. Look, I need to take my son to—"

"Which flat?"

"Four-one."

Further down the stairwell, the man in the sweatshirt was getting agitated. "I told you – I didn't see her last night!"

"Just answer the question, Mr Dawson," said the officer, noting his statement. His voice was devoid of emotion.

DC Rowan kept her eyes on Zoe. "Did you see anything unusual—" she began.

Ben tugged on Zoe's arm. "Just a minute, Ben," said Zoe. "I'm talking to the policewoman."

"—over the past twenty-four hours?" continued Rowan.

He tugged her sleeve again and looked up at his mother. "He's lying," he said quietly.

DC Rowan's gaze landed on him.

"I'm sorry," said Zoe as she turned back to Rowan. "Can you say that again?"

Rowan crouched down until she was eye level with Ben. "You think the man's lying?" she whispered.

He looked back at her in that way that children do, giving nothing away.

"What's your name?" asked Rowan.

The boy looked at his mother.

"His name's Ben," said Zoe.

"Why do you think he's lying, Ben?" said Rowan, softly.

Ben tugged on Zoe's sleeve. She bent down and he cupped a small hand to her ear as he whispered something.

Rowan watched Zoe expectantly as Zoe let out a nervous breath. "I think he has a good imagination," said Zoe.

Rowan did not indulge Zoe's opinion, nor did she smile. "What did he say?" she said.

Zoe glanced at the man on the stairs then sighed, speaking in a hushed voice. "He said the man's worried he didn't clean his car properly."

"Ben," said Rowan, her voice just a whisper as she eyed the man in the sweatshirt. "Do you know where his car is?"

Ben nodded.

"Ben?" said Zoe. "Look, I don't want him getting caught up in this," she said, rounding on Rowan.

"This is a murder investigation," said Rowan. "We're obliged to follow all leads."

Zoe opened her mouth to say something, but changed her mind.

"Can you show me, Ben?" asked Rowan.

Ben nodded again.

DC Rowan held her finger to her lips then led them down the stairwell past the man called Dawson and the officer, still in discussion. Zoe stole a brief glance and Dawson caught her eye, the corners of his thin mouth downturned, forcing her to look away. She didn't know him, nor did she want to. Ben was concentrating on the stairs at his feet.

They stepped out into the street.

"I really don't think you should be wasting your time," said Zoe as they reached the corner. "He's six. He doesn't know what he's saying."

Rowan ignored her. "Where's his car, Ben?"

He led them to the next street. It was narrow and lined with vehicles parked on both sides, between rows of dark sandstone tenement flats and an off-license on the corner behind barred windows. He stopped halfway along, his finger pointing to a Ford Cortina. Rust had eaten holes into its maroon coat.

The detective took out her radio and held it to her mouth. "This is DC Rowan. I need a vehicle check, over."

A crackle from the radio, then a voice. "Okay, send registration number…"

Zoe pulled Ben aside. "Ben," she said. "You shouldn't make things up. The policewoman's very busy. This isn't a time for games."

Ben, who was small for his age anyway, seemed to disappear as he withdrew into his hood and stared at the ground.

The radio crackled again. "It's registered to a Paul Dawson, 455 Newton Road. He's on record."

DC Rowan glanced at Ben. He was kicking a small stone around with the toe of his trainer. She walked towards them. "I think you'd better come with me."

*

It had been three hours. They sat in a small windowless room with a desk, four chairs and a CCTV camera mounted in the corner of the ceiling, Ben on Zoe's knee. Rowan had brought some toy cars and knights and placed them on the desk with some orange juice and a packet of chewy sweets. The ensemble amused Ben and he moved from one to the other in an imaginary game, keeping himself fed and watered, while the people behind the desk asked questions. Next to Rowan was a man with a dark beard and dark hair flopped to one side. His shirt and tie looked like an afterthought, the tie fat and loose and askew. He had introduced himself as Dr Raymond Locke, a doctor of psychology.

"Why do we need a psychologist?" asked Zoe.

Locke glanced briefly at Rowan. "It's become routine, recently," he said. "Ben?"

Ben was eye level with the table making a soft 'vvvvvgh' sound as he pushed one of the cars round the obstacle course he had set up with his sweets.

54

"Ben," said Zoe. "The doctor's talking to you."

Ben straightened up.

"How did you know about the man's car, Ben?" asked Locke.

Ben shrugged.

After a pause, Rowan slid a photograph across the table to him. It was Paul Dawson, the man in the stairwell. "How do you know this man, Ben?"

Ben stared at the photograph blankly.

"*Do* you know him?" asked Locke.

Ben shook his head.

"Have you met him before?" pushed Rowan.

Ben pushed his car slowly around a fried egg. "No."

Locke looked to Zoe. She shrugged. "Like I said, we don't know him. The first we saw of him was today."

"Is there any way Ben could have met him when you weren't around?" asked Rowan. She had a notepad in front of her with not much written on it.

"There's a woman who looks after him when I'm at work," said Zoe. "But she doesn't take him out. Anyway, he's been with me for the past two days, and we didn't see that man till this morning. Like I said."

Locke picked up a toy car and wheeled it round the gummy obstacles on the table. Ben watched him, the ghost of a smile appearing on his lips.

"Ben," said Locke, while he concentrated on his car, "how did you know what the man was thinking?"

Ben stared into space. He shrugged.

Locke studied him as Ben mirrored the route Locke's car had taken with his own, then turned to Zoe. "Have you noticed this kind of thing happening with Ben before?" he asked. "I mean, anything unusual?"

Zoe held his eye but said nothing.

Behind her, the door opened. A man in a suit stood in the

doorway. "Excuse me, Detective, Doctor… Can I have a word?"

They got up and Ben carried on with his game. "Excuse us," said Rowan.

Locke and Rowan followed the Chief Inspector into an adjacent room where, in the corner, a monitor on the desk showed Ben sitting on Zoe's knee. He closed the door.

"We've found traces of blood in the boot of Dawson's car," said the Chief. "He just signed a confession. I think we're done with these two."

"But how did Ben know about him?" asked Rowan.

"He must have seen something," said the Chief.

"He didn't," said Locke. "We've been over that."

The Chief was losing patience. "How else do you explain a six-year-old knowing we'd find evidence in Dawson's car?"

Locke stared at him but didn't answer. "I want to run a psychological profile on him."

"Not on my time," said the Chief. "We have Dawson's confession. Let them go."

*

Rowan held the door for Zoe and Ben. "Thanks for your time, Ms Philips. You too, Ben."

Ben threw her a glance from under his hood as he slipped the toy car into his hoodie pocket.

Locke watched them leave, mother and son, hand in hand.

"What do you think?" asked Rowan.

"I don't know," said Locke. "I might put it down to one of those things, if it was just him."

*

Cora opened Danny's laptop as they sat at the kitchen table. He had left it for them to use while he was out. They sat in the same room, amidst the communal clutter of everyday life – empty mugs stained with tea, the pile of unopened mail that grew larger every day, the scrawny plant on the windowsill that Cora had saved by watering it for the first time in a long time – seeing none of it, lost in the different realities of their own thoughts. "You okay?" she asked.

"Yeah," said Robert. He folded the blood-stained letter carefully and returned it to its envelope.

She gave his hand a sympathetic squeeze and they shared a smile that hurt. When she went back to the laptop, Robert said, "Don't use your email, or social media."

She threw him a look that said, *I'm not stupid,* and turned back to the screen. "I just want to catch up with the world."

Robert took out the flash-drive and turned it over in his hand, his mind returning to another place and time as Liam's words echoed in his mind... *there's no sign of it...*

Glancing up at him, Cora said, "You can talk about it, you know. If you want."

Can I? he thought. *How much could you handle before it's too much?*

She reached for his hand again. "Don't shut me out. I told you I'm with you."

Maybe you could... He glanced down at the flash-drive then said, "What do you remember, about Mindscape?"

She pulled back. It wasn't the question she was expecting.

"Why?" she asked.

Choosing his words carefully, he said, "Remember how you knew something was wrong after Sarah died?"

Cora's face paled. She had known. The dreams of her sister that had plagued her, were the same ones that had taken Robert to the edge of his sanity. He had long since crossed the line of what anyone could call normal but Cora, always more open-minded, always more willing to believe, had become convinced that Sarah was trying to reach them. Shame rose in Robert as he recalled how he had scorned her insistence. She had been right. Mindscape, it seemed, did not discriminate between the living and the dead.

"You think Elliot's in Mindscape?" she breathed.

"I don't know. It may not even exist anymore, but I have to be sure."

Cora bit her lip.

"I need to start somewhere," said Robert. "If I understand it better, it might help me know."

Her gaze fell to the floor again as she closed the lid on the laptop. "It was feelings, mainly. Abstract thoughts. An overwhelming sense of despair, like I was sinking into this black pit, and there was no way out..." She swallowed.

"Do you remember anything about when it first happened? About how they put you in there?"

The lines on her forehead deepened and she fidgeted with her sleeve. "There was a blue light... and then a kind of tunnel that emerged into..." She paused and Robert laid a hand on hers, feeling her skin cool and clammy to touch. "...into this field of trees. Thousands of them, all of them dead. I felt the trunk digging into my back, and I couldn't pull away from it. There was no sense of time; no day or night. Just grey. All of the things I'd been afraid of came back, and I was living them, drowning in them, over and over..." She drew breath and closed her eyes, as tears spilled onto her cheeks.

Robert held her, berating himself for what he had just done. "Hey, I'm sorry. You're safe, it's okay. It's okay." He smoothed her hair and kissed her head. "I'm sorry..." he said again.

The front door slammed.

"Hi honey, I'm home!" came Danny's voice. He strode into the kitchen, dumping his blue rucksack on a chair and taking off his jacket. "How about a pint?" he said. Dusk muted the colours outside the window as Cora wiped her cheek and avoided his eye. "You two look like you could use a drink," said Danny.

Robert glanced up. "Maybe another night."

"Thought you might say that." Danny reached into his rucksack and produced a bottle of whisky and some beer, which he landed heavily on the table. "We'll just stay in, then."

He dug out a deck of cards and a box of matches from a drawer then raked around in a cupboard and produced three shot glasses. He spilled the matches onto the table, counting out equal piles, and slid one to each of them.

"Texas hold'em. Fifty pence per chip," he said, filling the shot glasses. "And a shot for every time you lose or you swear." He clapped and rubbed his hands together then raised his glass. "Let's get warmed up." Their glasses clinked as they met over the table and they sank the first drink.

*

"For fuck's sake, Cora," said Danny as he pushed another pile of matches towards hers, which was substantially bigger than his own. The light outside had faded into darkness.

She threw him a schoolteacher look. "Penalty."

Danny shook his head and knocked back his drink, wincing as it hit the back of his throat. "You never told me she was a shark," he said, as Robert dealt the cards of the next game.

"I didn't know," said Robert. He winked at Cora.

A faint smile raised the corner of Cora's lips as she held Danny's eye. "Beginner's luck."

"Wait a minute…" said Danny, getting up and staggering to keep his balance. He rummaged around in the bookcase, ignoring the things that dropped onto the floor beside him and slumped down a moment later with a compass in his hand.

"Are you lost?" said Robert.

"My lucky compass," he said, clutching it as though this was about to change everything. Robert sniggered.

"You may scoff," Danny said, "but this has never let me down." He waved the plastic rectangle before them. "This little baby's got me out of more scrapes than you could imagine. You're shy, Cora. Small blind. Keep up."

"Yes, I am," she said, pushing a match forward with sarcastic sweetness. "You're absolutely right, Danny."

Robert surveyed his cards then slapped them on the table, face-down. "Why have I had such shitty hands all night?"

"Penalty," said Cora and Danny in unison.

Robert's sigh was thick with disgust. He sank his shot then dealt the flop, as Danny refilled his glass.

Cora slid three matches forward and Danny topped up his bet with another two. She nodded to Robert, who dealt the turn. They considered their cards, each scanning the others' faces, each doing what they could to mask their own.

"Four," said Cora, pushing her bet forwards.

Danny eyed the upturned cards on the table and the two in his hands. He studied Cora, and she winked at him. "Your four and up four," he said.

Cora pushed another four matches into the middle, meeting his bet.

"Happy?" said Robert.

Cora nodded and he dealt the last card.

"Eight," said Cora, carefully selecting eight matches from her oversized pile.

Danny's concentration moved from his hand, to the table, to Cora's face. A sly smile fractured his mask. "Your eight and up eight," he said.

"Careful, Cora," said Robert. "He's not bluffing this one."

Keeping her gaze fixed on Danny, Cora said, "I'll see you," and pushed forward another eight matches.

Robert sucked air in through his teeth as Cora and Danny locked eyes. "What have you got?" said Danny.

They did not blink or break the stare for an agonising moment before she laid out her cards.

"Two pairs?" said Danny in disbelief. "That's it?"

She didn't rise to it. "What have you got?" she said.

Danny's mouth tightened. "Fuck all," he said, throwing his cards onto the table. He picked up the compass, glowering at it like it had done him a great personal injustice and had just blown its chances of any future trust.

"Penalty," said Robert and Cora.

"Ah, shite," said Danny.

"Doubler," said Robert, holding up the bottle like a parent expecting a child to take his medicine. "Come on, now. Get it down you."

Danny winced as did the honourable thing. "How is she doing

this?" he said to Robert. "Even you didn't think I was bluffing that one." He hiccupped at her. "Were you cheating?"

"No!" said Cora, indignantly.

"So how come you knew I had a crap hand?"

She shrugged. "I just did."

Danny eyed her. "Alright then," he said, picking up the deck. His attempt to shuffle it resulted in a card explosion. Snorting like a pig, he keeled sideways, kick-starting a fit of giggles between him and Robert, as he tried to reassemble himself and the deck. Then, conjuring an appropriately serious expression he held up a card, its back to Cora. "What have I got here, then?"

"What is this?" she said.

"Think of it as a game," Danny replied.

Her eyes narrowed. "Bullshit. You're testing me."

Danny pointed a wavering finger at her glass with a look of *you know what to do…*

She straightened up and held him with a level stare. "Alright, then." Sinking her drink, she slammed her glass on the table upside down, and said, "Red. A face card."

Robert shuffled his chair next to Danny to see the card. They looked up at her.

"Lucky guess, but a bit general." Refilling her glass, Danny held up another card and she watched them as they peered at it.

"Two of spades," she said.

Danny's forehead crumpled into a frown and Robert stared at her. *Are you for real, Cora?* Danny turned the card to face her and the giggles seized them again.

"Wait, wait, wait," said Danny. He waved his arm across the space between them as though clearing away the past. "That could just be coincidence. Alright," he said, assuming control of the situation in the way that pissed people do. "How about this?" He swept the cards to one side and placed his elbow on the table, squaring up to her. "Wood-paper-scissors. Ready?"

"You're really can't let this go, can you?" she said.

"Nope."

She mirrored his pose. "Alright then. Ready. On three." They bounced closed fists in synchrony. On the third bounce, both produced scissors. Two more bounces, then both rocks. Another two bounces, both rocks. Both paper. Both scissors. Both paper.

Danny slumped back into his chair. "What the absolute fuck, Cora?" She pointed at the remnants of the whisky, but Danny didn't move. He, like Robert, just sat staring at her.

*

Seth Winters sat at his console and flicked through the updates his team had brought to his attention. They had all shared his disappointment in finding the trail and then being plucked out of the forest, but they had enough work to keep them going. Links between earthquakes and fracking, unprecedented summer warming in Arctic Canada... Seth scrolled through them, without really reading. His mind wasn't on it. He opened the GRACE link again. The gravitational anomaly showed no sign of losing its intensity. If anything, the readings were stronger, and it seemed to be spreading. Amos' dismissal of his involvement still burned. He felt like the star student who had been caned for the first time.

He wondered what Dana would have done. Picking up his phone, he selected her number, pausing as his eyes fell on the image of her sleek dark hair and red lips. He had taken the photo on one of the rare days they had gotten away from the place, into the outside world where people did normal things. They had spent the first day in the park, meandering in the sunshine, listening to music on a warm rug, sharing their favourite food. The second day they spent in bed. He remembered how he felt when he made her laugh and when she looked at him in that way she sometimes did, the bliss of being unable to resist the pull she had on him. Had she asked him anything confidential about his work, he'd have told her. But she wasn't like that. He respected her professionally as much as he lusted after her personally. His bliss was blemished with confusion now, and bitterness. He swallowed then dialled.

"*Hi, you've reached Dana Bishop. Please leave a message...*" He hung up. While the sound of her voice made him feel lighter, the recollection that she had not returned any of his many phone calls did not. He tapped his pen on the desk. Someone had to know where she'd gone.

"I'll be back soon," he said to Nadine as he stood up. He left his Hub and took an electric buggy to the sick bay, passing through the large contemporary tunnels with their bright panels flashing above as they drove. People weren't often sick in ORB, unless something had gone badly wrong with a trial, and he was not surprised to find the waiting room empty. Only Clay, the medic was there, restocking the shelves. Late forties, friendly and a little worn round the edges, Clay was the man Seth was hoping to find.

"Hi, Clay."

"Seth! How are you?"

"Have you got a minute?" said Seth, eyeing the new security camera above. The whole place was in the process of being rewired since the CERN incident.

Clay followed his gaze to the wall-mounted camera, whose loose wires dangled from the socket. "It's not connected," he said. "I opposed it on the basis of confidentiality."

"Whatever," said Seth. "Bring your tablet."

He led Clay down a back corridor into one of the service tunnels. It was dimmer than the main ones, grey, rather than white, its lighting an afterthought. More importantly it was out of sight of any cameras, connected or not. A buggy chugged past tugging a trailer. Perched on the back at an awkward angle was a busty manikin of a scantily-clad woman and a glass tank splattered with red droplets. Something that looked like a thick red-brown rope impaled on a knife, lay inside. They froze as they watched it pass.

"Jesus Christ, was that a snake?" breathed Clay. He shook his head.

Seth watched the truck disappear round a bend. He shivered then turned back to Clay. "There's someone I need to get in touch with," he said. "I haven't heard from her for a while."

"What," grinned Clay, "did she blow you off?"

"Maybe. But it's not like her to avoid contact. She's usually pretty straight talking." He paused as another buggy hummed past. "I thought maybe you'd have her contact details on medical record."

Clay sighed. "Hmm. We go back a long way. I mean, I know I still owe you for that thing with the guy in the pub, but... technically, I'm not meant to do that."

"I just want to know she's okay."

Clay chewed on his lip. "What's her name?"

"Dana Bishop."

"*Dana Bishop? The* Dana Bishop? You and her were..." He blew the air out from his puffed cheeks. "You're braver than I thought."

"Can you help me, Clay? Just have a look..."

Clay chuckled as he opened his tablet and scrolled through some details. Then he paused, hesitating, his eyes fixed on the screen.

"What is it?" asked Seth, moving to see what had changed Clay's expression.

Clay shut it down. "She's not on the system."

Seth stared at him. "You must have something..."

"Sorry, Seth. Maybe you should move on. Listen, I've got to go – I have a clinic in five minutes." He patted Seth's shoulder. "Good to see you, man."

Seth watched as Clay disappeared back up the corridor, clutching his tablet, his head hung low.

*

Victor Amos sat at the head of the polished, rectangular table. The room, sparsely furnished, was partly in shadow, lit only by cold white cones of up-lighting at intervals along the base of the walls. At the opposite end of the long table was a man with sallow skin. He sat motionless, his eyes veiled behind small round shades; matching omega signs on his black tee-shirt and baseball cap. Amos' eyes stayed on him as the door opened and a young man entered, wearing a black shirt and black trousers, a white cloth draped over his left arm. He was carrying a plate of food and a set of cutlery, which he placed in front of Mr Y.

"I'm told you have not eaten much since the CERN incident. Please, eat."

"I'm not hungry," said Mr Y. His voice was soft, a blend of Eastern and American.

Amos did not flinch or look away. "Eat."

Mr Y sat unmoving then picked up the fork and lifted a mouthful of flaked meat dressed in a sprinkling of green leaves, to his lips.

Amos watched him in silence. After the fifth mouthful, he said, "I expected more of you. Your pride cost this organisation a great deal of trouble. Were you anyone else, I would throw you to the lions. As it is, your expertise is second to none, therefore I am willing to forego a personal mistake for the greater good of our endeavours. However, do not assume I will be so forgiving should there be another transgression."

He pushed something leathery along the table. It spun slightly as it slid over the smooth surface, coming to stop in front of Mr Y's plate. A belt, made of snakeskin.

Mr Y stopped chewing and looked down at the meat on his plate.

"Mr condolences for Reggie," said Amos.

*

If hangovers were punishment, Robert must have been very bad. It took far longer than it should have just to sit up straight and see the world as a place that didn't move. When he finally surfaced, he found the space next to him empty.

He threw on some clothes and made his way into the kitchen wondering how, given that he had evolved in ways he could not have imagined, he could still end up with a thumping headache after drinking some whisky. It had been a lot of whisky though, he reflected, as he rubbed the pain behind his eyes.

Danny was at his laptop, his hair dishevelled. "How are we this fine morning?" he grinned.

"Rough."

Danny kicked out a chair for him and Robert flumped into it.

"You look like shit," said Danny. He got up and rummaged around in a cupboard as Robert closed his eyes and laid his head against the wall. Either the wall was pulsing and he could feel it in his brain, or his brain was bouncing and it was resonating in the plasterboard.

"This will sort you out." Danny plonked a can of orange fizzy juice and a blister pack of painkillers on the table. "Remind me never to play poker with Cora again. Or anything else. That was some weird shit last night."

"She's taking ages in the shower."

"She's not in the shower. She went out half an hour ago."

Robert straightened up.

"She should go pro with her luck," said Danny. "Couple of big games and you could both…"

Robert was on his feet. "Where did she go?"

"Relax, man," said Danny. "She just needed some air…" He followed Robert as he went back to their room, watching him pull on his boots. Robert whipped back the sleeping bags and picked up his mobile. He dialled, waited, then hung up. "Shit," he mumbled as he headed to the door. "Which way did she go?"

"Into town, I think. What's the problem?" said Danny, frowning.

"She shouldn't have gone out on her own…"

"Why not?"

"Call me if she comes back," said Robert.

"Wait," said Danny. "What's going on?"

"I'll talk to you later, Danny." He grabbed his jacket, leaving the door open and Danny bemused in the hallway.

*

Robert wrestled with his sleeve as he strode out, trying to fit his arm into it as he held his phone to his ear with his shoulder. He could feel the thud of his heart against his ribs, in time with the thud of his brain against his skull. The number rang out. "Fuck," he breathed, and dialled again. *Christ, Cora, you should know better…*

"Hello?" came her voice.

"Cora!" Robert stopped. "Where are you?"

"Eh, in a shop on Candlemarket," she said. "Shamans Cave, I think it's called…"

"Okay – I'll meet you there." He took his beanie from his pocket and pulled it over his forehead, picking up his pace as he walked. But he didn't run. Running might attract attention.

*

Robert glanced up at the name painted in loud purple above the shop entrance. Things competed with each other for space in the window – tarot cards, dream catchers, incense sticks… He felt his heart sink. For all of his own weirdness, he still had antibodies to stuff like this. It represented a world he couldn't relate to. *Another one,* he found himself thinking. A bell jangled above him as he pushed open the door.

He found her by a stand of prayer flags. "What were you thinking?" he whispered. There was no one else around but he kept his voice low. "You saw what they did to my dad…"

"I know," she said, avoiding his eye. "I just needed some air."

"Next time just tell me…" He put his arms round her, wanting to hold her and strangle her at the same time. She broke free, her eyes scanning the stuff.

"You see anything you like?" asked Robert.

Drawn to the display cabinet in the corner, she stopped in front of a box of black rocks. Her hand reached out slowly and she picked one of them up and turned it around, studying its contours. It was about the size of a small plum and glinted as it reflected the fairy lights coiled on the shelf. She put it back and lifted another. Five rocks later, she had forgotten Robert's question.

"Can I help you?" came a silky voice. A woman came gliding towards them, wearing a black dress that reached to her ankles, imprinted with white eyes. Her hair was an unnatural purple and an Egyptian ankh hung round her neck from a thick silver chain.

Cora turned to her, frowning, as though she were interrupting a dream.

"They're good for protection, security and transformation," said the woman, and her voice had the quality of air. "And they bring balance to the intestines."

"I'm sorry?" said Cora.

"Obsidian," she said, nodding to the crystal in Cora's hand.

Cora turned back to the box. "Do you mind if I…" she began, and lifted the box to the counter. She turned it upside down and the obsidian lumps rattled out over the glass.

"Not at all," said the woman, raising her eyebrows. She drifted behind the counter, moving aside an Indian headdress to make space, and watched as Cora raked through the selection of black volcanic glass. "We have a special on angels today," said the woman, lifting from the shelf a white winged statue, about the size of a coke bottle. "Two for the price of one."

Cora wasn't listening. She was examining each rock like it hid a treasure she was hunting. She turned them this way and that as the light glinted on their smooth black surfaces. Robert watched her. *She's still hungover,* he thought. *Spaced.* The woman behind the counter glanced at him and nodded sagely, while she filed her nails.

"Does this remind you of anything?" asked Cora, holding up a crystal she had been pondering for what seemed to Robert like far too long.

He considered answering but before he could, she turned back to the counter, peering at the crystal as she inverted it.

"Do you mind if I borrow that?" asked Cora, nodding to the metal nail file in the assistant's hand.

"Eh... no," said the woman, and handed it over.

Cora began to file the edge of the crystal.

Smiling, in that way people do when they think they have a direct line to wisdom that you don't, the woman said, "It's obsidian, dear. Volcanic rock. You'll be filing that for a very long time."

Cora ignored her and continued filing.

"Cora..." began Robert, as a phone rang from a back room.

"Excuse me," said the woman. She smiled mistily at Robert.

"Your son's okay," said Cora, glancing up briefly from her crystal filing.

The woman stopped and looked back, her serenity fractured as the phone bleeped its crescendoing pings. She bustled through the bead curtain and the pinging stopped.

"Cora?" said Robert.

Cora looked up, recalibrating herself to her surroundings. "Right," she said. "Eh..." She picked up a handful of rocks and reached for her purse. "I'm going to take these."

"Oh, thank God," came the woman's voice from the back of the shop. "Was anyone else hurt?"

*

"You want to tell me how you're doing this?" asked Robert as they stepped onto the street.

"What?" said Cora, as she put her paper bag of black crystals and the nail file, which the assistant had thrown in free of charge, into her pocket.

"The phone calls, the cards last night…"

"I don't know." She shrugged. "Intuition."

"It's more than that, Cora. Those weren't just random coincidences…" Robert's words fell away as his eyes were drawn to something behind her. As Cora turned to look, Robert caught her arm and steered her firmly into a café to their left.

"What's wrong?" she breathed, frowning at the force of his grip.

He said nothing until they reached a table in shadow, near enough to see out onto the street opposite, which sat bleached in sunlight.

Cora glanced sideways through the window, trying to see what had his attention.

"Don't stare," he said, urgently.

"What is it?" she said.

He faced her, but his gaze slid to the window again, as the man in the parked car lifted a phone to his ear and the snake-like scar appeared on his upper arm beneath his black T-shirt. "See the guy in the black car across the street?" said Robert.

Casually, she glanced round. When she looked back, angst had replaced her composure. "Oh my god, is that…"

"Peter Banks," finished Robert. He watched Banks run his hand through his hair, the hand that had forced Cora into the back of a van, and had held itself tight over Aiyana's mouth and nose until the life shuddered from her.

The waitress arrived with a pad, a pen and a smile. "Now, what can I get you folks?" she said.

"Just coffee," said Robert, with the briefest of glances in her direction before his gaze was drawn back to Banks.

"Same," said Cora.

"You alright, love?" said the waitress, her brow knotted.

"Yeah," said Cora, forcing a smile. "Fine, thanks." She became absorbed in a flyer that was lying on the table, an advert for computer repairs.

"Uh-huh," said the waitress as she walked off, with a look that suggested she would just play along with Cora's game. The glance she cast Robert was loaded with judgement.

They sat in silence, Robert's eyes on Banks and Cora's fixed on the flyer she wasn't reading. Banks' hand was on the wheel, his mobile still to his ear.

After a moment, she said, "How would I know?"

Robert turned back to her. "What?"

"I've never even seen it," she said.

"Seen what?" said Robert.

She looked up, vaguely irritated. "The stone."

"What stone?"

"Are you even listening?"

Robert sat back, perplexed. *What is she on about?*

"You know what I'm on about!" she said indignantly. "*You* asked *me!*"

He watched her, feeling suddenly queasy. "Cora, I didn't say a word. I didn't even think—"

The colour had drained from her face. "Amos?" she whispered. "Why?"

Robert froze, his gaze sliding back to Banks, who hung up and pulled out onto the road.

He reached for Cora's arm. "What else do you hear, Cora?" There was an edge to his voice.

"What do you mean?"

"It's not my words you're hearing. It's not even words…" He glanced after the car, which disappeared into the traffic. "You're hearing Bank's thoughts."

"*What?*" She looked appalled.

"Quickly," said Robert. "Where's he going?"

"Eh…" Cora squeezed her eyes shut, flustered and disturbed. "I dunno… it's hard to make out…"

Robert squeezed her hand. "Try," he breathed.

She opened her eyes. "The university."

*

Elijah Lazaro stood facing the pillar of mist. It was a thing of beauty to him, swirling as it did on its axis inside the protective casing that reached from below the floor of Area 9 to extend beyond the ceiling. The girth of the tank was as wide as a bus. The space was important and the dim chamber in which it stood, more than able to accommodate. Grey had many colours within it, thought Lazaro, his face tinged by the beam of blue light that sliced through the tank's centre. It was gathering more texture now, as proceedings advanced. He recalled the thrill he felt the first time he saw the fleck of things forming within. It made him feel like a god, watching the amniotic fluid that bathed his creations. As things progressed, he found himself gazing longer through the casing, marvelling at the glimpses he caught of the smooth arc of a head, the slender tapering of a finger as it drifted past in the spiralling current of mist. He loved them in the way a father loves a child, wanting to nurture them, to give them the best of what they needed to grow. It had to be right.

He turned to the test subject in the dome to his left. It glowed with a soft blue haze, like the semi-transparent surface of a living planet, encasing the trolley on which she lay. He recalled vaguely what she had once been – abrasive, aggressive, intolerant; willing to do whatever was necessary to advance her career and then failing at the critical moment. He had no compunction about it. The world did not need another woman like her. But she was not useless. It was a beautifully efficient service he offered, now that he thought about it. This way she could contribute to something worthwhile.

He leaned close to her, his breath misting on the blue dome that encased her, sending an eddy of neon spirals through it. "You should be grateful," he whispered.

Dana Bishop stared ahead, her eyes fixed on the things that haunted her.

Elijah turned to the technician in scrubs and a mask who recorded her stress responses on his tablet. "Take her below. And make sure she's well enough sedated. We'll begin the first test in an hour."

*

Dana was aware of blue above her. A dome of the sky, perhaps. Like that moment of emerging from sleep before you remember your place in space and time, she lay suspended. It seemed to darken in colour, like the sun setting too rapidly, and her awareness contracted in on itself. Memories seeped back – fear, loss, regret. She felt the unease of them coil about her like a snake sliding round her throat and squeezing. Fears she had suppressed from long ago, ones she thought she had left behind. They bubbled to the surface, forcing her to relive them, and left a scum on her mind. Why was it happening? She didn't know. The darkness was pierced by a bright light above her, a harsh clinical light. Her body was moving, but it was not her will that directed it. It felt like she was floating as things passed above her. There was a swish and a ping, a sound she recalled. An elevator. She felt the sensation of dropping. A masked face peered down at her and she became aware of a pain on the inside of her elbow. She found it in her to turn her face towards the sensation and saw the syringe full of white liquid pushing into her veins. It hit her just as the sedative hit her blood-brain barrier and seeped through the cracks in her capillaries to bathe her neurons. She felt her consciousness dissolve into black.

*

She was not aware of the basement cavern, or the technician as he placed the headband of electrodes onto her scalp. She did not see the blue dome that glowed around the trolley on which she lay, like a neon pod. She knew nothing of the pipe that led out from the casing that housed the swirling grey pillar of mist, the pipe that syphoned off a segment of its contents. She did not see Elijah Lazaro open the hatch at the end of the pipe or the look of affection in his eyes as he gazed on the shadow that drifted out. Smooth, black and insubstantial, it was the shape of a human, its domed head featureless, its movements fluid, like an eel in water. It penetrated the dome that encased her and came to rest above her, mirroring her pose as she lay supine, turning its head gently as it tuned into her mind. She did not see it but she felt it. She felt it draw her fears forwards from the recesses of her memories; felt the pain of them blister the surface of her mind as the blue glow of the dome above her intensified, pulsing with newfound energy. And she felt the thing above her sifting through those fears, absorbing them, expanding with them as a leech engorges with blood.

Elijah looked on, his pale grey eyes filled with pride and admiration. When it was full, he watched it drift to the casing surrounding the pillar of mist. It pressed its palms and forehead against it and issued a sound like a faint whispering. From inside the tank, through the cyclone of swirling grey, came glimpses of other things taking form, shapes resembling the curve of its back, the arc of its shoulder. More things like it.

CHAPTER FIVE

Zoe and Ben approached the door of the ground-floor flat. A pile of junk mail was wedged in the letterbox and a black bin bag that emitted a whiff of something off, sat to the side of the stained mat. A baby was bawling inside. Zoe glanced down at Ben who stood patiently beside her. His red hood was up and he stared at the floor.

She felt her heart sag. "Look," she said. "It's only for a wee while. I'll be back soon."

"Why can't I come with you?" said Ben.

"Because Mummy's got to go to work." She rang the doorbell. "You know that, Ben."

His head dropped again.

"It's not that bad, is it?" said Zoe.

"Tyler doesn't like me." Large hazel eyes stared up at her from under a spray of long eyelashes and blond hair. Zoe crouched down beside him. "Of course he does. But you've got to play normally, okay?"

Ben dropped his gaze to the floor as Zoe kissed his forehead and stood up.

A moment later, the door opened. A stout woman with dreadlocks stood before them, holding a snivelling toddler in a nappy.

"Thanks Shannon," said Zoe. "I'll call you when I'm heading back."

"That's alright, love. In you come, Ben."

Ben shuffled forward, his hood still up.

"See you soon, Ben," said Zoe. "Love you."

He turned away and shuffled inside.

*

"Be with you shortly," said Zoe to the customer at table three, balancing a pile of plates on her forearm. She offloaded the dishes onto the counter.

"Zoe, the specials board needs done." The tousled-haired manager turned to the customer who was waiting to pay and smiled, ingratiatingly.

"Yeah, I'll get it," said Zoe as she unhooked the blackboard from the wall.

The new-start, a waitress, who looked young enough to still be in primary school, approached the counter with some more empty dishes.

"Do you have table four's order?" The manager's tone was condescending, like he was addressing someone who didn't qualify for his respect.

"Eh… I don't think so… not yet…" she stammered, as she leafed through her order pad.

"Table four's having the big breakfast and orange juice." Zoe didn't look up as she chalked. "And table one's a skimmed latte."

"Yeah," said the young waitress, tearing off a sheet of paper and handing it to the manager as she glanced at Zoe. "A skimmed latte for table one."

"Okay," said the manager as he punched the orders into the till. "Table six?"

The young waitress frowned at her pad and leafed some more.

"Two bacon rolls and two black coffees." Zoe carried on chalking.

"Excuse me, miss?"

Zoe glanced up. The man sitting at table four, just between the counter and the window, was watching her. She put down the chalk and leaned across the counter. "What are you doing here?" she hissed.

"I wanted to speak to you," said Raymond Locke.

Zoe dusted her hands off on her apron and approached his table. She glanced back at the manager who was ringing up another bill. "I told you everything we knew," she said in a hushed voice.

"How did you know my order?" he asked.

"What?"

"I hadn't placed it yet. And I don't talk to myself, at least not in cafés, anyway. You were absolutely right – big breakfast and orange juice – but how did you know?"

Zoe stared at him.

"It is kinda weird," said the young waitress, eavesdropping.

"Haven't you got work to do?" glared Zoe. The new-start shrugged and wandered off with her pen and pad.

"It's not just Ben," said Locke. "Is it?"

Zoe said nothing.

"Listen, I don't usually work for the police. I'm a researcher. I'd like to speak to you and Ben again."

"No," said Zoe. "I don't want him being questioned anymore."

"Then how about you?" he asked.

She stared at the floor.

Locke leaned forwards, his voice lowering. "You're not the only ones—"

"Ben's always been like this," she said curtly. "It's taken me a long time to help him forget. I'm not undoing all that."

"Forget what?"

She glanced back at the counter, where the manager was sharing a story with another customer, then leaned on the table, an edge to her whisper. "Try to imagine what it feels like if your son told you that he had another mother." Locke watched her as her lip trembled. "Told

76

you every day since he could talk that this wasn't his real home, that he had another family and he missed them…" She straightened up. "We've had a good month. I'm not going to do anything that encourages those fantasies."

"You think they're fantasies?" asked Locke.

"What else could they be?"

Locke paused, then said, "Maybe it would help if you understood it."

Zoe snorted. "I doubt it."

"Just consider it," said Locke. He placed a business card on the table. "Call me if you change your mind."

*

Ben took out the car from his pocket and sat on the floor. The room was sparsely furnished – an old couch with a rip in the red cover, a TV and stack of games against the wall. He ran the car over the carpet on all fours, preferring his imagination to the games. Sometimes he liked just to look out of the window. Behind the flats lay wasteland and an old warehouse with broken windows and words Ben couldn't read sprayed on the crumbling walls. Beyond, the four red sandstone chimneys of an abandoned factory reached into the air, the ghosts of another era, but in the foreground was a small patch of grass with a tree in the middle. Now it was summer, white flowers appeared on its branches like handfuls of snow. It was nice in the winter too, when real snow laced the dark bark and frost drew pictures on the trunk. He liked it best then. It reminded him of home.

Ben did not see Shannon much unless she brought in some food and a drink. She was nice, but she usually stayed out of the way in another room with the baby and so did Tyler. He could always hear them, though.

"But I don't want to!" came Tyler's voice. "I don't see why I have to! He's *weird*."

Ben stopped pushing his car. When it moved again, it barely crawled.

"That's enough!" came Shannon's voice. "You're a big boy, Tyler, and you're meant to look after him. I want you to go through and play with him right now."

A door slammed. Ben's car inched along a ridge in the carpet, like a snail out of fuel. The door opened behind him then thudded shut. The TV snapped on and babbled a milieu of tuneless music and inane chatter as Tyler slumped down on the couch. Ben sneaked a peek at him. He was facing the other way, arms folded, a scowl firmly on his face in the flickering lights from the TV. Ben went back to pushing his car.

Tyler let out a harsh huff. He stomped to the window, undoing the lock at the hinge, until it swung open fully. He hopped up onto the windowsill. "Don't you tell my mum or you're dead. You hear me?" He swung his legs out and dropped onto the grass below then pushed the window shut behind him.

Ben got up and ran to the window and pressed his nose to the glass. Outside, Tyler jumped at the tree as he ran and tore off a branch. It lay with its flowers on the grass like an offering. Tyler ran off towards the warehouse.

The glass misted and cleared, misted and cleared as Ben breathed, the elusive promise of freedom beckoning. He felt for the catch, as he had seen Tyler do, and it clicked beneath his fingers. The window swung out and the world opened up.

Ben touched the tree trunk as he passed then began to run. He ran across the wasteland, over the rubble, the remnants of another dream, over the rusty remains of bits of things that mattered once. He felt the air on his face and tasted it. It carried the scent of rubbish, of things abandoned to rot into the building blocks of another idea. He stopped, finding a perfect ramp for his car – a plank of wood – and launched it in an explosion of speed, imagination and a loud *sploosh!* into the ocean – a large puddle – that lay at the base of the ramp. He didn't know how long he stayed there, or how many times the superhero at the wheel catapulted the car into the tumultuous sea. Sometime later, voices drew his attention. He looked up and saw a flickering light from within the warehouse. Shaking the muddy water from his car, he went to investigate.

Finding a doorframe that opened into the building, he followed the sounds that led him up the stairwell to a higher floor. The shadows on the walls, cast by an orange light, led him further in.

There were three voices.

"Do it." A boy's voice, gruff; testy.

"You better not." It was Tyler. "It could explode."

"You do it," said a third.

Ben peeked around a corner to see a large open space. Three boys were standing around a metal bucket. Large dark pillars propped up the ceiling and the musty smell of decay hung on the air. The light came from the fire that crackled inside the bucket, casting a glow on the graffiti in the shadows and the shards of glass that poked through the rotting window frames. One of the boys thrust a metal canister at Tyler. Tyler took it, but his look told Ben that he was scared. As Ben moved closer, his foot slipped on a rough stone and the sound carried. The boys turned.

Tyler's fear hardened into anger. "What are you doing here?" he barked.

Ben said nothing as he backed away.

"Who's he?" said the boy with the gruff voice. He was bigger than the others, with a large face and small, hostile eyes and he was closing in on Ben.

"Just some kid my mum looks after sometimes," said Tyler. "Go home, Ben."

"So your name's Ben?" said the gruff boy. He turned back to Tyler. "Is this the weird kid you told us about?"

"Yeah, that's him," said Tyler, who looked thoroughly annoyed at the interruption. "Just ignore him, Darren."

"The one who's got two mummies?" said Darren, in a sing-song voice. "How does that work then?" He towered over Ben like a thundercloud, threatening to spoil his day. He looked like he was beginning to enjoy this. Ben said nothing as he stared back.

"Just leave him alone," said Tyler.

Darren ignored him. "What's that you've got there?" he said, his head cocked to one side as he frowned at Ben's hand. Ben moved his hand and his car behind his back and stared up at Darren.

Darren spun Ben's small frame round and snatched the car from him. "So, you want to play with the big boys?" he said. As he backed away, he waved the car at Ben. "Then you won't be needing any toys."

He grabbed the metal canister from Tyler, opened it and sloshed some of its contents over the flames. They flashed, erupting furious heat and light that engulfed the air above in a roar of blue and orange. The other boys shielded their faces with their arms as they turned, but Darren stared on in triumph. He glanced back at Ben, holding up his car, then dropped it theatrically into the blazing bucket.

"Don't be a shithead!" said Tyler. "What'd you do that for?"

"If he wants his car," mocked Darren, "he can come and get it."

Ben stared at him then, slowly, began walking towards the bucket.

"I'm taking you home, Ben," said Tyler as he strode towards him, but Darren's fist grabbed Tyler's hoodie and pulled him back.

"He wants his car, Tyler," Darren said again, sounding reasonable, "Let him have it."

Ben kept his eyes on the bucket as he crossed the floor. The flames were twice his height and he could feel his skin prickle with the heat.

"Get back, Ben!" shouted Tyler, wresting with Darren's grip. "*No! —*"

Ben was kneeling down next to the flames, now jettisoning from the container like the after-burn of a small jet engine. He leaned into them, reaching an arm inside the bucket, his face unflinching. A moment later, he retrieved a lump of metal.

Darren's grip on Tyler fell limp.

Ben shuffled a few feet away from the bucket, the smoking, deformed car on the floor, and not a mark on him. The skin of his hands, his face, unblemished, his red hoodie unburned. He stared at the car. Slowly the smoke fizzled out. The melting metal began to reform, morphing from a blob of blue into the body of the car. Black rubber took shape, reassembling itself into wheels. Ben tested them on the surface of the floor and they rolled the car around, like wheels should.

"What are you? Some kind of freak?" shouted Darren. "How'd you do that?"

Ben felt Darren's anger first but when he turned, he saw it in his eyes. He was coming for him, an ominous mix of fury and fear in his face. Ben's hand slipped into his hoodie pocket, his fingers curling round the stone.

"No!" shouted Tyler as Darren swiped at Ben.

Suddenly everything stopped.

"Darren?" said Tyler. "What happened? Where'd he go?"

Darren was backing away, his eyes on the space where Ben was. Only now, it looked like he couldn't see him at all. He turned on Tyler, gripping the front of his hoodie and twisting it. "This is *your* fault! Why'd you bring him here?"

"I didn't!" shouted Tyler indignantly.

"You did!" Darren pushed Tyler so hard that he fell back onto the floor and skimmed along the dusty concrete. Then he turned to the boy with no name. "Let's get out of here."

But the boy with no name did not move. Darren turned back to him. "Are you deaf? We're leaving."

The boy stood motionless, watching him. Slowly, deliberately he walked towards Darren, holding him with a level stare. Something about his eyes was different. Unflustered, unblinking, they seemed to have taken on an iridescence that was not there before. He reached down and helped Tyler to his feet then stood facing Darren, his expression unflinching.

"Leave," commanded the boy. His voice was layered, like it wasn't the only one speaking.

Darren backed away, stumbling as he retreated, then turned and bolted for the door.

Glancing warily at the boy, Tyler said, "Thanks… Are you okay? What happened to Ben?"

The boy with no name turned his impassive gaze on him. A breeze seemed to breathe through Tyler as the boy lowered his eyes, blinking like the light was too bright. He looked up. "Tyler?" he said. "What happened? Where's Darren?"

Tyler's eyes scanned the space around them. "Let's get out of here," he breathed.

Ben watched from the window as they ran across the waste ground, back to the street. He looked down at his car, his heart heavy, then sat down and wheeled it slowly around a broken plant pot. He reached for the stone in his pocket. It wasn't the real one but as his fingers curled round its surface, it reminded him, and he remembered what it was like to have a friend.

*

Zoe pushed aside her plate and picked up the business card. *Dr Raymond Locke, Psy.D. Psychologist, Innovatics Institute.* She turned it over in her hand and looked up at Ben. He was still working on his macaroni but was more interested in making shapes with it than eating it. Carefully, he drew all of the pasta tubes to the middle of the plate, forming a tapering lump. A mountain.

Zoe watched him, deep in concentration, his small hand awkward with the large spoon. It was becoming a habit. "Come on, Ben," she said. "Eat your food."

He glanced up, catching the uncomfortable expression on his mother's face, and squished his mountain with his spoon.

Zoe sighed. "You want to tell me what happened today?"

Ben looked at his plate and shrugged.

"Ben?" Zoe leaned forward and waited until he raised his eyes.

"Tyler's scared of me."

"Why?"

"I don't know. His friends called me a freak." He poked at his macaroni.

"Come here," said Zoe.

He clambered down from the seat and Zoe picked him up and sat him on her knee. He buried his face in her neck, the spikes of his blond hair soft on her skin and his breath puffs of warm air on her shoulder.

"Remember the man we met at the police station, the one who gave you your car?" said Zoe as she stroked his hair.

Ben nodded.

"I think we should go back and see him. You can tell him about

82

your mountain."

Ben nodded again and wiped his runny nose.

*

They set off early. Ben liked the walk through the park and although he usually stopped to feed the ducks, today they were in a hurry.

"Dr Locke's a nice man," said Zoe. "It's okay to tell him about things."

Ben glanced up at her. Normally it wasn't okay for him to talk about 'things' – it made her uncomfortable and he didn't like that. Sometimes he wondered if she believed him at all. He wondered if Dr Locke would be the same.

They took the bus and got off at a long road with grand buildings. Following directions from a skinny boy with spots and glasses, they stopped outside of a large dark building. Ben stared up at its glass walls, squinting as the sunlight glinted on its panels. It did not look like a place to have fun.

Inside a woman directed them to an elevator, past people busy arranging tables in the atrium. A man followed the table-shifters, sticking red tape between the table-tops, making a paper fence. The elevator took them to the second floor. They followed the corridor to the door at the end marked *Dr R Locke*. Zoe knocked and waited. It opened and the man who had played cars with Ben's obstacle course at the police station, smiled at them through his beard.

He did seem nice, like his mum said. And he had more toys in the corner of the room by the window. Ben busied himself with them while his mum talked to the doctor, although he wasn't a normal doctor, as far as Ben could work out – he had no stethoscope and the room didn't stink of that smell he'd remembered about doctors, like the stinging cream his mum insisted on rubbing on his skin if he cut himself. There were plenty of toys, though. He set about piling them up.

"And when did you first notice this?" asked Locke.

"Almost as soon as he could talk," said Zoe. They were sitting away from his desk on a couple of armchairs inclined towards each other. Locke had a notepad on his lap.

"Has he ever changed his story?"

"No. It's always the same."

"And have you noticed anything else unusual?"

"Not really. Something happened yesterday, but he won't say what. And neither will the boy who was with him."

Locke made a few notes, nodding slowly. He put down his pen, stood up and walked to the toy corner, where he crouched down beside Ben.

"What are you making, Ben?" he asked.

"A mountain." Ben was on his knees, a teddy bear in one hand, as he studied the pile. He placed the bear carefully halfway up.

"Uh-huh. Can I help?" Locke picked up a toy truck and handed it to Ben. Ben watched him then smiled, taking the truck from him.

"Do you know this mountain, Ben?" asked Locke.

"Mmhmm," said Ben, wondering what to do with the truck. He crawled round the pile and placed it at the base.

"How do you know it?"

Locke handed him a stuffed blue owl. "I could see it from my window in my old house."

"When did you live there, Ben?"

"Before I came here," said Ben.

"What do you remember about that place?"

Ben stilled for a moment, then pulled at the feathers on the owl's ears. "It was cold, and it snowed a lot."

"Uh-huh?"

"I lived in a place with lots of other boys."

"What did you do there?"

"I served rice. And I looked after the stone."

"The stone?"

Ben traced the outline of the owl's eyes with the tip of his finger. "I had a friend. I miss him."

"Do you? What was his name?" asked Locke.

84

"Tenzin."

"What happened to him?"

"He died in the fire."

Locke paused. Ben bounced the owl on his knee then lifted it into flight.

"Do you remember your family, Ben?"

Ben nodded, steering the owl through the air. "My mum had long hair. She liked music."

Locke glanced at Zoe. She watched in silence, her hands over her mouth.

"How did you come here, Ben?" asked Locke.

Ben studied him. He was a doctor, wasn't he? He should know this stuff. "I fell through the hole," he said.

*

"Take a seat, Zoe. I'll just be a couple of minutes." Locke held the door for them and ruffled Ben's hair as he passed. "You can keep the owl, Ben," he said.

Ben smiled at his owl. He glanced back as his mother led him to the seats in the corridor.

Locke closed the door and walked to the pile of toys in the corner. He crouched down again, studying the seemingly haphazard structure before him, as the branches of the tree outside swayed in a soft breeze. He took out his phone and dialled.

"Ron, it's Raymond. Listen, do you have room for one more?"

There was a sigh on the other end of the phone. "We've been inundated, Ray. We're barely keeping up with the program as it is. And Jack's still insisting that we open it up to the public—"

"You need to see this child. He has something."

"So do a lot of people. I don't know what the fuck is happening." The voice on the phone sighed. "Alright. Bring him along on today. 2.00pm."

CHAPTER SIX

"Keep the change." Robert dropped some pound coins on the café counter, paced for the door and held it open for Cora.

"Do you hear anything else?" he asked as he hailed a taxi. "Whereabouts on the campus?"

She shook her head. "It's like a radio signal breaking up... I can't make it out..."

*

The taxi dropped them at the main gate and they stepped out into the sunlight.

"Which way?" asked Robert.

"I don't know," Cora shrugged. "I didn't even know he was in my head."

They stood for a moment in the shadow of the stone gate, Cora scanning the surroundings.

"Nothing?" said Robert, watching her face for any sign of reaction.

"If I knew how I was doing it, maybe I could figure it out, but..." She turned to him, her eyes flecked with anxiety. "What's happening to me, Robert?"

He smoothed her hair. "I don't know. But try to stay open to it. We need to find Banks."

They attached themselves to a small crowd of students and followed them into the nearest building. Daylight speckled in through old stained-glass windows onto the dark wooden panels lining the walls. Robert glanced up and down the corridor, but there was no sign of Banks. They took the spiral staircase that curved towards the ceiling, coming to an empty corridor on the next level, and followed its narrow contours to another stairwell. Some students hurried towards them, but Banks was not amongst them. They bustled past, pushing open the heavy doors of an old lecture hall to the left.

"Robert?" Cora was staring at a digital display. It read *Today's Lecture: INTP – Dr Jack Harley discusses the recent unexplained surge in Telepathic Accounts.*

"Cora, we don't have time to…" Robert stopped as he processed the information. "Jack Harley?"

*

Robert eased the door closed at the back of the lecture theatre. It was an old-fashioned amphitheatre – hard wooden benches reminiscent of church pews, that fell away steeply to the stage below, each row divided by a thin wooden ledge that was too narrow to hold anything much bigger than a pencil, and useful only as a place on which students could rest their heads while they slept off their hangovers. There were no recovering students today, though. The audience was attentive and fully engaged with the speaker. Jack Harley had not changed since Robert last saw him at CERN – tall, easy in his stride as he crossed the stage, his long grey ponytail trailing down his back. His delivery, like everything about him, was relaxed. Behind him, an MRI image of a human brain lit up the overbearing projector screen.

They slipped into the back row next to a burly student in a rugby shirt, who was leaning forwards on the pitiful ledge, frowning. Robert scanned the audience but Banks was not amongst it.

Jack was in full flow in his soft American accent. "We've been working on synthetic telepathy for four years and getting some good results." Jack glanced back at the screen, which showed a graph of accuracy against time. The line bumped along around the thirty per-cent mark. "Until this," he said, and clicked onto the next slide. The line climbed straight up to the high nineties and levelled out. A murmur rippled through the audience and Cora leaned forwards.

"For the past few weeks, we've had hit rates beyond anything we've seen before – accuracy that makes our first attempts look like kindergarten. And we're not the only ones. These results are being reported in centres all over Europe.

"So my question is: why is this happening? The technology hasn't changed, and neither have the subjects."

The next image was one of a trilobite. It looked like it belonged on another planet with its pincer-shaped feelers and spiny thorax. "There was a time when life on Earth couldn't see. Then it developed eyes." A fish replaced the trilobite. "A time when it couldn't breathe..." A man replaced the fish. "Then it developed lungs."

The screen changed to a cross-sectional image of a brain with tiny white flecks scattered throughout its substance. "A recent study in the European Journal of Brain Pathology showed that the concentration of magnetite in human brain tissue has doubled over the last decade. Is it possible we are in the middle of another evolutionary shift – one that allows us to connect to a subtler force of nature?" He scanned the audience, who sat transfixed.

"We operate within the four fundamental forces – electromagnetism allows us to interact with the world; the strong nuclear force binds nuclei together; the weak force allows subatomic particles to change into one another; gravity attracts objects of mass together. Perhaps there is a fifth force we're missing, one that could help explain what we're seeing here."

The letters INTP appeared on the screen. "We're in the process of compiling a database of telepathic accounts in conjunction with other centres. The International Telepathy Database is up and running and growing every day. We've put out a public appeal for volunteers to assist in further studies and we're running open days in our lab at the Innovatics Institute from this afternoon. Perhaps it will help us answer some of the many questions we now have. I certainly hope so. Thank you for your time." He stepped back and nodded as the audience applauded.

Cora stood up. "I need to speak to him," she said.

"Wait," said Robert, catching her arm. "We need to find Banks."

"This is important, Robert. I have to understand what's happening to me." She pulled away and weaved through the crowd to the front of the lecture hall. Robert held back, eying the people as they exited, on the off-chance Banks was amongst them.

By the time Robert made his way through the line of questioners, Cora was engaged in conversation with Jack, who was listening intently.

"I'm sorry, I didn't catch your name," said Jack, as Robert approached.

"Cora," she said. "Cora Martin. And this is Robert Strong," she said, as Robert joined them.

"Robert?" Jack broke into a smile. "What are you doing here?"

"You know each other?" said Cora.

Robert shook Jack's hand. "Good to see you, Jack."

"Cora," said Jack. "You could really help us with this research. I'm heading to the lab at Innovatics, now. Do you have time?"

She turned to Robert and lowered her voice so that only he could hear. "It might help me tap into Banks."

Robert was hesitant. "Alright. Look after her, Jack. I'll meet you later." As he kissed her cheek, he breathed, "Stay with him, understand?"

*

Seth sat alone at his desk, the link to the GRACE satellites waiting patiently on his computer. His Hub's access to GRACE had been restricted, now that their involvement was curtailed; the final insult to their hard work. But it helped to know people. His mind was not on his pen as it bounced its nervous repetitions on the surface of his desk – his mind was wrestling with his curiosity and a feeling that warned him against it. It felt dangerous. He tapped the pen a few more times, like he was drumming up his courage then, steeling himself, typed in the restricted access code he had acquired and struck the return key. The program began to run. He watched the image collate as the earth's gravitational changes revealed themselves before his eyes. The turquoise gravity mountain was still spreading – now approaching the eastern seaboard of the USA to the west and Japan to the east. He copied the updated data onto a flash-drive – a memory of a global secret that he was in on, albeit one he watched from the side-lines. Whatever the GRACE ground station engineers were looking at, it was not this. His geophysics hub had seen to that. It was a shame – they were out in the cold on their own secret too. He put down the pen and leaned closer, tapping the key to zoom in on the spinning the globe, examining the substance of the mountain in more detail. Something had changed. He peered closer, then froze the screen.

Nadine Proust paused as she passed Seth's screen. "I thought we weren't on GRACE anymore?" she said, eying the feedback globe.

Seth peered at the screen. "We're not, I'm just... Nadine, what does this look like to you?"

She leaned closer. Something interrupted its uniformity – a dark inky patch marred the turquoise haze over northern Britain.

"If I were to use my imagination," she said, " I'd say it looked like a sinkhole has appeared filled with heavy water, or lead." She glanced at the data on the right. "That reading's off the chart."

He zoomed further in on the location of the density, right down to the empty fields surrounding it.

"Wait," she said, staring at the image. "Is that... *here?*"

He studied the screen. "You know of anything going on here that would cause this?" he asked.

She shook her head and turned a parental look on him. "He doesn't want us on this anymore, remember?"

"I know," said Seth. "We're not. I was just curious."

"Yeah, well," she straightened her glasses, "you know he likes curiosity, as long as it's inside his box. And from what you said, he seemed pretty definite about leaving this one alone."

Seth looked up at her. "You're right. Yeah. We should back off." He shut down the program and summoned a plastic smile.

*

Robert left the building uneasy. He trusted Jack, but the uncertainty of leaving Cora behind, out of sight, made him nervous. For all she could take care of herself, he still felt responsible for dragging her into all this. A few students lay around on the grass in the middle of the quadrangle, soaking up the sun's rays. Robert kept to the shadows, out of the heat and glare of the midday sunlight, scanning the names on the plaques screwed into the stone of the buildings as he passed. *Alan Hunter Building, Bryson Lecture Theatre, Hillsworth Business School.* He didn't know what he was looking for.

He backtracked to the Innovatics Institute and followed the road to an underpass that took him to a quiet cobbled street. Then, in the glare of the sunlight, he saw him. Cropped hair, purposeful stride, his snake scar just visible beneath the sleeve on his upper arm. Banks disappeared into the stone building to his right. Stepping into the shadow of a doorway, Robert let out a slow, controlled breath. He closed his eyes, surrendering to the feeling of emptiness, feeling the substance of his cells fade into insubstantiality. There was no space for fear this time, no time for doubt. He glanced down, seeing the cobbles where his legs should be. When he was confident in his nothingness, he stepped out and followed.

It took a moment to adjust to the dimness. He was in a cloistered area that opened to the corner of a large lawn, flanked on four sides by imposing old buildings. The echo of Banks' footsteps slowed and stopped. He was drawing on a cigarette, his mobile to his ear.

"You're gonna have to give me more than this," said Banks. "It's chasing a myth."

A pause.

"As far as he knows. It's been lost for centuries. What makes Amos so sure it's here?"

Another pause. "Yeah, well I need more than intuition to go on." He ground out his cigarette on a pillar and flicked it onto the lawn. "Get back to me." He hung up and walked from the cloisters.

Banks took the path to the side of the grass, bathed in sunlight. He crossed to the shadowed gateway at the other side of the quadrangle and Robert followed, steering clear of a group of tourists coming the other way. Banks glanced back once or twice, his gaze sweeping through Robert. Three huge, deep arches sheltered the dark paved steps that spilled down to the street beyond. Stone columns and black wrought-iron gates gave the passageway the sense of Victorian judgement. Robert slipped after him, pausing against the cold stone of a column, watching Banks below him on the steps. He wouldn't be so naive this time round. Banks was his link to ORB, to

Mindscape, and he wasn't about to let him go. He closed the distance between them, drawing confidence from his insubstantiality.

But as a woman and a small boy walked towards him, hand in hand, Robert double-checked. The boy looked up at him from under his red hood. His head turned and his eyes stayed on the space where Robert stood as they passed, and he stumbled a little, resisting his mother's pull. Robert glanced down – he was still invisible – and yet the boy was looking right at him…

"What is it?" asked the woman.

"That man," said the boy, pointing at the space where Robert stood frozen. "He's…"

She frowned at him. "What man? That's a pillar, Ben. Come on, we don't have time for games. We're late." She tugged his hand until he followed and he trotted behind her, his neck craned as his eyes stayed fixed on Robert. The intensity of the boy's stare shook Robert to his core and he felt his grip on nothingness slip, the weight of substance flooding back as his body reformed. *Shit,* he thought, trying to clear his mind again. But the more he struggled, the more his energy crystallised into matter.

"He didn't mention that." Banks had turned back, his phone to his ear. "Lying bastard. I *knew* he was hiding something…"

Robert stood rooted to the spot as Banks drew closer. And then he saw it – that moment when recognition dawned in Banks' eyes and a sneer raised the corner of his mouth. Banks hung up.

"Well, well," said Banks. "This is a coincidence. What are you doing here, Robert Strong…?"

Robert opened his mouth to speak but before he could, Banks froze, the colour draining from his face as he backed away down the steps onto the street.

"Stop!" shouted Robert, instinct trumping rivalry, as Banks stumbled backwards onto the road. There was a screech, a sickening double thud, the blast of a horn, too late. Banks' body lay on the tarmac, his legs bent in a way that made Robert want to throw up. A pool of blood oozed from his right ear and from the cracks in his elongated skull, now a fractured eggshell. There was no need to go any closer to know.

What the absolute fuck? Robert turned back, shaken by Banks' obtuse retreat. "*Aiyana?*" She stood behind him, fully visible.

"Disappear," she ordered, as she faded like a rainbow in sunlight.

He backed into the shadows and summoned his focus with everything he had.

Both ghosts left unseen as a small crowd gathered round the mangled remains of the man on the road and discord fractured the sound of a chime. In a final glance back, Robert saw Banks' silhouette arc towards a tendril of dark air and disappear.

"What the fuck just happened, Aiyana?" hissed Robert, as they stole back across the green.

She said nothing until they reached the shadows of the cloisters. Leaning both hands on a pillar, she hung her head, drawing breaths from deep in her lungs. "Shit," was all she could say. She slapped the pillar hard.

"I could have used him!" Robert kicked the wall. "Jesus Christ, Aiyana, he was my link to Amos – to finding my dad…"

"Want to tell us what that was all about?" They turned to the voice. Casimir walked towards them, followed by Sattva.

"I didn't mean it to happen like that," she said. "I felt Robert's signal and I showed up…"

"Fully visible?" said Casimir, his eyebrows raised. "To the man who murdered you? This is exactly why we don't—"

"I know, I know," she said, still staring at the ground. She drew another breath and faced Casimir. Her expression traded guilt for resolve. "But he had it coming."

Robert rounded on her. "Your determination to get even just cost me the chance to—"

"Enough!" snapped Sattva, with uncommon curtness. When he spoke again, his voice was measured. "Aiyana's intention was not for Banks to die. It was to help you, Robert."

Robert lowered his gaze as he fought to release his resentment.

"All the same," said Sattva. "Casimir is right. The living should not see the dead. It dislocates their sense of reality, especially when they're not ready for it. But there's nothing we can do about it now."

"Can you reach him?" asked Aiyana.

Sattva closed his eyes and breathed out a long slow breath. He shook his head. "I can't sense him."

"Something took him," said Robert. "I saw it. The same thing that took my father."

"Mindscape," said Sattva.

"No," said Robert. "According to Liam's findings, Mindscape doesn't exist anymore. At least not as Aiyana detected it before." He glowered at her. "We may never find out now."

Aiyana let out a harsh sigh and avoided Robert's eye as she stomped back to the quadrangle, unseen.

Sattva turned to Robert. "What I want to know is what Banks was doing here. Because if Banks was involved, my guess is Amos is not far behind."

"He's after a stone of some kind," said Robert. "Cora..." he struggled to think of the right word, "*heard* Banks' thoughts."

"She is a Sentient," said Casimir.

"She's off the chart, lately," said Robert. "And she's no idea how to use it."

"From what I understand, she's not the only one," said Sattva.

"What's going on?" said Robert. "How come all these people are suddenly mind readers?"

Sattva considered the question before he answered. "I don't know. This is unprecedented. But if Cora is going to help us, she needs to learn how to control it." He placed a hand on Robert's shoulder as the amulet round his neck glowed red. "Give her some support," he said. A second later he was gone.

Footsteps echoed behind and Robert turned to see Aiyana holding a phone towards him. "This belonged to Banks," she said. "It might help us Tunnel to ORB."

"They'll be tracking it," said Robert.

"I'm not stupid, Robert," she spat. "I threw the battery away. We only need it as a focal object. I'm not planning on calling them."

Robert eyed the phone.

"For Christ's sake, Robert," said Aiyana. She shifted uncomfortably. "I'm trying to make this up to you."

He diffused a little then reached out and took the phone. "Thanks."

"Alright," said Casimir. "So when do we do this?"

"Tonight," said Robert. "After dark."

*

Zoe and Ben returned to the Innovatics Institute as Dr Locke had asked them to do when he called. Ben stared up at its glass walls again, watching the sun's rays bounce off its panes like gold lasers. It was much busier this time – a queue bulged from the main doors onto the wide pavement. People were camped out on the concrete and on the grass in the square opposite. A man stood wearing pink shades and a white sunhat, holding a wooden placard with the words:

THE ALIENS HAVE LANDED –

THEY'RE INSIDE YOUR HEAD

painted in silver. Locke waved at Zoe and Ben from the other side of the glass when he saw them, ushering them in, passing the throng of people waiting to get inside.

Sunlight spilled through the glass atrium from a ceiling too high up to see. Ben looked up at the lattice of mezzanines above and the staircases that climbed between them like white corkscrews. Locke pushed through the crowd, cutting a path for them and Zoe kept her hands on Ben's shoulders as she followed, until they reached the table at the end. It was one of many – a line of desks cornered off a large section of the atrium, each manned by someone with a laptop. The red tape attached to the corners of the tables separated the crowd from the quieter area behind. "Wait here, just a moment," said Locke. He undid the tape and walked between the desks towards a man with a long grey ponytail.

Behind the reception area, on the other side, a small group of people were gathering. Every so often someone from the queue would be ushered beyond the red tape to join them. A young woman with a clipboard stood by them, waving her pen around officiously, as she counted out five heads then marched to the elevator, the group trailing behind her as she led them somewhere higher up. All the while, more people trickled in from the other side of the tape to replenish the ones that had been invited upstairs.

Ben glanced at the woman with pink hair at the next table. The man on the laptop opposite stopped typing.

"I'm sorry, you what?" said the man.

"I can communicate with my dog – he's a Weimaraner. Purebred. I hear what he thinks. His favourite TV program is The Big Bang Theory."

"Right…" He ran his fingers through his unruly red hair. "Eh, we're really looking for human accounts."

"Oh, it didn't say that in the ad…"

"Yeah, I know, eh… how about you leave your number and we may call you back?"

She seemed happy with that. She wrote her details with concentrated precision on a piece of paper as the man stood up.

"Thanks for coming along," he said, shaking her hand.

"Gaia loves you too," she nodded knowingly, then turned and smiled her way through the crowd.

"Uh-huh." He picked up the paper and dropped it in the bin as he approached the man with the grey ponytail, who was deep in conversation with Raymond Locke. He interrupted anyway.

"This is out of control, Jack. They're coming out of the woodwork. Fucking dog telepathy?"

"I know, Ron," said Jack. "It was bound to attract a few questionables."

"Questionables? They're unhinged, that's what. Hi, Raymond."

Locke grinned and raised an eyebrow. "Busy day, Ron?"

Ron rolled his eyes and sighed. "I can't even tell you…"

"How about you take Locke's kid upstairs?" said Jack.

"Gladly," said Ron.

Locke waved Zoe and Ben towards them. The man with the grey

ponytail smiled at Ben and shook his small hand with a large paw. "Good to meet you Ben. I've heard lots about you. My name is Jack Harley."

*

Robert skirted the edge of the throng in the atrium of Innovatics, scanning for Cora. The crowd jostled against him as he caught sight of a boy in a red hoodie, hand in hand with a woman, following a man to the elevator. The boy peeked round the doors as they slid closed, his eyes fixed on Robert.

"Hey." Cora squeezed his arm.

"Hey," he said, placing a hand on her back. "You okay?"

"Yeah."

"You didn't register your details on the database, did you?" he asked.

"Of course I didn't," said Cora. "Jack's okay with that. I've... heard nothing from Banks, though. At least, not that I'm aware of."

"You won't," said Robert. "Banks is dead."

"*What?*" she breathed.

"He was just hit by a car."

"Jesus."

The events replayed themselves in Robert's mind, detail by detail, despite his attempts to repress them.

Cora pulled away, eying him with an air of iciness. "Who's Aiyana?" she said.

Robert's thoughts scattered as he scrambled for an answer. "Eh…"

"Miss Martin?" Cora drew her frown from him and turned to the woman with the clipboard who was approaching from behind the red tape. Perhaps there was a god after all, thought Robert. One with perfect timing.

"Yes?" said Cora.

"Come with me," said the woman, undoing the barrier. The look she gave Robert was apologetic but stern when he tried to follow.

"I'm afraid there's no room for visitors."

"You look after Miss Martin," said Jack as he walked towards them. "I'll take care of Robert." He shook Robert's hand as the woman led Cora towards an elevator. "She'll be fine," said Jack, reading Robert's concern. "We're not going to dissect her."

Robert grinned at the floor.

"So how are you doing, anyway?" asked Jack.

A bang interrupted Robert's reply, as the grey-haired man at the next table slammed his fist on the desk. "I'm not leaving until someone tells me how my mother can hear my thoughts!" He was white-faced and shaking, his voice straining at the upper limits of male pitch. "*Do you have any idea how intrusive that is?*"

"Let's go somewhere quieter," said Jack.

They took the elevator to the seventh floor. A square mezzanine, it was lined with glass offices, separated by solid walls, each of them staffed. Desks were pushed up against the mezzanine railings, maximising the use of space, with desktops and laptops on their surfaces.

"So when did you come over here?" asked Robert.

"Just after the launch at CERN. I'd left a PhD student running the quantum biology project here while I was on secondment. I thought they were going to shut us down, but when we started getting results, he needed me back. How come you left so quickly?"

CERN was so long ago that it felt like another lifetime. *It was*, Robert realised. He had to pinpoint the memories, compose the lie and evaluate it against other lies he may have told, all within a fraction of a second. And remain composed. He marvelled at the capacity and audacity of his own brain. "I had a family emergency," he said. As it turned out, the lie was true.

"Sorry to hear that," said Jack as they walked along the mezzanine past the glass offices. "Things okay now?"

"Yeah," said Robert. "Pretty much."

They paused outside the third glass office. On one side of the room sat a man with a white headset that reached across the top of his scalp and half of his forehead. On the other side, a technician studied a computer screen.

"So how come a physicist ends up working on telepathy?" asked Robert.

"We're investigating the quantum biological events involved in the Mind-Machine Interface."

"The what?"

"Synthetic telepathy. Now we can literally record people's thoughts and dreams and implant them into someone else's brain by linking them through computers. We're mapping thoughts. At first we got only mediocre results. But this past month we've had an explosion of data."

"Yeah, your presentation was pretty impressive," said Robert.

"I mean, look at this…" Jack tapped his tablet and an image formed of Michelangelo's *David*, crystal clear in its contours. "This isn't a photograph," said Jack. "It's a reconstruction of an implanted thought – seen through one person's eyes, reconstructed in someone else's brain then picked up by fMRI and decoded. This kind of detail we wouldn't have believed possible a year ago."

"That's crazy," said Robert.

"I know. It feels like we've just opened a box of tricks, and we've no idea what's inside. We know that neurons communicate information between different areas of the brain at speeds faster than it takes to conduct electrical impulses. So we think there's a kind of neuronal quantum entanglement process going on. We're beginning to look at the brain as a kind of quantum computer. I mean, quantum processes seem to control navigation, photosynthesis, the sense of smell, so it makes sense."

"So how come Cora's suddenly picking up stuff inside other people's heads?"

"That's where it gets intriguing. Even empty space contains information." Jack lowered his voice as if he were about to swear in church. "What if our neurons become entangled with a network outside the brain? A universal network?"

"Dr Harley? Need your signature." A bespectacled student thrust a clipboard in front of him. Jack scrawled his approval, apparently accustomed to interruptions, and the student bustled off.

"We've had to relocate due to the workload," said Jack. "The Institute gave us this whole floor for six months until we work out what's going on. This place has become our lab."

They stopped outside the next room. "We're amplifying brain waves through those headsets," he said. "They pick up thoughts and transmit them to a 'listener' via computer."

Robert approached the glass. Two men sat with their backs to the mezzanine window, a monitor in front of them, which displayed a pink rose. Further inside the room sat a blonde woman and the boy who could see him when there was nothing there to see.

Jack nodded towards the man with a flop of dark hair and a brown suit. "That's Raymond Locke, psychologist. He's helping us out with things. Ron's our chief technician."

"Who's the boy?" asked Robert.

"His name's Ben." Jack tapped his tablet, turning on the speaker that allowed them to eavesdrop on the room. "This should be interesting," he said.

*

Ben saw the men stop outside the glass wall. He couldn't see their faces for the reflection of the room on the glass, but he knew they were watching.

"Ben?" said Ron from behind his computer screen. Dr Locke sat next to him. The headset felt cumbersome on Ben's head and it kept slipping, its white flat arm sliding down towards his eyes. He pushed it back up to the middle of his forehead like they had asked him to do. They had offered him a chair, but he preferred to sit on the floor. It was more space to play with his owl.

Zoe adjusted her headset and studied the rose on her screen, the same image that had appeared on Ron's monitor. From where he sat, Ben could not see either of them.

"A pink flower," said Ben, as he flapped his stuffed owl's wings up and down.

"That's good," said Ron, who was busy typing notes. He tapped return and a new image replaced the rose on both his and Zoe's screens.

"A blue boat," said Ben.

Ron glanced at his screen. "That's right," he said. He struck return again. Zoe stared at a whale underwater.

"A big fish," said Ben. "A whale."

Ron glanced up. "You're doing great, Ben," he said, and continued typing.

"A polar bear," said Ben.

"Hold on, buddy," smiled Ron. "Don't get ahead of yourself." He tapped the return key and the whale disappeared from the screens. In its place, a snow-scape – and a polar bear by an ice-hole, blood on its white fur.

Ron glanced at Locke.

Ben bounced his owl on his knee and chuckled. "Ice cream!"

Ron's finger hovered over return. He checked Zoe's screen – the polar bear was still there. He struck the key. An ice cream cone appeared, drizzled in chocolate sauce.

"Oh, my god," whispered Ron. "He's anticipating?" He knocked on the glass window behind him, where Jack and Robert were already looking in. "Are you getting this?" he mouthed.

Jack circled his index finger. "Keep going."

"A balloon," came Ben's voice over the speaker. A moment later, the image appeared on Ron's screen just as Ben had described.

"A cow," said Ben. The image changed but this time to a church. Ron glanced round at Jack.

"A red racing car," said Ben, whizzing his owl through the air.

Ron shook his head as the image of a policeman appeared. Ben took off his headset and tried to fit it onto his owl's head.

Jack was staring through the glass at Ben. "That was incredible," he breathed.

"He's not done yet," said Robert. He had moved to look inside the next office. Cora sat wearing a headset, a laptop on the table before her, her partner for the experiment, a teenage girl with short dark hair, facing the other way. "Jack?" said Robert.

Jack's pace slowed when he saw the red car with a black stripe on Cora's screen.

"Now can I play with my owl?" came Ben's voice through Jack's tablet.

Jack knocked on the glass, catching Ron's attention. "Keep him going."

"Eh... just a few more, Ben," said Ron. "And put your headset back on."

Ben sighed but left the headset on his owl. "A spaceship."

USS *Enterprise* appeared on Cora's screen, in the next room.

"A Christmas tree!" came Ben's voice.

Jack glanced from the tinsel-covered tree on Cora's laptop to the small boy in the next room, whose headset now lay on the floor. "Jesus," he breathed.

It went on for several minutes. Ron, Locke and Zoe stepped out into the mezzanine corridor while Ben played with his owl on the floor of the room and stated whatever image would then show itself on Cora's screen next door. The headset was redundant.

"How is he doing this?" whispered Zoe.

"There's some kind of connection between them," said Locke. "Any ideas, Jack?"

Jack shook his head.

Ben sat back on the floor, suddenly quiet, his owl by his side.

"I think he's had enough," said Zoe. She opened the door and went inside, crouching down beside him.

Cora appeared from the other room. "How did it go?" she asked.

"Better than you could imagine," said Jack, as Ben and Zoe emerged hand in hand into the corridor. "I think it's time we went home," said Zoe.

"Do you mind if Ben comes back for some more tests?" asked Jack.

"No," said Zoe. "You have my phone number." She turned to

move away but Ben stayed still. Zoe felt the tug on her arm and looked back. Ben was rooted to the spot, staring at Cora.

"That's a nice owl," said Cora.

Ben broke from Zoe's grasp and walked slowly towards Cora. She knelt down, eyelevel with him as he stopped in front of her. Neither of them spoke. He closed his eyes and rested his forehead against hers and they stayed there, silent and unmoving, as the others shared uncertain glances between them. Then, without warning, Ben threw his arms around her. She found herself clasping the back of his head. He was smiling although his eyes were wet.

Locke read the look on Zoe's face and the thin tight line of her mouth. Gently, he disentangled Ben from Cora. Reaching for Ben's hand, Zoe snapped, "Come on, Ben. Time to go." She turned and marched away as Ben stumbled behind her, glancing back over his shoulder.

Cora stared after them.

"Are you alright?" asked Robert.

"I just need a minute," she breathed and walked the other way, her hand on her stomach.

Robert followed her down the corridor, pausing outside the door of the women's toilets. He knocked. "Cora?"

She didn't answer.

He pushed the door open. The tap was running and she stood beside the sinks, her forehead against the wall, her face in her hands.

*

"Alright, Patsy. And we're live in three, two…" The producer mouthed the word *one* as the presenter straightened her hair at the entrance to the Innovatics Institute.

"Scientists report that they have been overwhelmed with the public response to their appeal for assistance in Synthetic Telepathy research. Just hours ago, this atrium was filled with people who all independently report a recent telepathic experience. Chief researchers here at the Innovatics Institute are at a loss to explain the sudden surge in the number of reported events. But they claim that studies will help future developments, such as electrical implants to help the blind 'see' the world again, and implanting memories into people with Alzheimer's…"

*

In the large screen projection, the sun glinted off the glass panels of the Institute building. "…This is Patsy Drummond, Science Correspondent…" Amos watched the image fade from the wall. He stared at the white space for a moment, unmoving but for the faintest clench of his jaw.

He reached for his intercom. "Get me Baroness Avonsbury."

*

Amos sat on the decking of the lodge house overlooking the small lake. The sun was beginning to set and made the shadows of the trees far taller than the trees themselves, which already towered like sentinels guarding a secret place. The quiet words spoken here were heard by few but felt by millions, as the intentions they carried played out in the politics of time. The trees had been growing for centuries on the estate, cared for by generations of one family on behalf of another. The woman who sat next to him dangled a goblet of red wine elegantly over the arm of her chair. A silver cigarette holder sat perched between the manicured fingers of her other hand, a trickle of purplish smoke rising into the air beside her. They watched the swans on the lake glide over its glassy surface, as the sun turned it gold.

"It seems I only ever see you when there is something you want," she said smoothly, and sipped her wine.

"Oh come now, Lucia, that's not the case." He paused. "And who's to say I don't have something to offer you today?"

"Do you?" she said, her voice teasing a little.

Amos breathed in the evening air and the scent of wine mingled with her perfume. "What would you say to something that guaranteed you the advantage in any political debate?" he asked. "Something that your opponent did not have?"

"I would be intrigued," she said. "Does such a thing exist?"

"It does," smiled Amos. "And once it's fully developed, you would be welcome to test it for yourself."

"I look forward to it."

He watched the graceful arc of her arm as she lifted the glass to her lips again.

"And in return?" she said.

"Some assistance in finding the perpetrator of our recent security breach."

She raised an eyebrow. "I thought ORB was above security breaches."

"It would seem we are not. We lost several weeks of development from making that same assumption."

"Clumsy," she said in a sing-song voice and sipped her wine. "Do you know who the perpetrator is?"

"I have my suspicions." He spoke slowly, allowing his words to seep in. "It would be a shame if he were to disrupt our project before you had the chance to enjoy it."

"I see. By removing the perpetrator I'm protecting my political advantage."

He watched her look out over the lake. The sweep of her short whitish blonde hair across her forehead, the smooth, slim line of her chin, the intriguing mix of certainty and femininity in her eyes. What she saw in front of her was not the tranquillity of the scene, but political opportunity. And he could see that she wanted it.

"An activist?" she said.

"Possibly," said Amos.

She shook her head. "Activists. Running the country would be so much easier without them."

"Indeed. It would have to be handled delicately, of course."

"Of course," she said, her eyes still on the lake but her mind on the seed he had planted. She took another sip. "Anything else?"

"There is one more thing," said Amos.

"Yes?"

"How is your artefact collection coming along?"

*

Max Guthrie checked the text message again as he leaned on the brass railing of the balcony inside the museum. A school trip straggled in below, kids just six or seven, who pointed and ogled at the tyrannosaurus skeleton that gaped down at them. Max was about level with its skull from up here and was relieved that no one had managed to clone a real one, yet. He took out a hairband from the pocket of his green trench-jacket, hooking his tangle of dark hair into a top-knot, then reached for his phone. 10.03am. Footsteps came from behind. Heels. He didn't turn round as the woman came to stand next to him and looked out at the bones. He didn't have to. He recognised her from her scent and the measure of her gait. "You're late," said Max.

The woman did not look at him as she slipped him a small envelope beneath the solid wall of the balcony.

"Why me?" asked Max.

"I don't have the staff to spare for this one." She paused. "And it's off the record."

"Ah," said Max. "What is it?" he asked.

She turned her back on the dinosaur and leaned on the railing, her fair shoulder-length hair tucked behind one ear, her dark eyes unflustered as they stared at the wall behind. "The suspect of a company security breach."

"Which company?"

"The name's classified."

He snorted. "No name? I'm shovelling shit in the dark?"

Turning to him for the first time, she let her gaze move from his mouth to his eyes. "You look better clean-shaven," she said.

He rubbed his hand over his stubbly chin. "So you keep telling me."

Her gaze slid back to the wall. "It's a government asset," she continued. "One that's worth protecting."

Max watched the children below, now sitting on the floor drawing pictures of the dinosaur, their pencils and notepads scattered around them. "You're telling me you don't know?" he asked.

"I'm telling you it's classified. You have the suspect's name. Do what you do best. See what you can find."

The woman walked off and did not look back.

*

Max bolted the door inside his flat and took out the envelope. It lay on the desk as he made himself a coffee, and waited to be opened. A modern apartment, it was clean and functional, a place for work, not entertaining. Max sat down and cleared a space on the desk, as he cleared a space inside his head. The laptop, reading glasses, ashtray and mug of coffee were ergonomically arranged for easy reach and minimal disturbance.

It was a kind of ritual, whenever a new story crossed his path, and it allowed him to see things his eyes couldn't. In his earlier days as an investigative journalist, he dived right in, driven by enthusiasm, judgement and deadlines. But as he matured, he found that he could accomplish more by doing less. Time seemed to work better for him when he slowed down. Those few moments of preparation, of opening his mind, allowed him to see what was really important. Whatever action he then took usually led him down the right trail. It had paid off in other ways too. He was in demand from many of the major newspapers, all willing to pay above the odds to have him on their team. And it had flagged him to the attention of the Security Services. He preferred the freedom of freelance writing and the rewards of intelligence gathering that made a difference in ways people would never know about. The direction of fire was steered by his senior at MI5, but he called the shots.

He met her for the first time at a party one night, a highbrow charity fundraiser for London's elite. He had got in through the back door – a favour from a rising defence lawyer on whom he had reported favourably in a high-profile case. Max's articles simply reflected how he saw things, but the publicity had done the lawyer no harm, and the two had remained acquainted from then on.

He had checked himself in the mirrored wall as he walked in, unaccustomed to seeing himself in a suit and clean shaven, and thinking how he should have had a haircut. Olive skin and green eyes stared back under a mop of shoulder-length dark hair. He found her at the bar in a silvery dress that shimmered as the lights caught it, as did her hair which gleamed like pale silk. She regarded him with appraising eyes that allured him from the beginning. Emily Hastings was the consummate professional, for a while. Their relationship was passionate and sporadic, too volatile for any stability, but intense enough to allow a bond to grow between them. One based loosely on trust. He was her link to the media and she, his link to information.

He put on his glasses, adjusting the thick black rims so that they sat square on his face, then opened the envelope. A flash-drive toppled onto the table as he slid out a single folded sheet of paper. Printed on the top was the name: *Robert Strong,* and a passport number.

He turned on his laptop and plugged in the flash-drive. CCTV footage appeared on his screen – a man in his thirties it looked like, sandy hair and an oval face, coming out of the men's room into a corridor. Halfway along was a door marked *Operator's Room.* The man glanced both ways, walked towards it, then stopped. He turned back as a door opened in front of him and a bespectacled assertive-looking blonde woman strode out. After a brief conversation, she walked away and he dithered on the spot, undecided about something, then took out his phone, agitated. Max didn't need sound to interpret the expletives. He zoomed in on the CCTV information in the corner of the screen. It had come from CERN.

Taking a sip of coffee, he typed in the name and passport number, linking it to a basic sweep of databanks. His hand froze, the mug suspended in mid-air. According to the Social Security Death Index, Robert Strong was dead.

*

The panels from the consoles glowed in the dim room, the only light. Data flashed up on four of them, alerting the watcher to Max Guthrie's login to the databanks. The watcher uploaded the amendments and pressed enter. Easing back in his leather chair, he grinned. He reached to the fruit bowl for a handful of chewy cola bottles, tossed one in the air and caught it between his rotting teeth. He had been waiting for this. It had begun.

CHAPTER SEVEN

Max put down his mug of coffee and lit up a cigarette, blinking away the smoke trail that drifted past his eyes. He sat staring at the screen, lost in thought, wondering why Emily would have him chasing a dead man. Placing the cigarette carefully in the ashtray, he dug some more. Employment history, online references, papers published, financial transactions, close relationships, he scanned through them all. The owner of the property he had rented was now looking for new tenants, after he and his partner, Cora Martin, failed to pay the rent two months in a row. He showed up on Interpol a few weeks earlier when he first entered Geneva, around the same time as he appeared on Romfield Lab's payroll. After that, the trail went cold. No credit card transactions, no return plane tickets, no mobile phone trace, no social media activity. He had a Facebook account, deleted, Max discovered, two weeks prior. The UK passport database showed the biometric image of Robert Strong – an oval face, blue eyes, a mole on his right cheek. Max flicked back to the CCTV footage – the same man that was caught on camera in the CERN corridor. He closed in on him – his gait, his slightly uncertain posture, the way he clenched and unclenched his right fist. He froze the screen and studied the tense expression in his eyes.

The date was in white at the bottom left of the image. He flicked back to the Social Security Death Index, peering closer at the screen. Robert Strong's death was registered *before* he appeared at CERN.

Before he was added to Romfield's payroll. Max dug some more, his search taking him to the medical records of a private hospital in the southwest. He scanned through Robert's file until a summary appeared. It stated Robert Strong sustained unsurvivable injuries following a helicopter crash.

Max kept digging, sipping his coffee, as he accessed deeper files from databanks that only a few are privileged to view. It seemed that rent payment should not have been an issue for Robert Strong, not with the amount that had been in his offshore account. Just after he died though, the money was transferred to another bank account, again offshore, in the name of Damien Volker. Other than one payment coming in the week after Robert Strong was in CERN, Max hit dead ends. The only contact detail for Damien Volker was an email address. Max picked up the phone. "Josh? It's Max."

"Hi Max, what's up?"

"I need a favour. Take a note of this email, would you?" He read it out. A longstanding friend on the inside, Josh was someone he trusted. "I need you to monitor any traffic to or from this address," said Max. "Let me know what comes up."

"Sure." The good thing about Josh was that his social awkwardness meant he didn't ask too many questions.

Max returned to the accounts, going deeper into the rabbit hole of unauthorised data. All of the transactions, with both Robert Strong and Damien Volker, came from one source – *Sipherghast*.

Max sat back, picked up his phone again and dialled. "It's me. We need to meet."

*

"They're not ready," said Lazaro. "They need more time."

"I don't want excuses, Elijah. I want results. This is getting out of hand." Amos marched down the corridor that led to Area 9, while Elijah trotted to keep up. They passed through the upper chamber, the dim empty space surrounding the huge central tank, and took the elevator to the subbasement. Neon blue shimmered at the periphery of his vision from the domes encasing the subjects on their trolleys. Data flashed from the bank of computer screens on the wall behind them, but Amos' eyes were on the shifting darkness that dominated the room. He slowed as he approached the tank.

"They're not mature enough to hold their ground," said Elijah. "We've had only limited success with habitation. Revenants don't like being confined to flesh."

Behind the casing, the entities drifted smoothly on the current of the mist. Their heads turned as they passed, like they were watching.

"Revenants are messengers, Elijah. Information carriers," said Amos. "We have to play to their strengths." Their movements were almost meditative and Amos stood transfixed, absorbing the sight before him. As a gardener might regard seedlings, he saw more than the fragile stalks, the frailty of the leaves. Instead, he saw what they could become. "Have a little more faith," he said. "They will mature with experience. If they progress to habitation, consider it a bonus. In the meantime, let them do what they do best."

He stepped aside as Elijah unlocked the circular hatch at the end of the pipe, which let out a soft hiss as it swung open. Silently, the entities drifted out one by one, moving as though a steady current of air carried them across the room. They paused, surveying the neon domes around them which encased the twelve test subjects then, as though a silent collective decision was made, they dispersed, each moving towards their chosen dome. A hum reverberated in the room as they penetrated the domes, one by one, and the surfaces swirled in eddies of neon blue. Like a reflection on the under-surface of an invisible pool, they hovered above their subjects, the smooth arc of their heads staring down at the faces beneath them.

The monitor alarms began to ping. Elijah nodded to the female med-tech who walked from one bed-space to another, topping up the subjects' sedation. He watched as the Revenants tuned into the subjects' minds, mining them for the things they strove to forget. It was a thing of beauty to Elijah, but to Amos was more than that. To him, it was anticipation. His appetite was growing and they promised a feast.

One by one, the Revenants withdrew from the domes and came to rest outside the cylindrical tank, pressing their heads and hands against it. Its contents had grown darker, with clumps of things congealing within. One by one they returned to the cylinder through the pipe. Elijah closed the hatch and Amos stepped up to the side of the tank.

Inside, one of them moved towards him. The largest and the first, it felt to Elijah like a first-born son. It drew level with Amos, drifting gently, suspended as the mist swirled around it. Its featureless face watched Amos and they stared at one another, locked in silent communication. Then, as though fuelled with something unseen, it seemed to grow in stature. It turned its head upwards, looking into the dark tunnel of the tank, as though it knew what to do.

Amos stepped back and Elijah, with the knot of pain and pride that comes with releasing something nurtured into the wild, tapped the code into the control panel on the side of the tank. The swirling of the mist picked up its pace, like a cyclone gathering energy, then spun upwards, upwards, and disappeared.

*

Above the fields and hills and farms and settlements, a plume of mist ejected into the cold air, mingling with the clouds.

*

"It was like I knew him," whispered Cora. She stood as Robert held her, the tap still running in the sink in the women's toilets.

"Where from?"

He felt her shake her head on his chest. "I don't know. But he knew me, I could feel it."

"How come it upset you?"

"I can't explain it. It was beautiful, but... I can't remember."

He reached over and turned off the tap. "Let's get some air."

*

They cut through Queen's Drive that tracked the base of the steep mossy slopes of Salisbury Crags, where the city surrendered to nature. Far quieter than the streets, the open green space felt like they were miles away. They walked in silence, Cora absorbed in her thoughts.

Following the path down to the park, they found a band playing on the small stage – electronic music from India, heavy on rhythm. A guitarist, a tabla player and a man playing sitar on his knees, sat between the amps. A bracket of stage lights hung above them, casting neon blue and pink on the stage, muted by the sunshine.

They kept to the back of the small crowd that sat around on the grass capitalising on the Scottish sunshine, and skirted the perimeter fence of the park. Cora glanced back.

"You're making me nervous," said Robert.

She was fidgeting with something in her pocket as she walked. "Shit," she said, as her collection of obsidian crystals scattered onto the grass. "Hold on a moment." She stopped to pick them up and Robert crouched down to help her, his eyes scanning the crowd.

Nearby, a woman in a floral sundress lay on her front reading a magazine, her shoulders crimson, while her partner snored beside her under a sunhat and a large belly. She nudged him and he snorted then rolled onto his side, still asleep. A family sat next to them, having a picnic. The boy, who looked to be about Ben's age, was immersed in his own world with his plastic pirate. A girl with blonde pigtails, who looked like his younger sister, babbled to herself as she flicked through a picture book, while their parents shared out the food.

Cora shivered as she drew her hand over the surface of the grass. "There was one more," she said.

"You want my jacket?" asked Robert.

"Yeah," she said. "Please. I'm cold."

As Robert took off his jacket and wrapped it round her shoulders, she stopped. Following her gaze, now fixed on the park, he stood up slowly. He glanced at the sky. Clouds were approaching, but the sky was still summer blue above.

It's not the sky, he realised. *It's the air.* It was condensing into a soft grey mist. Like a haar that rolls in from the sea to the coast, it brought with it not just a change in the light, but a chill that clung to the particles of air itself. But it was more than that. It was the feeling that hangs on the air when it knows a thunderstorm is coming. It settled on the crowd, like an intangible shroud.

The birds fell silent and the air grew tight. Waiting.

The girl with pigtails raised her eyes. She dropped her book and lifted herself to her knees, turning to look over her shoulder. Staring at the air behind her, the edges of her mouth curled down and her small chest moved in and out faster than it should. She crawled onto her father's knees and wrapped her arms around his neck.

"What is it, Melissa?" he asked. "Are you cold?" He rubbed her bare arms.

Quietly, as though trying to stifle it, she began to cry.

"What's the matter?" said her father, hugging her close. "Did you not like your story?"

On the stage, the music stuttered to an awkward silence as the musicians stopped playing. Getting to his feet, the sitar player eyed the sky.

A shout from the side made Robert jump. The man under the sunhat bolted upright, his hands covering his face, his breaths punching holes in the stillness.

"Jesus, Marty!" his wife snapped, her hand clutching her chest. "You scared me!" Marty stared at her, haunted, as though he didn't know who she was.

"Something's wrong," breathed Robert.

Before Cora could speak, the amp on the stage exploded and the lights blew out one by one. Sharp screams pierced the air and the band shielded their faces from shards of glass. Melissa's cries crescendoed as agitation seized the crowd.

"Let's get out of here," said Robert, grabbing Cora's hand. They took to the path as the crows cawed and scattered from a towering copper beach overheard, their black wings scoring the sky.

"Do you feel that?" she shouted, running beside him.

"Yes." He felt it. It was as though his insides were souring.

"What is it?" she called.

He glanced round the darkening park. "I don't know. Come on."

*

Max stood up as Emily walked in and closed the door behind her. The true professional, she shook his hand and invited him to take a seat, while he eyed the activity behind the glass in Thames House. He only came here when he had to and was thankful that his job did not involve clocking in for compulsory desk duty or wearing a suit. Not like the people here, chasing phantoms from their consoles.

She sat down on the opposite side of the desk and crossed her legs. "What do you have for me?" she asked.

"You mean apart from the fact that our suspect died last month?"

"That can't be right. The company's security breach was this month." She froze, her eyes on him. "Are you saying he didn't do it?"

He watched her, trying to work out if she already knew. "No. I'm saying he staged his own death. This guy's had dirty fingers on more than one occasion. Just after he appeared on Romfield Lab's payroll for the first time several years ago, a lab in China pipped Romfield to the post in announcing a major breakthrough in high-performance computation. It's based on supercomputer network analysis – taking humans out of the loop and cutting research time from years to months. The algorithm produced by the Chinese and Romfield was the same.

"Six months after Strong started at SightLabs, their xenon dark matter studies were replicated in a rival lab in Chile. And just after he appeared in CERN, the design for a tool that CERN had been developing to examine magnets in a vacuum was leaked to a private lab in the US.

"On each of these occasions, a large sum of money was deposited into Strong's offshore account. After he died the funds were moved to an account owned by Damien Volker. He's using the name as a cover."

Emily stared at him. "He's selling sensitive scientific information?"

"It's bigger than that," said Max. "He's selling it through an underground broker. What do you know about *Sipherghast*?"

*

The helicopter touched down amidst the dusty rocks, stirring up a cloud of billowing sand. Sunlight glinted on its blades and the silver landing skids as the figure in the black coat stepped down.

"Boss?" Inside the dark room, lined wall to wall with consoles of flickering data, the soldier who sat manning the bank of computers glanced round.

Jason de Vrise was cleaning his rifle, the metalwork on its body burnished from overuse. His face impassive, he lifted his gaze slowly and his hand stilled. He put down the rifle. Walking towards the screen, he peered over the soldier's shoulder.

"Zoom in," said de Vrise, quietly. His physique, like his voice, was unmistakably commanding: broad shoulders and sculpted musculature beneath black webbing, his jaw chiselled, a neat moustache above his upper lip, his lidded eyes a blue so pale that it was as though the years had erased the colour, as well as the emotion. A faded scar cut from the right side of his nose across his eyelid to his temple.

The soldier glanced at de Vrise who watched, silent and unmoving, as the figure on the screen approached. Turning abruptly, de Vrise grabbed his rifle and strode from the room.

He marched down the dim corridors, loading a magazine into the rifle then slung it onto his shoulder, his hand resting on the grip. Passing the classrooms lined with maps, the climbing hall where men in black webbing scaled the walls, and the smell of cordite from the indoor range, he reached the main gate. He punched the code into the control panel on the wall and the metal heaved and groaned as the gate lifted and sunlight burst through between the large metallic teeth at its base. He stepped out into the barren land.

Victor Amos stopped, a stone's throw from de Vrise, waiting.

"I told you never to come here," said de Vrise. "You know the protocol."

"Some things are better discussed face to face."

De Vrise's cold eyes remained fixed on Amos, unflinching as the sand whipped at his scar in a gust of wind.

*

Inside the complex, de Vrise and Amos sat in the windowless room. Amos slid the document across the table and watched as de Vrise digested its details.

"There is no physical threat?" said de Vrise.

Amos appraised him – he had expected more. "Physical threat is a crude weapon. Target the mind and you cripple from within. No man can fight when he is afraid, not even your men, I would venture."

De Vrise met Amos with his empty stare. "It's a non-issue. My men have mastered fear."

Amos did not look away, but leaned forward and spoke softly. "You misunderstand me, General. I'm talking about the kind of fear that paralyses. The kind of fear the goat feels when you hold it down and pull back its head – that moment when it stops struggling because it knows what is coming next."

De Vrise's eyes narrowed. He glanced down at the document again. "And your agent is ready for large-scale ops?"

"In due course," said Amos. "What I'm suggesting is a trial. A few small-scale operations to test the water."

"And how are my men protected?"

"If they truly have mastered fear, as you say they have, they will need no protection." Amos watched for a sign of weakness but de Vrise's stare was impassive. "Regardless, it is a target-specific agent," continued Amos. "It knows which side it's on."

De Vrise raised an eyebrow. "It's intelligent?"

Amos nodded.

The General studied him then leafed through the paper again and Amos saw the seed take root.

"When will it be ready?"

"We're finalising alpha testing," replied Amos. "On completion, your men will have the opportunity to test in it the field, should you wish."

De Vrise said nothing.

"In the meantime," continued Amos, "I have a favour to ask of you." He slid a photograph across the table.

De Vrise picked it up. "An old woman?"

"Unharmed," said Amos.

De Vrise nodded and pushed the photograph aside. "And for these trial operations, who chooses the target?"

The hint of a smile appeared on Amos' lips. Moments like these were what life was about. He had him. "I do," he said.

*

Seth sat at his desk. To his team, it appeared that he was reviewing his round-up for the next Heads of Sectors meeting. His review had taken only a short time to compile and it left him the space to return to the thoughts that were beginning to plague him. He realised he was breaking his own rule about not knowing what you shouldn't. But, he reflected, his rapid rise through the ranks had been partly a result of taking the initiative. He rarely discussed anything to do with his projects with people outwith his sector, unless it was in an official capacity, but having contacts in other branches of ORB had its uses. They had helped him in the past and in turn, he had helped them when he could. While both parties respected the other's professional position, there was no doubt that it was useful to know people. And in this case, he reasoned, following his gut may satisfy his curiosity and offer something of value to the company. Sometimes rules were there to be broken, provided you picked the right rule.

He found Francis Diamond, from electronics, over lunch and asked him about it. Diamond was something of a legend, being able to create almost anything from almost anything that had wires attached. He looked at the mountain of food on Diamond's plate and wondered if he'd ever considered building himself an exercise bike.

"I'm looking for a microgravimeter," Seth said. "Something small, that I can put in my pocket, that can detect local changes in gravity."

Diamond munched his bagel as he considered Seth's request. "How sensitive do you want it?" he asked.

"Sensitive. And a generous scale. I'm looking for fluctuations in big surges over a small area."

"On a local level?"

"Yeah."

Diamond frowned and munched some more. It didn't make sense to him, but he didn't need to know the whys, just the whats. "You have a mandate for this?"

"Not exactly," said Seth.

"Hmm." Diamond slurped his hot chocolate. "Give me a few days, I'll see what I can come up with."

*

True to his word, a few days later a package arrived for Seth. He closed the door in his office, cut open the seal and tipped out something resembling a mobile phone. He smiled – it was intuitive, as were all of Diamond's inventions. He pressed the switch at the side. A dial lit up, a progressive circular band of yellow, orange and red lights above a digital panel that displayed a number. He zeroed it. There was a single earplug whose wire fitted into a corresponding socket. He twisted the plug into his ear, placed the device in his pocket and went for a walk.

He tried the obvious places he could think of first. Marshall gave him a lukewarm reception when he wandered into Astrophysics and Space Engineering carrying a hefty document and armed with a trivial question to which he already knew the answer. All the while he listened to the feedback beeps in his ear, which told him there were no significant gravity surges here. Same for the Environmental Sciences and Material Sciences hubs – the readings, reflected in the orange dial and the constancy of the beep pitch, were higher than normal but fairly uniform. It was when he turned from C Sector to the atrium that he caught sight of Lazaro. It occurred to him then that he didn't know where he was based. This gave him the opportunity to find out.

Seth adopted a purposeful stride yet kept his distance as he tailed Lazaro's slight build through the pedestrian traffic. When Lazaro stepped into a buggy, he watched it disappear into D Sector, then followed. Disembarking further along, he paced up the main corridor. He had lost sight of Lazaro, but it was worth it – the rising pitch of the beeps in his ear told him he was on the right path. He followed them, playing hot and cold, until he found a stairwell that took him to a basement level he never knew existed. He stopped outside a corridor marked:

AREA 9 – RESTRICTED

and pulled out the gravimeter from his pocket. High-pitched beeps jabbed at his ear and the dial hit red. He pulled out the earplug and tried the retinal scanner by the entrance, but his retina was not on the guest list. Whatever was causing the gravity surge he had detected was behind those doors. He turned and walked back up the stairs, wondering what to do with this information, now that he had it.

From beneath the metal stairwell, Elijah Lazaro's pale grey eyes watched him leave.

*

A knock stirred Zoe from her thoughts as she sat alone in the kitchen. She glanced at the cooker clock – 21.45. Too late for visitors. Zoe unlocked the front door and peeped through the crack above the security chain.

"Dr Locke?" She opened the door and let him in.

He looked apologetic. "I hope I'm not disturbing – I was worried about you and just wanted to see you were both doing okay. I tried phoning but…"

"I'm sorry," said Zoe, not meeting his eye. "I turned it off. It's just been a lot to take in over the past few days."

"Yeah," said Locke, "I can imagine. How's Ben doing?"

"He's been quiet, but he seems okay. He's sleeping now. Do you want some tea?"

"Yes. Tea would be good, thanks."

She led him through to the kitchen. "Please, have a seat." The room was small and clean, with a few things lying scattered on the worktop – magazines, unopened envelopes, plastic bricks piled in the shape of a mountain. A pin board displayed some of Ben's paintings of red and yellow things.

Locke glanced at it as he sat down. "And how are you doing?"

Zoe took a deep breath as she filled the kettle. "I met a friend of mine on the way home yesterday. As she came towards me, I just knew her father had died. No one had told me. She didn't speak about it when we talked because she didn't find out till later. But when she did, she called me. Like I said, I already knew."

Locke watched as she placed the teabags into the mugs, her hand trembling.

"And when my sister called tonight, I knew she was going to tell me that her husband was having an affair, even though I haven't seen either of them for six months. And sure enough, that's what she told me." She turned to him. "So how am I doing? I don't know." She sighed harshly. "Whatever this is, I don't want it."

"So why did you take part in the INTP study?" asked Locke.

She shrugged. "I hoped you'd be right. That maybe if I understood it, I'd be okay with it."

"Doesn't it help knowing that it's not just you and Ben?"

She lifted the mugs to the table and sat down. "I don't care about other people. What matters is that it's affecting us." She paused, her gaze running over his face. "Do you have a family, Dr Locke?"

"Raymond, please," he said. "No. I'm kind of married to my work."

Zoe nodded. "I see. And what does your work tell you about Ben?"

"He's special. His connectivity, his obsession with the mountain… Honestly? I think he could be remembering a past life."

Some milk splashed onto the table as she poured it into the mugs. She reached for a cloth, but Locke took it from her and mopped it up. "You really believe that?" she asked.

"There are documented cases around the world – children who are very attached to memories they believe are real and from a former life. They're afraid to let go but, usually by the age of six or seven, the memories begin to fade."

"You don't know they're memories," said Zoe, sharply.

"No," said Locke, "I don't. Have you asked him directly?"

Zoe hesitated. "I don't want to."

"It might help him if you encourage him to talk about it."

She did not look at him as she stirred her mug, watching the teabag bleed its brown stain into the milky water. "I don't know if I can deal with it," she said quietly. "I hate myself for it, but it's so against everything I grew up believing."

Locke watched her, stirring her tea and avoiding his eye.

"Had he met Cora before?" asked Locke.

"Who?"

"The woman from the lab."

Her face grew tight. "No. I don't know what that was about."

Locke left her space to expand, but she shut down. He changed tack. "What about the stone he mentioned?"

She shrugged. "He used to talk about it. It was important to him. Sometimes he'd wake up with nightmares that he'd lost it."

"Did he ever tell you what it was for?"

"No," she said. "He used to carry a pebble around with him, saying it was like his real stone. I never told him, but I didn't like it."

"Why?"

"Because it made me think that maybe the stone was real once, in another life, and so maybe his stories about another mother were too…" She dropped her gaze. "It just made me feel sad."

In the next room, Ben lay on his side on his single bed, his head on his owl. He got up and walked to the window, clambering onto the small table beneath it, and opened the latch. Outside it was colder now than it had been all summer. He could barely see the street for the mist that lay over it as he leaned out over the sill. He took the pebble from his pocket, feeling the groove where his thumb and forefinger had rubbed comfort from it, from as long ago as he could hold it. He knew it wasn't the real one but in his mind, he made it so, and just pretending had helped. His heart clenched as he held the stone over the window ledge and for a moment he thought he couldn't do it. But then there were other things that could remind him, like his red paintings on the walls or the snow in the wintertime. He opened his fingers and let his stone go. It dropped to the ground like the weight in his heart, with a soft thud, and when he looked down, he couldn't distinguish it from the other pebbles on the ground. That weight would be his memory and it wouldn't hurt her anymore.

"Let me know if you need any help," said Dr Locke's voice from the hallway. "When you're up to it, I think it would help Ben if we worked with him some more." Ben heard them walk past his door.

"Alright, I will," said his mum. "Thanks for coming round." Ben heard the front door close as he stared down at the ground outside the flat for the last time. He closed the window and walked slowly back to his bed with his empty hand and his heavy heart.

Zoe washed up the mugs and dried them, slow movements, of which she was barely cognisant. Her mind was on their discussion and the chasm that had reopened. She had been here before, on the edge. Like before, she was afraid to look down for fear of what might be inside.

She opened Ben's door. He was asleep on his bed, his arm round his owl. She knelt down next to him and tucked his small arm under the duvet. He rubbed his nose with his free hand, his eyes still shut as she kissed his forehead, then closed the door quietly behind her.

She changed into her nightshirt and brushed her teeth, staring into her eyes in the mirror. The furrow on her brow seemed to have become her default expression. Did she always look this worried? She spat out the toothpaste and wiped her mouth without looking up.

When she turned out her light, she lay with open eyes for some time, trying to quell the chorus of anxiety that usually struck up round about now. Daytime was easier with so much to do, but this time of night was much harder. Her body stopped, but her mind didn't, and she did not have any say in it. Sleep would come – it usually did – but she wished that it would hurry up.

Sleep did come, and with it, something else. The night breathed through the net curtains and blew around some featherweight clutter in the room. It carried a passenger that slipped in through the crack in the window and came to rest above her, its sleek form rippling slightly in the soft breeze. It turned its head as it watched her, listening... searching... waiting... She began to whimper, as something unbidden mined her memories. It stilled as it found it, tuning in to the thing it sought, absorbing the feeling of her mounting fear; growing from it.

When it was full, it left the way it came in and stole through the quiet streets to a deserted warehouse in wasteland. It moved to the old chimneystack at the end of the building, where the red sandstone bricks were crumbling a slow death. A breeze whipped up the sheets of an old newspaper and they fluttered around like paper birds. Resting its hands and its forehead against the bricks, it began to whisper.

If whispers could harmonise, that would be the sound, as its sibling rested its head and hands on the trunk of the single tree that stood in the rubble of the open ground beyond the chimneystack. The crows nesting in the branches flapped away silently into the night, as the tips of the leaves began to blacken and wither.

Together, their whispers trickled down through the substance of the stones, rippling through the grains of sand that formed them, vibrating their way deeper into the earth. Like an invisible river feeling its way through the gaps in the rocks, the whispers relayed their message from one molecule to the next, drawn towards the place that was calling them.

*

The mist inside the tank became agitated, clouding its contents as they swirled within. The technician put down her tablet and stepped up to the side of the tank, now refilled with a fresh batch of mist, and read the panel attached to its surface, waiting for the measurements to settle. As they did, Elijah Lazaro stood up and walked from his seat in the corner. This was the moment he had been waiting for.

He nodded to the technician, who opened the hatch in the extension pipe. A single entity drifted out, penetrating the dome over Dana Bishop's bed, coming to rest above her. It began to whisper, words that were incomprehensible to its onlookers. Dana's eyes shot open. The technician moved to her bedside and checked the numbers on the monitor that reflected her responses, the window to her physiology.

"Well?" asked Elijah.

"Her heart rate's up but other than that, she's stable."

"Good," said Elijah. "Plug her in."

The technician pressed a command key on her tablet and the green light on the side of Dana's headset lit up. Elijah moved to the bank of monitors behind her, watching the cross-sectional image of Dana's brain, as her limbic system flashed in a cacophony of red and yellow lights. "Turn on the Holopod," he said.

The technician selected the control on her tablet and enabled it. They turned to the sleek black pillar that stood next to Dana's bed, about the same height as the bed itself, as a holographic image stammered into life above it.

Elijah leaned in, frowning. "Sharpen the image," he said.

As the technician experimented with the controls, a holographic room appeared, circular and dimly lit above the pod. A woman stood in the middle of the floor, as someone walked away through a door in the wall. She ran to the door but it slammed shut before she could reach it. She tried the handle but it was locked. Another door squeaked then banged as someone else left the room and she ran to this one, but the same thing happened. One by one, the doors all around the circular walls slammed shut. She ran to each of them, but never in time. Then she backed into the middle of the room and sat down on the floor, under a single cold white spotlight. She wrapped her arms around her knees, rocking slightly, and hung her head.

The corner of Elijah's mouth smiled thinly. "Abandonment," he said. His eyes slid to the technician. "Can you feel it?"

The technician nodded, her expression blank, but her face draining to the colour of damp clay. The electronic tablet in her hand was trembling.

"Categorise it," he said. "Then take a break."

*

A long distance away, above the ground, a chimneystack stood at the end of a derelict building. A bird's nest lay abandoned in the cracks of its stone. Nearby, the skeleton of a Rowan tree stood alone, its blackened branches reaching through the mist for something it could not remember.

*

Cora sat on the floor of their room, propped up against the sofa. She wasn't hungry, and picked at the meal Robert had made for her. Had it been a culinary masterpiece, he might have been offended. As it was beans on toast, he let it slide. Besides, it was nothing to do with the food and he knew it. Since their return from the park she had become withdrawn.

"You okay?" asked Robert.

"Yeah," she said, pushing the plate away. "Now we're indoors." She emerged from behind the veil of her thoughts. "What was that?" she asked.

"I don't know."

The front door slammed. Footsteps in the corridor and the thud of a cupboard door closing.

Robert stood up. But as he reached for the door handle, she caught his arm. The look on her face made him lower his voice.

"What is it?"

"He's angry," she whispered.

"What?"

She paused then said, "He doesn't trust us."

*

When Robert walked into the kitchen, Danny glanced round but did not meet his eye.

"Hey," said Robert. "What's up?"

Danny opened the fridge, took out a single beer and slammed the door shut. "Well, we could spend half an hour exchanging small talk about how our days went, or we could cut the crap."

"Huh?"

Danny faced him. "What's going on, Robert?"

Shit, thought Robert. *He's serious.* "What do you mean?"

'How come you got so edged with Cora going out on her own today?" He stared at Robert, his mouth a tight line.

"She's been through a lot lately and I just—"

"She's an adult, for Christ's sake. And how come you show up in the middle of the night just after your dad was murdered?"

"Danny, look, a lot has happened that I want to tell you about but it's... safer if you don't know—"

"*Safer?*" As Danny stepped closer, his hostility was tangible. "Safer for who? Who are you running from, Robert?"

Robert stared at him, his mind numb as he tried to figure out if he should level with him.

"Did you kill him?" asked Danny.

"Who?"

"Did you kill your father?"

"*What?* No! What the fuck's got into you? Jesus Christ, Danny, do you really think I'd kill my own father?"

Danny eyed him, trembling, his face white. The ice in his stare was new to Robert and it scared him.

126

"I told you," said Robert, trying to regain some sort of control but wary of triggering the side of Danny he had never met before, despite years of shared experiences. "My dad got wrapped up in the wrong kind of company. I'm just trying to find out what happened." He paused, suddenly seeing Danny's perspective. "Look, if you're not happy with all this, I get it. It's fine. We'll find somewhere else to stay. But I didn't kill him – you have to know that."

As though a memory tricked in and thawed his mind, Danny blinked then lowered his eyes. "Yeah," he said. "Yeah. I'm sorry, man, I…" He ran his hands through his tangled hair, pulling at it in a way that looked painful. "I just… I dunno. Not been myself today."

He opened the fridge again and handed Robert a beer. "Course you can stay. I'm just being an asshole. Sorry, man."

*

They stood in the shadow of the brick building. The headlights of a car skewered the mist, the sound of its engine muffled as it purred along the street nearby. Robert waited until it passed then took out Banks' phone and handed it to Casimir.

"You take it," he said. "I don't know what I'm doing." It was true, but he was more distracted by Danny's outburst earlier. It wasn't like him. He had waited until Cora was asleep and Danny's snores were audible through the wall before he slipped out.

"You know the feeling of surrendering to the drop?" said Casimir, taking the phone.

Robert nodded. What came to mind more clearly was the sickening anxiety of standing at the edge of a roof, while any sense of control and everything that defined you trickled away in strands of light.

Casimir read him. "I'm talking about the surrender," he said. "Not the panic. That feeling of trust, of letting the bird carry you."

"You mean that feeling of having no other option," said Robert.

Casimir grinned. "Just keep your mind on where we're going and relax. We'll drive this one."

Aiyana placed her fingertips on the phone and looked expectantly at Robert. "Tunnelling's easier than a Jump," she said. "Trust me."

Robert's eyes moved from Aiyana to Casimir as he placed his fingertips on the glass screen.

"Ready?" said Casimir.

"Ready," said Aiyana.

Robert nodded, breathed out and closed his eyes.

A gut-twisting cyclone gripped him, wrenching him, it felt like, inside out, sucking the breath from his chest and the blood from his brain. There was a moment of intense pressure, like he was being squeezed into his own singularity, with no point of reference other than how sick he felt. Then, like he had been vomited out of some porthole, his face hit soil. He could taste the grains of dirt in his mouth, damp grass on his cheeks. He got to his knees, the darkness still spinning around him, and threw up.

A hand slapped his shoulder.

"Rough ride?" Casimir's voice, from somewhere outside of him. He opened his eyes, trying to catch the whirling disc that was everything around him. "You'll get used to it."

It took a moment, but the world slowed down and let him back on. When he managed to focus on Aiyana, she looked vaguely appalled. "God, Robert, you look like shit."

"Thanks," he said. "Just so you know, Tunnelling is worse than a Jump."

Casimir helped him to his feet and he glanced around. The darkness was beginning to take shape. The sky swept above them, distant suns puncturing a black velvet dome, laced with inky clouds. Ahead was a large open field and, a hundred metres or so away, a bunker. *The substation,* thought Robert. He shivered. *I boarded the helicopter here.* His mind drifted back to that one moment in time when everything changed. A flashback to someone else's life.

"This way," he said, heading towards the bunker that was the door to ORB's subterranean labyrinth. He staggered as he walked, his limbs remembering what it was to move him through space. The silence of the countryside was thick without the buffers of city noise, and the stillness crystallised every sound. An owl hooted from a distant place, warping the void of the night.

They paced ahead, the grass uneven tufts under their feet, as the moon drifted out from behind the shadow of a cloud, then disappeared again.

"Stop!" Aiyana grasped Robert's arm. She stood rooted to the spot, staring ahead.

Robert froze then followed her gaze. "What?"

The carcass of a sheep lay on the grass a few feet in front of them, its head shrivelled and blackened, as though it had decayed faster than the rest of the corpse. Small dark clumps lay scattered around, each about the size of a fist.

"What are those?" said Robert.

Cautiously, they approached and Casimir crouched down, peering at one of the small things that lay motionless on the grass. An unseeing eye stared up at him amidst black feathers. "Starlings," he said.

Robert's gaze swept across the field where a curved line of dead birds was scattered over it. He stepped back.

Only when the veil of cloud inched aside, yielding to the moonlight, did he see it. Insubstantial, almost invisible, it was as though part of the landscape before them was darker than its surroundings. He scanned the field, the bunker, the sky in the background, all in denser shadow than seemed right. It was as though something encased them.

"Is it my imagination, or is that…" The cloud cleared the moon as Casimir's eyes traced the high arc barely perceptible in the soft light.

"A dome?" finished Robert. He took a step closer, looking up to where the pallid moonlight spilled onto its smooth curvature. "Yeah, I think it is."

Aiyana reached a hand out towards it. As her fingers drew closer, a soft whispering rose on the air. It could have been a breeze but for the chill Robert felt inside him. He grasped her hand. "No."

Plucking the stalk of a fern plant from the ground, tentatively he held it forwards. The whispering rose again, quietly, as the fern neared the dome, and as it touched, its leaves curled and blackened. Robert dropped the stalk and backed away.

They paced round the circumference, following the trail of small dark carcasses and the faint line of dead grass that betrayed the dome's presence and led them back to where they started.

"There's no way in," said Aiyana.

"There's got to be," said Casimir. "They'd need supplies…"

"So what do we do," she said. "Wait?"

"*Fuck!*" Robert kicked the earth and a clod of dirt launched into the air. "How am I supposed to find him?"

"What about Banks' home?" said Aiyana. "Like the first time you got in?"

"I suspect this field is activated to cover all ways in and out of there," said Casimir.

"We don't know that, Casimir. We could—" Robert began. "What?"

Aiyana was pointing at his neck. She glanced at Casimir. "Your amulets…"

A sharp pain seared the hollow above Robert's breastbone at the same time as he heard Casimir say her name.

"*Marion…*"

He felt Casimir grab his hoodie as the world caved in on itself in a sickening cyclone.

*

They were in a narrow street above a sleeping village. Moonlight danced on the dark sea that lay beyond the mountains, silhouetting distant inky islands. Robert felt Casimir grasp his armpit and drag him upright, staggering as he hustled him up the hill.

"What just—" began Robert.

"Did you see it?" Casimir cut through his words. 'The Ominence?"

"The what? No, I…" He took in his bearings. The white petals of magnolia flowers clinging to the front wall of a cottage shone in the pale light. A *For Sale* sign stood by the fence and a beehive at the edge of the lawn. "Wait, are we… Casimir is that your home?"

Aiyana glanced behind them. "They're coming."

Robert turned to see a car pull in at the bottom of the hill. The white beams of its headlights went out.

"Move!" hissed Casimir. "We don't have much time."

He led them to the top of the hill where Robert's mother's cottage stood in darkness apart from a yellow glow from the upstairs window. Panic surged in Robert chest. *Jesus, they're coming for her?*

They followed Casimir down the narrow passageway to the rear of the house, under a canopy of hawthorn trees, on the flagstones Robert had walked a thousand times as a child. A frayed rope still hung from a branch of the old beach tree in the back garden where he used to swing back and forth, stargazing. The moon cast deep shadows in secret corners of the garden. Casimir spoke in an urgent whisper but there was no mistaking his authority. "Robert, get her out of the house."

"Where to?" said Robert.

"My cottage. There's a key at the base of the beehive. Leave through the front door. They'll come in through the back. Aiyana, you're with me."

Robert passed unseen into the kitchen of his childhood home, shrouded from sight but cloaked in dread. He tore upstairs, passing the photographs of his past, and stopped outside his mother's door, reforming to his physical self. He knocked before it hit him. *What the fuck do I say?*

"Who's there?" Her voice was tense.

"Mum? It's me." He pushed open the door to see Marion Strong sitting bolt upright in bed, wide eyes staring out over half-moon specs, her dressing gown still on, a book lying open to one side.

"*Robert?* What—"

"I'll explain," he said, moving to the window, "but right now you have to come with me."

"Why? What's—"

He teased back the curtain. Two shadows stole from the street to the narrow passageway at the side of the house. "*Now*, Mum!"

He held her hand as he led her silently down the dark stairs. Gently, he unlocked the front door and took out the key as a soft thud came from the kitchen. She froze. He shook his head, raising a finger to his lips then opened the door and followed her outside, locking it quietly after them. She padded behind him, barefoot, as they crossed the street in the moonlight.

*

Two men moved through the house. Clad in black, toned, their heads covered in dark woollen hats, each had a holster strapped to his waist and a pistol in his hand. A coiled rope hung from the belt of man at the rear. They crept silently from one room to the next, with only a nod of communication between them. *Clear.*

The taller of the two led the way upstairs, pausing as the stair creaked beneath his foot. Silence returned and they moved again, stopping by the line of yellow light that escaped from the base of the closed door. He gestured to his buddy, who checked the next bedroom and returned a moment later, shaking his head. A curt nod and the taller man opened the door. He scanned the room. Empty. They moved inside, stealing to the old dark wooden wardrobe which lay ajar, exchanging a glance as they paused beside it.

In the background, the bedroom door slammed shut. They spun round, pistols aimed. Slowly, painstakingly, the key turned in the lock. They stared, transfixed, as the lock bolted itself and the key dislodged and dropped to the floor. The wardrobe doors flew open, clattering on their hinges and they spun round again, aimed to fire. The few clothes inside swung back and forth on their hangers. Their rapid breathing and the beads of sweat on their foreheads betrayed their crumbling composure. Easing forward, the shorter man held his pistol steady as he parted the clothes with his other hand. Nothing was there.

"Are you looking for me?" A woman's voice came from the corner of the room; soft, steady.

Their eyes darted towards it, scanning the empty space before they shot a glance to each other.

"You're too late." The voice came again, this time from behind them and they turned abruptly, backing away. A lipstick lifted itself from the dresser. Slowly, it raised itself to the mirror and scrawled letters in red across the glass: *ALREADY DEAD*

"*Jesus H. Christ,*" breathed the tall man.

His accomplice circled an index finger in the air as he moved towards the door. *Bail out.* But something violent and unseen pushed him onto the bed. He fired his pistol, the silencer muffling the shots as feathers exploded from the large cushion in the corner. The pistol flew out of his hand, something tearing it from him. A sudden *crash*, as the mirror dropped from the wall, shattering on the dresser, splinters of glass showering the room. He yelled and backed against the wall.

The light snapped out. Only the haze of moonlight siphoning in from the crack between the curtains made the shapes in the room vaguely discernible. The taller man scanned the darkness, his pistol following his line of sight, his breaths punching at the silence. Something stroked the side of his cheek and he turned, swiping the air beside him.

"Leave the dead to rest," whispered the woman's voice.

As the grip on his pistol fell loose, the weapon took itself from his hand, turning on him, levelling itself between his eyes.

"Now, tell me." Her voice was like silk. "How does one get into ORB?"

*

Robert watched his mother as she sat in her dressing gown by the fireplace in Casimir's old living room, the blood-stained letter and photograph on her lap. A single reading lamp poured weak light on the words as she stared at them through her half-moon glasses. She looked smaller, fidgeting with her tissue; a little girl in an old woman's body. He could feel the ache in her heart, and his own heart swelled as he saw her fragility for the first time.

Eventually she swallowed and met his eye. "I'm not leaving."

"You can't stay here. Christ, Mum, they're in your house right now."

"And yet they didn't find me."

"What if I'm not around next time? I can't stay here with you... I have to fix this."

"I understand, Robert, but this is my choice. I'm not afraid, no matter what happens. I've had a good life."

"Please Mum, you have no idea... what they did to Dad..."

"You think they can break my spirit after all I've been through?"

"Yes, I do. You don't know what they're capable of. They broke Dad, and he was a strong man. Please. Just for a couple of months, until things settle. For me."

She said nothing as she leaned back in the chair. Her eyes closed and for a moment she sat motionless, then tears began to spill down her cheeks. He knelt down and held her and she surrendered to it, sobbing into his shoulder. Vulnerability she had never admitted to or shared, until now.

"I'm sorry," she sniffed, straightening up and pulling another tissue from her dressing gown pocket. She wiped her dripping nose. "Alright. I'll do it." Smiling through watery eyes, she handed him the photograph. "You can keep that," she said. "I have the same one."

Something tapped the window and Robert tensed. He stole to the curtain, easing it back. In the moonlight, he saw Aiyana and the shadow of Casimir, and breathed out a long breath.

"It's okay," he said to Marion. "Give me a minute." He left her sitting in her thoughts.

Opening the front door, he saw Casimir pause as he passed the beehive, a faint smile on his lips. *Another life.*

"What happened?" asked Robert.

"They're gone," said Aiyana. "And they won't be coming back."

"What about getting inside ORB?" asked Robert.

Casimir shook his head. "They didn't know what ORB was."

"And you believed them?" said Robert.

"They were truly afraid, Robert," said Casimir. He glanced at Aiyana. "She'd scare the life out of me if I weren't already dead." He glanced at the living room door. "How is she?"

"As you'd expect," said Robert. "But at least she agreed to go away for a while."

"How much did you tell her?" he whispered.

"Only what she can handle," said Robert. "I was flexible with the truth."

Casimir nodded. "I'd better stay out of sight."

Robert led Aiyana into the living room, and as Casimir's shadow followed on, Robert could feel his tenderness as he saw Marion again.

"This is Aiyana," said Robert. "Our other colleague, Mike, had to take care of a few things, but maybe you'll meet him some other time."

"I can't thank you enough," said Marion, getting up and hugging Aiyana. "And I'm grateful that your surveillance team are so efficient."

"Any time," said Aiyana, glancing at Robert. "Can we, eh... can we help you get your things?"

*

They left her with Tam, the proprietor of the Stone Circle pub who took her in for the night. A man of few words and loyal to his core, he would drive her to a friend's place, deep in the neighbouring glen at first light, and say nothing to anyone.

"Look after yourself, Robert," said Marion as Robert held her close. "I'll be alright." He didn't want to let her go. How often do we abandon those we love for things that seem to matter more?

*

Cora was sitting up, her back against the wall, her fingers rolling a black obsidian crystal slowly in her palm. The grey light from the gap between the curtains sliced across her chest but left her face in shadow. The remnants of nausea lined Robert's head and stomach as he woke.

A hangover?

No.

What then?

Ah, yes. Tunnelling. And the taste of fear on his mind. The feeling of gulping air from the surface as the surge of an ocean much bigger than he threatened to pull him under.

"Where were you last night?" said Cora.

He propped himself up on his elbow. "Huh?"

"I got up when you didn't come back to bed. You weren't in the

135

flat."

Things started to fall into place. "I needed some air." He didn't know what else to say.

"In the middle of the night?"

"I had a busy head." He rubbed his eyes, still not fully awake. This double life was beginning to wear thin. Fragments of the night's events slipped back to him unbidden... ORB, his mother, Aiyana... He sat up and pulled on a T-shirt.

"That's the second time you've mentioned her," said Cora. Her words were loaded with accusation.

"What?"

She fixed him with a cold stare. "Robert, are you seeing someone else?"

"Christ, Cora. Of course not!" *Like there's any space in my head for that.*

"Then who's Aiyana?"

Shit. He guarded his thoughts then shuffled over so that he sat level with her. "Look," he said, running his hand through his messy hair. "Alright, I wasn't just getting some air. Aiyana's someone I met who knows about Mindscape. She used to work in a company that monitors electromagnetic output and she accidentally picked up the medium ORB is using for Mindscape – she's helping me understand it, that's all."

"When did you meet her?"

"When I was in Geneva."

Cora studied him through narrowed eyes. "Why didn't you tell me about all this?"

He hesitated. "You've had enough to worry about."

"We're a team, Robert!" She slapped the floor next to her, seized by a flash of fierceness, and held him with an icy stare. "At least I thought we were."

"We are." He reached for her hand but she swiped his arm away, her gaze fixed on the floor. "Cora?" he said gently. "We are." He lifted her chin so that her eyes met his.

He saw beyond the ice wall, to her vulnerability. "So," said Cora. "When do I meet her?"

"Well… that might be tricky."

She pulled away. "Really. Why?"

"Logistically… She's not always easy to get hold of."

"You seemed to manage last night."

"Look, okay," he said. "I'll see if I can arrange something."

"Fine," said Cora, in a way that made it clear that it was not. She stood up. "I'm going for a shower."

Well that's just great, thought Robert. *Like things aren't complex enough.*

Robert knocked on Danny's door. No answer. He pushed it open and saw the bed unmade, but no sign of him. The kitchen, too, was empty. Robert boiled the kettle as the sound of the shower pattered in the next room. Steam rose onto the window. A layer of grey mist cloaked the back yard, where yellow dandelions pushed through the cracks in the gravel beneath the rusty whirligig. One of its plastic green lines trailed across the ground, rising in the soft breeze like a blind tentacle. A crow sat perched on the central pole, doing that odd scooping movement they do, cawing at the world. It stilled, then turned to him, like it was looking right at him.

He became aware of a heat in the hollow of his neck. It grew to a burning, searing his skin. Grasping the amulet, it felt like a hot coal in his fingers, as the world around him dislocated and something unbidden gatecrashed his mind.

He saw Danny.

He was walking down a side street, through the fog, his blue rucksack tucked in closely on his back. As he turned onto Grassmarket, a thin figure stepped out of the dimness, its face concealed beneath the hood of a dark sweatshirt, hands in pockets, shoulders hunched. Danny glanced back and picked up his pace. The figure kept its distance amongst the straggling pedestrians. It hung back as Danny stopped beside a red and white take-away shop and a vintage clothes store that flanked a dim alleyway. Danny cast his eyes over his shoulder then glanced down at a piece of paper he pulled from his pocket. He started down the passage ahead of him.

As the figure closed in, Danny looked back then turned and ran, the gap between them narrowing in the dim alleyway. He almost reached the other end before there was a scuffle – the hooded man pinned Danny to the wall beside a large waste bin.

A glint of silver in the fog, as the figure reached under his sweatshirt. In one swift movement, almost too quick for a man, he thrust the knife into Danny's solar plexus, his hooded face almost touching Danny's, their breaths mingling in the damp air, as he pushed a second, a third time in sharp, deliberate twists. Danny's eyes widened as his lips paled and he slumped to the ground, the pool of maroon staining the pavement, the smell of copper rising on the air. The hooded man picked up the blue rucksack, glancing along the deserted alleyway. He wiped the blade on Danny's leg then disappeared into the shadows.

CHAPTER EIGHT

*F*uck! Robert leaned over the sink, grasping the cold metal edges, his breaths punching at his lungs, the cawing of the crow outside pulsing in his ears. The world relocated as he stumbled to the hallway.

Cora was coming out of the bathroom wrapped in a towel. She froze. "What's wrong?"

"Danny's in trouble. Lock the door. I'll be back when I can."

"Wait, Robert—"

He slammed the door behind him.

He ran like he had never run before, along the damp streets, through the mist that would not lift. It was ten o'clock in the morning, but it may as well have been dusk – the street lamps were still lit and the mist swallowed most of the light. His feet pounded on the ground as he darted between the straggles of people on the pavement, his head turning over and over the image of the dark ooze on the concrete... *What have you done, Danny?*

He stopped dead, almost colliding with a businessman as he turned onto Grassmarket. Fair tousled hair bobbed ahead, a blue rucksack tight against his back. Danny looked over his shoulder, but didn't see him. *He's alive...*

Crossing the street, not far behind Danny, was the thin hooded figure. Robert could make out the back of his hunched shoulders, weaving through the crowd. Danny had stopped by the red and white take-away shop. He cast his eyes over his shoulder then glanced down at the piece of paper he pulled from his pocket. He started down the passage ahead of him.

The Hood was on his tail as Robert sprinted after them, knocking into a dawdling woman whose shopping bag spilled its contents onto the damp pavement. She shouted a barrage of abuse at him as he turned into the darkened alleyway.

He was not prepared for what he saw. In the distance, Danny was rounding a corner at the other end, disappearing into the next lane. But halfway along the alleyway, Danny's stalker was pinned against the wall beside the bin, the assailant's forearm fixed under his throat. The Hood's right hand slid under his sweatshirt, slipping the slivery blade to his side.

"Casimir!" shouted Robert.

Casimir's left hand gripped the Hood's wrist, as slowly, painfully, the blade inched higher. With a burst of strength, the Hood thrust Casimir backwards. He tumbled to the ground as the figure turned the blade on itself, slicing it upwards, into his own chest. Shuddering, it slid down the wall to the cobbles. Robert stood there, frozen in the shadows of the fog, as the figure's twitches faded to stillness. Casimir looked up.

Cautiously, Robert approached, his eyes on the thin unmoving body which was half propped against the wall, its hooded head bent at an odd angle against its chest as a pool of black blood oozed onto the concrete.

"What took you so long?" asked Casimir.

"I couldn't run any faster—"

"You *ran?*"

"Yeah, I…" Robert stopped, feeling suddenly stupid.

"Running won't cut it, Robert. When you feel an Ominence, you Tunnel. There's no time for anything else."

"Ominence?"

"The warning… the premonition. The signal of what's about to happen. If it calls us, something major is about to disrupt the Field. It's our chance to stop the disruption." He watched Robert digest the words. "It's what we do, Robert. As Eidolon, we have the gift of foresight. Even if it's only a few moments in time, those moments change lives. If you're beginning to see them, you have no choice but to follow them."

Robert's gaze fell to the body slumped on the ground. Tentatively, he reached towards its hood.

"No!" snapped Sattva. He appeared without warning behind him. "Don't touch it."

Robert backed away then froze. In the way that the eye is drawn to something moving that should not be, he stared at the blood on the pavement. Black, the colour of tar, it was shifting, quivering, congealing. A sound weaved on the air, the faint echo of whispering; unintelligible voices too distant and weak to decipher. A thin black vapour rose and came to hover a few inches above the pool of blood. With a movement resembling a bead of dark ink dropped into a glass of water, it snaked above the ground and dispersed into the fog. They stood in silence staring after it.

"What *was* that?" breathed Robert.

Sattva said nothing as he crouched down by the corpse.

Robert took a step closer. "I don't understand. He killed himself?"

Sattva studied the thin face inside the hood. "He was already dead."

"What?" said Robert.

He followed Sattva as he paced to the end of the alleyway.

Further down the dank lane to the right, Danny was standing beneath a brown sign swinging from an iron bracket which read: *Ingles' Books Old and New*. He hitched his rucksack tighter onto his back and checked the paper in his hand.

"Any idea what's in that rucksack of his?" asked Casimir.

"No," said Robert. He glanced back up the alleyway. The corpse was crumbling into dust on the cobblestones. A soft breeze scattered its fragments until they dispersed on the air, leaving nothing behind.

Sattva's eyes remained fixed on Danny. "Find out."

*

Robert crossed the lane, unseen, to where Danny stared up at the windows of Ingles' Bookstore. Unaware of his friend at his shoulder, Danny rested his hand on the brass door handle, dulled by too many years of use, and pushed. A bell jangled above as it swung open.

Dust danced on the shard of daylight that filtered in from the skylight and the room smelled of the past. Bookshelves stacked with old tomes, their leather bindings faded and peeling, lined the walls around a wooden desk and an empty wooden chair. A table lamp with a metal stem leaned over a large book, shining a cone of light onto it, as though peering at the faint remaining text. On the book's open pages lay a magnifying glass and next to it, a mug of steaming coffee and a phone. A cast iron spiral staircase twisted to an upper level crammed with more books on shelves.

A thud came from upstairs. "Sorry, I'll just be down. Make yourself at home."

"Sure," said Danny. "Take your time." He ran his fingers over the books in the shelf next to him. *The Upanishads,* the *Tao Te Ching,* the *Bhagavad Gita...* He picked up a copy of *The Tibetan Book of the Dead* and flicked it open, and a loose page fluttered to the floor. "Shit," he whispered as he picked it up and stuffed it back between the pages.

Footsteps clanged on the stairs. An older man with thinning hair waddled down, as though trying not to topple onto the belly bulging inside his brown jumper. He smiled over his spectacles. "Now, how can I help you?"

"My name's Danny Mitchell." Danny extended a hand.

"Ah. Nice to meet you. Wilbert Ingles," said the man, shaking hands. "Sorry to keep you waiting – I was cataloguing some intriguing manuscripts I've just had sent in from Bolivia."

"No problem," said Danny.

"What can I do for you, Mr Mitchell?"

"I understand you're an expert in old texts?"

"Well," said Mr Ingles, his pink face flushing to a deeper red. "Yes, well, I suppose you could say that."

"I wondered if you'd take a look at something I found," said

Danny. He took a hexagonal wooden box from his rucksack and placed it on the desk.

The old man sighed and flumped down into his chair. He reached into the drawer under the desk and put on a pair of white silken gloves. His chubby fingers lifted the lid of the box carefully then teased out the material. He unfolded it delicately, respectfully, until its charred edges lay flat on the table.

Mr Ingles peered over his specs, frowning as he pushed them up onto the bridge of his nose. Then he flipped them onto his head and picked up the magnifying glass. The lines on his forehead deepened as he concentrated and his jowls hung over his down-turned lips, giving him the look of an ageing cherub.

His gaze rose to rest on Danny. "May I ask where you got this?"

"Tibet – the western plateau. I found it near a monastery I stayed in."

The book dealer's eyes flickered momentarily to the material then back to Danny. "Did you find anything else with it?"

"No," said Danny. "Why?"

Ignoring the question, Mr Ingles continued to study the cloth. "Who else knows about this?" he asked.

Danny shrugged. "Just me. Is it worth anything?"

"It's a mandala. A geometric pattern; a chart, if you like, which represents the cosmos metaphysically or symbolically. A microcosm of the universe."

"Can you read it?"

"My grasp of mandalas is limited but it's in remarkable shape. A Tibetan Vajrayana, seventh century, I'd estimate. Very unusual." He glanced up at Danny. "Most of the manuscripts from that era were lost when the temples were destroyed."

He adjusted the lamp and wrinkled his nose as he studied it. "Let's see. It's a typical format – this square surrounding an inner circle and a centre point, and these 'domes' on the sides of the square represent four gates. But it is a little unusual..." His voice tailed off as he adjusted his glasses and squinted back at the document.

Danny peered closer, nodding. "So what does it mean?"

The book dealer stared through the magnifying glass, but he did not answer.

"How much do you think it's worth?" pushed Danny.

Mr Ingles glanced up then folded the cloth, placing it back inside the box. He stared down at it before he spoke. "What line of work are you in, Mr Mitchell?"

"I'm a journalist – I'm writing a piece on the history of Tibet," he said.

Robert was impressed by the ease with which Danny could come up with bullshit.

"How fascinating. What makes a journalist interested in Tibetan history?"

"I read history at Oxford."

Now you're digging, Danny.

"Really? Tell me, how is Professor Shanti these days?"

"I… haven't seen him for a while, but I believe he's doing well."

"That's good to hear." Ingles glanced down at the box again. "Have you taken this to the museum?"

"No."

"I see. And I take it the Chinese Authorities are aware of this."

"Not exactly."

"What makes you think I won't inform them?"

"Because that's not how you work. I know you have links to collectors."

Mr Ingles removed his silk gloves slowly as he studied him. "Leave it with me. I'll make some enquiries."

"Thanks," said Danny, "but I'll hold on to it in the meantime."

"Well then I'm afraid I can't help you. My understanding of mandalas is limited, and without an interpretation of what it represents, I cannot give you a price."

"If I get you an interpretation, will you find me a buyer?"

Mr Ingles let out a slow breath. He searched for a pen and

scribbled a name and an address then gave the scrap of paper to Danny. "A Professor of Sanskrit. He should be able to help."

Danny reached to pick up the box, but Mr Ingles got there first.

"I trust you will look after this," said the old man. "As a scholar of history, I don't need to explain to you that this," he looked down at the relic, "this *is* History." He handed the box to Danny but as Danny's hand folded round it, the book dealer did not relinquish his grip. He held Danny's eye. "Don't forget you're only borrowing it, Mr Mitchell. You don't own it."

"Of course," said Danny.

Mr Ingles let go.

Danny pushed the box into his rucksack and turned to walk out, blowing the air quietly from his lips. As he reached the door, Mr Ingles spoke again. "Do give Professor Shanti my regards if you see her again. She was always a good friend."

Danny hesitated, lowering his eyes, then walked out without looking back.

Robert followed on then paused, as a phone beeped behind him.

"It's me," said Mr Ingles, his voice hushed this time. "We need to meet." A beep, then silence.

*

Still unseen, Robert followed Danny as he crossed onto a tree-lined avenue, shrouded in a quilt of grey mist. He cut through the square, passing the Innovatics Institute at the corner, still bustling with activity. A group of students straggling the whole width of the pavement was coming towards him, giving him no room to move aside. He froze as two of them passed through the space that was him and felt a ripple shudder through him, like he was suddenly immersed in invisible treacle. The sounds of the world became muffled for a second but it took longer for him to shake off the feeling of confusion, like he still had bits of them in him. When he got his bearings again, he glanced up at the Innovatics building, whose glass walls and bold architecture clashed eras with the grey tenements and wrought-iron fences that lined the small leafy park in the middle. Danny stopped outside one of the tenements and squinted at the plaque on the wall, which read: *International College of*

Sanskrit Studies.

The door swung shut behind Danny and Robert passed through its substance, faintly tasting dust and wood and glass and varnish as he came through on the other side. A mandala in a glass frame decorated the wall at the foot of the staircase.

Sitting at the desk behind a computer was a plump middle-aged woman with dyed blonde hair and fingernails painted pink. She peered at him over her gold-rimmed glasses. "Can I help you?"

"I'm looking for Professor Ganesh," said Danny.

She blinked her unfeasibly long lashes. "Do you have an appointment?"

"No, I don't. Is he available?"

She raised her eyebrows in preference to smiling and they seemed to climb a long way up on her forehead. "You've just missed him," she said. "He's in a meeting."

Danny adjusted his rucksack on his shoulder. "What about later – is he around?"

She let out a tight-lipped sigh and reached forward, moving aside a badge to pick up a large desk diary, and flicked through the pages with her pink talons. The badge sat by the edge of the desk, showing a picture of a man with greying hair and the words: *Professor P. Ganesh.*

"He's free after 2.00pm. Can I take your name?"

"Danny Mitchell."

He didn't know what made him do it but as they spoke, Robert slipped the badge from the desk. It disappeared as his fingers folded round it.

"Can I ask what it's concerning?"

"No," said Danny, "But thanks for your help."

It looked like an invisible string was pulling her face into her nose. Danny beamed at her then walked for the door.

"You need a good shag," he muttered under his breath.

"Excuse me?" came her high-pitched voice.

"I need a fag," he beamed back, gesturing an imaginary cigarette to his lips, then walked out.

*

Danny left the square and found a diner on Chapel Row, its neon red sign stark in the damp mist. Robert waited outside, watching through the window as Danny took a table near the back wall and unpacked his laptop. Only a handful of customers were inside, each absorbed in their newspapers, conversations or phones. Robert barely noticed the ripple of passers-by as they walked through the space where he stood. When Danny was taken up with his bacon roll and whatever he was reading on his computer, Robert walked in and headed for the men's room. Moments later, he reappeared, fully formed, and bought a coffee.

"I thought that was you," said Robert, placing his mug on the table.

Danny looked up. "Hey! What are you doing here?"

"I'm stalking you," said Robert, grinning. He sat down. "What are you up to?"

"Trying to get a buyer for this mandala. Flights to Tibet aren't cheap, you know."

"Any luck?"

"I'm seeing some professor this afternoon. If I can get him to translate it, I'll get more cash for it." He scoured the laptop screen. "And then I just need to find the right buyer…"

Robert's phone beeped in his pocket. "Hi, Cora," he said, standing up and walking out of earshot of Danny. "Yeah, I found him, he's okay. Listen, I can't talk right now…" He glanced back at Danny who was still absorbed in his screen. "I'm going to stay with him for a bit, so I'll be back later. Keep the doors locked, okay?" He paused, absorbing her words. "I will. I… I love you too." He stared at the phone.

"Alright?" asked Danny, as Robert sat down again.

"Eh, yeah," said Robert.

"Look, man, I'm sorry about yesterday," said Danny. "Don't know what got into me."

"It's okay," said Robert. "You're not the only one who's been jumpy recently. Forget about it."

Danny nodded. "Watch my stuff, will you?" he said, standing up.

"Why, what's it gonna do?" asked Robert. The same retort had travelled with them through many journeys like an old friend. Danny grinned as he walked off to the men's room.

Robert eyed the open rucksack on the seat opposite, where the wooden box peeped out over the zip. Glancing back, he saw the men's room door close behind Danny. He reached across and lifted the box onto the table, pushing the coffee cups aside to make space, then opened the lid and laid the mandala on the flat surface. The material felt rough against his fingers – old, faded and yet oddly robust. A series of circles inside squares. Dulled characters that he couldn't make out followed the uneven lines of the central spirals. The edges of the cloth were blackened and misshapen. He ran his hand over its roughened surface, his fingers brushing the markings...

The world flicked a switch and the room flashed red.

Scorching heat, a fierce orange roar, the groan and crash of falling timbers... the stench of singeing flesh lacing his nostrils in smoke, choking his breath, scalding the lining of his mouth and throat and lungs... a searing pain on his back... the suffocating feeling of fear, dread... *death*...

He yanked his hand away, as the world righted itself, becoming the diner again. He coughed, the taste of carbon still on his tongue, his back hard against the chair, panting, trembling, staring at the material that sat quietly on the table. He turned his hand over, slowly, wincing at the feel of a blistered, blackened palm. But there was nothing. Not a mark. Shaken, he glanced around. No one noticed, or showed any signs that something catastrophic had just happened in his world.

Robert folded the material hurriedly, holding its edges with a napkin to avoid its markings then crammed it into the box. He slid the box back into the rucksack as the door to the men's room opened.

"You want some more coffee?" asked Danny.

*

Max made his way from the station along the village street, its terraced cottages and snug doors huddled low against the chill. Between the gaps in the buildings he glimpsed a murky sea undulating in the distance, shadowy islands swelling the horizon. Mountains stood silent and commanding around the bay, breathing to a cycle that spanned eons. Mountain Time. It was colder this far north, even in the summer, especially in a suit. He passed the glow from the Stone Circle pub and checked the map on his phone. The reception was intermittent, but it was a straight road up the track to the houses at the edge of the village. A cottage for sale stood to his left, a snowfall of white climbing flowers clinging to its walls and a beehive in the front garden. Further up the lane, he found the place he wanted.

He knocked on the door and waited. No answer. He gave it a minute then tried again. Still nothing. Glancing back, the road was still empty. He crouched down and flicked open the letterbox, glimpsing a pile of unopened mail on the mat below.

He took the narrow passageway to the rear of the cottage, ducking to avoid the hawthorn branches that straggled across it. As at the front, the windows at the back were unlit. Peering through one of them, he saw a tidy kitchen. The fridge door sat open, revealing empty shelves.

He returned to the village and found the local shop on the main street, where plastic yellow sunflowers sat in a vase at the window. A small door opened through a thick stone wall into the cramped store. It appeared to sell everything you might need on the west coast of Scotland, including what seemed to Max to be an excessive supply of insect repellent. He scratched the back of his neck and picked up a can. The woman behind the counter watched him approach.

"So it's true what they say about midgies," said Max, now clawing at his scalp.

She grinned as she rang up the bill. "It is."

He handed over the cash. "I wonder if you can help me. I'm looking for Marion Strong."

The smile on the shopkeeper's lips faltered and Max read her hesitation.

"You see, I work with a law firm that's looking to settle a family matter that relates to her," he said. "She's not at the address we have on our records... does she still live here?"

Her mouth still smiled but it was as though a portcullis had come down and she appraised him from behind it. He was an Outsider. "No, she doesn't," she said.

"Do you know where she is?" he said.

The till clanged shut. "No."

Aside from confirming the viciousness of the Scottish midgie, the only thing he came away with, from his long trip to the remote Highland village, was a glimpse of the wall the villagers had made around Marion and Robert Strong.

*

Robert pulled up his collar, feeling the bite of the mist droplets as they settled into the nape of his neck. The streetlights were still on and cars emerged and disappeared on the road beside them like ghosts. "Feels like January, here," he said.

"I know," said Danny. "Even more incentive to get some cash together and go somewhere that isn't strangled by fucking fog. I hate this weather. You okay?"

Robert was glancing behind them. "Fine, yeah."

"Don't get jumpy on me. You're making me nervous."

They walked back to the square, passing the trees and shrubs of the small fenced-off park.

Ganesh's secretary, who now sat wrapped in a fluffy cerise cardigan, picked up the phone as they entered. "He's free just now. Top floor, second on the right."

They climbed the small staircase, where relics of another place and time decorated the shelves on each floor. Ganesh's office has his name on a faded brass plaque. Danny knocked on the door and a voice came from inside. "Come in."

The door opened into an old spacious room. Dark wood lined the floors, the panelled walls and the bookcases. A desk sat by the window that overlooked the square below and the man sitting at the desk looked up at him. Sallow skin, grey hair that sat somewhat wildly on his head and dressed in a tweed suit, he looked to be in his early sixties. He peered at them over his glasses. "How can I help you?"

"I'm Danny Mitchell," said Danny, extending a hand. "This is my friend, Robert. Mr Ingles, the book dealer, suggested I contact you."

"Oh?" Professor Ganesh closed his notebook. "Well then, please, take a seat." He stood up and gestured to the chairs on the other side of his desk.

"Thanks," said Danny. "I wondered if you would have a look at something for me." He reached into his rucksack and handed the professor the box. Robert tensed as the professor extracted it from its casing and smoothed out the material. He showed no reaction as his hands brushed its markings, but neither did he seem comfortable. It lay quietly on his desk as he stared down at it. For a moment, he neither moved nor spoke.

"Professor?" said Danny.

He glanced up, distracted.

"I was hoping you could translate it," said Danny. He pulled out a piece of paper and a pen from his rucksack.

Ganesh took a breath then he studied the material again. "The outer ring here is fire, a Buddhist representation of wisdom – to be always mindful of death. The gates on the sides of the squares point to the shadows of confusion of samsara—"

"Samsara?" asked Danny, scribbling notes.

"The repeating cycles of birth, life and death," replied Ganesh. "Or in Vajrayana teachings, the impurity of the outer world. The spirals represent the descent into samsara."

"What are those?" asked Danny, pointing to the broken markings within the spirals. The professor peered down at them.

"It's hard to say." He shrugged. "It's a straightforward aid to meditation. Very common for its time."

"Is it worth anything?"

"I doubt it."

Danny shifted in his seat. "Well, is there anything else you can tell me about it?" he pushed.

Ganesh studied him for a moment. "No."

Robert glanced at Danny.

"I'd recommend you don't hold on to it, though," said the

professor quietly.

"What do you mean by that?" asked Robert.

Turning to him, the professor said, "Stolen artefacts are not good karma."

"Thanks for your time, Professor," said Danny, visibly deflated. He packed the mandala into its box and returned it to his rucksack with his measly notes, then stood up and headed for the door.

Robert studied the professor before he got up and Ganesh returned his stare, but said nothing more.

*

They made their way downstairs, Danny scowling at the receptionist as he went by, who afforded him a pinched pout.

They paused on the outside steps.

"Not much help, then," said Robert, sensing Danny's disappointment.

"You don't believe that bullshit, do you?"

Robert shrugged. "You heard what he said."

"Come on, Robert," said Danny. "You saw his reaction. He was hiding something."

Robert had seen it, and had hoped it might be enough to dissuade Danny. "Yeah, well maybe it's for the best. Let it go, Danny. Give it to the museum or something."

Danny marched down the remaining steps. "No way. It just confirms that it's valuable. I'll find my own buyer."

"How?"

Stomping off towards the square, he said, "I'll figure it out."

Robert hung back. "I'll see you back at the flat, then," he said.

"Fine, whatever," called Danny, without looking back. When he had disappeared into the mist, Robert turned and retraced his steps.

"Hi," said Robert. "I need to speak to the professor again."

The secretary straightened up and regarded him with lofty distain, a look it seemed she had taken time to perfect. "I'm sorry, but he has another engagement. He said to tell you he had no more information for you, should you come back." She raised her eyebrows in expectation of him leaving, glowing in her little victory.

"Right," said Robert.

*

He wasn't about to be dissuaded by a sour-faced, sugar-coated secretary. Robert waited outside the building, finding a spot on a low wall to sit. People came and went; students, lecturers, tourists, inside their own worlds, as the day wound to a close. The secretary left the building, tottering in heels and a red winter coat, and the light from Ganesh's office glowed a little brighter as the mist darkened. Half an hour later the professor walked down the steps lost in thought. Robert crossed the space to join him.

"Professor?"

He jumped, startled by Robert's sudden appearance then walked on, his pace brisker.

"Please," said Robert. "Danny doesn't know I'm here. I need your help."

Ahead of him, the professor stopped and lowered his head. He looked up as Robert drew level with him. "Your friend would do well to leave the mandala behind him. He is not the only one with an interest in it."

"I don't care about him selling it," said Robert. "But I know that someone planned to kill him for it. And I know that when I touched the markings on it, it felt like I was on fire. I want to know why."

Ganesh stared at him, the colour draining from his face. Finally, he said, "Come with me."

*

He took Robert to a small backstreet tea-house and chose the space furthest from the door with a low table and cushions scattered on the floor. Bamboo screens partitioned the seating areas, giving an exaggerated sense of privacy. No one looked up when they came in. Dim lamps cast shadows on the faded tapestries and eastern artwork on the stone walls. Music lilted on a pentatonic scale in the background.

"Are you comfortable sitting on the floor?" asked Ganesh.

153

"Yeah, fine," said Robert, taking a seat on a faded burgundy cushion.

A young man with dark hair and Asian eyes came and took their order.

Ganesh sat with his back against the wall and took off his glasses, cleaning them slowly with a tissue. "Do you know much about mandalas, Mr Strong?"

Robert shook his head. "Only what I've overheard."

"So you have no understanding of what your friend has in his possession."

"No."

Ganesh nodded slowly. "They are a common means of symbolising our imperfect relationship with the perfection of the cosmos."

"What's special about this one?"

"It is the Imperfect Mandala."

"I don't follow."

Ganesh put on his glasses, took out a pen from his pocket and smoothed out a piece of paper on the low table. He began to draw. "Mandalas tend to follow the same basic pattern – an outer circle and inner square with four gates, surrounding perfect inner circles." He raised the pen, pausing as he spoke. "But your mandala has spirals in the centre – broken, uneven spirals."

"So what does that mean?"

"Its true meaning has been lost with time but myth has it that, when it shows itself, it heralds a human shift on a seismic scale."

"What do you mean by shift?" asked Robert.

"No one really knows, but many believe it is ultimately destructive. The end of an era, so to speak. The cosmos creates and destroy itself in cycles."

"Ingles asked if Danny had found anything else with it. What was he talking about?"

Ganesh shifted in his seat and studied the table.

"Please, Professor."

The professor raised his eyes to meet Robert, his expression unfathomable. "Another artefact was originally thought to accompany the mandala – a jewel of some kind, we think. It was once believed that understanding the Imperfect Mandala and possessing the jewel would empower the owner in some way. Protect them, perhaps, from things to come. It is even rumoured that Hitler was searching for them."

"Do you know where it is now?"

"No one knows. It was never found."

Robert's eyes fell to the cloth on the table. "Can you read the mandala?"

Ganesh shook his head. "I studied its legend for years and it haunted me for many more. I even dreamt about it recently." He shrugged. "In the end, it's all just speculation. Only two men understood its symbolism. Together they were its original guardians, fourteen-hundred years ago, but the name of only one of them survived. He was Tenzin Chodron, one of the first monks charged with its protection."

"What happened to him?" asked Robert.

"He burned to death."

It was as though winter had blown in through an open window as Robert digested his words, the chill snaking its way from his neck to the back of his knees. He recalled the flash of blistering heat, the stench of singeing flesh, the hissing and bubbling of scorching skin. He stared at Ganesh without really seeing him.

When he found his focus, he saw Ganesh observe him with a strange expression. "I don't know what you experienced when you touched the mandala, but somehow it spoke to you. Perhaps you should listen to what it has to say."

*

They shook hands at the shadowed entrance to the tea-house.

"Thank you," said Robert.

The professor nodded graciously. "I'm going back to my office now, so if you'll excuse me..."

"A bit late for work, isn't it?" said Robert. The streets were already quieter and the night was settling in.

Ganesh shook his head. "I have not been sleeping well these past few nights. Tonight, I don't think I'll try. Fortunately, I have plenty of work to keep my mind occupied." His smile was burdened. "If I can be of any more assistance, you know where to find me."

Robert watched the professor walk away, his shoulders hunched, as he blended with the fog.

*

A fox trotted along a high garden wall to Robert's right and light from a street lamp etched orange circles in the mist, as black branches bobbed up and down in front of it. His thoughts seeped back to the monk he never knew and the memory of his death. *Memory*. As though it was something he had lived himself.

He rounded the corner near Danny's street and hesitated. A figure was ahead, leaning against a lamppost in the fog. He slowed as he approached.

"Jesus, Casimir. You spooked me." Robert let out a long breath.

Casimir grinned. "You're a bit edgy. So, what's in Danny's rucksack?"

"A mandala," said Robert. He relayed the conversation with Ganesh as Casimir listened intently.

"The hard part will be persuading him to give it up," said Robert. "I don't know anyone more pig-headed. He won't listen to me when he gets hold of an idea…"

"What about Cora? Could she talk to him?"

"Yeah, but how much do I tell her?" Robert shook his head. "I'm trying to be as normal as I can with her but it's not easy. She picks up random thoughts. She even accused me of cheating on her… with Aiyana."

Casimir snorted. "I can't wait to tell her."

"It's not funny, Casimir."

"Lighten up, Robert. Look, your thoughts are broadcast into the Field. She's managed to tune in to some of them. Just watch your focus, that's all, but be light with it. I thought you two shared everything anyway?"

"Be real, Casimir. You know I can't share everything with her. Not now."

"Even after what she went through in Mindscape?"

"Especially after that. She won't admit it but she's fragile. It would be too much, even for her. She'd go, and I wouldn't blame her."

"Maybe you're underestimating her."

Robert shook his head. "No. I'm looking out for her." He reached into his pocket, warming his hands from the bite on the air. His fingers brushed against something sharp, and he pulled out Ganesh's badge.

"Have you been stealing?" said Casimir, his eyebrow raised in reprimand. He paused. "Robert, your amulet..."

It was beginning to glow like a hot coal. Reaching for the sear in the hollow of his neck, Robert's fingers closed round it and the night world fractured.

The street became an office lined with books. Ganesh was slumped over his desk, his head resting on his arm. His eyes were closed but, in the yellow pool of light from his desk lamp, his face betrayed what his mind was witnessing. He twitched, snatching breaths from the air as something hovered above him. The details were blurred but Robert could feel it as it hung there, dark and curious. It was watching Ganesh.

The professor jolted awake. He gasped, his face sprinkled with sweat, adjusting to his surroundings to find that his nightmare was real. Fear sculpted his face as he recoiled from the thing that leaned in towards him. He stumbled to his feet and backed away, his eyes wide, his skin clammy and drained of colour. He was trembling uncontrollably.

With an invisible force that was almost seizure-like, he was thrust against a shelf, books clattering to the floor around him. The door of the office opened and four men in black balaclavas and webbing stole in as Ganesh slid to the floor and closed his eyes, cowering from what hovered above.

CHAPTER NINE

R obert's eyes shot open. "What was that?"

Casimir wasn't listening. Robert knew by his face that he was staring at the image he had just witnessed, emblazoned in space.

"We have to go back!" Robert turned to run but Casimir caught his arm.

"When will you learn?" Casimir reached for the badge in Robert's hand and grasped Robert's shoulder with his fist. Dominated by Casimir's certainty, Robert closed his eyes and surrendered to the Ominence.

*

They found themselves by a gnarled tree at the edge of a darkened green. Robert steadied himself on the trunk before catching up with Casimir, who was halfway across the street. He glanced up at Ganesh's open window, from which a pool of light leaked into the shadows. A breeze breathed past the window and Robert froze. Something dark and unformed snaked from it into the night.

"Did you see that?" he whispered.

"Quickly!" said Casimir.

Racing for the entrance, they jumped through the substance of the old wooden doors, into the dim, empty hallway. They bolted the stairs, past the eastern statues and wall art, pausing only when they reached the deserted corridor. Straining to hear beyond the thick silence, they found Ganesh's door lying open. They stepped inside.

A soft glow emanated from the lamp on Ganesh's desk. Beyond, Sattva was looking out of the open window. The bookshelf lay in disarray.

"Where is he?" said Robert.

Sattva did not answer.

"You saw it?" asked Casimir.

"Yes," said Sattva. "I saw it."

"There were men – I saw armed men come in through this door..." Robert glanced back to the empty hallway.

"Crowley is searching for them," said Sattva, still staring out into the night.

Robert's eyes fell to Ganesh's empty chair. An old tome lay open on the desk before it, Ganesh's glasses to one side. The Buddhas in the paintings and the statues on the shelves looked down, silent witnesses to his abduction.

Sattva turned from the open window. He paced the room, passing the large-scale map pinned to the wall displaying the Tibetan Plateau, and the books that lay scattered on the floor. "Even with Tunnelling," he said, "we were late. That's never happened before." He returned to the desk, his fingers moving across the pages of the open tome. "The Imperfect Mandala..." he breathed.

"Those things are hunting it," said Robert. "Only Ganesh doesn't have it – Danny does." Sattva's eyes fixed on Robert.

The door clattered against the panelled wall as Arcos Crowley appeared at the entrance, his burly form dominating the space. Dark tangled hair fell to the collar of his leather coat, which reached almost to the floor. It flapped behind him, fanning his irritation as he limped across the room, the sound echoing against the wooden walls in the uncomfortable silence. His face, like his body, was lopsided – twisted, Robert thought, by the acrid drips of lifetimes of an embittered personality. Crowley had little patience with the world, and no compunction to hide it. His mentoring techniques involved pushing any and all of Robert's buttons until the pressure inflamed a response and ignited his rage. He had learned from him but he didn't have to like him.

"There's no sign of him," said Crowley. He stomped towards the desk in uneven thuds and slumped into Ganesh's chair. Lifting the professor's glasses, he turned them around in his chunky fingers, staring at them between the strands of unruly hair that straggled across his face.

"Did you find the thing that took him?" asked Casimir.

Crowley eyed the window. "No."

"It was the same thing that hunted Danny in the alleyway," said Robert.

"Only this time, it didn't need a corpse," added Sattva.

Crowley froze, his eyes on Sattva. "What are you saying?"

"I'm saying it was a Revenant," Sattva replied calmly.

"A what?" said Robert.

Crowley's eyes narrowed, his right eyelid beginning to twitch. "It could not have been."

"No?" said Sattva. "Then what do you suggest, Arcos?"

Crowley put down the glasses and leaned forward, his elbows on his knees, the light from the desk lamp catching the side of his face that was contorted by contempt. His voice was quiet, almost threatening. "Revenants haven't existed for centuries. You know that."

"Once something is created, it never really goes away." Sattva returned his stare. He was not about to back down.

As Crowley stood up and pointed to the open window, the edge to his demeanour cut through the room. "That thing had purpose, Sattva. Intention. That is not how Revenants work."

Sattva remained composed. "Then perhaps, in their absence, they have evolved."

"Wait," said Robert. "Would someone explain what a Revenant is?"

Casimir turned to him. "A migrant soul that can inhabit the body of someone newly dead."

"*What?*" breathed Robert. He glanced at the others, who did not appear to be as appalled as he felt.

Crowley cut in with his signatory sarcasm. The twitch around his right eye was so marked now that it looked like one half of his face was blinking against a sandstorm. "That thing was untethered, Sattva. See any dead bodies around here? Hmm? I don't."

"Perhaps they no longer need them," said Sattva. "I think your memories of past lives are haunting you, Arcos. It was a painful time, but it should not cloud our judgement of the here and now."

Crowley's mouth tightened into a thin line.

Walking to the window, Casimir stared out into the night. "If Revenants have returned," he said, "what brought them back?"

*

Their bedroom was in darkness, but the light was still on in the kitchen when Robert got home. Danny was on his laptop, the mandala spread out on the table next to the scanty lines of notes he had taken in Ganesh's office.

"Danny…" began Robert.

"Hi," said Danny, barely looking up from the screen.

"Danny, we need to talk."

"That translation was useless," he said. "It's just a bog-standard explanation for a mandala. I need something that makes it stand out…"

Robert sat down and pushed the lid of the laptop closed, which got Danny's attention.

"Hey," said Danny, scowling. "What are you doing?"

"I went back to see Ganesh," said Robert. "He told me more than he did first time round."

Danny straightened up. "What did he tell you?"

"You were right – it is valuable, but—"

"I knew it," said Danny.

"*But*, it's dangerous."

Danny snorted. "Dangerous? It's not a weapon I'm selling, for fuck's sake. It's a piece of cloth."

"I'm serious Danny. There are people who'd be prepared to kill you to get it. It's not a world you want to mess with. You need to get rid of it."

Danny's gaze fell to the faded material lying in front of him. He shook his head. "Old fucker. I *knew* he was lying. I'm going back to see him tomorrow."

"You can't," said Robert. "He was abducted from his office an hour ago."

"What?"

Robert leaned closer. "Whoever took Ganesh was after the mandala. It's only a matter of time before they come after you. You need to get rid of it," he said again.

The muscles on the side of Danny's cheek clenched as he looked down at the cloth.

"I know some people who can help," said Robert, "if you let me take it to them."

Danny sat back, studying Robert through narrowed eyes. "Wait… I get it," he said slowly. "You want it, don't you? Is that what this is about?"

"No, I—"

"Bit of a coincidence you showing up here just when I bring it back into the country…"

"Jesus, Danny, I'm trying to help you!"

Danny said nothing but he looked at Robert like he was a thief. He rolled up the mandala, placed it in its box and stood up.

"Where are you going?" asked Robert.

"To get some sleep." He gripped the box in his fist. "I appreciate your help, Robert, but stay out of this." The edge in his voice lingered in the room after he left.

Robert sat alone in the kitchen, numbed by their exchange. He stared into space, as his mind scoured for options. What he did not give a name to was the undercurrent of unease, which sat beneath his thoughts, around Danny's unpredictable hostility. *Maybe Casimir was right – maybe Cora could persuade him. She couldn't do any worse than your attempt.* A few moments later, he got up and went to their room.

He closed their bedroom door quietly, his gut a tight coil inside him. Something rolled away as his boot touched it and he paused, turning on his phone to illuminate the floor. Crouching down, he picked up a small lumpy piece of gravel. The torchlight fell onto another. A sweep of the beam revealed dozens of them scattered round the floor, across the table, on the chair. It was like they were breeding. Robert turned the light towards their bed. Cora wasn't there.

Panic tightened round his throat. He checked the bathroom, the kitchen, but found them empty. Then something caught his eye and he turned back, pacing slowly to the kitchen window. In the darkness outside, a light swept slowly over the ground. As he opened the door, the light jolted up, blinding him as it met his eye. He raised his arm to block it.

"Sorry." The light lowered.

"Cora?" said Robert as he switched on the outside light. She was crouched down wearing one of Danny's shirts and a head-torch.

"Cora, what are you doing?"

She glanced down at the pile of gravel chips in her hand. "Couldn't sleep," she said.

*

Robert flicked on the lamp when they got back to their room.

Kneeling down, Cora placed her collection of chips on the floor, next to the nail file. A line of dark grey gravel was laid out against the wall, pieces of about the same size, all shaped like tiny pyramids. "Sorry," she said, as she gathered the ones scattered around the room into a pile.

"What are you doing?" asked Robert.

"Just something I have in my head." She picked up a gravel chip and began to file its surface. "Seems stupid, I know, but..." She shook her head and set the rock down again, as though clearing away the thought.

Robert eyed her. "Are you alright?"

"Yeah, I'm fine," she said, as if the question were absurd.

Robert sat down next to her, wary. "Cora, what's in your head?"

She stared at him, her veneer of cheeriness faltering. "I can't explain it... it's like when you have a word on the tip of your tongue, but you can't remember it... I know it's important, it means something." She picked up the gravel chip again. "This means something."

"What?" asked Robert.

She shook her head, deflated. "I don't know." She sat for a moment, staring around at her scattered rocks then, as though seeing the absurdity of it, she seemed suddenly embarrassed. Straightening up, she changed the subject. "So, what happened with Danny today?"

Robert took a breath and chose his words and his thoughts carefully. "I had this really strong... vision, that he was in trouble... so I followed him. I mean, he was okay, obviously, but... I don't think it's over yet. It's something to do with the mandala."

She eyed him. "Vision? That's not like you."

He picked up one of her pyramids. "I could say the same about you."

She watched as he turned it over in his fingers. "What's happening to us?" she breathed.

He took her hand and they sat in silence.

Eventually Robert said, "Something's wrong with Danny."

"I know."

"Have you picked up anything from him? Any thoughts?"

"Just feelings," she said. "It's like he's contracted inside, like he doesn't trust anyone. He's... afraid."

"Afraid? Of what?"

"I don't know."

*

There were nineteen messages on Ron's phone the next morning as he sat at his desk on the edge of the Innovatics mezzanine on level seven.

"Ron, hi, this is Katie Crookshank." The voice on the other end of the phone was shaky. "You said to get in touch if there were any problems and, well… it's the nightmares. I've been afraid to sleep for days. Is this anything to do with the study? I mean, is it just me?" There was a pause. Then, her voice constricted with emotion, she said, "You know I can't speak to my parents about any of this. I'm seventeen years old and I feel like I'm losing my mind. Please, just give me a call."

It wasn't just Katie. The other eighteen messages were more or less the same. He played them back for Jack to hear.

"I called all the people on our list," said Ron. "Eighty-five per cent of them report nightmares over the past few days."

"What about the other centres?" asked Jack. "We should contact them."

"I already did that," said Ron. "It's not just us."

Jack let out an irritated sigh and slumped on the end of the desk. "Is it the interface?" he asked, picking up a headset.

"That equipment has been used for years around various centres," said Ron. "Why would it suddenly cause problems with so many people at the same time?"

"So what's causing it then?" asked Jack.

Ron shook his head. He scrolled through the INTP database on his computer, where he had highlighted the affected people. There was a lot of yellow on his screen.

Jack took out his phone and dialled. "Raymond?" he said. "It's Jack. Listen, we have a problem. Do you have time to run a few emergency clinics up here?"

*

Cora was filing a piece of gravel when Robert woke. She sat cross-legged, still in Danny's shirt, which was far too big for her, her back against the wall. The floor surrounding her was like a weird pyramid factory.

"Cora?" said Robert, squinting in the grey light from the window. "Did you get any sleep?"

She looked up at him, blankly, as though she was working to process his words. Heavy bags sat under her eyes and her hair was tangled and matted. Dirt smudged her fingertips and nails, like she'd

165

been digging in the soil. She had, Robert recalled. "Not much," she said.

"What time is it?" he asked, reaching for his phone.

"I'm not sure." She went back to her filing.

"10.15?" said Robert, squinting at the numbers on his phone. He got up and pulled on some clothes, dazed with oversleeping. "Is Danny still here?" he asked.

"I don't think so," she said without looking up.

Robert checked the kitchen and knocked on Danny's door before he pushed it open. The bed lay unmade and the rucksack was gone. "Shit," he breathed.

His phone rang from the bedroom.

"Robert?" said a voice when he answered. "It's Jack. Are you free?"

"Eh…" began Robert.

"Remember the boy, Ben?"

"Yeah?"

"He's here with us now, and he's… he's not doing so well."

"What do you mean?"

"Do you think you could bring Cora up to the lab?"

Robert watched Cora, lost in her pyramid assembly. "I'll see what I can do." He hung up and crouched down beside her. "Cora?" She did not look up, but continued scraping bits from the corners of the gravel lump in her hand. "Cora, Jack's asked us to go back to the lab."

"You go on," she said squinting at the small rock. "I've just got a bit more to do here."

He steadied her hand. "Please, Cora," he said. "It's about Ben."

She lowered the pyramid and met his eye.

*

Seth Winters clicked off his tablet and stood up. The others were shuffling out of the weekly briefing back to their silos but he held back, working up the courage to speak. Like jumping into the deep end of a pool for the first time, it was better not to think about it.

"Mr Amos?"

Amos glanced up. "Yes, Seth?"

"Do you have a minute?"

"Of course."

Seth glanced at Elijah Lazaro who showed no signs of getting up from his place and, as Amos showed no signs of encouraging him, Seth had to accept he was part of the conversation.

"I hope you don't mind but I had a look at the most recent data from GRACE."

Amos regarded him with no visible change of expression. His voice, however, was fractionally less smooth than usual. "I thought I made it clear that GRACE was no longer your concern."

"You did, yes, you did," said Seth apologetically. "And maybe I shouldn't have done it, but I found something."

Amos and Elijah exchanged a glance subtle enough to miss, if Seth had not been looking for it. Amos nodded, his air of courtesy as pronounced as ever. "Then do tell us what you found."

"Another gravitational layer has appeared, beneath the first one. It's different – more like pockets of intense gravitational pull." Amos watched him, giving no indication of his reaction. Seth pushed through his growing unease, pushing on. "I reversed the time frames, like we did with the first wave, and found its source." He hesitated, still uncertain if he had the balls to say what was coming next. "It's coming from here."

A silence descended on the room.

Amos breathed in slowly as he observed him. "We know," he said. "We created it."

Seth stared at him. All of his instincts warned against it but his curiosity would not back down. "Created it?" he breathed. "How?"

"That is not your concern, Seth," said Amos.

"Forgive me, Mr Amos. I know you oversee a lot of incredible work here. I'll respect your opinion, of course but, as a geophysicist, I can help. This is my field—"

"That won't be necessary," said Amos.

"Actually," said Elijah, in his thin quiet voice, "another assistant may be useful. We have a lot of work yet to do."

Amos' gaze settled on Elijah, before returning to Seth. "It would mean you give up your post as Sector Head."

"I know," said Seth. "That's okay."

Amos nodded graciously. "Very well. Then we have a solution."

Elijah's lidded eyes stayed on Seth. "Provided you have the stomach for it."

*

Seth followed Elijah down the metal staircase to the subbasement. The retinal scanner now permitted him entry and the door swung open onto a long white corridor lined with dimly lit panels. Seth had to consciously shorten his stride to avoid stepping ahead of Elijah, barely able to contain the anticipation that tugged him on like an eager child. How did they create something that had such gravitational density, something that was on the move? He burned to ask the question but held his tongue, conscious that Elijah did not pander to his enthusiasm. He would have to content himself with waiting another few minutes. They reached the end of the corridor and a large steel door. Elijah held his eye to the scanner. There was a clang then a blue mist hissed from the door's edges, like a pressure release. Seth felt his intrigue swell. They stepped into the chamber.

Elijah watched as Seth approached the tank, his pace slowing, his neck craning to take in its full height.

"What is it?" asked Seth.

Elijah gave a flicker of a smile.

"It is a memory bank," said Elijah. "A collection of consciousness."

Seth's intrigue, like the blood in his face, drained from him, and was replaced by a cold sweat. He came to see that there were things in this tank that resembled humans.

"Each is individual," said Lazaro, "self-aware, yet bound to the others and to us. Each has will, intention and loyalty. We give them the freedom not just to know those qualities, but to live them."

Seth waited, afraid to ask. Afraid to hear.

The shadows flickered across Elijah's pale face as he paced slowly round the cylinder, marvelling. "Einstein's most famous equation is not simply a mathematical work of beauty. It is a recipe that reminds us that matter and energy are interchangeable. Consciousness is energy. And now we have the technology to change its form."

Seth swallowed, his throat uncomfortably dry. "How do you do that?"

Elijah stopped, staring into the cylinder's depths. A blue laser beam cut through the centre of the tank from somewhere in its murky depths to as high up as could be seen, glimpses of its soft pulsation visible between the strands of mist that encircled it. "We use light."

Seth tried to keep his eyes on Elijah's face, but the tank seethed at the edge of his vision. "What do they do?"

Elijah considered him before answering. "There is one thing that hinders evolution more than any other. Fear. Think what we could do if we understood it better. These beautiful creatures are like bees. Instead of harvesting pollen, they harvest—"

Seth glanced at the tank, despite himself. "Fear? You're collecting fear? From people?"

"The world is advancing at a rapid pace," continued Elijah. "And our work here, at ORB, is a silent champion that leads the way. Imagine what could be possible if we understood what holds mankind back."

Seth tried to reason with it all. It could be considered a noble intention. "What do you do with the... fear?"

"We study it, using the mind-machine interface."

Seth did not know what that meant, but he couldn't bring himself to ask. Instead, he said, "So, what is it you want me to do?"

"The changes you detected from the GRACE readings have already demonstrated their collective gravitational properties. We want you to measure their gravitomagnetism here, in the lab."

"Why? What will that tell you?"

"It will tell us how strong they are."

*

Max returned to his flat. Lost in thought, he turned on a single lamp which cast a feeble glow across the room, and dropped his jacket on the sofa. Robert Strong, it seemed, had covered his tracks, but not that well. He was operating under a new identity, and he was still active. But where? Max poured himself a whisky and stood by the window, where the mist strangled the turrets of Tower Bridge and deadened the water of the Thames below. Someone had to know where he was.

He downed the drink and opened his laptop. Settling into his chair, he put on his glasses and reviewed the results of his searches. Interpol had shown Strong's partner, Cora Martin, had turned up in Geneva while he was there. But she, too, had dropped off the grid since then. A detailed search of Strong's credit card history showed a ticket purchased to Tibet. Max accessed the passenger list of the flight and found the names of the people who sat nearby. The first was a woman in her twenties from Manchester, travelling with a baby. Then there was a couple with the same surname in their sixties. The next was Daniel Mitchell, a man of similar age to Strong. A little digging revealed they had graduated from the same university around the same time. Max took what he had on Mitchell and cross-referenced it to social media sites. It was not long before he came across a photograph of two men in climbing gear on a peak in the Pyrenees. Max recognised the untagged man with the oval face, blue eyes and sandy hair as Robert Strong. Beside him was a weird-looking guy tagged as Danny Mitchell.

He picked up the phone. "Emily? It's me. I'm going to need a flight to Edinburgh and a place to stay."

*

The fog that clung to the streets made the air murky. It was hard to tell if the dawn had slipped in, but Max assumed it had, given that he could now make out the faces of the early morning pedestrians in the Scottish capital. The flight had been bumpy and the pilot had to circle several times before they lined up to land in the unseasonal weather. Max sat in his compact grey car, a block away from the flat he had been watching for the past two hours. With any luck, he would see Danny Mitchell and find a way to tap him. The door opened and a woman and a bearded man wearing a beanie, walked out. Max straightened up. This was better than Daniel Mitchell – this was Robert Strong himself.

He left his car and kept his distance as Robert Strong and the woman made their way through the urban backstreets. He followed them as they cut west through Hill Place, blending with the tourists and the students and the mist.

*

Robert glanced back into the crowd behind them.

"What is it?" asked Cora.

"I dunno, I just..." His eyes fell on the man with dark hair and olive skin, who looked away as Robert turned. As they turned into the next street, Robert glanced back again, but the man was no longer there.

"Robert?" asked Cora, turning to look behind her.

"It's nothing," said Robert. "Just me being paranoid."

*

Max stepped into a doorway as the woman glanced back, and breathed out a mixture of relief and annoyance. He was cutting this too fine. Tailing was meant for teamwork, not one man. You couldn't get close enough for long enough without attracting attention. But it had told him something else. Cora Martin was now a brunette.

When it felt like enough time had passed, he stepped out into the pedestrian traffic again, scanning the waves of people. *Shit.* He'd lost them. He picked up his pace, sharpening his focus, then fate cut him a break. Between a throng of yabbering students, he saw them as they turned into a glass building at the edge of a grassy square.

Max overshot the building then doubled back, slowing his pace and glancing through the windows as he approached. Inside the atrium was bustling with people on the escalators and at the desks. He glimpsed Robert's beanie as he walked towards the elevators. Latching onto a group of students as they entered the building, Max stayed with them as they made their way across the open space. Strong and Martin boarded an elevator and Max hung back as the doors swished shut. He watched the numbers above them light up and pause at the seventh floor, then he took the next elevator to the eighth.

Standing at the edge of the mezzanine, Max peered down. Below him, on level seven, was an air of disorganised activity. Staff bustled about, like they were all up against a deadline that threatened their jobs if they overshot it. They came and went from the desks wedged up against the mezzanine railings, which were scattered with laptops, bits of paper and clipboards. A flustered-looking man sat at one of them, caught in a cycle of typing, peering at his screen and running his hands almost aggressively through his red hair. Behind him, through the glass walls of offices, Max saw Strong and Martin sitting with their backs to him. He squinted to try to see what they were doing.

"Can I help you?" A woman in her fifties, with a greying hair and glasses, passed behind him.

"Thanks," said Max, adopting a relaxed smile. "You know, I think I'm on the wrong floor."

He walked to the exit, his heart hammering. He was getting clumsy, but this was an opportunity he couldn't afford to miss. He took the stairs to level seven, put on his glasses and removed his jacket, leaving it behind a plant pot in the stairwell, home to a sprawling, sad-looking yucca. As he pushed open the door on level seven, he rolled up the sleeves of his shirt and grabbed a clipboard and pen from an empty desk as he passed.

Staring intently at his clipboard on which he made some notes about nothing, his pace slowed as he reached the red-haired man at the desk. He kept scribbling as he glanced sideways at his computer screen. It always surprised him how much information was readily accessible if you just look. The man, who was entering details into a data-sheet entitled INTP, glanced up briefly, before his work absorbed him again. Max walked past and circled round to the exit.

By the time Max reached the eighth floor again, Robert was leaning on the mezzanine railings, peering down to the floors below, as he spoke with the harassed red-headed guy. But neither of them noticed the man who stood watching him from the shadows of level eight, or see him lift the phone to his ear.

"I've found him," said Max to his phone. "I'm going to need access to the INTP database."

"I'll get on it," said Emily's voice in his ear. "I found something too. We're getting the next flight."

"We?"

"I hope you packed a suit."

*

"You're sure she's not on the list?" said Robert.

Ron sat back and rolled his eyes to the ceiling. "For the last time, Robert, Cora Martin is not on the list, okay? Ask Jack if you don't believe me."

"Okay, okay," said Robert. "Sorry, I just want to be sure."

"Paranoid, more like," said Ron. "What's the big deal anyway?"

"Nothing. It's just… she's kind of private about stuff. Doesn't like the idea of the government checking up on her."

"Well, I get that," said Ron. " But we aren't the government. Chill out."

The door opened and Locke came out from the office to join them.

"How is he?" asked Robert, relieved to shift the spotlight from his obsessiveness.

Locke turned, his back resting on the mezzanine railings, as he watched Ben and Zoe through the glass.

"I still think he has something," said Locke.

"Yeah?" said Robert.

"It's more than just telepathy."

"What do you mean?"

Locke's eyes stayed on Ben who stood by the windows inside the office, staring out onto the street. His owl lay on its side by his feet.

"I think he's trying to tell us he has experience of a past life."

Ron looked up from his screen, about to dismiss the comment but stopped, his gaze turning to the small boy who stood motionless looking out at the world.

"And I'm worried about Zoe," said Locke. She sat at the other side of the office, behind a computer screen, her head in her hands. Jack was manning the control computer. Cora looked on from the corner nearest Jack, biting a nail of one hand and pulling at a twisted strand of hair with the other.

Jack knocked on the glass and waved them through. He caught Locke's eye as they entered, and nodded towards Zoe. Reading him, Locke approached her, crouching down so that they were eye level. He put a hand on her shoulder. "Why don't you take a break?" he said. "We'll look after Ben for a while."

Slowly, she stood up. "Alright." She threw a sideways glance at Cora as she passed but did look at her. Dark shadows circled the skin under her eyes and her cheeks had hollowed.

"What do you think's wrong with Ben?" whispered Robert, as Zoe closed the door behind her.

"His aura's changed," said Cora without looking up.

"Sorry?" said Jack.

She sighed heavily then said, "It was green – vivid – before. Now it's like it's going out."

Ron raised an eyebrow as Jack glanced at Robert.

Robert nodded. *She can see them.* He recalled the scorn he felt when she first told him, thinking she had lost her mind, because things like that weren't possible. *Humble pie, Robert?* he thought.

"What do you think that means?" asked Jack.

"I don't know," she said. "I just see them." She looked away.

"Cora, can we try again?" said Jack. He gestured to the empty seat by the computer screen and placed the headset carefully on her forehead as she sat down. "Just like before, alright?"

She nodded and turned to look at the image of a dolphin that appeared on her screen.

"Ben?" said Locke.

Ben continued to stare out of the window. He was watching the fog.

"Ben, can you tell us what you're thinking about?" said Locke.

Ben said nothing.

The image on Cora's screen changed to a fireworks display.

Silence.

A crocodile in a swamp.

When Ben did not answer, Jack sighed. He pinched the bridge of his nose and closed his eyes.

"What's happened?" asked Robert.

"We'd hoped he'd retain some connection with Cora, given it was so strong before," said Jack. "But he's lost it. They all have." He picked up his tablet and tapped. A graph appeared showing a line near the top of the page that dropped off like a cliff edge. "Every centre investigating telepathic events is showing the same thing. That intense connection people had? They're losing it."

"What's more," said Locke in a low voice, "they're feeling it. It's like separation anxiety – sleep disturbance, irritability, irrational behaviour…"

A door slammed from the office next door. Glancing up, Robert saw a teenage girl with short dark hair, ripped jeans and clumpy boots, as she stomped across the mezzanine followed by a flustered-looking lab tech, clutching a clipboard, and a young guy with a ginger beard. The teenager stopped and turned on them. "I've had it with this!" she shouted. "I can't do it anymore, alright? Just find someone else!"

The lab tech turned to Jack and opened her hands in an I-don't-know-what-else-to-do kind of gesture. Jack got up but Locke intervened. "It's Katie," he said. "Let her go."

Watching Katie through the glass, as she slapped the elevator button and tapped her boot on the carpet, Jack seemed uneasy about doing so.

"I spent the morning speaking to her," said Locke. "There's no point. She'll come back when she's ready."

Robert glanced at Cora, who was staring at the image of a monkey, as she pulled at her strand of hair.

From the other side of the room, Ben whispered something.

The adults turned to him. "What was that, Ben?" asked Locke.

"A stone," he said.

Jack shook his head as he looked at the monkey on Cora's screen.

"He's right," breathed Cora.

"Sorry?" said Jack.

"It's not on the computer, but it's in my head." She reached into her bag and pulled out one of her gravel pyramids, holding it out as Locke approached. He lifted it from her palm, peering at it.

"Do you mind if I...?" said Locke. Cora shook her head.

Locke pulled up a chair beside Ben as he stood at the window.

"Ben?" he said gently. "Is this your stone?"

Ben took the stone from Locke's hand and rubbed his fingers over its surfaces. A tear trickled down his cheek. "It's like it."

As Cora walked towards him and knelt down, he turned, wrapping his arms around her neck. His voice was muffled as he whispered into her shoulder. "Do you remember?"

She just held him, her eyes closed.

He sniffed. "You look different."

The door opened and Zoe froze, her face fixed in accusation. "What's going on?" she demanded.

Ben stepped back from Cora and bit his lower lip.

"Nothing," said Cora, "he just—"

"Get away from him," snapped Zoe as she crossed the room. Her bitter stare forced Cora's eyes to the floor. She grabbed her son's hand and pulled him away. "Ben, get your things. It's time to go."

"Wait," said Locke, "not like this..."

Zoe turned on him. "Enough. No more of this. We're going home and we're going to live a normal life. And you're going to let us, do you hear?" Her hand tightened around Ben's and she marched from the room as he stumbled behind. This time he didn't look back. Locke and Jack went after them.

"Zoe—" said Jack but Locke caught his arm. The elevator doors slid together as Ben stood with his head to the floor inside his hood.

"Let her go," said Locke. "It'll just make things worse."

"Is he safe with her?" asked Jack.

Locke chewed on his cheek as he considered. "She loves him," he said. "But I'll keep a check on things."

A woman bustled towards them and held out a clipboard. "Dr Locke? Your list for this afternoon."

"Thanks," said Locke as she walked away. "Those emergency clinics you asked me to run, Jack?" he said, as he glanced across to the other side of the mezzanine. The chairs in the waiting area were full and people were standing in the spaces around them. "I'm going to need a bigger office."

*

In the glass office lab, Robert put an arm round Cora and gently swept the hair from her brow. "You okay?" he asked.

She nodded but didn't speak. Then she pulled away from him and sat down, taking out her stone and her nail file.

The phone in Robert's pocket buzzed. He stared at the screen and moved to the corner before he answered, his voice a whisper. "Liam?" He froze. "When? …Okay. I'm on my way." He ended the call, becoming aware of something sinking in his gut, as two concepts collided in his mind.

"Everything okay?" asked Jack as Robert strode towards him.

"You said that other centres showed similar changes in results?" said Robert.

"Yes."

"Can you get an accurate picture? I mean a map of all the places that do this work and an update on their success rates?"

"Why?" asked Jack. "What are you thinking?"

"What if it's something environmental?" said Robert.

"Like what?"

"Do you mind if I take this?" asked Robert as he lifted the pen from the breast pocket of Jack's shirt, and leaned towards his ear. "Look after Cora till I come back," he whispered. "Don't let her leave on her own."

*

Max glanced up at the ornate steeples and stained-glass windows of St Giles's Cathedral as Emily led him across the Royal Mile to the cobbled square. Her heels struck purpose into the ground with each stride despite the constraints of her tight skirt. The high statue of a cloaked man rose out of the fog like a noble spectre, its grandeur scoffed by the red and white traffic cone perched on its head. Max silently applauded the humour of the Scottish public. Behind the statue stood the sombre chambers of Parliament House.

"So, what is she doing up here?" asked Max.

"She's being efficient," said Emily. "She's here on other business. What's the background on Strong's roommate?"

"Mitchell? He's clean. What about INTP?"

"You've got your access," she said, her pace picking up. "My team will get the details to you by the end of the day."

"Will you relax?" he said. He checked his phone then returned it to his jeans' pocket, and pulled his collar up round his neck against the chill.

"We can't be late. She's not known for her patience." She threw him a disapproving glance. "You should have worn a suit."

*

"Sipherghast?" The Baroness peered at them over the gold rim of her glasses across a large oak desk. She smoothed aside her whitish blonde hair that swept elegantly across one side of her forehead. The bookshelves were lined with rows of bound books, navy with gold writing, and oil portraits in heavy bronze frames hung from the dark wooden wall panels. She had listened intently to their findings, taking occasional deep draws from a cigarette mounted on an engraved silver holder. A trail of smoke, tinged with a hint of purple, trickled into the air above her.

Max took a packet of cigarettes from his pocket. "Do you mind if I—"

"Yes I do," said the Baroness. "This is a no-smoking room."

She held his eye as she sat motionless, her elbow resting on the arm of her chair, her wrist delicately extended with the cigarette holder poised between her manicured fingernails. "You may smoke one of my mine, if you wish. They are designed to boost neutrophil function. Not the filth that clogs up the lungs."

"That's okay, thanks," said Max, returning the packet to his pocket.

Emily threw Max a scowl and cleared her throat. "Anyway, Sipherghast," she said as the Baroness' cool gaze lingered on Max before returning to her.

"It's the codename of an underground organisation," continued Emily. "They sell sensitive scientific information—"

"To which country?" interrupted the Baroness.

"Not one country," said Emily. "To the highest bidder. It's an open market."

"And you think Strong is associated with this?" said the Baroness.

"Everything points towards it," said Emily. "He's a scientific spy."

"He may be more than that." The Baroness' sharp eyes held hers. "My source believes he is responsible for a cyber-attack on his company. That would suggest to me that this is more than just trading information for cash."

"Exactly," said Emily. "Two years ago, Sipherghast was associated with the abduction of an Argentinian molecular biologist who was working on cloning research. Rumour has it that he was about to announce a breakthrough in stem cell processing. Just after he disappeared, an Austrian group made the announcement and took the credit. We believe Sipherghast operates an active wing."

"And Strong is here, in Edinburgh?" asked the Baroness.

"Yes," said Max. "He's involved with the INTP study."

The Baroness' eyes narrowed. "In Synthetic Telepathy?"

Max nodded. "This research is way more advanced, more accurate and more successful than the CIA attempts in the sixties."

The Baroness sat back into the folds of her high leather chair. "That could be viewed as a valuable commodity. Do you have enough to convict him?"

Max glanced at Emily.

"Not yet," said Emily. "But that may work in our favour. He's using another identity, so we're tracking communications from his source email. And now we've found him, he may lead us to Sipherghast."

*

Robert's shadow took the service stairs to the roof of the Innovatics

Institute. With nothing to link him to Liam Bradbury, the knot in his stomach was tightening. *How do I Tunnel?*

When he stepped outside, the air was dank and cool against his skin. The open space was enclosed in a single railing on top of a ledge. Large curved vents emitted a steady hum as they churned warm air into the atmosphere. Clambering onto the ledge, Robert peered over the edge to the pedestrians weaving along the street below, none of them thinking to look up. He realised it was a very long way down.

Closing his eyes, he tried thinking of Liam, but could barely recall what he looked like. All he felt was static in his head as his mind offered him blanks, its bandwidth taken up by one thought – *How the fuck do I Tunnel?* He glanced up to the sky. No birds. *No option.* He took out his phone and stared at the number which delivered Liam's last call. Closing his eyes again, he saw only blackness. He couldn't even remember the colour of Liam's hair.

Shit, Robert. You don't have time to piss about. Breathe.

He steadied himself, trying to remember the last time he saw him. Images and feelings came to him – Aiyana's ache when she laid an invisible hand on Liam's cheek… holding her in the corridor afterwards and the hurt that radiated from a wound that would never really heal… The scent of her hair… how small she felt in his arms… the feel of her head on his chest…

He felt himself falling.

A sharp jolt yanked him back. He slammed onto the concrete, rolling onto his back. Aiyana stood above him looking down, one eyebrow raised. "Did you miss me?" she asked coyly.

"What are you trying to do, Robert? Kill yourself?" Casimir offered him a hand up and Robert dusted himself down.

"I'm no good at this," mumbled Robert.

"You're trying too hard," said Casimir. "You focus, purely, but once you feel the right tension in the bow, you have to let the arrow go. You have to trust it. You can't force it."

Robert frowned, irritated by his failure and how easy it seemed to everyone but him.

"I think you did miss me." Aiyana held his eye for a moment too long and he couldn't tell if she meant it or if she was mocking him. "But you're not my type," she added, reverting to her familiar insolence. Casimir was grinning.

"Thanks Casimir," said Robert.

"So?" said Casimir. "Why are you trying to throw yourself off a ledge?"

"Liam found something," said Robert. "I have to get back to him." He turned to Aiyana. "I need your help."

She hesitated, her arrogance suddenly deflated. "Eh, okay."

*

They Tunnelled to the technology park, to the roof of the tall white building whose windows glinted in the sunshine. Passing through the fire escape door, they made their way down the stairwell, unseen.

Liam's office corridor was brighter and busier than the last time Robert had been here. A woman in a skirt and heels clumped past, frowning at the sheaf of papers she carried, her phone to her ear, oblivious to the three ghosts who stood silently watching her.

When she was out of earshot, Aiyana whispered, "Listen, I really want to speak to him again. Just one last time."

"*What?* No." Casimir was emphatic. "There's a reason the living can't see the dead."

"Robert does it every day. And anyway, we're not dead," said Aiyana. "It can't be that big a deal."

"Robert made that choice and stuck with it," said Casimir. Aiyana tutted and looked away. "And yes, it is a big deal," said Casimir. "It would complicate everything."

"Besides," said Robert, "he has something for us. The last thing we want to do is spook him."

Aiyana sulked at the floor. "Fine. Have it your way."

Inside the office, Liam sat behind his desk, a dark-haired man in a suit opposite. A moment later, Liam stood up, shook the man's hand and showed him the door.

"Thanks, Graham. I'll be in touch."

Graham passed through them as he left, his pace slowing as he strode along the corridor. Glancing back, he scanned the space behind him, then walked on. When he turned the corner and Liam was absorbed in his computer, the substance flooded back into Robert and Casimir's bodies. Robert knocked on the glass door.

"You didn't waste any time," said Liam. "How'd you get here so quickly?"

"We had another meeting in the area," said Robert. "But I cut it short." His bullshitting skills were improving, an achievement about which he had mixed feelings. "Liam, this is Michael Casimir," said Robert as Liam held open the door for them. "He's an associate and he also knew Aiyana." Aiyana stood behind, quiet and invisible, as they shook hands.

"I'm so sorry about what happened," said Casimir.

Liam nodded at the floor. "Thanks," he said. "Me too."

"So," said Robert. "what have you found?"

Liam closed the door. "Let me show you." He took a seat at the desk while Robert, Casimir and Aiyana's shadow moved to join him, watching as he loaded the program onto his screen.

"This is what Aiyana discovered when she first scanned for ultralow electromagnetic frequencies." The world map appeared and over it, a dark haze shrouding parts of North America and Western Europe.

"And this is what's happened since." Liam pressed the return key and the screen began to change. At first the haze receded, fading like a stain being washed clean. But then, from a corner of Western Europe, it appeared again, reforming and spreading. "I picked it up yesterday but wanted to run it for twenty-four hours to make sure."

"It looks denser this time," said Casimir.

"Yeah," said Liam. "And the pattern's changed. It's the same low frequencies, but they're scrambled, like it's coming from multiple small sources, close together."

"Take it back," said Robert. "To the point where it first emerges." He leaned closer as the image on the screen magnified, and its source revealed itself.

"ORB," whispered Aiyana.

Liam straightened up. "What did you say?"

"Odd," said Casimir. "Odd that it's changed." He glowered in Aiyana's direction. Liam glanced back, his gaze lingering on the space where Aiyana stood.

Robert cut in. "Can you give me copy of this?"

Taking a flash-drive from the drawer, Liam saved the file and handed it to Robert. "Do you have any idea what's causing it?" he asked.

"We're still working on it – I'll let you know when we do." Robert held out his hand. "Thanks, Liam. What you're doing here…" He paused, trying to find the right words. "Well, it means it won't all have been for nothing."

Liam lowered his eyes, frowning, and nodded.

As he walked them to the door, Robert felt Liam stop behind him. Turning, Robert followed Liam's gaze towards the windowsill where Aiyana's shadow touched a photograph of Liam with his arm around her. Except, as she stood there, she was more than a shadow – she was reforming, hesitantly, like static on a TV. Her slender outline stuttered in and out of existence against the daylight of the outside world, neither fully one thing nor the other.

"We should go." Casimir's voice smacked of authority.

"Aiyana?" breathed Liam. He stepped towards her. She looked up, startled, then closed her eyes and melted into nothing.

Liam stood motionless, staring at the space where she had been, then picked up the photograph. Robert shot Casimir a look that said *Fuck.*

Slowly, Liam turned towards them. His voice was barely above a whisper. "What are you?"

"Sorry?" said Robert.

"I saw—"

"Saw what?" said Casimir.

Liam glanced back to the window where nothing but tepid sunlight spilled through the glass onto the photograph in his hand of Aiyana as she once was.

Casimir opened the door. "Thanks, Liam. Keep in touch."

They left Liam to his questions and the discomfort of his doubt.

*

"What were you thinking?" Casimir was pacing the roof space of the technology building. In their agitation, all three were fully formed.

"I'm sorry," Aiyana said. "I don't know what happened…"

Robert had rarely witnessed Casimir angry; he was always the one who found the middle ground, easing tension with his broader perspective. Now fury simmered behind the tight line of his mouth and flashed in his eyes as he strode to the perimeter and kicked the wall. "You know the rules!" He turned to face her. "You're either non-physical or physical – nothing in between. It's too much for people!"

"I know…" She slumped down on an air vent, sending two pigeons flapping off into the grey.

Casimir was still pacing. "The consequences…"

"I get it, Casimir," she snapped. A pause spread between them; an uncomfortable void. She looked down. "I don't know how I lost my focus."

"Alright, enough," said Robert. "She made a mistake. But right now, we don't have time to argue. Do you know what this means?" He held up the flash-drive. "This means that ORB is recreating Mindscape."

His words silenced them. He stared out over the flat countryside, barely blinking. All he saw was his memory of the dark stain smearing the earth's landmass and all he felt was the creep of nausea in his gut. "We need to get back," he said. He took Jack's pen from his pocket and held it out as a thick bank of fog drifted in, obscuring the view. "Ready?" he asked.

They touched their fingertips to the pen, their eyes meeting briefly before they closed.

Nothing happened.

Robert opened his eyes to see Casimir frowning.

"Try again," said Casimir. He shifted, getting comfortable in his stance.

184

Again, nothing.

"Shit," breathed Robert. "Why can't I do this?

"Let me try." Casimir took the pen from Robert and held it out. "Okay, everyone. Just relax."

Robert grounded his stance and in the blackness of his mind, he let go, feeling a wave of surrender wash through him. A few seconds later, he sneaked a peek. Still nothing had changed. "Something's wrong," he said.

"I don't understand…" replied Casimir, his brow knotted.

"Then we'll have to Jump," said Robert, clambering onto the ledge and over the small railing, that was all there was between him and the ground. "We've got to get back."

Holding out a hand, he helped them to the edge and they lined up beside him, waiting. Heavy clouds inched past above them, dialling down the daylight, and the cool air pressed against their skin. From the murky sky above came the rhythmic beating of wings as two buzzards appeared through the mist. But only two. Robert and Casimir raised their arms as Aiyana scanned the skies. The birds spread their full wingspan and friction slowed their descent, their talons reaching towards the outstretched arms beneath them. Their wings beat the fragments of mist, like fanning the tendrils of smoke from a fire. But none came to her. *This is wrong*, thought Robert. The fog, which had crept up over the roof seemed thicker around her, like it was singling her out.

"Where's the other one?" Robert's arm bounced with the buzzard's weight as it landed and turned its silver eyes towards him. The chime struck up.

"You go on," said Casimir, as the fabric of Robert's body began blending with the bird in a trickle of shimmering light. "I'll stay with Aiyana…"

But as Robert glanced at her, he saw her veneer of confidence dissolve as the fog snaked round her. He had not imagined it – she was afraid.

*

A bird broke through the clouds above the Innovatics' roof, circling.

The lightening rod of a nearby church steeple skewered the fog; an antenna broadcasting God. Robert transformed as he hit the roof, and tumbled.

Pain burst across his temple and he heard something crack as it struck the concrete. He steadied himself, but the world continued to spin as a wave of nausea washed over him. He lay on the cold chipped rooftop, unable to keep up with the pace of the sky as it rushed overhead again and again. He closed his eyes, waiting for it to stop. Why did he have such a problem with this? Didn't being dead qualify him for some benevolent protection against travel sickness? Maybe Sattva had got it wrong. Maybe the enlightened people were the ones who blocked out their last life, on purpose. Remembering just seemed to bring bigger problems. Something Aiyana had once said about it came back to him: "It's overrated." *Aiyana...*

He got to his feet, gingerly, giving the world time to stop, then paced the perimeter, waiting, scanning the skies through the tatters of fog. Edinburgh bustled about its business beneath him and did not look up. A different city was up here on a different timescale, one that did not identify with the urgency of the streets below.

A billow of air and a brief flash of light made him turn. Sattva and Casimir came towards him, fully visible, and he could tell from the look on Casimir's face and the sudden weight in his chest that the news was not good.

"Where is she?" he asked.

Casimir shook his head.

"We don't know," said Sattva. "I feel no sense of her presence in the Field."

"I shouldn't have argued with her." Casimir leaned on the railings, his brow knotted, his fists gripping the metal with a force that whitened the skin that stretched over his knuckles.

"Your disagreement is not the reason for it," said Sattva, gently.

"Maybe. But it didn't help," said Casimir. "I should have known that seeing Liam would shake her. Even when she was in his office she was showing signs of it..."

"But why?" asked Robert. "What happened to her?"

"She lost her focus," said Sattva. "When you doubt – when you lose sight of truth – you lose your power."

Casimir lowered his head and Robert heard the guilt in his sigh. "It was too much for her, seeing him again. I shouldn't have been so harsh…"

"We all miss things from our lives before, if we choose to dwell on them," said Sattva. "But it takes more than a sense of loss to shake our core so severely that we forget what we really are. No. Something else got to her."

Robert stiffened, staring at the city below him. "The fog…" He watched as it oozed silently through the streets. "There's something in this fog." He stepped back from the edge and the others followed his gaze over the spires and turrets that reached up through a suffocating sea of mist.

"It singled her out," said Robert. "We both saw it, Casimir. Shit," he breathed. "It's everywhere. Messing with people's heads…"

Sattva met Robert's eye. "Splitting their minds…" he breathed.

It was as though the chill air sunk deep into his bones as Robert absorbed his own deductions. "This fog is the medium for Mindscape."

Casimir backed away. Below them, the fog continued its creep. It clung to the streets like a blanket, tucking into corners and moulding into spaces. Now that they saw it, it was clear. It was alive.

CHAPTER TEN

T he feeling of the fine droplets of mist as they settled on Robert's skin took on a new meaning now. It felt like a thin film of grime was clinging to his pores as they stood in silence on the rooftop staring out over the city and its unsuspecting inhabitants. His phone rang and he jumped, startled by the intrusion into the pit of his thoughts.

"Robert?" It was Jack's voice. "We've mapped that data."

"I'll be right there." Robert hung up and turned to Sattva and Casimir. "I have to get back to the lab."

"And we must find Aiyana," said Sattva. He eyed the creeping fog. "Keep your guard up and stay focused."

*

"So these are all the centres working on the mind-machine interface?" asked Robert. He was sitting at Jack's computer, a sheen of sweat on his face, Jack and Ron leaning in behind him as they peered at the map on the screen.

"Yeah," said Ron. "For the past two months, all of them had reported telepathic hits that exceeded anything we've seen before. Until last week. Then these ones here…" he said, pointing to red dots on the screen, "all reported that their results had bombed."

Robert inserted his flash-drive and pulled up Liam's map. The correlation was unmistakable.

"What is that?" asked Jack.

"What if I told you that something had been manufactured that can block thought?" said Robert.

Jack stared at him. "Are you serious?"

Cora looked up from across the room. She lowered her gravel pyramid and nail file, her hands trembling.

*

Seth mounted the meter on the side of the tank, doing his best to ignore the dark shapes inside that glanced off the casing at the edge of his vision. The meter was only the size of a mobile phone and wasn't much use in blocking them out, but he had found another way to do the same thing – he tried to see it differently. *It's a privilege to be part of something as... forward thinking as this*, he told himself. He had told himself the same thing every day since Elijah first opened the door and let him inside. He should be grateful.

He took a reading. The globe in the gravimeter began to spin... wildly. As it gathered momentum, the circumferential dial lit up in a succession of red lights. Gravity, compared to the other forces, was weak, but even on this scale, the contents of the cylinder showed readings far higher than Seth would have expected for something with such little substance.

As Elijah walked up behind him, Seth became aware of a slight change in the scent of the air; a hint of tooth decay.

"I don't understand," said Seth. "This whole place should be stuck to the tank. With this reading, we should be measuring the gravitational pull of a mountain, not a vapour. What are they made of?"

Elijah watched the shapes drift behind the glass, his head slightly inclined, his eyes filled with something approaching awe. "Mass is not the only thing that attracts," he said.

*

Ben woke to a sound. He looked around his darkened room, unable to place it. It sounded like a dog, or a child, whimpering...

He got up and padded to his door, pulling it open quietly. The hall was empty and the sound seemed to be coming from further down.

189

He crept along in the blackness, feeling his way along the wall, his pyjama legs bunched at his ankles, waiting for him to grow into them. He stopped outside his mother's room; the sound was coming from inside. Listening, he tried to recognise it but it was not one he had heard before. He reached for the handle and twisted, slowly. The door creaked a little as it swung open.

His mother was lying in bed. Around her, the glow of a faint blue dome was fading as something dark and insubstantial snaked through the crack in the open window. He did not know what it was, but when it had gone and the blue dome vanished, his eyes fell on his mother again, who lay whimpering. The noise was coming from her. Her eyes were wide open, staring above her, but it looked like she couldn't see. Softly, he approached the bed and laid a hand on her arm, feeling the film of moisture that shrouded her skin. He watched as she mumbled words he could barely hear and could not understand. Her face was wet and her hair was stuck to her forehead.

"Mummy?" he whispered.

She screamed and he jumped back, stumbling onto his bottom on the floor. She turned to him, and her eyes seemed to see him this time.

His lip trembling, he sniffed back a sob.

"Ben?" she said, through her tears. "What..." But she could not finish the words. She picked him up and hugged him and he wrapped his arms around her neck.

"I'm sorry," she said as she rocked him back and forth. "It was a bad dream. That's all. Just a bad dream."

He didn't know you could see someone else's bad dream, but he said nothing about it to her.

*

It was a bad dream that came back. Soon, his mum didn't go to sleep. She stayed awake until dawn, then closed her eyes as the first weak rays of sunlight penetrated the mist outside her window. Ben took his owl and left the house when he knew she was sleeping soundly. The dreams only came in the night.

He made his way to Shannon's house. He knew it well and it wasn't far. But he didn't stop there. He went past it, round the other side, to the wasteland. Tyler and his friends had not come back, but their bucket, singed and ash-filled, still sat in the middle of the floor. Muted sunlight trickled in through the broken windows, settling on a corner of the wide, open space. The rubble had formed a natural wall there. He made it his den and set about collecting things to keep in it.

There was plenty to choose from. Bits of things that people once owned lay everywhere. He wondered who they were and where they were now, and if they remembered, like he did. Who owned the rusty bicycle chain? Or the torn light-shade? Or the pencil case? He took them to his den and showed his owl, arranging them between the bits of rubble as he told his owl the stories he made up about where those things had come from. But he made sure they were home before dark.

*

Robert held Cora's hand as they made their way home. They barely spoke as they weaved their way through the evening pedestrians who hurried past, heads down, coats wrapped tight around them, like they were trying to disappear into themselves.

Danny was not home when they arrived. Robert closed the curtains in their room and rolled down the blinds in the kitchen, feeling the relief of shutting out the night, although he was still aware of it pressing against the glass. Cora turned on the lights and brought through another lamp from the hall. They made some food and sat at the table, where Cora pushed her rice about her plate.

Eventually she spoke. "Is it back?"

Robert put down his fork and saw the tremble in the spirit behind her eyes. "Yes."

She bit her lip and dropped her gaze at the floor, as Robert took her hand.

"But you're stronger than it is, Cora. You know that."

She did not look up.

*

Dreams plagued Robert that night.

A feeling… something dark pressing down on his supine body, squeezing the will from him, desiccating him of happiness. The only warmth was in the hollow of his neck, a heat that burned until it began to hurt. He woke to find his amulet glowing and a singular thought in his mind: *Danny...*

He got up and crept to Danny's door, listening for something beyond the silence. Quietly, he pushed it open then froze. Danny lay on his back, his eyes open, but not seeing the thing that levitated above him. Inky black, lean, the humanoid silhouette with its elongated head floated as though balancing on a breeze Robert could not feel. Its movements were fluid, swaying like a snake, undulating as though dancing to a slow silent lilt. Around it, around Danny, was the faint glow of a blue dome. The thing had no discernible features as it inched its head round, turning towards the open doorway where Robert stood rooted to the spot. *A Revenant...?*

Robert's heart hammered as he stood his ground, his eyes flicking to the space under Danny's bed where the mandala lay in its box. Danny's chest rose and fell as he sucked air deep into his lungs too fast for comfort. The Revenant reached down, extending long darkened fingers that folded around the box, its head still inclined towards Robert, even though it had no eyes. The dark wood of the hexagonal box was becoming insubstantial in the grip of the Revenant's shadowy form.

Robert lunged for it but the Revenant recoiled, startled, then as if it had no spine or joints to constrain its movements, it snaked round. The window burst open, its curtains billowing, as the thing fled into the night. Robert bolted out after it.

*

It was ahead of him in the mist. Out on the street, it moved like a primate, using its hands and feet to propel itself over the ground, writhing smoothly with each bound, its shoulder blades rising and falling like a chimp on the chase. For all of its athetoid movements, it covered the ground at a pace. It seemed to cut through the mist, as though the fog parted for it, forming an empty rim around its lunging form. It turned its head, looking back without breaking stride, as Robert tore after it. The streets were quiet, the pubs long closed. Puddles of limp light seeped through the fog onto the empty pavements.

He struggled to keep up. On the long straight of the Royal Mile, Robert held back, stepping into a doorway of a T-shirt shop to stay out of sight, although he wasn't sure sight was a sense it deployed. He cleared his mind, and his body drained of substance. Unseen, he peered round the corner. Ahead, the Revenant slowed, its head turned back in an awkward stretch as it scanned for Robert. It came to a stop in the middle of the road and the mist oozed round it, lit by the white lights hanging on the walls of the buildings. It swayed for a moment, rising up on its legs, then turned and slunk into an alleyway.

Robert kept to the shadows, despite his immaterialism, as he stepped out of the doorway and back onto the cobbled street. He reached the narrow passage and peered round the corner. The flagstones sloped downwards in steps, worn out by centuries of walking that had caused them to sag in the middle. On either side, brick walls leaned in towards each other, close enough to whisper secrets from one window across to the next. Pipes hugged the length and height of the buildings like black veins. A lamp shone from a bracket in the stone, but the fog, thick in the narrow alley, strangled its light into a tense white ball. The Revenant slunk on ahead. It glanced back every so often, sometimes rising to its full height as though smelling the breeze, before moving on.

Robert followed as it rounded a corner, descending further into the darkness, past some bushes and a wrought-iron staircase clinging to a wall. Tucked at the base of the alley was a windowless building with a low door. The Revenant paused outside and Robert flattened himself against the wall as it scanned the alleyway. It may not have seen him, but he had the feeling it sensed him. It passed through the door and disappeared.

Robert crept towards the entrance. The wood was chipped and old, and the door fit for the height of a child. He passed through its substance, the taste of sawdust and fear rising in the ghost of his throat.

On the other side was a stone corridor and his eyes struggled to make out the details in the dimness. He had to stoop to walk along it, feeling the soft crumbling of sandstone beneath the shadow of his fingers as he inched his way forwards. He passed several entrances leading to darkened rooms, but he sensed that whatever he had followed was not inside them. The corridor wound a tortuous route into the shadows and the ground sloped downwards beneath his feet. He was descending. The heavy, damp stillness was punctuated only by his hammering heartbeat and the soft rapid sound of his breaths.

Ahead, a faint yellow glow and a faint whispering beckoned him deeper.

At first he couldn't make it out. He paused, peering closer through the edge of the archway ahead. The chamber beyond it was round, old, abandoned. A shaft of streetlight sliced through a gap in the stonework above, casting an odd glow on the crumbling walls. Shadow shrouded the ceiling, but Robert had the impression that it extended further up than he could see. Beyond, the Revenant stood facing a wall inside the large chamber. Its hands and forehead rested on the stone, and it was whispering something Robert could not decipher. As he inched closer to the archway and the room came into view, he drew breath. There was more than one of them.

They stood facing the cold curved stone, whispering things into it. He counted at least five of the entities but most of the chamber was in darkness, and there could have been more. Behind them, in the middle of the stone floor, sat the wooden box.

Robert inched towards it, hardly daring to breathe, and lifted it slowly. The box disappeared into nothingness in his grip as he backed away.

The whispering stopped.

Robert felt himself beginning to tremble as he edged back into the passageway, his rising unease bringing with it the heaviness of physicality. *No,* he thought, as he saw his right arm begin to reform. *Not now...* Sweat broke out on his forehead and as he wiped it from his eye, his arm brushed the wall, dislodging a soft fragment of sandstone. It hit the ground with a *thunk,* which echoed through the air like bad news. One by one, their heads turned.

Robert ran.

Breathing like a train, he bolted along the passageway, steeling himself for the jump through the door, willing his body to blend, *to be nothing, to be nothing...* Behind him, their agitated whispering grew on the air, closing in. He shut his eyes as he raced at the door and passed through its substance into the night.

Bolting down the alleyway, he turned into another that opened to a widened space, poorly illuminated by a single bracketed wall lamp – a dead end. Ahead were high metal railings and on either side, dark buildings, their lower windows boarded up. He turned, seeing the faceless heads of his pursuers inclined towards him in an awkward bend as their shoulders rose and fell with each lurch. *What are you worried about, Robert? That they'll kill you?* The single remaining humour-neuron fizzled out when he remembered that there are things worse than death. The fear of that memory rose in him as he ran at the railings. He hit them hard, the force knocking him back and sending a searing pain across his nose.

Fuck!

He turned. They were breaking to form a circle around him, the whispers rising as the creatures closed in. The wall lamp flickered and went out. Robert backed away, stumbling, and the box fell from his hand, the lid bouncing open as it hit the ground. He dived for it at the same time as the closest Revenant lunged for it too, and as he wrenched it away, his fingers fell inside the wood, touching the ink of the mandala. The world shook as though a depth charge had gone off, then flames and smoke consumed him. He dropped to his knees.

He was on fire.

*

The wind picked up in the cul-de-sac. The Revenants sniffed at the air, pacing the space where Robert had been. They passed through the boarded windows into the disused building. One by one, they leaned their foreheads and hands on the walls and whispered to them.

*

The grey mist swirling in the tank clouded, and Elijah Lazaro glanced up. Its agitation was a sign of their anticipation, he had learned. New fears were coming, new things on which they could feed. He stood up and walked to the edge of the tank, as the technician opened the hatch at the end of the pipe, allowing them to exit. They drifted over to the test subjects on the beds, penetrating the blue domes that held them rigid. Floating above them, their smooth black heads swayed gently just inches above their faces, as one by one the subjects twitched and their eyes opened. The technician was standing by and had made the preparations to receive the dreams. They would be sharpened here, before transmission to the library upstairs. Elijah watched as the bank of computers flashed the subjects' brain activity and the holographic pods at their bed-spaces lit up.

"Sir?" said the technician. He glanced behind him. "Subject Two is getting restless..."

Elijah approached and frowned. Something unusual was happening: Subject Two was trying to speak.

"Shall I up her sedation?" asked the technician.

"No," said Elijah. "Not yet." He leaned closer, straining to hear, watching as Dana Bishop tried to form the words.

"Ma... Mandala..."

Elijah froze. "Where is it?" he said.

Her lips tried to articulate the words, but no sound came out.

"Dana," breathed Elijah. "Who has the mandala?"

"Rob... Robert Strong."

*

A white glow illuminated Robert's closed eyelids. A gentle coolness breathed on his face; a balm after the scorching flames that seared his skin only a moment ago. The soft breeze trickled across his cheeks. He opened his eyes and saw the moon, almost in its fullness, against a sky speckled with stars. He lay for a moment, lost in time and space, not caring particularly, just surrendering to it. It felt like it had been a while since he'd seen the stars. He became aware of grass under his hands; small soft spikes between his fingers. A shadow crossed in front of him and the moon went out.

A face stared down. Round, bald, clean-shaven with eastern eyes, it peered at him with a faint frown. "You want a blanket?" it asked. "It can get cold at night."

Robert sat up, feeling his brain wobble, like it was too small for his skull and was moving around more than it should. He was lying on a grassy slope that led down to a pebbled beach, the sea like glass stretching out to the shadow of an island in the distance. His conscious mind caught up with his surroundings. "What the fuck?" he breathed.

The bald man eyed him with suspicion. "You been drinking?"

"No, I..." Robert's voice tailed off. "How did I get here?"

The man adjusted his red and yellow robes and sat down beside him. "I'm thinking it was the ferry. Only way on and off the island."

"Island? Which island?" Robert felt anxiety creep around his throat and begin to tighten.

The man's frown deepened. "The Holy Isle. You sure you've not been drinking?"

"Holy Isle." Robert ran his hands over his scalp. His eyes fell onto the wooden box by his foot. *I must have Tunnelled,* he thought. Life before death was so much simpler.

"People come here to find themselves," said the monk, chuckling and shaking his head. "But they usually know where they are before they start." He straightened up. "Every day is a surprise to me," he said. "Maybe tomorrow I win the lottery!" He let out a belly laugh, doubling over at his own joke. "You want some tea?"

"No," said Robert. "Thanks, but I need to get back." He picked up the box and stood up. The monk's laughter stopped abruptly when his eyes fell on it. He leaned closer, peering at it as his voice faded to a whisper. "Where did you get that?"

*

Robert followed the monk up the slope towards a large building surrounded by a stone wall. Prayer flags fluttered in the moonlight, flittering their requests onto the breeze. The building was modern, its white façade a soft glow in the night. Robert followed him to a small outbuilding on one side, with stone walls and wooden floors. A Buddha statue sat by the window and incense trickled into the air from a burning stick. A table less than a foot high sat on a rug, with a string of metallic prayer beads resting on its surface and plump cushions scattered around it. The monk switched on a dumpy lamp and a kettle, perched on a shelf next to some books. A mandala hung on the wall, perfect circles inside a perfect square. Gathering his robes around him, he gestured for Robert to sit down. Lifting the lamp, he placed it next to them. Outside, the sound of the tide washed against the shore in rhythmic swishes, the engine of the world.

When he settled on the cushion opposite, Robert removed the mandala from its box, taking care not to touch the markings. He spread it out on the table.

The monk looked across at Robert, his mouth slightly open.

"How do you know this?" asked Robert.

The old man sank back, unfocused, and did not answer.

"Are you alright?" asked Robert.

"I do not know how this came to you. But then it was the same for me."

"So you've seen it before?"

He nodded and Robert felt something plunge in his gut. "What's your name?"

The monk raised his eyes to meet Robert's and the lines on his face cut deeper than before. "My name is Tenzin Chodron."

CHAPTER ELEVEN

T he first time I saw the monastery, I was seven years old.

It was a great honour, my parents told me, to go to the monastery. I said I would like to stay with them instead. They told me, you are our first-born son. That is The Way of Things. The Way of Things sometimes does not agree with your way of things, but there is nothing one can do to stop it. It took us two days to walk to the monastery from my home, up through the wooded hillside and onto the dusty plateau, the longest walk I had ever taken. And over that time, I thought that it might be a good thing to be a monk, because that is The Way of Things. You learn to read and chant and find enlightenment, and it is a special thing to do. And I would meet other boys there who were as lucky as I was and the monks would take good care of me and my parents would be proud.

But as the miles walked under our feet, my hand gripped my mother's more tightly as I thought of what it would mean. I would not hear her voice to wake me in the morning or to send me to sleep at the end of the day, or to sing to me at night when I woke with demons in my dreams. And I would not listen to my father's stories any more as I helped him with the goats and the yak.

When we saw the monastery in the distance I thought what a grand place it was, with its prayer flags fluttering in the mountain breeze, but when we reached its steps I looked up at it and wondered if anyone would find me in there if I got lost, it was such a big place. My fingers were swollen from gripping my mother's hand and she crouched down beside me and opened them out and rubbed them between her hands. There were other boys in red robes playing on the steps and they looked happy, my mother said, and I would be too. But they were them and not me, I thought, and they were not leaving everything that I was.

Then a big monk with great yellow and red robes came out and smiled at me with his eyes. My mother and father bowed to him and I copied them. My father patted my head and told me I made them very proud and my mother kissed my cheeks and held her forehead against mine and smiled with her mouth, although her eyes were sad. I kept looking back at them as the big monk took me inside and they stood there, watching me until the shadows of the monastery came between us.

The first night I met Sonam Dorje. He had been there for a year when I arrived. He was eight and he knew everything there was to know about the monastery, and he told me how to behave. He told me that the pain I felt inside would soon get better, and one day I would not have it any more at all.

"Don't be lazy in your bed, Tenzin," Sonam told me. "You get up early, when you hear the morning bell. That is my job, to ring the morning bell." He must be very important, I thought. "Then you come to the shrine room for the morning prayer. You don't make a noise in the shrine room, you must not talk and when you go in, you stand and bow, holding your hands in prayer, like this," he pressed his small palms together, his face very serious, his eyes cast to the ground, "until the teacher sits down." Then he glanced up at me with mischievous eyes. "You just do what I do and you will be fine."

It was a lot to remember. I did not sleep that night for fear of sleeping in or making a noise in the shrine room. When I got to the shrine room, with its dark wooden floors and polished statues and butter lamps, I would have been too afraid to speak anyway. The teacher came in, a great big man in flowing red and yellow robes that made him look like he had all the answers to everything. I held my hands in prayer, like Sonam said, and I sneaked sideways glances as I tried to follow him when he lay on his belly and face on the hard wooden floor. When the teacher sat down, I peeked at Sonam and sat up. But Sonam shook his head in tiny violent movements and his eyes grew as wide as rice bowls and he pointed with one finger hidden beneath his robe towards my feet. They were stretched out in front of me, so I thought that this must be wrong and I folded my legs under me, as Sonam did, but it was uncomfortable and I wriggled and shuffled on that one spot whilst the teacher spoke. He spoke of many things that morning, but I did not hear much of it, for the pain in my numb, tingling legs.

"You never point your feet at the altar," said Sonam later. He was very wise.

When it was time to eat, I was hungrier than I ever remembered being and went to sit down at the table, but Sonam pulled the sleeve of my robe. "You must serve the rice to others first," he said. I had to try hard not to steal a mouthful as I carried the bowls to the table, for if they caught me they would throw me out and then how would I find my way home?

There were classes after that to memorise the ritual texts. I did not know the order of the words, and so to begin with, I just opened and closed my mouth and sometimes made a sound as if I knew the right words to say.

"You have to learn the words," Sonam told me after the class when we sat on the steps outside. "They write them down, but you must remember them in here." He pointed to my heart.

"Why?" I asked him.

"They tell you how to live," he said.

"Oh."

"Do you want to know a secret?" he asked me, and his eyes twinkled.

I nodded.

He grinned and ran round the outside of the monastery towards the side entrance that led to the room with the prayer wheel. The prayer wheel was bigger than me, bigger than the monk who took the morning prayer: it was as wide as two yaks standing nose to tail and just as high. Sonam spun the wheel as he passed and I put my hand on it to spin it too, and its writings blurred in front of my face and it creaked and clicked as it went round. I followed Sonam behind the wheel where he crept to the back wall and crouched on the ground. He touched his finger to his lips and lifted aside a flat piece of wood. He grinned at me again and crawled into the black space behind it like a cat, and his red robe and the dusty soles of his feet disappeared inside.

I crawled after him into the tunnel, my knees catching on the robes beneath them. For some of it, the tunnel was too narrow to crawl on our knees, so we shuffled forwards on our elbows, wriggling like red snakes on the earth. At the end of the tunnel there was an orange light, like fire. Sonam shuffled towards the light and I saw that it came from a hole in the tunnel. He waved to me to come closer and I wriggled towards him on my knees until my eyes were level with the hole. I peered through the gap, my face next to Sonam's to see where the fire came from.

An old monk, with a face as wrinkled as a yak's nose, was kneeling on the ground, bent over a piece of cloth on the stone floor. He was whispering words I could not hear and his eyes were closed. The light was from a fire torch on a metal stand, and it made shadows on the walls like a demon. Those demons danced on the small black stone that sat in front of the cloth.

"That is where they keep the mandala," Sonam whispered.

"What is it?"

"It is the Nag Khung Mandala. It is kept away from the others. There is always a monk in there, reading it. It is never left alone."

"What does the mandala say?" I asked him.

He looked at me in a strange way and shook his head. "You would not want to know."

In the evening there was a quiet time to spend in reflection. I thought of my mother and my father and the pain came back to me. But I also thought that even if the monastery was a grand place, which could swallow you up with the size of it, I already knew one of its secrets, and that made me smile.

Over the days and months, the words of the ritual texts came more easily to me, although they were difficult to understand. And as the months grew into years, my legs grew accustomed to sitting for long stretches of time in one place, and I began to unravel a little of what the words meant. The pain stayed with me but I accepted it, and it became a friend, a reminder of home.

*

Change can be thrust upon us, turning what is a calm sea into a turbulent storm. The day that Sonam came running to speak to me after evening prayer, I knew that the world would not be the same again. He led me out of the main hall to the hillside in the dusk, and something in the urgency of his movements and the look in his eyes made me want to turn away, to go back to quiet reflection of the day, and not listen to what he had to say. But his fist gripped my robe and he cast his eyes behind him before he spoke.

"They've burned the Tsozong monastery," he whispered.

"Who?"

"Men came with torches. Many monks were killed. They say they are coming here, too."

I heard his words, but it was difficult to believe that men would do such things. It was in the stories passed down to us from before and in the history texts; the suffering caused by the actions of men, but to hear it spoken as Sonam spoke, it made me think that it could not be real.

That night, I meditated on the suffering of the Tsozong monks.

*

Twenty-six years after I arrived at the monastery, my master, Thubten Tashi, woke me from sleep one night. We stepped over the monks sleeping on their mats as he led me out of the room. Sonam was waiting outside. It was dark, but he did not light a fire torch. My master did not speak to us as we stole down the corridor and his steps were quicker than usual. He opened a door at the end of the corridor and led us down some stone steps. I thought I knew the monastery well but I had never been down these steps before. At the bottom of the steps was a dark passage and at the end of that, a door. A flicker of light shone from the gap underneath it.

Thubten Tashi pushed open the door to the small room inside where an old monk looked up at me. He was kneeling on the floor next to the mandala, a small black stone cupped in his hand, like two pyramids joined at their bases. The light from the fire torch glinted on its many flat surfaces and as he looked back at it, he sighed and the weight of the world was in that sigh. He put down the stone and rolled the mandala carefully around it, placing them inside a wooden box. It was then that he told us their secrets. His old hands were trembling as he pushed the lid into place. He got to his feet and handed me the box.

Thubten Tashi said, "Tenzin, you and Sonam must take the mandala and the stone from here. Evil is coming."

"Where should we go?" I asked.

"Go to the west, to the Chiu Gomba monastery. The temples there may be safe for a little longer. Do not let them be parted from you, for if they are found…" Thubten Tashi shook his head. "Go now."

We bowed to him and I strapped the box to my back in a strip of material. My heart did not want to leave and it told me so, but that is The Way of Things.

*

As we left, I saw the monks running from the shrine room as the smell of charcoal and the plumage of smoke rose from it. Thubten Tashi saw me and he stopped on the steps while the other monks ran past him. We shared something in that moment, and I knew we would not see him again. He smiled at us then and nodded and we turned, with the mandala and stone on my back, and ran into the night.

*

We saw no one on our journey to begin with, but we kept off the tracks and in the shadows. We looked back at the track behind us and listened for sounds of anyone on our trail but there was nothing. After two days, we passed along the route that led past my family home. I saw my mother outside milking a goat and my father fixing a hole in the wall of the house. It filled me with joy to see them, older, greyer, perhaps a little empty, but overflowing with love to see me. Was what followed worth all the love I saw in their faces then?

We changed our robes for the clothes of herders and although it was only one night, we stayed too long. Evil came to the house when we slept, and my mother and father would not wake up. We choked on the thick putrid air as we tried to rouse them, but they were asleep in their smoke-filled room, a sleep that would last forever. I was shaking as I left them and I thought how could this be The Way of Things? How can men inflict such suffering on others and walk away from it? A part of me wanted to find them and stop the cycle of suffering with my bare hands, but that is something I would have to carry with me through many lifetimes. That was not my part to play in things. We ran from the blazing wreck into the forest and when I looked back, I saw the hillside alight in all the colours of the sunset and the smoke rising like a giant black snake into the dawn sky. We ran, and kept on running.

We ran for days at a time. We took the stone out of the box and left the mandala inside, then took turns to carry each of them. Sonam preferred the stone, he told me. It felt like a comfort in his hand. We stopped only briefly for rest amongst the thickets, long enough to drink some water from the streams and to remove the leaches from our arms and legs. We could not see our hunters but we knew they were behind us, in the dark. And so we ran and ran, driven by fear but not consumed by it.

I have known fear. I have looked into the eyes of it and felt its sickening swell within my stomach, the drain of warmth from my limbs and the clammy tremble that remains. If you give in to fear, it will wither your strength like a drought withers the branch, but if you master fear, master the release of it, you peel away another layer of yourself and you will find a place where you have a strength beyond anything you could have imagined. I found that when I ran. It was as though I watched myself run – the leaps and bounds, the certainty of my stride carrying me onwards, almost in flight. The running made me free. I would not have believed it possible, yet I ran with the wind, as part of it.

Some nights later, we could hear them in the distance behind us. We had been on foot across the mountains for days, with only berries and roots to eat, and soon the snow would be coming. On the nights with no moon, we would run on the open plains, but when the moonlight was bright, we stayed under cover of the trees. The thick undergrowth and gnarled roots made running impossible, but then it also did for them. The leeches were thick there, in that moist dim world under the canopy, but we could not stop for them. Some dropped off, fat and satiated with our blood, others clung on to our legs, growing plumper with every stride. We ate very little – there was only time to gather a handful of berries with each stop – and I could feel the bones in my ribs like blunt teeth protruding from under my tunic. Sonam's cheeks were hollow and his jaw was like a flat blade in his face. He stumbled more often, weakened by fatigue and hunger, until the time that he could not get up. Blood oozed from the hole the branch made in his thigh, and he winced with pain as his clothes turned red. I tried to pick him up but he was too heavy and I was too weak. It was then that Sonam made me stop.

"We can't outrun them," he said. "This is where our paths must part."

"I won't leave you!" I said.

"You have no choice. They cannot find the stone." He smiled as he handed it to me. "We both know the eternity of things, Tenzin. I will see you in another life." He squeezed my hand. "You must go. Now."

I tried to smile but my eyes were blinded by tears at the sight of my friend lying helpless in a pool of red. How often do we abandon those we love for things that seem to matter more? As I held his hand and squeezed it, I felt like a traitor, even though I knew he was right. I turned and ran and did not look back.

They found me by the next nightfall. There were four of them, and although I tried to run, I was weak and dizzy and they caught up with me easily. It is a terrible feeling, that moment of realisation, when defeat looks down at you with pity and contempt, as though there really was no other end to this, and did you really think you could succeed?

They took the box from my back and forced me to my knees. The biggest of them, with hands like shovels and a bearded face stepped up to me. I remember the smell of sweat from him and the coldness in his eyes. I was an animal to him; feral, vermin. The first blow broke blood from my lips as they burst against my teeth. The second swelled my right eye with a pain that felt like my head was split in two, and I could not see through my puffed-up eyelid. I spat out blood and swayed on my knees. The third brought no pain, only darkness.

I woke with the snow in my face, and the moon high above. Dried blood caked my cheek and it felt like a mask when I moved it. A trickle of wet blood found its way to my lips. I was lying on my right side with my swollen eye nearest the ground, so I could see above the rocks. There were voices in the distance, smoke from a fire and raucous laughter. I lay there for an hour, maybe two, while they drank their spirits and slurred their words and then fell into a chorus of noisy sleep. When I was sure they were sound, I crept up from my place, my head pounding with its bloody swelling, and inched towards them. I moved like a ghost on the earth, each step a painstaking effort to be unheard. When I reached the edge of their camp, I saw them sprawled on the ground, mouths open, snoring like pigs. The fire in the middle had gone out and only a feeble whisper of smoke rose from its centre and my wooden box lay cast aside by the embers. I lifted it gently, pausing whilst the big pig snorted and rolled over, and I looked inside.

Neither the stone nor the mandala was there.

And then something in the ashes, beneath the unburned sticks piled on top, called to me. The corner of a cloth, its edges charred, protruded from the twigs. My heart leapt so violently that I thought they might hear it, but they snored on in their drunken chorus. I lifted it gently from the embers, and a flame flashed as it moved, curling up its borders, but it did not burn. Its edges were the colour of charcoal, but the flame, for all it was hot to touch and the colour of fire, did not encroach on the markings. Not an inch of the cloth was lost. In the flicker of light from its flames, I saw it. There, in the open palm of one of the drunken pigs, lay the stone. It glinted in the firelight from the cloth, as the flame dwindled and went out. Carefully, with more precision than I have ever called upon, I lifted the small angled stone from the creases of his hand.

I took the mandala, the stone and the box and stepped past the drunkards like a shadow, then broke out onto the mountain. I ran for miles without stopping, despite the pummelling inside my head and the screaming of my muscles.

And then I stopped. They would be after me before sunrise and if they found me again they would not be so forgiving. They knew my face now and they would kill me and take the mandala and the stone if they set eyes on me again. I thought on Thubten Tashi's words, that I should not be parted from it, but things had changed now. Sonam had come to the end of this life and I could protect the mandala and the stone only if I separated myself from them and led the hunters away. And so, as the moon began to fade in the sky, I searched for their resting place. I found it under a boulder, which was narrow at its base and flat and wide at its top so that it sat like a shelf above the ground. I dug the earth under it with my hands and a stick until I could reach into the hole with my whole arm. Before I laid them to rest, something made me take the stone out of the box. I put it in my tunic pocket. I closed the box on the mandala and placed it in the hole, and I piled the dirt back into it under the boulder. I prayed for protection for the mandala, that it would outlast me.

*

I waited until dark before I climbed the wooden steps that led inside the Chiu Gomba monastery. It had been weeks since I was parted from Sonam and the mandala. When the door opened I bowed to the monk who stood there. He bowed to me and stepped aside to let me enter. For three cycles of the moon I stayed there, and the monks were kind to me. I did not speak of the mandala or the stone because then they would know, and knowing can be a dangerous thing. Instead I worked in the gardens and served the rice and enjoyed the company and the peace of staying in one place. I buried the stone beneath a Yunnan tree and thought of Sonam. For a while I thought that I could stay there forever and that it could be a place that would be home to me. But it was not to be.

I woke with the smell of smoke in my nose the night that evil came to Chiu Gomba. It drifted like a serpent on the air and wakened my senses in an instant. I was on my feet prodding the monks as they slept on their mats.

"Go! Go!" I shouted to them, and I ran through the corridors until I found the great cast iron bell that sat in a frame on the terrace, and I struck the bell again and again, and it rang out in the darkness until they all were wakened. I shouted to them all to leave now as the smoke thickened and the timbers creaked, and I thought that I had done this, I had brought the evil upon this place. How could I have become complacent? When the last of them left through the blazing beams, I stumbled to the shrine room through the swirling black smoke, and I sat down to wait. I would not run from this evil any more.

The flames sought me out along the wooden floor planks like a blind monster feeling for food. The timbers crashed from the ceiling

208

behind me, and the whispering drone burrowed into my mind. Evil was embodied in that sound, etching its claws deeper with every visitation. It encircled my soul like a vulture waiting for the last gasp.

Raised voices came from outside as the burning timbers crashed to the floor, only this time I understood. They were ordering the destruction of books and manuscripts, all the ancient texts which cradled the wisdom of man's existence and which we strove to protect. I heard the sound of tearing scrolls and the swelling roar of the flames as they fed on them like frenzied wolves, consuming them as they would consume me. But they had not found the mandala they sought. If they had, they would not be here. It was a glimmer of light in the darkness to me. And so I sat motionless amidst the smoke, and waited. And I yearned for it, the Oblivion and the Unknown. Anything else but the pain. The flames scorched my flesh and I fought to remember that *it is only my body, it is only my body. It is not who I am.* Everything is temporary, everything changes with time, except that which I am. It would change again soon.

I closed my eyes and let the fire lick my neck and the smoke snake deep inside me. As my flesh bubbled, a shadow crossed the orange glow. I opened my eyes and saw him.

*

Tenzin stared at the mandala without really seeing it. "It was the first lifetime I remembered with any clarity," he said. "The ones before and since are like echoes, but this one stays with me as though I lived it yesterday, not fourteen-hundred years ago. Time, it seems, is a construct of the mind."

Robert sat motionless, watching him. "It's like I live your death," he said. "Whenever I touch the markings."

"We are both entangled with the mandala now. It is its way to connect us."

"Why?" asked Robert.

"Realities shift over time. Just as we each repeat our cycles of birth, life and death, so does our collective consciousness. Every so often, the earth's consciousness, like its crust, undergoes seismic shifts. It evolves. The mandala shows itself when it does. That it has shown itself to you, means that you have a part to play in this."

Robert stared down at the material. "What do the symbols mean?"

"Its markings are a record of man's collective intentions," said Tenzin. "My masters, and all those who studied it, were searching for its lessons.

"But it is not the mandala you must understand," said the monk. He reached for a pot on the shelf, tipped it upright and caught the dark object that toppled out. It was jet black, little more than an inch long, with eight surfaces, like two pyramids joined together at their bases. He handed it to Robert. "It is the Stone."

Cautious that it might inflict some kind of painful connection with him, Robert took it from him hesitantly, but felt nothing. Just the cool feel of its many angles and smooth faces, ones that he recognised.

Tenzin watched him as he turned the rock over in his hand. "This is the Intention Stone."

Robert glanced up, frowning.

"It amplifies intention," explained Tenzin. "The stone hears your intention and draws to you what you are asking for."

Robert rested his hand on the table, still rolling the stone in his fingers, and as he did so, the metallic prayer beads coiled at the corner of the table began to tremble. Robert eyed them as their vibrations became more violent until suddenly they shot across the wooden surface and stuck to the stone in his palm. He stared down at it.

"It is also magnetic," said Tenzin.

Disentangling the beads, Robert placed them on a cushion. "So why did Sonam die, if he had the stone?" he asked. "That wasn't his intention, was it?"

The creases around Tenzin's eyes deepened. "Not consciously," he said. "But the stone does not hear your words. It hears your innermost thoughts and feelings, your deepest beliefs. While we believed we could outrun our hunters, we did. But when we traded certainty for fear, the stone heard and gave us what our hearts were thinking."

"But how do you know what your beliefs really are?"

"By listening to how you feel. All intentions, when the details are stripped away, are rooted in only two – fear or love. You know when you feel love, and you know when you feel fear. The stone makes no judgment about which one you choose. But," he held Robert's eye, "it is powerful. That is why you must know your truth, *be* your truth, before you use it."

Robert glanced down at the small object in his hand, like it might detonate. He placed it on the table. "How did you find it?" he asked.

"As I said, the details of that lifetime stayed with me." Tenzin winked. "Things are easy to find when you know where to look." The lines on the old monk's face, the signatures of many lives, etched deeper, as he stared at the stone.

"I think I've found Sonam," said Robert.

A smile settled on Tenzin's lips and his eyes softened. "I always hoped our paths would cross again. Perhaps, someday, they will." He turned to look out of the window where the sun was clearing the cusp of the horizon and the ocean was a vat of golden liquid.

Robert leaned forward, his voice barely a whisper. "Who was hunting you, Tenzin?"

Tenzin studied him for a long moment, then slowly reached out and took his hand. Robert pulled back but the monk's grip tightened as he placed it on the markings of the mandala.

Pain burst across Robert's palm. Red consumed the room as he smelled his singed flesh and choked on the carbon-laden air and the furnace roared and crackled in his ears. He opened his eyes and saw the shadow standing before him, flames dancing around him as though they were prayer flags and not fire. The shadow's eyes glinted like blue ice in the blaze. His face timeless, his smile void of compassion, the dark figure reached out, into him...

The room righted itself and Robert faced Tenzin again, gasping for breath.

"*Amos...*" Robert rubbed the flesh of his palm that only a moment ago was charred and hissing.

"There is no name for what he is," said Tenzin. He placed the stone in the centre of the mandala, carefully folding the four corners of the cloth so that they met over its pyramidal smoothness, then lifted them into the box and handed it to Robert.

As Robert's hand closed round the box, the light changed outside. Almost imperceptibly, the colours dulled and faded, like the sun was going out. Robert stood up and walked to the window. A mist crept in above the surface of the water. It was making its way to the land.

"Tenzin," said Robert, backing away. "We have to leave. They're coming."

"I am too old to run, Robert."

"No," said Robert. "I can get you out of here if we go now."

Tenzin stood up. His face was calm, his eyes settled. "Take the stone to Sonam. Tell him it's his turn." He rested his hands on Robert's shoulders. "I may see you in another life, but I'm glad I met you in this one. Go now."

*

Robert ran to the main building, tall enough to give him the drop he needed. He was too distracted to Tunnel. His hands and feet found holds on the windowsills and drainpipes, guiding him with a speed that seemed unnatural towards the roof, as the land darkened behind him. He swayed and regained his balance as he climbed onto the tiles. From here he could see the ocean spread out in its vastness, the mist hovering above like a spreading stain. It drifted in to the beach where Tenzin stood alone and waiting. As the mist struck the land, they began to take form, emerging from the dark haze like eels from water. Two speedboats broke through the fog, turning in a spray of white water to land on the shore. Men dressed in black, their faces covered, waded from the boats to the shore as the things circled Tenzin, the arc of their necks smooth as they watched, prowling, testing, waiting. As the bird descended from the clear sky, Robert held out his arm. The old monk looked up at him as the circle closed in, then closed his eyes.

CHAPTER TWELVE

T he sun may have risen over the city, but very little of its light made it through to the streets below. The bird circled above, high enough to feel the heat on its wings, high enough to ride the thermals that kept it up here, in the light. It was another world. There was purity in the blue, tranquillity in the soft rays from the sun. A space to breathe. Below, through the gaps in the mist, was the dead-end alleyway where Robert had Tunnelled. It lay empty in the bleak light, the Revenants gone. The bird soared higher, banking as it navigated the sleepy streets towards Danny's home. It circled one last time in the limitless sky, then dived. The air rushed at him, the sinking feeling inside him more than just gravity. It was a plummeting of his spirit as he descended into the fog, like it was dragging him down into a world that had turned grey.

*

Cora was sitting on the floor of their bedroom when Robert got back, her head resting on her knees, her arms clutching her legs, her gravel and obsidian crystals scattered around her in disarray. The window was open and the curtain wafted back and forth as the grey breeze stole inside.

"Cora?" Robert moved towards her but she didn't look up. "Cora, are you alright?" He crouched down and put a hand on her arm but she pulled away. "What's wrong?"

She lifted her head. Her face was smudged with tears and gravel dust, and her eyes were red. "It's not right," she whispered. "It isn't right…"

"What isn't?"

She picked up the nail file and the nearest gravel chip, an almost perfect pyramid, and filed furiously. Then she got onto all fours grabbing at the other stones in what became a frenzy, throwing them across the floor until they littered the room. In her eyes was something he had not seen before – the look of someone who had opened fire on her own internal war. There was no sign of the Cora he knew, even accounting for her recent weirdness, nothing of the Cora who had first seized his attention with the steadiness of her inner metronome. The woman before him now was rabid; a stranger.

"I hate this!" she shouted. "I *hate* it!"

Robert slammed the window shut, locking out the fog. He knelt down and grabbed her forearms and she wrestled against his grip. "Just leave me alone! Get out of my head…"

"Cora!" He tried to steady her, staring into her through the layers of her intruder, until she finally saw him and her struggling slowed. "It's alright," he said gently as she shook in his arms. "It's alright." He held her until the storm abated then said, "There's something you should see."

He sat her down and opened the lid of the box then teased aside the corners of the mandala. Cora froze. She gasped as he took out the stone, inching closer, her eyes poring over it. "That's it," she breathed. Tears trickled down her cheek and she smiled as she raised the two gravel pyramids in her hands and placed their bases together. Her gaze turned back to the stone. It was the same shape. The gravel dropped from her grip and she lifted the stone from Robert's palm, holding it level with her eyes and turning it slowly, her gaze following its dark facets. "I can't believe it's real…" she whispered.

She looked up at Robert then around at the gravel replicas littering the room.

Robert smoothed her hair from her eyes. "It is real," he said. "You were right." He stood up as her eyes were drawn back to the black rock in her palm. "Let's take it to Ben," he said. He offered her a hand but, as she reached for it, Danny's bedroom door slammed.

Robert's smile faded. He took the stone from Cora, wrapped it in the mandala and sealed them in their box. "Wait here," he said.

Danny was standing in the kitchen when Robert walked in. His jaw was set. "Where is it?" he snapped.

Robert said nothing.

"Where's the mandala?"

"It's safe," said Robert.

Danny rounded on him. "You *stole* it? You came into my room and you stole it? I thought we were mates! You turn up in the middle of the night with some bullshit shady story and I don't push you. I give you a place to stay to get yourself together and then this happens? I never had you figured as a thief but that's what you are!"

"Wait, Danny—"

Danny lowered his voice, pointing a finger at Robert's face. "I'm warning you, Robert. If you fuck this up for me, I will never forgive you. I'm giving you one chance to hand it over." He waited, the small muscles at the sides of his cheeks flexing, the veins that crossed his temples standing out like purple ropes. Robert said nothing.

Danny's face soured and he turned and strode out. A door clattered – the door to Robert's room – as Danny threw it open. Robert's heart lurched as he went after him.

Danny spied the box on the floor and as Cora lunged for it, he pushed her away, his arm striking her face, blood spilling from her lip. Robert launched himself at Danny, knocking him through the table, which splintered under him, and sunk a punch hard into Danny's cheek. Danny brought the heel of his palm up under Robert's chin, knocking him backwards, and in the space it gave him, Danny scrambled to his feet and kicked Robert solidly in the stomach then planted a fist in his temple. Blood burst from the blow as Robert's vision danced with white lights then went black. He hit the floor. Cora scrambled towards Danny, screaming, but he pushed her aside. He scooped up the wooden box and bolted, slamming the door behind him.

When Robert came to a moment later, his eyes found Cora leaning over him. She helped him up and he staggered to his feet, reaching for the wall for support through the ringing in his ear. He clasped her face. "Are you alright?"

She nodded, shaken, her lip swollen and bruised.

"Keep the doors locked and the windows shut." He frowned as he kissed her forehead, burning inside at what he had let happen.

Stumbling out of the front door, his palm reached for the wet warmth oozing from the side of his head. Blood on his hand. He scanned the street. Danny was approaching the end of the road and as he reached the corner, a sleek silver car pulled up beside him. The door opened and Danny stepped inside.

"Shit," breathed Robert. He tore after the car but it purred away out of sight. He searched his pockets – there was nothing to link him directly to Danny. Taking out his mobile, he dialled. "Jack? I need your help."

"Sure. What's up?" came Jack's voice.

"I need you to come and get Cora – take her to the lab. I'll explain later."

He hung up and ran back to the house, unaware of the grey car that sat on the other side of the road.

*

From inside the car, Max watched Robert return to the flat, seeing the blood on his face and the tight line of his mouth. When Robert closed the door, Max glanced down at his tablet, where he had entered the registration number of the silver car. He took a swig of coffee from his flask and waited. The vehicle check was almost complete.

*

Cora was leaning over the bathroom sink, dabbing her bloody lip. She lifted the towel to his temple, wiping away a trickle of blood.

"Jack's coming to get you," he said. "I'll meet you at the lab."

"You're going after him, aren't you?"

"I have to get it back, Cora."

Robert took the towel from her, ran it under the tap then held it gently against her mouth. "I'm fine," she said. "It's nothing."

"It's not nothing," he said. "When I find him I'll…" His fury strangled the words in his throat.

"No," she said. "Don't perpetuate bad karma. Promise me."

He lowered his gaze unable to do as she asked.

"Robert, he's not himself. None of us is."

He handed her the towel again and kissed her forehead before closing the bathroom door behind him. When he reached the kitchen, he closed that door too, giving him the privacy he needed in the empty room. He turned to the bookshelf and rummaged through the clutter to retrieved Danny's 'lucky' compass. His fingers closed around it as he shut his eyes and pictured Danny. The image came with a feeling of white rage.

The last time he Tunnelled, it was by accident. The times before that, he had help. Now, he had no room for error or doubt. He settled into himself, slowing his breathing, until he felt a twinge in his gut. Nausea rose within him and he became aware of the substance of his body lighten. It rippled through him but it was intermittent, like a stuttering car engine trying to ignite. He breathed out, trying to ignore the resistance in his mind; to let go of the rage until he felt it again – the rushing feeling in his solar plexus as the particles that were his body began to morph into light... He grasped at the feeling, but it faltered and flickered as fury intercepted it, until it ebbed away.

Fuck.

"Robert?"

He opened his eyes. Cora was standing in the doorway. The bloody towel dropped from her limp hand as he glanced down to see the solidity flood back into his body and the last of the light go out. His eyes met hers.

"Cora, I..." he began.

She backed away, her face ashen.

"It's alright..." he said.

She shook her head and recoiled when he came closer. Her back hit the wall and her legs gave under her as she slid to the floor.

Robert knelt down beside her and reached for her face. She trembled at his touch and stared at him with frightened, questioning eyes.

"Don't be afraid," he whispered. "It's me. It's still me."

"What are you?" Her voice was barely a whisper.

"I will explain but right now I need to find Danny. Please. Do you know where he went?" He reached for her hair, but she pulled back. Hurting, torn between the urge to tell her everything and the urgency of what he had to do, he swallowed and squeezed her hand, then got up.

He went to Danny's room. The window lay wide open and droplets of mist hung on the air. Reaching for the handle, he slammed the window shut and drew the curtains. The laptop sat on his bedside table, displaying a map search – the Castle Grand Hotel. The door opened and Cora walked in. She was still staring at him, her eyes searching for an answer.

"Wait for Jack," he said. "But don't tell him or anyone… about me. Please. I'll be back for you." He kissed her and left, taking the compass with him.

When she followed him into the hallway, he was gone. Her fingers touched the links in the chain slung between the front door and the wall – the door that was locked from the inside.

*

Things were not as he left them when Seth arrived in the chamber. The engineers had been in overnight and were still working, five of them on their knees wiring things together. The empty space surrounding the cylinder was now populated with holographic pods. They stood at intervals about waist height, small black balls suspended on their upper surface, loose wires coming from their bases and disappearing into the newly drilled holes in the floor. He walked over to the nearest one.

"Watch your feet," said the engineer, pulling aside a wire.

Seth skipped over it, glancing back at the blue light that glowed from the hole in the floor that took the wire somewhere else. The same neon light emanated from all of them.

"You're just in time," said the engineer as he stood up. "We're just about to test."

He tapped his headset. "All set here, Freddie. Whenever you're ready."

The elevator doors slid open and Elijah stepped out followed by seven technicians each holding electronic tablets. Seth wondered what they had that he didn't that allowed them access to the areas Elijah had forbidden him. The pods simultaneously cast their cones of light into the space, and the room filled with their red holographic glow. A soft babble of incomprehensible words breathed on the air, stabbed occasionally by a muted cry or muffled scream.

Elijah walked towards Seth as the technicians dispersed between the pods. "Quite something," he said. "Isn't it?"

Seth peered at the nearest hologram, seeing the details of the image it broadcast. A man was inside a dark room backing away from the walls that advanced towards him from all sides. The ceiling inched downwards or the floor crept up – it was difficult to tell – but soon he was pressing his hands on the structures that encroached on him on all sides, trying to stop their creep. Seth felt a tightening in his chest, like someone had wrapped a belt round it and was pulling it taught. Finally, when Seth felt he could hardly breathe, the man was reduced to kneeling face-down, in something the size of a small box.

"Entrapment," said Elijah. The technician next to him made a note. The hologram faded and Seth's chest expanded.

He turned to the next pod: a woman wrapped in a blanket in a damp kitchen, walls peeling, cupboards and drawers open and empty, a bare light bulb dangling from a wire in the ceiling. The light bulb went out and the walls fell away and she was on the street, the legs of people passing her by as she sat there in her insignificance. Seth felt a black hole in his heart open up, like he had sunk into desolation.

"Poverty," said Elijah.

"I can feel it," whispered Seth, as the woman faded from view.

"Good," said Elijah. "Then it's working. And this one?" He gestured to another pod.

A man lay on a bed, his frame ageing and emaciating before his eyes until he was old and no more than decaying skin stretched over bone. Seth caught his breath as the old man stilled and did not move again. The doctor closed the door behind him and the man faded from view.

Seth turned away.

"Sir?" said one of the technicians.

As they walked towards her, Seth caught Elijah's expression change from smug satisfaction to a frown. The pod she was monitoring showed a woman sitting on a chair in a darkened room. Behind her, a small ball of light glowed on a table. White in colour, it pulsed in time with her breath. The woman sat frozen, her eyes wide. Seth's heart contracted, gripped with fear, sensing something so ominous that he dared not turn round.

"It's coming up a lot," said the technician.

Seth glanced round the room. Other pods showed the same scene – sometimes a woman, sometimes a man, but all afraid to look back.

"What category do we give it?" asked the technician.

Elijah hesitated. Then, gathering himself, he said, "Unclassified." He turned to Seth. "I need you to measure them. We can then categorise them according to the strength of their attraction." Faint amusement flickered in Elijah's eyes as he watched Seth's face, then a look that said, *you asked for this.* He turned and walked to the elevator, followed by the technicians.

"I think that went pretty well," said the engineer as he packed up his tools. "Nice clear signal. We'll tidy up those wires once they've re-plumbed the subjects."

Seth stared at him. *Subjects?*

The engineer picked up his bag and walked away, leaving Seth standing amidst the glowing pods of other people's fears.

Seth glanced around him. It felt like his mind had been dropped into the deep freeze and was just beginning to thaw, as his senses took things in again. The engineers and the technicians had gone and he stood alone in the chamber, the tank on one side with its column of swirling grey-blue fog and the red glow from the pods on the other. It flickered and shimmered as they played out their fears, giving the room an uneasy feeling of jarred disconnection. He kept coming back to Lazaro's explanation for the motivation for all this. He was right – understanding fear was the first step to overcoming it, but Seth found little solace in this. He was not just witnessing those fears as a curious observer – he was feeling them.

He took out the gravimeter and set it beside the first hologram –

220

entrapment. He found himself taking several deep breaths to overcome the claustrophobia that squeezed in on him again as the globe on the meter swung about its axis. The dots on the surrounding circle lit up in succession, reaching the orange zone before settling. He set up a table on his tablet and noted the result. The requirement to focus on the technical details helped take his mind off the more disturbing issue of what it all represented. He moved to the next pod – death, it looked like – and noted the reading, while he did his best to ignore the hollow emptiness that gnawed inside his gut. As he moved around the room, he came to see that there were not that many categories. There was a sprinkling of very specific ones like fear of rats or spiders, or fear of drowning, but most were broad generalisations that could be easily grouped together.

He sat down at his station, as the room hummed and flickered around him, and began to rank them in order. He worked away, absorbed in the technicalities of arranging his table, feeling a little lighter now that he was not standing right in the midst of them. When he had finished, he sat back and looked at the result. It surprised him. The *Uncategorised* fear ranked highest, outstripping all of them, even death.

*

Max sat in his car as the mist hugged it, watching as Cora Martin followed a man with a long grey ponytail into an old Vauxhall. It was registered to Jack Harley, chief researcher in the INTP study. Strong had not come out again.

The vehicle check for the silver car was taking much longer than usual. He glanced down at his tablet again, but when the small circle stopped chasing its tail and the registration details appeared, he froze.

He reached for his phone. "It's me. We need to meet."

*

Max leaned on the railings overlooking the Forth and waited. He pulled up his collar around his neck to stop the chill of the air getting in and watched the football that bobbed past beneath the fog on the dull waves. The sounds of the city were muted, like echoes of a different time. Emily arrived a few minutes later, announced by her perfume. He glanced at her and wondered when they might take their next excursion beyond a professional understanding. But as she stared up at him, waiting for his information, her mind clearly was not where his was going. She was on duty.

"I saw Daniel Mitchell today," he began.

"Strong's housemate?"

"Yeah. They'd had some kind of bust up. Mitchell left and got into a car."

"And?"

"It was a government vehicle."

She stared at him. "Could you trace the owner?"

"It's restricted," he said. "I don't have that level of access."

Emily turned to the murky water.

"Something's not hanging together," said Max.

"What do you mean?"

"With Strong. It's too clumsy. If you go to the trouble of staging your own death, you don't leave any loose ends. You make your new identity more concrete. Something's not right. I need more people."

"I can't do that."

"Why not?"

"I have my orders too," she said. "This is just you."

"Come on, Emily, you know you can't run surveillance with just one—"

"Do what you can," she interrupted. "Stay on Strong. Leave Mitchell to me – I'll take it from here."

The trouble with these dealings, Max reflected after she left, was that you could never really trust anyone, or know where their true loyalties lay. He watched the river undulate beneath the fog, then turned and walked away.

*

Seth had been alone in the chamber for several hours, tinkering with the table on his tablet. He had grown used to the dimness and the faint blue glow that flickered as the shapes passed in front of the beam of light inside the tank. He had even grown used to the pods that glowed their red nightmares. He tapped his pen on the desk.

There was one thing that sat uneasily at the back of his mind since his conversation with the engineer. *What subjects?*

He cast around the room. Dominated by the tank and the pods, both quiet at the moment, there was little else here. A few control panels on the curved walls, some consoles, and a lot of floor space. Seth stepped up to the tank, doing what he could to ignore the entities within. They had no eyes he could discern, although as they passed in the swirling current, there were times he felt like they were watching him. Their heads would pause momentarily as they passed the place where he stood on the outside, looking in. He looked past them, down to the floor. There was no doubt that the tank and its laser came from down there, from somewhere on a lower level. It was hard to make out, but it seemed to extend a long way down. He glanced at the silver elevator against the wall. Elijah would be at the Progress Meeting for a while yet, he thought, as he crossed the room. He could get away with it. He stepped inside and pressed the button marked *Subbasement*. For some reason, until today, he had always assumed the elevator would go up, not down.

There would be a lot of pipes, he expected. He wondered if he would need a hard hat. As the door slid open, he froze, taking it in. The doors began gliding towards one another again, shutting out what he thought he saw. He punched the hold button. This time he stepped out.

There was a lot of blue. Not just from the core of the tank, but from the neon domes that sat to one side of it. It looked like a ward: monitors beeped quietly next to trolleys, drip stands held bags of fluid that trickled inside tubes, wires snaked up to the holes in the ceiling. And the tubes and wires passed through the blue domes to whatever was inside. He took a step closer. People. He could make out their shapes inside the blue haze, under the white sheets draped over them – the points of their feet, the swell of their thighs, the rise and fall of their chests. There were people in the domes and they were alive.

Something approaching panic set in. *What is this?*

"Can I help you?"

Seth jumped at the voice. He turned to see a female technician in blue scrubs, her fair hair pulled back from her face. She stared at him

over her glasses, one arm holding a digital tablet.

Seth mustered as much confidence and poise as he could. He had to dig deep – he wanted to run. Instead he extended a hand. "I'm Seth Winters, geophysicist from upstairs. Just seeing how you're doing down here."

She looked hesitant. "I don't think you're meant to be here. This is restricted—"

"I know," he said, "but I'm looking at the gravitational readings in the tank for Mr Lazaro, and I wonder if there's a difference in density down here." He wandered over to the tank, appearing to study it.

"Well, Mr Lazaro will be back soon. Maybe you could come back then…"

"Sure," said Seth. "No problem." He ambled towards the elevator then, with his skin of ease and authority beginning to fit more comfortably, paused and said, "How are the subjects doing anyway?"

She glanced around at her patients, frowning. "They're needing a lot of sedation."

"Yeah?" Seth turned back.

"Yeah, they just seem more agitated than usual." She tapped on her tablet and shook her head. "It always peaks between 3 and 4 a.m. but it usually settles by now."

"What do you think's causing it?" he asked casually. *Anything to do with the fucking monsters in the tank, by any chance?*

"I really don't know," she said. She paused then asked, "Have you noticed anything in your…" she recalled his words, "gravitational readings then?"

He shrugged. "Not that I can think, offhand. But I'll look into it."

"I suppose, now that they've started receiving, it's really pushing them," she considered. "I just hope it doesn't push them too far…"

"Hmm," nodded Seth, with an appropriate air of gravitas. "That would be too bad." He pushed things a little further himself. "So how does the 'receiving' work, exactly?"

"Well, they're the human interface, you know? Whatever information the Revenants harvest has to be translated. The subject's mind is the translator, then we read their thoughts through a simple mind-machine interface." She pointed to the banks of data screens on the back wall.

Seth walked towards the twelve screens with rotating images of brains. On one side, coloured lights flickering across the contours of the hemispheres; on the other, indistinct images – people, places, objects – flashing too rapidly to make out.

"These are their fears?" asked Seth.

"No, not the subjects' fears. They're from the population."

"What population?"

She stared at him. "The general population."

He digested that.

"Well," she corrected. "The ones we can access anyway."

Seth swallowed. "Of course."

He was beginning to feel sick. He turned, retracing his steps. "I should go back and get on with—"

Suddenly he stopped. Close enough to see into the nearest dome, he saw what lay inside.

"Mr Winters? Are you alright?" The technician's voice was muffled in his head. Background.

He was hardly aware of her when she came to stand next to him. He felt a tightening in his throat, a flush in his face, a film of moisture smarting across his eyes – emotions that threatened to hijack him, as he stared at the woman inside the dome. It was Dana.

CHAPTER THIRTEEN

S eth made his way along the service tunnel, stumbling, breathing too hard, processing what he had just seen, only he couldn't. The decorum he maintained in the subbasement had fallen away, leaving him raw and appalled. He avoided the main corridors for fear of running into someone he knew. The last thing he needed right now was Marshall telling him he looked like shit and should see a doctor. He was heading to the medical bay anyway, but not for a consultation. He emerged onto the back entrance of the medical corridor, where some people were lined up in chairs, waiting for something. A vaccination, perhaps, for some other godawful monstrosity they had created here.

"Are you alright, sir?" asked the nurse. She offered him a seat.

"Where's Clay?" he said.

"He's with a patient. Can I help?"

"No. Just get me Clay."

Clay emerged from a consulting room a moment later looking a little annoyed, until his eyes fell on Seth.

"We need to talk," said Seth. "Now."

*

They stood alone in the service corridor. Neither spoke as an electric buggy chugged past, dragging a small trailer of linen, and disappeared around a corner.

"Clay," said Seth, facing the medic, whose back was against the wall. "Have you been into Area 9 before?"

Clay paused then said, "Yes."

"Have you seen what they're doing there?"

Clay took a deep breath. "My job is to run a physical on the subjects every twenty-four hours. We monitor their vitals continuously from the—"

"Subjects? Dana's in there!"

"I know."

Seth pulled back. "You *know?*"

"She volunteered, Seth."

"What?"

"I have it right here, her consent…" He scrolled through his tablet to find the page, and turned it towards Seth as proof. It showed a signature scrawled at the bottom of the scanned document.

Seth shook his head. "She could not have consented to this. Do you have any idea what it is they're doing? They're taking people's nightmares and transplanting them into her fucking head and making her live them—"

"Seth," said Clay. "She consented."

"*Bullshit!* Did you see her sign that document? Did you? Or do you think, maybe, that that document exists to salve your guilt?"

"Hey, don't start on me. You're a bigger player in this than I am."

"Yeah? Well, not any more, I'm not. I'm out of this."

"Wait, Seth – think about this." Clay leaned closer, choosing his words carefully. "If you blow the whistle, they'll put you in there to join her. You're no use to her there."

"You've got to help me get her out."

"No way," said Clay. "I've got a family to think of. I'm no use to them if I don't come home."

Seth grasped his shirt and twisted it. "You son of a bitch. You can't leave them like that."

Clay shrugged off his grip. "I'm sorry, Seth. I can't help you." He turned and walked off.

*

Seth was waiting for Clay when he did his rounds. The anger he felt had burned like a white-hot ember in his gut since their last conversation. Outbursts and vitriol wouldn't help. It would feel good, but he had to be smarter than that if he wanted results. He lingered in the shadows of the chamber, watching as Clay crossed the space between the Holopods and boarded the elevator. He gave him a few minutes then followed him down to the subbasement. It was 10.30 at night, which was why Seth had never run into him here.

The elevator doors opened. Seth held back, his finger on the hold button behind him, then peered round the door. Clay and the technician were at the other end of the room, preparing for the physicals. Waiting until they were absorbed in their equipment, he slipped to the shadow of the tank, which shielded him from view. He placed the gravimeter on the side of the tank, his eyes on Clay as he moved between the subjects. The technician switched off their domes one at a time before Clay scanned their hearts with an echo machine, listened to their lungs, took their blood. When he had finished with the last subject, he packed up his things and walked to the elevator.

The doors were closing when Seth placed a hand between them. "Evening," he said. "Mind if I join you?"

Clay breathed out an irritated sigh as Seth stepped inside.

*

The upper chamber glowed red when they disembarked. Seth steered Clay forcefully round the Holopods, his fist gripping the back of Clay's shirt.

"You see this?" he said, pushing him close enough so that he saw the details of the dreamer's face; the fright in her eyes. Clay resisted, trying to pull back, but Seth's fist held fast. "Do you feel it? Do you feel her fear? Because that's what they're living down there in the subbasement, all day, every day. Now you tell me they consented to this."

Clay was trembling but Seth held him a little longer before he let his grip fall loose.

228

"You take their bloods, you run their tests and you justify that it's okay because you're looking after their bodies. But what about their minds? Do you give a shit? Or is caring just a convenient stamp for your job description?"

"I have kids, Seth, I can't—"

"No," said Seth. "That's exactly why you can, why you *must*. What kind of father would they rather have? A coward with his head in the sand or man who did the right thing?"

Clay hung his head. For a moment, he said nothing. When he looked up, he met Seth's eye. "Alright. I need time to come up with something, but we'll start with Dana."

*

Seth had not slept properly since he found the subbasement. Any snatches of sleep he caught were troubled, and he preferred to run on caffeine and the tension of exhaustion, fuelled by his body's excess of adrenalin, than to try to sleep. He felt its effects in almost everything he did. When a door closed, he jumped. When someone asked him a question, he tensed. His whole body was alert to threat, whether or not it was in any sense real. It felt like the scrape of a bow over the high strings of an untuned violin, discordant and unpleasant, playing out against the bass drum of his heart that thundered too fast and never let up, just under his skin. As a result, he kept his interactions to a minimum. He had to fight the urge to demand a solution from Clay, having to trust that he would come up with something. The fragment of Seth's rational mind knew he needed time, but his patience was at breaking point. When he grew too uncomfortable in the clammy sweat he lay in, he got up. It was 2.45am. He might as well do something useful.

The conversation he had with the technician replayed in his mind, that the subjects had a predictable pattern of agitation each night. Most of him railed against the idea of knowing any more about this, but he was in so deep now and felt so at sea with everything that his grip was slipping. He had to regain control. *Knowledge is power*, he thought, *even if you don't like what you learn*. He got up and went back to Area 9.

The chamber glowed with its usual red haze as he walked in. He crossed the floor where the Holopods stood like sinister sentinels, casting their fears into the space around them. He did not look at them. Instead he went to his desk and took out the gravimeter. He walked over to the tank, pacing round it to its far side, as its shapes swirled and drifted inside. As he placed the meter on its casing, a hissing made him jump. At the opposite end of the room, the door of the chamber was opening. He could not see it from where he was but he recognised the sound as he stood, frozen, his hand on the meter and the tank, afraid that any movement might draw attention. There was a hum and a buzz and the light in the room began to change. The red haze was still there, but it was moving. Silencing his breathing and commanding absolute precision, he inched sideways to allow him to see.

Standing in the central space among the pods was Victor Amos. The black balls on the surface of the Holopods swivelled and were now angling their holograms at him. He stood at their focal point, his head back, his eyes closed, his arms raised slightly, as the soft babble of distress and anguish around him crescendoed and the red haze intensified. It was as though he were drawing them to him. In the swirling contrast of crossing light beams, it was hard to make out, but it seemed as though his solidity had exchanged itself for something more like dark smoke, that rippled as the projections danced their fears on it.

Seth stood paralysed, afraid to move, afraid to breathe. He didn't know how long he remained there – time has no meaning in a mind gone numb. Then, without warning, the black balls on the pods swivelled again in unison, casting their holograms upwards. The intensity of the red haze softened and their sounds died away. Amos stood for a moment, his eyes still closed, his breaths deep and hungry before falling into an even rhythm, like he was resetting after something intensely pleasurable. He was still for a moment then his eyes opened and he turned and left the chamber.

Seth did not sleep that night.

*

In the subbasement of Area 9, the technician on night duty got up from his seat. The monitors binged their alerts and the subjects twitched and struggled, their eyes wide open. He bolused their sedation, as he did at the same time every night, wondering what it was that got them so hyped.

*

Danny followed the man in the suit into the hotel suite, wiping the blood stain from his knuckles as he caught sight of it, hoping that no one else had. He was shown to a seat in a large opulent room. Heavy beige drapes framed the broad windows that overlooked the street below. The man in the suit did not sit down. He was older than Danny, with grey flecks in his dark hair and the beginnings of a portly belly.

"I'm Clarence Jenkins," he said. "Thank you for coming." His accent came from somewhere like Eton. "My client prefers to remain anonymous, so I will be acting on her behalf. May I offer you something to drink?" he asked.

"No thanks," said Danny. He reached into his rucksack and took out the wooden box. As he handed it to Jenkins, his grip tightened.

"Just out of interest, how much would your client be offering?"

"If this is the original, it would be six figures."

Danny released his grip and forced his face to remain impassive.

"But let's find out, shall we?" Jenkins took the box and walked through the connecting door, beyond which Danny glimpsed a younger man standing in a suit that struggled to contain his biceps. There was no potbelly on him. He turned to Danny, watching him, his eyes void of human connection. The door closed and Danny was on his own.

He blew the air from his lips and slumped back in the cushioned chair. *Six figures?* He began to think about that. This could cover not just one climbing trip, but countless. The world suddenly opened up. He could buy some new kit, fly first class even...

He glanced at his knuckles again where only a few specks of blood remained. Robert's blood, or maybe even Cora's – he would never know. His gaze fell to the floor, his excitement fractured by the gnaw of guilt. What had he done?

The door opened and Jenkins appeared carrying a small card with a number written on it. He handed it to Danny. Danny glanced at it, reading it three or four times to makes sure he got it right.

"Do we have a deal?" said Jenkins.

Danny looked up. "We have a deal."

*

In the adjoining room, a woman, slender and composed, sat on a beige velvet sofa. The room was spacious with the feel of understated wealth. An open fire crackled in the marble fireplace. She looked to be in her early fifties but may have been older, for it seemed that life had graced her the gift of indulging in its finery. She wore a cream skirted suit and matching heels and her short hair, whitish blonde, was swept elegantly to one side of her forehead. The stub of a cigarette, tucked inside an engraved silver holder, sat in a marble ashtray on the table before her, trickling a tinge of purple smoke into the air. She was made up, but subtly so. Her hand reached for the gold-framed glasses on her thin nose, adjusting them as she studied the mandala on her lap. Her bodyguard stood by and observed, a background to which she had become accustomed. Another suited man stood at the other end of the room next to Jenkins, hands clasped in front of him, a metal briefcase handcuffed to his wrist. All of them remained silent as her eyes swept over the mandala.

She was drawn in by its delicate markings, etchings of significance from a forgotten time. She could feel the weight of the centuries it had endured, and wondered who had pondered it before. She rested it on her knee and picked up the stone, turning it over in her fingers. Its black surface glinted in the soft white light from the chandelier above and the red glow from the fire. Her bodyguard glanced out of the window, observing the pedestrians on Princes Street.

Slowly, she folded the mandala around the stone and returned them to their box. When she spoke, her voice had a softness and an assurance that suggested she rarely had to raise it. "I'm ready now. Call the driver." She held the box to one side and the man with the briefcase approached and took it from her. He put his case on the table, entered the code and it clicked open. He placed the box inside then clicked the case shut.

*

The hotel was elaborate; luxurious. Unseen, Robert passed the kilted doorman standing beneath the canopy and went inside.

The reception hall bustled with business people and tourists, none of them registering Robert as his shadow slipped past them. He clutched the compass as he climbed the sweeping staircase to the next floor, which was quieter than below. He felt nothing here, so he moved on, climbing to the second floor; pausing, listening, feeling. When he got to floor five, his fingers tightened round the compass. Danny was here, somewhere on this level. He paced slowly, feeling his way, letting the compass guide him towards its owner. He found himself outside a door marked *Suite 552* in brass lettering. Danny was in here – he could feel it. He passed through the door's substance into the plush room.

Danny was alone, standing over his unzipped rucksack which was propped on a chair, as he leafed through an envelope thick with notes. He was smiling, shaking his head, as he thumbed the cash in his hand. Robert felt cold rage well up inside as he watched him, every fibre of him wanting to punch Danny till he blacked out. Cora's plea was the only thing that held him back. He walked closer, his eyes on the rucksack. It lay open and empty – there was no box inside.

Stuffing the fat envelope into the rucksack, Danny zipped it up and slung it over his shoulder. He turned and strode past Robert, his right arm brushing into the substance of Robert's being, causing the unsettling rippling sensation as their two existences collided. He paused at the door, glancing back, searching the space where Robert stood seething in his bitterness. Danny lowered his eyes and walked out.

Voices were coming from the other side of the connecting door. Robert watched Danny go then turned to the wooden panels and stood listening. Holding his breath, he passed through the substance of the door to the other side.

"Thank you, Jenkins," said a woman's silky voice. "I'll be in touch."

As Robert's shadow entered, he saw a man leave through the main door, the glint of a metal briefcase chained to him. Two people were in the room now. A young man, suited and toned, held out a camel-coloured coat. The elegant woman sitting on the sofa removed the stub of a cigarette from a silver holder and dropped it in the ashtray then placed the holder in her bag. She uncrossed her legs and stood up, her movements assured and feminine. Slipping her arms into the sleeves, she pulled the collar around her neck. Robert scanned the room for the box, but there was no sign of it. As he stole past the fireplace, the flames flickering in his wake, the woman glanced up, her pale eyes sharp over the rim of her glasses. Robert froze as she scanned the air between them. She fastened her coat and picked up her handbag, pausing again, as though reading the air. Then she turned and strode from the room. Robert lifted the cigarette stub from the sprinkle of purple ash, absorbing it into his nothingness, and followed.

The woman and her bodyguard stalked past the reception desk and Robert weaved his way, unseen, behind them.

"Have a good day, Baroness," said the doorman as he held the door for her. She nodded from behind her sunglasses but did not reply as she walked down the steps to the silver car waiting outside. Her bodyguard held the door for her as she stepped inside with elegant swiftness.

"Robert!"

Robert turned to the voice behind him to see a stout woman in a tweed dress and pearls wrap her arms around an apprehensive-looking teenager in a suit, who recoiled as she planted a kiss on his cheek. "I've missed you *so* much, darling boy!"

When Robert turned back, the car was pulling away. He bolted after it but it sped off into the clear road.

Shit!

He slowed to a stop, berating himself. *How could you have been so stupid?*

*

Robert took the steps down to Princes Street Gardens, away from the bustle of the city. It was like descending into an ethereal valley, its trees and shrubs just suggestions in the moist air. Castle Rock rose out of the sea of mist, an imposing island bathed in still grey waters. Opposite, the sharp Gothic spires of the Scott Monument pierced the fog. He found a quiet corner of the park, where the bushes and trees shrouded him from the path. An old bearded tramp lay asleep on a bench by a litter bin but otherwise, he was alone.

His fist gripped the cigarette stub as his eyes closed and his mind turned to the Baroness. He tried to recall her features, the softness of her voice, the elegance of her movements…

Judgement butted in. *She was right there — you could have got in the car and stayed with the stone if you hadn't been such a fucking airhead...*

He opened his eyes. That the mist still clung to the trees and the grey clouds still pebbledashed the sky, did not surprise him. He let out an irritated sigh, closed his eyes again and tried to let go.

Why are you always such a fuckup? Judgement was in full flow. *Do you even realise the consequences of losing the stone? Face it, Robert, you've not got what it takes...*

He looked up, his heart hammering inside his chest, his skin clammy in response to his mind's bitter onslaught. The old tramp was on his feet now, rummaging around inside the bin next to his bench.

Robert glanced down at the remains of the Baroness' cigarette, hating her almost as much as he hated himself. Shaking himself loose, he tried to see past the wall Judgement had built between him and Clarity.

There is no wall. Clarity found a crack in the stonework.

He felt himself relax. This time, he turned his mind to Casimir and Sattva.

*

"So this monk, Tenzin, is the stone's guardian?" said Casimir.

Their shadows had appeared through the gap in the trees and they walked like ghosts through the mist to where Robert stood. Huddled in a corner of the park, between clumps of rhododendron bushes whose withered blue petals lay fallen on the grass, they listened as Robert told them every detail he could recall.

"He was," said Robert, "until the Revenants took him. Now it rests on a six-year-old boy."

"And the Baroness has the stone?" said Sattva.

Robert nodded. "And the mandala. If Amos finds her..." His words tailed off into silence as a young couple approached arm-in-arm. Robert watched them stroll past, their worlds sculpted by only each other. Innocence seemed absurd in his own world now, a memory so alien to him that he could barely recall it. When they were out of earshot, he held up the cigarette stub. "I have a link, but I

235

need help to Tunnel."

Peering at the purplish filter, Casimir frowned. "That's your link?"

"It's the best I could do, Casimir," glowered Robert. He turned to Sattva. "Any sign of her?"

Sattva shook his head. "Not yet. But we will find her." He spoke with conviction, but Casimir's glance was laced with doubt.

"In the meantime, we must not let her suffering be in vain," said Sattva.

"What do you mean?" asked Robert.

"Aiyana's fate reminds us that we must be absolute in our focus — we cannot afford to split our energy." He reached for the amulet round his neck which pulsed an amber haze. "From now on, we must not Tunnel alone. Those are our most vulnerable moments. Now, if you will excuse me…"

"Wait, what about you? You just said it — we shouldn't Tunnel alone," said Robert.

Sattva winked. "I'm not alone." He held Robert's gaze as he faded into the mist. A few brown leaves spiralled on the grass where he stood only seconds before. Somewhere nearby, a dog started barking and would not stop.

"He'll be alright," said Casimir.

"I hope so," said Robert, staring after him. He looked down at the cigarette stub in his hand.

"Ready?" said Casimir.

"Ready."

∗

A stiff breeze cut through Robert. He found himself outside, on concrete, the hum of machines nearby. Casimir helped him to his feet and pointed to the small jet next to a silver car on the tarmac. Its engine whined and its propellers blurred as the car purred away.

"Quick," said Robert. "We can't lose her."

"Relax," said Casimir. "Let her get to wherever she's going. We found her once — we can find her again."

*

Danny walked in through the unlocked door. The house was quiet and he did not have to go far to feel its emptiness. He opened the door to the living room – Cora and Robert's bedroom – and it squeaked on its hinges as it swung open. He walked inside, slowly, his eyes falling on the debris on the floor, the blood stains on the rug. He picked up one of Cora's stones, his fingers folding round it as he closed his eyes and hung his head.

*

Robert and Casimir's Tunnelling took them to the middle of a wood. Towering trees spread a canopy over soft mossy undergrowth, and lichen hugged the scattered rocks and boulders. They glanced around. In the distance, visible through the gaps in the trees, stood a large mansion. Casimir started towards it but Robert held back.

"No," said Robert. "It's this way." He walked off in the opposite direction. Casimir paused, the shadow of a smile on his lips at Robert's certainty.

In the distance was a lodge and beyond it, the glimpse of a small lake. Casimir followed him, unseen and silent. The low wooden building stood nestled among the bushes and trees, its windows peeping out over clumps of green. There was no fog here.

They climbed the wooden steps and passed through the red door into a spacious room with an unlit open fire flanked by armchairs. A wall-mounted stag's head stared down at them through hollow eyes. Large glass doors opened onto a decking at the rear.

The tranquillity was unsettled by a soft growling. Turning, Robert saw two Dobermans, teeth bared, hackles rising, poised at the entrance to a small kitchen off to the left. He glanced down – both Casimir and he were unseen – *but dogs sense things*, he remembered. An older man dressed in shooting attire appeared behind the dogs, scowling as he hobbled towards them. He scanned the room, his brow knotted, as Robert held his breath. Finding nothing, he went back to the dogs. "Daft animals," he said gruffly. "There's nothing there."

He dealt them a clip and they followed him, still growling softly, as he opened the front door. "Outside with you. Go on." The dogs slunk through the door and he closed it behind them and went back to the kitchen. A moment later he re-appeared with a tray of red wine and two glasses and opened the doors onto the decking. Two people sat on the chairs outside, overlooking the lake. He served the wine and placed the bottle on the table between them. Robert's eyes fixed on the glass surface where the stone and the mandala and the open wooden box lay.

Robert saw the sleeve of a tailored jacket resting on the arm of one of the chairs; on the other, a delicate hand with manicured fingers holding a glass. He heard the soft voice of the woman from the hotel. "Thank you, Williams," she said.

"Will that be all, Ma'am?" he asked.

"Yes."

He nodded and returned the tray to the kitchen before he left through the front door.

"You trust him," said the man.

Robert froze at the voice, feeling suddenly clammy, and Casimir caught his eye as the thought spread between them.

"Williams?" she laughed. "Don't worry about him. His family has served mine for generations. And since I paid for his drug-addicted son to clean up, his loyalty has been unimpeachable. Not that it was ever in question."

"And the transaction?" The man's voice was like silk. "Did the seller negotiate?"

"He settled on the first offer. Clearly he had no idea what it's really worth."

"Everyone has his price." Victor Amos picked up the stone and walked to the edge of the decking. Standing in his dark suit, his raven black hair swept back from his face, he was taller than Robert recalled. He studied the stone's black surfaces as they glinted in the sunlight.

"And now for mine," said the Baroness. "You have the mandala. You have the stone. I believe there is something you owe me."

"All in good time, Lucia." He was turning the stone over in his hands, running his fingers across its triangular faces, his eyes narrowed.

"You have nothing for me today?" She sounded offended. "Am I

238

to think that you're losing your touch?"

Amos did not rise to her taunt. He turned towards her, placing the stone on the table. Resting both hands on the arms of her chair, he leaned closer, his face inches from hers. His gaze slid over her cheeks and skin, studying the contours. Robert edged forwards and saw her veneer of flirtation crumble, succumbing to a flicker of fear.

Amos spoke softly. "You are free to think as you wish." He ran the back of his hand down her cheek and she closed her eyes, trembling slightly. He watched her reaction with what looked like curiosity, moving closer still until his breath mingled with hers. His tongue traced the outline of her lips before he began the kiss.

Robert seized the chance. Nodding to Casimir, he bolted forward, grasping the stone and the mandala from the table, but the cloth slipped from the shadow of his fingers. It fluttered into the air and Casimir lunged for it as he followed, knocking over the bottle of wine which glugged its red liquid onto the decking, as Amos reached for the mandala and snatched it first.

Robert looked back. *Leave it, Casimir! We have the stone!* Casimir leapt from the decking onto the shores of the lake, as Amos strode forward, his narrowed eyes scanning the space.

The two ghosts ran, doubling back around the side of the lodge, back into the woods.

They bolted past the dogs, now locked in a large wire enclosure, and set them off in a frenzy of barking. The animals threw themselves at their metal prison, their bared teeth gnashing at the air.

Tearing through the forest, Robert felt the dark tree trunks, the thorny bushes, whipping past his vision as he blended with whatever crossed his path. The woods seemed endless, sprawling like a maze in all directions. They ran onwards, not knowing where they were going, other than away.

"We need to Tunnel!" shouted Casimir.

"I can't think straight!" Robert glanced back. Amos was approaching the kennel, reaching for the gate. "The dogs…" he gasped between breaths.

"They can't harm us," shouted Casimir. "Just stay unseen. Keep focused…"

Robert looked back again but as he saw the dogs burst free from the kennel, he felt like prey. Certainty drained from him and he felt the heaviness of substance as it flooded back into his body. He stumbled on a large root and fell, the stone dropping from his grip as Casimir, further ahead, stopped and turned back.

Robert lifted his head. The dogs were in full gallop towards them, teeth bared, muscles rippling under the gleam of their black coats.

Shit!

"Focus!" bellowed Casimir.

Robert closed his eyes, blocking the vision of the impending dogs, doing what he could to *let go, trust, allow…*

He heard them snapping and snarling the air where he stood, but he shut out the sound, tuning his mind to *let go, trust…*

Suddenly, as though he could see through a refocused lens, the world became clear and time stopped. He became someone else, someone in control, as certainty and clarity seeped into him. When he looked down at the dogs gnashing at the space that had defined him only seconds ago, he was no longer afraid. The animals, suddenly contrite, backed away, panting and whining, their savagery gone. Robert let out a slow breath as for the first time, he realised his power. There was no shred of doubt in his mind: it was absolute knowing.

I did this.

He watched the dogs slink away then picked up the stone that lay on an upturned leaf and turned to Casimir. "Let's go."

Casimir's eyes were trained on something beyond him. "Robert…"

Robert turned. In the distance Amos' dark lean figure was pacing through the forest, followed by Williams, who held a shotgun.

Robert took off after Casimir over the undergrowth and fallen branches towards the open space that beckoned through the gaps between the trees. He glanced up, seeing Casimir's substance becoming visible, like a broken transmission.

Fear nailed a crack in Robert's power. "Casimir!" he shouted. "Keep focused!"

Casimir was beginning to stumble, his material self gaining

240

precedence, as his pace began to slow. He stopped abruptly and dropped to his knees, clutching his scalp. "He's inside my head!" he shouted, his eyes screwed up against it.

Behind them, the dogs began to bark.

"Don't let him in!" Robert grasped his arm as he drew level, dragging Casimir to his feet. "You control this, remember?"

Wincing, Casimir's eyes were still closed.

"Look at me." Robert held his eye for only a splinter of time but enough to reach through the pain into his soul. "Go."

As though suddenly seeing him, Casimir nodded, then took off into the shadowed woodland and Robert glanced back again before following, keeping Casimir in his sight. They gained speed, and the more distance that came between them and Amos, the more Casimir regained command over his body. By the time they reached the last of the trees, he was unseen.

They tore over the lawns, bolting over the flagstones and flowerbeds, passing the hedged maze that dominated the front grounds until they saw the driveway. They went for it, the dogs still behind them, all reconciliation forgotten. Robert steeled himself for the jump through the wrought-iron gates that were clamped shut ahead, willing, with all that he was, that they both had it in them to make it. They hurled themselves at the solid metal, bursting out into a country lane, and bolted on. Behind them, the dogs leapt at the gates, clattering into them, barking, snarling, yelping.

"Keep going!" shouted Robert as they raced down the lane that cut through flat farmland. He was shaken by Casimir's tenuous grip on his focus. "Can you Tunnel?"

"I don't know..." panted Casimir.

Behind them, in the distance, was the clang of metal, the hum of an electric hinge. The dogs were barking again. The gates were opening.

Robert felt his lungs about to burst as they ran on at a pace that would outstrip any athlete, tapping into a resource neither of them knew they had. Only when the sound of the dogs faded to silence behind them, did they slow to a stop. Casimir doubled up, leaning on his knees, fully physical.

"You okay?" said Robert.

Casimir nodded, sucking air into his chest. "Just need... a minute." He straightened up, scanning the road behind and listening. "I think we're clear." The only sound was the cawing of crows that had settled in the nearby trees.

As they walked on over the flat landscape that stretched out over endless fields, Casimir said, "I can't *believe* I dropped the Mandala." He kicked a small rock that bounced off into the grass. "I'm sorry."

"We did what we could. We have the stone," said Robert. He stopped, opening his palm and the stone's black surfaces stared up at them. Casimir reached for it, but Robert's fingers closed round it first. "No, not yet," he said. "Not until your head is clear."

Casimir lowered his eyes.

"What happened to you back there?" asked Robert.

Casimir reached for his temple. "I heard him... inside my mind," he said. "I felt his rage, and I saw..." He swallowed. "...Aiyana. He has them."

"Them?" Robert took a step closer. "Who, Casimir?"

Casimir brought himself to meet Robert's eye. "You were right. He has Elliot and Aiyana and he wants the stone. An exchange."

Robert's gaze fell to the black rock in his hand then back to the road that led to the mansion. Closing Robert's fingers round the stone again, Casimir held his eye. "You don't do deals with him, Robert," he said. "We'll find another way."

Robert felt the shard in his chest, the tear between loyalty and duty. *I can't just let them...* But his angst was scattered by a flurry of disruption. Suddenly restless, the crows in the trees flapped into the air, cutting the stillness with their *caws* and their clumsy wings. Casimir paced slowly into the field, his eyes narrowing as he turned to the sky.

Robert followed his gaze and froze. The sky was darkening, from the west.

Fog oozed over the fields, not just a layer this time, but a thick wall that stretched to the stratosphere. Like the swell of a large body of turbulent water in the open ocean, it crept steadily and deliberately towards them.

"Get inside!" shouted Robert.

Ahead of them, in the next field, was a large metal cowshed. They sprinted towards it as the air thickened and darkened around them. Robert heaved the huge door along its railings, shutting out the waning daylight. The image of the straw bales behind them faded as the door slid to a close with a *clang*. Darkness fell. Their harsh breaths punctured the dense silence and it took a moment to adjust to the black and the musty air inside.

"You okay?" Robert panted.

Casimir nodded as Robert held out the stone. "This will take us to Ben," he said. "Do you think you can Tunnel?"

"Yes."

Robert breathed out, settling himself into his focus, his mind on the stone and on Ben. Nothing else.

Silence descended. They stood, eyes closed, waiting.

A whisper fractured the stillness. Opening his eyes, Robert saw Casimir's gaze shift to the shadows behind him. The darkness deepened as Robert turned to see something moving inside it. Stretching to its full height, the entity's curved, faceless head inclined as it observed them. It was suddenly cold.

"Go," whispered Casimir.

"No." Panic rose inside Robert as Casimir held his eye. He read the thought and felt his heart tear. "I'm not leaving you!"

"*Go!*" shouted Casimir.

Squeezing his eyes shut, Robert turned his thoughts to Ben, but the image, etched on his mind, went with him too. The last thing he saw was Casimir's face as the Revenant closed in. The last thing he felt was his fear.

CHAPTER FOURTEEN

R on yawned and scratched his head, his eyes aching from too long staring at the screen on his computer. He took a swig of coffee and grimaced – it was cold. There were only a few more details left to transfer, but his muffled concentration made them seem insurmountable. He had already added the long list of names, contact numbers and codes that described their telepathic experience and the final results of their studies. Now all that was needed was an update on whether they had reported nightmares. He added a description of Locke's clinics in the free text area, to show how the centre was managing things, *or not,* he thought. Sitting back, he scrolled through their contribution to the INTP database. It was considerable. He forced his eyelids open a little wider and continued typing.

*

In the same way that the data from the GRACE satellites could not resist another journey, neither could this. The information, classified and data-protected as it was, found a plughole down which it trickled, one that led to another destination. In the darkened room, its new observer sat back, a smile crossing his lips as he stared at the screen. He adjusted his black baseball cap, centring the omega sign over his small round shades, and picked up another handful of cola bottles to chew on as he straightened up. His fingers flexed and extended over the keyboard, as though he were about to begin a concert piece on a grand piano. They went to work, de-encrypting, laying bare the email addresses and phone numbers the data was meant to protect. He grinned, relishing the addictive thrill of manipulation, as he created doorways through which the next round of information would pass. Information that came from him.

*

Zoe closed the curtains in her bedroom, blocking the tepid light from outside. Even though it was midday, it felt like dusk. She had had another night of sleeplessness and a morning of trying to snatch more rest through the weight of exhaustion, but the nightmares had found her again, this time in the day. Until now, she had relied on the daylight to bring her some peace, but the nightmares were becoming less selective. She picked up the phone, the business card shaking in her other hand. It felt like she was stretched thin; like she would snap or fold up with the slightest provocation. She was overtired and under-slept, but most of all she was afraid. "Dr Locke?" she said when the call connected. "It's Zoe."

"Zoe?" said Locke's voice in her ear. "Hi. Are you alright?"

"No," said Zoe, her voice trembling. "I need to see you."

"Sure," he said. "Can you come down now?"

*

When Zoe arrived at the lab, Locke took her into his office. He closed the door and pulled the blinds, separating them from the hubbub of activity on the mezzanine. Showing her to one of the two armchairs, he watched her sit down. She had lost weight, her arms like fragile sticks, her hair matted in thick tangles, her face haunted. It was a look he had seen in too many of his clients of late. "Would you like something to drink?" he asked.

She shook her head.

He sat down in the other chair. "Where's Ben?" he asked.

"With the child minder."

"Have you let her know you're here?"

Zoe shook her head. "I forgot my phone. She won't mind if I'm late."

Locke nodded. "So, how can I help you Zoe?"

She stared at the floor, her lip trembling. He sat back, giving her space to find the words. When she spoke, her voice was weak, like she was afraid to use it. "Your email said you'd changed the venue."

"Email?" asked Locke.

"I wanted to call you to make sure, but... I had to see you." She looked up at him through hollow eyes. "It's the nightmares. I can't take it anymore."

*

Robert stood in a dim alleyway, his hands on the cold stone wall, his head hung low, gasping for breath. Large metal dustbins lined one side, their contents overflowing onto the cobblestones, and the air carried the whiff of stale rubbish. He threw up next to one of them and wiped the acidy taste from his lips. *Casimir...* Closing his eyes, he clutched his amulet, willing Sattva or Crowley to hear him, but his hope felt hollow. It bounced back at him like an echo in the mist. This time, no one came. Alone in the shadows of the alleyway, his isolation held a mirror to his vulnerability. Shaken, he headed out onto the street, back to the lab.

He kept to the backstreets as he made his way to the campus, avoiding eye contact with the passers-by, locked inside the prison of his own thoughts. An old ache resurfaced in his heart, the same one he first felt when his mother told him Michael Casimir was dead. But life had taught him that nothing was certain, not even death. It was little comfort in a reality which shifted the goalposts, just when you thought you knew where they were. Ahead, the dark glass panels of the Innovatics Institute were muted in the fog. As he approached and glanced inside, he glimpsed the reflection of someone in the street behind him, getting out of a grey car. *I know him.*

Glancing back, Robert saw a dark-haired man with olive skin. He couldn't be sure but as approached the entrance, he hesitated. Perhaps it was irrational, but something in his gut nudged him onwards and he listened. Instead of turning into the building, he carried on walking. When he crossed into the tree-lined path of the park, the man was behind him.

Robert blended into the small crowd queuing beside a burger van then slipped behind the vehicle. There, out of sight amongst the weeds and the bins smelling of grease, he let the substance drain from him, pouring all of his focus into nothingness. When he stepped out a moment later, he saw the man slow as he approached, his eyes surveying the paths as he joined the queue. Robert felt his hunch vindicated and icy relief that the same hunch had urged him to lead the man away from Innovatics; away from Cora. He watched as the man bought a burger and munched it, still scanning the walkways.

*

Max had lost him. Single-person surveillance was shit, but what could he do? If they weren't going to put some more manpower into the operation, they couldn't expect results. He caught some ketchup escaping from the bun with his tongue as his phone rang. "Max?" said the voice in his ear. "It's Josh. We've just picked up an email from Damien Volker."

Max threw the burger in the dustbin. "On my way. I'll call you when I'm back."

*

Robert stayed with him, not far behind him on the street. He followed him under the dank arch of a bridge that passed over Cowgate, its orange uplights barely illuminating the stains that smeared the surface of the black stones and the silent screams of injustice in the graffiti sprayed on them. A bus thundered overhead, its brakes squealing as the bridge shook. The man turned into the entrance of a narrow block of modern flats just beyond the arch.

He climbed the stairs to the first floor, unlocked the door and closed it behind him, bolting it shut. Robert passed through its substance into the apartment where the living room had become an office. Notebooks and papers were scattered across the dining table beside an ashtray holding a few cigarette butts. He watched as the man turned on his laptop and took off his coat, tossing it onto a chair in the corner while the computer booted up. Lying next to it was an ID badge, which read: *Press – Max Guthrie, Freelance Journalist*. Robert glanced at the man in front of him, now scrolling through his phone. So, this was Max Guthrie. He slipped the badge from the table into his nothingness. Personal objects, he was finding, had their uses.

"Josh? Hi. Okay, what do you have?" Max pulled up a chair and sat down, laying the phone on the table and tapping it onto speaker mode. Both hands now free, he typed on the keyboard.

"It was bcc'd to a lot of people," said the voice over the speaker, "but I've decoded it to show the recipients. It was personalised to each of them."

"I recognise those names," said Max. "Hold on a moment." He opened another page, and a database of names and contact details sprang up. "Yeah," said Max. "They're on the INTP database for this area."

Robert leaned in and read over Max's shoulder as he clicked back to the email.

Dear Katie,

Due to a high demand, we have had to move the location of tomorrow's clinic to the Gosford Building, just off Richard Square. Your appointment time is 10 a.m. A link to the map and the full address is below. I hope this will not be too inconvenient. It is important you attend, as we will be discussing a recent breakthrough that may help your case. I look forward to seeing you then.

Yours sincerely,

Dr R Locke

Psy.D.

"And this came from Damien Volker's email?" asked Max.

"It was under a few layers, but yeah. It originated there. There's one more thing," said the voice. "All the appointments are at the same time."

"Why does Strong want to change the location of—" He stiffened suddenly. "Shit. Has there been any activity from Sipherghast?"

"Not so far," said the voice.

"Alright. Keep me posted." Max hung up. He lit a cigarette and inhaled deeply, then opened the files he had accumulated and scrolled through them. The image of Robert Strong's passport photograph appeared on his screen and Max sat staring at it, squinting through the smoke as he took another drag.

Behind him, Robert's shadow stood motionless.

Max got up, went to the fridge and raked around. Unseen, Robert approached the laptop and his gaze swept over the screen as he scrolled through the files. He froze as he saw the photo of a small boy in a red hooded jacket. Below the next image, the words *Cora Martin: contact details not registered,* beside her passport photograph. Then another photo of Cora and Robert, outside Danny's house. Robert felt himself tremble, his focus slipping away in a tide of tight rage.

Max emerged from the kitchen eating an oversized sandwich and stopped. Robert stood before him, fully materialised. The plate dropped from Max's hand and smashed on the tiled floor as Robert rounded on him, taking him by the throat and pinning him to the wall.

"What the fuck is this?" he said. "What is Sipherghast?"

Max coughed and spluttered and Robert eased his grip, but not enough to let him loose. He frowned like he didn't understand the question.

"What is Sipherghast?" said Robert again, forcing Max's head back so that it thudded against the wall.

"I – I was hoping you'd tell me—"

"Who is Damien Volker?" said Robert.

"What?"

"*Answer me!*" Robert forced his grip again as Max screwed up his eyes and reached for Robert's tightening fingers.

"He's…" he gasped. "He's you…"

"What do you mean he's me?" Robert let him go and Max clasped his throat, doubling over, coughing and drawing in noisy air.

"How did you get in here?" said Max when he managed to breathe.

Robert kept his eyes on Max. "Your door was open."

Max's gaze slid to the bolted door as he straightened up. He eyed Robert, wary.

Robert pulled a wooden chair out from the table, slammed it down and pushed Max into it. "Are you working for Amos?"

"Who?"

"ORB. Are you working for ORB?"

"I don't know who that is," said Max.

Robert studied him. He didn't look like he was lying. Either that or he had perfected its art. "Who are you working for?"

"I'm a journalist. I get paid to find things out."

"Who's paying you?"

Max took a deep breath. "The government."

"I want a name."

Max shook his head. "I don't get names. I just get instructions."

"So why are you tailing me?"

Max weighed up his options as he watched Robert. He could make up some bullshit story and sell it to him and he may even buy it, but this time, levelling with him felt like would get him further. "You're suspected of selling scientific information through an organisation called Sipherghast."

Robert stared at him.

"Are you?" asked Max.

"What? No! Who told you that?"

"We have bank accounts, transactions, email correspondence…"

"*What?*"

Max read Robert's incredulity. Things weren't adding up and the doubts resurfaced in his mind. "Well, someone has gone to a lot of trouble to make it look like you're behind it," he said. "They even staged your death."

"My death?"

"Your medical notes said you died in a helicopter crash."

Robert paused, choosing his words carefully. "It was a bad crash," he said. "But as you can see, I walked away."

This time, Max could not read him. Either Strong was way better than he was, or he was telling the truth.

"I'm not behind this," said Robert. "But whoever is wants the INTP subjects to attend this meeting. Why?"

Max shook his head. "I don't know."

"Give me a copy of that email," said Robert.

Max could have refused. He could have called it in and had Robert arrested for breaking and entering and assault, but he didn't. Experience had taught him to trust his gut, and his gut believed Robert Strong, even if his head didn't. He printed out the email and handed it to him. It was only afterwards, when he was alone in his small flat, that the thought unsettled him again. How did he get in?

*

"Hi," said Clay. "How are we all doing?"

The technician smiled as he walked from the subbasement elevator. "Fine," she said. "How are you?"

"Couldn't be better. So," he said, stopping between the trolleys. "Who's first?"

"Could you take a look at Subject Six?" she asked. "He's had a rough couple of hours."

"Sure," said Clay, following the technician to the bed-space and unpacking his medical kit. "What's up?"

"He's had a temperature and his CO_2 levels are a little high, but his respiratory rate is normal."

"Have you upped his sedation?"

"Not yet," she said. "I wanted you to see him first."

"Let's take a look," said Clay.

The elevator doors swished open again and the technician turned to see Seth stroll in. "We've just had a flux in our readings upstairs," he said. "Do you mind if I check things down here?"

"Eh... No," said the technician. "That should be fine."

"Actually," said Seth, "would you mind giving me a hand with this?"

"We're in the middle of physicals," she said. "Maybe you could come back later."

"It's fine," said Clay. "I'll keep an eye on them." He nodded reassuringly. "Go ahead."

The technician hesitated then walked over to Seth. "Thanks," he said as he held the meter to the tank. "I just need you to hold this here for a moment, while I check a couple of things."

251

She placed her hand on the meter as Seth took out his tablet. He peered at the readings on the tank as she glanced back towards her patients.

"I just need to see this number, here…" He moved her fingers gently and took a note, a shy smile on his lips. "So, I never did get your name."

"Nancy," she said.

"Nancy. So where are you from, Nancy?"

Behind them, Clay slipped to Dana's bed space. He checked the bag of fluid on the drip stand and tapped the small syringe in his fingers, clearing the bubbles. Then he injected it into the bag and returned to his first patient.

"How come I've never seen you in the canteen?" said Seth, holding her eye as she blushed.

"I, eh…" she began, but her words were curtailed by a rattling behind her. She turned and dropped the meter. "Oh Jesus. *Clay!*"

Clay ran to Dana's trolley. Her limbs were jerking and her face twitching, as saliva frothed from her mouth.

"Turn off the dome," snapped Clay.

Nancy punched in the code and the blue haze vanished.

"Push her sedation," he said. "Double it. And get me a nasopharyngeal and suction." He put an oxygen mask on Dana's face and reached under her trolley, turning the valve in the cylinder up full, then clasped the sides of her jaw with tense fingers. Gas filled the bag below the mask, but the bag barely moved as Dana's breaths came in shallow erratic bursts and foam emerged between her clenched teeth.

Nancy adjusted the controls on the pump, her hand shaking, then grabbed a slim rubber tube from the shelf on the wall and stood back as Clay twisted it deep into Dana's nostril.

"I need to get her to the med centre now," said Clay.

"I can't authorise that. Mr Lazaro's the only one who can—"

"We don't have time for authorisation, Nancy. Can you give me a push?"

"I can't leave the others…"

"I'll help you," said Seth, as he approached. He clasped the end of the trolley as Nancy disconnected the wires and tubes.

"Keep her sedation running," said Clay, as they steered Dana's trolley towards the elevator.

"I'll call Mr Lazaro," said Nancy.

"*No*," said Clay, firmly. "Wait until I have things under control, then you can give him an update. I don't need any interruptions. Understood?"

As the doors swished closed, Dana's jerking was subsiding. By the time they opened again, it had stopped.

"What did you do to her?" whispered Seth.

"A small dose of reversal," said Clay. "It overrides the effects of sedation, except if you're on it long term. Then it can cause seizures. Risky – they're usually intractable." He glanced down at Dana who was now lying still. He turned off the sedation trickling in through her drip then wiped the beads of sweat from his brow with the back of his hand. "Jesus, if my old boss saw what I just did… We were lucky."

They took the service corridor to the med centre and locked the door behind them. Clay replaced the tape that barely held the cannula in place on Dana's wet skin while her monitor beeped the sound of her racing heart. Seth held her hand, standing beside her in the cold white room. A bank of monitors lined one wall; remote readings of the internal worlds of the subjects in Area 9. As Dana began to move, her face folding into a frown.

"Clay?" said Seth. Her breathing was high pitched and laboured and she mumbled words Seth couldn't understand as her eyelids fought against their own weight to stay open.

"Shh," said Seth, stroking her hair. "It's okay." He kissed her forehead.

When her focus found Seth's face, he saw inside her, to the terror that had taken hold. She gripped his hand with both of hers, her nails digging into his skin.

"It's okay, Dana," he said again. "We're going to get you out of here…"

She shook her head. "Find…" she began, but her voice was weak. He leaned closer.

"Find Robert Strong."

*

Robert took the elevator to the seventh floor inside the Innovatics Institute. All of the glass offices were closed down for the evening, except the last one, where Cora sat wearing a headset, her back to the window. Robert tapped on the glass. Cora, locked in concentration, did not look up but Jack did. He stood up and came out to the mezzanine to join him.

"You said Cora wouldn't be on the database," said Robert.

"She isn't," said Jack, wary of Robert's edge.

"Where's Locke?" demanded Robert.

"He's with Zoe. What's wrong with you?"

"I need to speak to him."

Jack shook his head. "We can't interrupt his consultation."

"Yes we can. There's something you both need to see."

"Alright," said Jack. "Give me a minute." As he walked away he glanced over his shoulder, frowning, to where Robert paced the floor.

A moment later Jack returned with Locke and they followed Robert into an empty office.

Robert unfolded the printed email and handed it to them.

"I didn't send any emails…" said Locke. "Maybe this is what Zoe…" His voice tailed off as he read the words.

"Someone wants to get the telepaths together in one place," said Robert. "And I'm guessing it's not for a clinic. Whoever they are, they're using your name Locke, and they've hacked into INTP to get those details."

Locke stared at him. "We've got to get in touch with the participants…"

"Where's Ben?" asked Robert.

"At his childminder's," Locke replied.

"Shit," breathed Robert, as Jack stepped out into the corridor and bellowed, "Ron!"

Ron appeared from another office, frowning at Jack's tone, then read the paper Locke handed him. "What the…" he began. "I didn't-—"

"I know," said Jack as he took back the sheet. "Call them all. Tell them they should only attend clinics here at Innovatics. Don't alarm them but make it clear that they should not go to this meeting tomorrow."

"I'm on it," said Ron, and disappeared from the office.

"We need to find out who's behind this," said Jack. He began pacing the room, running his hands through his hair.

"Then we go tomorrow and find out," said Robert.

Jack nodded. "I agree." He took out his mobile. "And we should inform the police."

"*No!*" said Robert. "No police."

"But what if—" began Jack.

"Please, Jack. Trust me on this. Let's just find out what we can tomorrow."

Jack hesitated then placed his phone back in his pocket.

"Get the address of Ben's childminder," said Robert, turning to Locke. "And ask if Zoe has anything with her that belongs to Ben."

Locke left the room and crossed the mezzanine to his office as Jack studied the email again. The muscles on the side of his cheeks clenched and unclenched. "I'm looking forward to finding this fucker," he said.

When Locke returned, he handed Robert a note with an address scribbled on it, and a toy car.

"Stay here," said Robert. "And don't let Cora leave. I'll be back soon."

*

Ben's name is on the list — they're going to find him… Robert clutched Ben's toy car as he took the back stairs to the roof, his mind seized by the thought. His feet clanged on the metal steps and the sound echoed in the tall, empty stairwell, but he lost his footing as a surge of heat seared the hollow of his neck and his amulet glowed red. Something uninvited sliced his vision.

A white room. He stumbled against the handrail – a woman on a trolley, her eyes wide with terror, she was saying his name...

Dana Bishop? He clung to the railing and what was left of his balance. *Shit. Not now...* Her face flashed before him again and he felt her anguish pierce his head. *Christ, I don't have time for...* The vision took hold, its presence engulfing him, leaving him no choice but to surrender to the Ominence and its nauseating revolving pressure. Gathering speed, the internal cyclone consumed him.

*

He found himself in a dim tunnel. Steadying himself, he caught his breath, sickened and disturbed. He had had enough of Tunnelling. He hated it. At least this time, he didn't throw up. A hum came from his right, growing louder as it approached. He backed against the curved wall, feeling its cold stone behind him, as an electric buggy chugged round the corner, its driver hidden under a skip cap. His heart lurched as he recognised the vehicle and he pressed himself further against the wall.

This is ORB.

The whine of its engine deepened as it slowed to a stop beside him and his pulse quickened. He was still fully visible. *Shit, shit, shit...*

"She call you too?" The driver raised his head and Robert saw the face under the cap.

"*Sattva?*"

He smiled at Robert. "Get in."

Robert climbed on board and the buggy took off again.

"I have to get back to Ben," he said. As Sattva drove on in silence, Robert glanced at him. "Casimir..." he began. "He didn't make it back..."

Sattva stared ahead as he steered the buggy round a bend. He nodded and Robert wondered if Sattva's mastery of himself had disconnected him from his emotions. They seemed to barely register, no more than ripples on the flat-calm of his being.

"I know," said Sattva. "But right now, life has brought us here.

We have to concentrate on Dana."

"How did we get inside when we couldn't get past the dome before?"

"You weren't invited last time," said Sattva. "The power of an Ominence can break through most barriers of spacetime, including, it would seem, ORB's dome. Do you have the stone?"

Robert pulled the small rock from his pocket and glanced down at its smooth triangular surfaces. "Where is she?"

"She's in the sickbay. Didn't you see the monitor beside her?"

"No," said Robert. "I was trying to stay upright."

Sattva snorted. "You'll get used to it."

"What's wrong with her?" asked Robert.

Sattva steered the buggy to the side of the tunnel, just short of a sign that read *Med Centre* and an arrow pointing to the right. He stepped off. "Let's find out, shall we?" he said as his substance faded to nothing.

*

Robert and Sattva's shadows stole along the dim corridor that led from the service tunnel, inclining upwards and ending at a closed door. They passed through it to the white clinical corridor beyond. The reception desk sat empty, as did the chairs in the waiting room, but the sound of whimpering came from a room further along. They followed it and as Robert passed through the door, he felt Sattva yank him back.

"She's in here," said Robert, frowning.

"How do you think she's going to react if you appear right in front of her?" said Sattva. His material body flooded back and he knocked on the door.

After a moment of silence, a lock clicked and the door opened a crack. Clay's face peeped out. "Can I help you?" he said.

"We're here to see Dana Bishop," said Sattva.

"I'm sorry, I'm with a patient right now..." He closed the door but Robert pushed against it.

"She asked to see me," said Robert.

"*Robert?*" said Dana from inside the room. "Let him in."

Clay glanced back then held the door open for them, before closing and locking it again.

This was not the Dana Bishop that Robert remembered. Not the sleek, composed, commanding woman who first accompanied him through the corridors of ORB. The woman on the trolley was a shell. She sat up, weakened, thin, but gripping the rail of the trolley so tightly that it trembled.

"Robert?" she whispered. "Is that really you?" She stared at him through haunted eyes that for a moment vaguely recalled peace, then looked at it like a curiosity.

Seth stepped aside, frowning as Robert took her outstretched hand. "What happened, Dana?" he asked.

She let go of his hand, wrapped her arms around her knees and did not speak.

"Which sector are you from?" asked Seth.

"We're not," said Robert.

Seth froze. "Then… how did you get in? This whole place is locked down…"

"It's a long story," said Robert. He glanced at the ceiling. "No cameras in here?" he asked.

"Not yet," said Clay. He caught Seth's eye and Robert read their silent communication. *Do we trust them?*

"We have no affinity for ORB," said Sattva quietly. "Or Victor Amos. We're here to help Dana."

"You can help us get her out of here?" asked Seth.

"Yes," said Sattva.

Seth breathed out but Clay watched them through narrowed eyes. "What, you just happened to show up? How did you know she was in trouble?"

"She invited us," said Sattva.

Clay frowned. "What do you—"

"We don't have time for this," said Seth. "Let's just get moving."

258

Levelling him with his even stare, Sattva said, "We will help you, but first we must understand what happened to Dana."

Clay glanced at Seth, poised on the knife-edge of the decision. Seth held his eye then said, "She trusts them."

Sattva nodded. "Now, bring us up to speed."

Seth looked like he didn't know where to begin. He didn't. "They were using her as a test subject," he said.

"She's not the only one," said Clay. "We got Dana out, but there are eleven others still in there."

Robert froze. "Do you have a list of their names?" he asked.

"Well," mumbled Clay, tapping on the tablet, "I think we've passed the point of data protection here." He handed the tablet to Robert.

Robert's eyes scanned the names. "They're not on the list," he said.

"Who?" asked Seth.

"Aiyana, Casimir …" Robert checked it again.

"What about Ganesh and Tenzin?" asked Sattva.

Robert shook his head as he returned the tablet to Clay. "Is there anywhere else they're holding people here?" he asked.

"No," said Clay. "If they were, I'd know about it. I do all the medical checks."

"What about people who aren't being tested?" asked Robert. "What about prisoners?"

Clay glanced at Seth who shook his head. "I've never seen them hold prisoners," said Clay. "They wouldn't do that."

"Wouldn't they?" asked Robert.

Clay considered that. "I'd still know about it," he said. "No, they're all in Area 9."

"Area 9?" said Robert. "With the tank?"

Clay nodded.

"It's where they're growing them," said Seth.

"Growing what?" said Robert.

Seth stared at them and bit his lip, reflecting on how there were things in his world now that, only a few weeks ago, he could not have imagined. Somewhere along the line he had gone with it; accepted it, although, looking back, he could not see where that point was. How did he let it get this far? Shame turned over inside him and tightened in his throat.

"Maybe you should start by telling us what you know," said Sattva.

Seth swallowed and looked at the floor. "I got involved when I found some changes in global gravitational readings…" he began.

"What do you mean?" asked Robert.

Turning to Clay, Seth said, "Can I use your computer?"

*

Clay logged into the computer in his office and pulled the chair out for Seth, who took the flash-drive from his pocket and plugged it in. The earth appeared as a lumpy globe. An evolving turquoise haze spread to distort the contours, cloaking Europe and the western Asian continent. "These gravitational changes are equivalent to this whole landmass becoming a new mountain range, I mean, like, Himalayan scale," said Seth. "I traced it back to its origin," he continued, rewinding the image, as the haze funnelled into one single point. "In Switzerland."

Robert glanced at Sattva, then peered at the date in the corner of the screen. "Sattva that's when…" His voice tailed off.

Sattva leaned closer, his eyes absorbed in the image. "Can you run that again?" he breathed.

Seth reran the program, and they watched as the world's gravity surge spread out across the continents. "I never thought I'd see it," whispered Sattva. "It's beautiful."

Frowning, Seth seemed unsure of what to make of him. "So, anyway, then Amos took me off the project," he continued. "But I kept following its spread. Then I noticed another signal, here." He froze the next frame where the dark blue density had appeared over ORB's location. "It matched what I was finding here on the ground. The gravitational readings in this place are off the chart, and it all comes from what they're making in Area 9."

The program looped to the start and Switzerland exploded all over again.

"But they still don't know what caused this initial surge," said Seth, watching the turquoise bulge spread out from the Swiss countryside.

"I suspect they do," said Sattva. "And I think you'll find that this is the reason they're working so hard in Area 9."

Seth stared at him. "You know what this is?"

"Yes," said Sattva, his eyes on the screen.

Robert and Sattva locked eyes. "Jack needs to see this," breathed Robert. Sattva nodded.

Turning to Seth, Robert said, "Can you give me a copy of this?"

"Take it," said Seth, handing him the flash-drive. "I just want out."

"We need to see what they're making in Area 9," said Robert.

"No, we've got to get Dana out of here." Seth's jaw was clenching and a cool sweat had broken out on his forehead. "We only have so much time until—"

"Time will wait." Sattva's certainty silenced Seth. "We have to understand what we're dealing with."

Seth took a deep breath. "I can't even begin to tell you."

*

Their shadows passed unseen along the maze of service tunnels, as Robert and Sattva followed the map Seth had sketched. It took them to the sign that read *Area 9 Restricted*. They walked the long, dim corridor towards the metal door at the end, hearing the whispering and feeling the air press in around them. Then they passed through the door into the chamber.

Red glows danced from the Holopods as they projected images and dark feelings into the space above them. Robert held back, feeling the oppression of the room sink his spirit further. It was worse than Seth had described. Slowly, they walked among the pods, pausing every so often as other people's nightmares played out before them.

Robert turned away from the image of a woman running from a rabid crowd, their eyes filled with hatred and intent, as they tore across an endless wasteland after her. "These are all fears?" he whispered.

He walked to where Sattva had been standing for some time, studying a single pod. Robert peered at the image of a man who sat trembling with his back to a table, on which was a small glowing ball of light.

Sattva nodded, his eyes still on the man in the hologram. Robert stared around at the pods, feeling their red haze drag the essence from him.

Slowly, Sattva walked towards the tank. "So now we know where the Revenants have come from," he said.

Robert froze as he followed Sattva's gaze. He hadn't looked at it properly till now. Dark shapes glanced off the casing on the inside – shapes he had seen before.

"Jesus," breathed Robert as he crossed the room. "They're making them?" Every fibre in him wanted to leave, to be as far away from them as possible, but he felt himself drawn closer to the tank.

"What we don't know is how." Sattva looked up at the casing's upper limit, which extended beyond the ceiling, then down to where it disappeared into the floor. Robert followed him into the elevator. Inside, neither of them spoke.

*

Nancy glanced up as the elevator pinged and the doors opened then swished closed. She expected to see someone, possibly Seth or hopefully Clay returning her subject, but no one came out. A beeping monitor called her away and she moved to silence it.

The shadows of Robert and Sattva stood taking it in: the people on the trolleys, the blue domes encasing them, the wires leading to the banks of computers and the pods beside them...

"This is sick," breathed Robert.

Behind him, Sattva was examining the tank again.

"So this is where they create them," whispered Robert.

"No," said Sattva. He was studying the base of the tank, which extended deeper into the earth. "That's where they create them."

*

The elevator descended deep into the earth, the journey taking much longer than Robert expected. The doors slid open and Robert and Sattva stepped out.

They were inside a vast cavern shrouded in mist, the elevator shaft standing on an island surrounded by an underground lake. Its surface was grey, glass-like, and yet it appeared to be moving as though a slow current took it deeper into the cavern to places they could not see. Above the lake, mist hung like a layered, billowing curtain, its density changing almost imperceptibly. And then there was the silence. Strangled by the mist, it felt like words or sounds could not penetrate it. The place was devoid of colour, except for a single blue beam of light that rose up from the lake, piercing the base of the tank above, which seemed disproportionately far away.

Sattva walked towards the edge of the lake, his eyes on something that was coming into view. As Robert followed, a shape was taking form on the billowing grey curtain, lighter in shade, like the projection of a beam of light on smoke. It was a man. His features indistinguishable, his age indiscernible, he turned away and faded from view as Sattva approached. Another appeared, a woman this time and she too, turned from him, lowering her head as her hands rose to cover her face. The misty curtain billowed softly and she was gone. More of them formed and faded, formed and faded, until it seemed like their projections were what made the substance of the mist itself.

The blue beam hissed and buzzed, brightening suddenly, its light spreading out in a fierce flash, catching the faces of the projections in the fog as they turned away from it.

"What is this place?" whispered Robert. The faces turned towards his voice, disturbed by the intrusion, then looked away as Robert returned their gaze.

Sattva had been standing motionless, his eyes on the undulating fog. "We should go," he breathed, backing off as the blue flash faded and the mist closed around its secret again. Robert watched him as they walked towards the elevator. Sattva's eyes, normally the signature of his stillness, were haunted. As Robert glanced back, three more projections began forming in the curtain – two men and one woman. Only these ones did not look away. Instead, they watched silently and Robert's heart lunged as their features crystallised. He ran back to the shore.

"*Dad?*" The figure wavered on the curtain, his eyes hollow and filled with sadness. He lifted a hand, holding it steady in the sway of the moving mist, as though touching the curtain's outer boundary. Robert raised his hand to meet his father's. Despite its intangibility, the mist had the feel of a solid object, like he was pressing on a glass window. As his hand touched the space opposite his father's open palm, a surge of emotions swept through him like a tidal wave – *regret, loss, fear...* he could not name them all but he felt his heart contract under their pressure. He pulled his hand away and the figure lowered his head and turned, disappearing into the mist. Behind him, a little deeper inside the folds of the curtain, two other figures looked on.

"Casimir? Aiyana!" Robert placed his hand on the billowing mist again and it pushed back at him, but he felt nothing until Casimir's figure drifted forward and placed his hand against Robert's, on the opposite side of the impenetrable boundary. A bolt of sadness hit Robert, crippling his heart, and he pulled his hand away. Casimir lowered his hand and his eyes then turned away. Aiyana dropped her gaze and followed, and they faded like distant memories as the mist enveloped them.

"The Valley," breathed Sattva.

Robert slapped the curtain with the edge of his fist. It billowed in indifference as his hand stuck the invisible barrier.

"We must leave," whispered Sattva.

Robert turned to him. "We can't leave them here."

"We have no option."

"We're inside ORB – we have a chance to—"

Sattva's stare was firm. "*How?*"

"I don't know, but..."

"We don't know what we're dealing with, Robert."

"Yes we do. We know enough about Mindscape. I got in before..."

"That was not Mindscape," said Sattva.

THE FIFTH FORCE: QUANTUM GHOSTS TRILOGY

Robert's agitation froze in a wave of cold stillness. "Then what was it?"

The change in Sattva's expression chilled Robert more than his words. "Something far worse," he breathed. "If you want to see them again, we need to regroup."

*

Raw betrayal seared through the dread that had settled inside Robert as they reached the med centre. "Whatever that place is, we can't leave them there."

Sattva turned on him with unusual curtness. "We get Dana out then come back for the others. Understood?"

Robert's eyes narrowed. "Are you afraid?" He took a step closer as Sattva lowered his gaze. "What are you not telling me?"

"Robert, trust me. We must keep focused."

"For fuck's sake, Sattva! If you would—"

"Diffuse your anger!" snapped Sattva. "It's of no use to them."

With a harsh sigh, Robert turned away.

Sattva closed his eyes and exhaled. When he spoke, his voice was steady again. "What did you see in the mist?"

Robert could not bring himself to look at him. "I told you. I saw Casimir, Aiyana and my father."

"You did not see the other?"

Robert turned to him. "What other?"

When Sattva met his eye, Robert saw his stillness restored, but behind it something else. The look of a man who has made peace with atrocity. "Robert," said Sattva quietly. "We must get the stone to Ben. You know where they are. You will come back for them."

In the uneasy silence, Robert's questions fell away.

"You will come back for them," said Sattva again.

*

When they entered the Med Centre, Seth was pacing. "We have to get moving," he said in a low voice as he pulled them aside.

"What's your plan?" asked Robert.

"As soon as she's settled, I'll take her to the surface."

"Past the dome?"

"We've made arrangements. The supplies vehicles have access. We'll get her out on a supplies truck."

"And then what?" asked Robert, glancing at Dana who was hugging her knees and rocking back and forth on the trolley.

"I'll figure it out," said Seth.

Robert shook his head. "It won't work," he said.

Seth froze. "What?"

"The minute you leave here, they'll be all over you. They'll hunt you down and bring you both back as subjects."

Bristling, Seth said, "I don't have a choice. I'm not leaving here without her."

"You don't understand," said Robert. "You can't leave."

"No, *you* don't understand. I can't stay in this place – you saw what's going on down there…"

Clay, who had been riffling through paperwork on his desk, stopped and looked up.

"If you leave now," said Robert, "you jeopardise any hope of us getting the others out."

"That's not my problem," said Seth.

Robert faced him. "You'll be looking over your shoulder for the rest of your life. Believe me, I know what I'm talking about. We have to break this from the inside, and we have a chance to do that now. We need you here."

"He's right," said Clay.

"For fuck's sake, Clay!" spat Seth. "Whose side are you on?"

"We started this," said Clay. "We may as well finish it properly."

Seth turned from them and smacked his hand against the wall. "Jesus Christ…"

"You think you can get her out of here alive?" said Clay.

"Maybe not alive," said Sattva.

Seth turned on him. "*What?*"

"This is a med centre," said Sattva calmly. "You must have a procedure for moving a corpse."

"Ah," said Clay, "I see where you're going. I have the paperwork but I would need some signatures…" He disappeared into his office and returned a moment later with some forms. He handed one to Sattva along with a pen. "Okay, here…"

"Cause of death?" asked Sattva, his pen poised.

Clay glanced at Dana. "Fright?" he suggested. "No, don't write that," he said before Sattva committed his words to paper. "Make it… status epilepticus secondary to…" he searched for the right term. "… Sustained sympathetic activity," he said.

"How do we get to the supplies truck?" asked Robert, turning to Seth.

Seth, his face still taught from the derailment of his plan, took a piece of paper from the desk. "I need a pen."

Searching his pockets, Robert took out the stone and placed it on the desk. The paper clips at the opposite end began trembling in their plastic container then one by one shot across the surface and stuck to the stone.

Seth stood rooted to the spot.

Poised over the death certificate, Sattva stopped writing and stared at the dark rock.

"That's a lodestone," said Seth. He lifted it up, peering at it through the silver loops. "Magnetite. The most strongly magnetic mineral found in nature." He picked the paper clips from its surface. "But this… this is way too magnetic." His brow furrowed as he studied it. "Even for a lodestone."

Sattva handed the paperwork to Clay. "Mind if we keep this?" asked Robert as he took the pen from Sattva's hand. "Might come in handy."

Clay frowned and shrugged; the pen was the least of his worries. The phone rang from the back office, and Clay disappeared to answer it.

Sattva watched as Seth turned over the glossy black lump in his hand. "What's special about a lodestone?" he asked.

"Ordinary magnetite is attracted to magnetic fields," said Seth, "but it tends not to become magnetised itself. The crystalline structure of a lodestone means that the crystal itself remains magnetic. It attracts anything with a magnetic field."

"Maybe that's what Tenzin meant," said Robert.

"Who?" asked Seth.

Robert took the stone from Seth and turned to Sattva. "*The stone hears your intention and draws to you what you are asking for.*'" His eyes fell to the octahedron in his fingers. "It's a prism that focuses thought."

Seth snorted, but Sattva's gaze was still on the stone in Robert's hand. He nodded slowly. "It's an amplifier – it focuses intention and projects a stronger signal into the Field." He met Robert's eye. "That's why Amos wants it."

The stone drew Robert's gaze back to it. "I wonder…" began Robert. "Could we use it now?"

Sattva's eyes narrowed. "Only if you're sure you know what you're doing. What else did Tenzin tell you?"

"It doesn't read your words," said Robert. "It reads your deepest thoughts and feelings, your innermost beliefs. He said it hears what your heart is thinking."

"Are you clear about what you believe," asked Sattva, "beyond any fear or doubt?"

Robert met his eye then lowered his gaze. "No," he breathed.

"Then we need to get this back to Ben," said Sattva as Clay entered the room.

Robert glanced up, registering Clay's ashen face. "What?"

"Nancy's spooked," said Clay. "She's going to inform Lazaro. I've bought us some time, but not much. You have to leave. Now."

*

Two men in white overalls, masks and hoods pushed a trolley down the service tunnel. A shape lay motionless on the thin mattress – motionless, that is, apart from the faintest rise and fall of the white sheet that shrouded it. They followed the map they carried to the underground deliveries area. It was quiet at this time in the evening. The white suits pushed the trolley into a small enclave, out of sight of the security cameras.

A black van backed up into the space and the driver got out. He opened the back doors of the vehicle and offloaded some linen trolleys down a metal ramp, lining them against the wall beside the enclave. Then he paused, lighting up a cigarette, and wandered off for a smoke. Behind him, in the shelter of the enclave, the men in suits lifted the shrouded figure into the nearest linen basket. The two white suits wriggled and fell to the floor, as though something had been standing inside them, although nothing was. Somehow the white garments lifted themselves into the linen basket too.

Moments later, the driver stubbed out his cigarette against the wall and returned to the vehicle, where he pushed the linen basket up the ramp into the back of the van. *Look after her*, Clay had said. He would. Clay was an old friend who had looked after him. The green light flashed ahead, signalling that the security shield was deactivated, and he drove through the long dark tunnel that took them back up to the surface.

*

In the med Centre, Clay sat down at his desk and glanced up at Seth. "You okay?" he asked.

Staring at the floor, Seth did not answer.

"You did the right thing," said Clay, watching Seth adrift in his thoughts. Lost. "You'd better get going," he said, gently.

Seth held his eye before walking out, numbed by what had come to pass. The idea that he was condemned to keep playing an active part in it made him want to throw up. Still, he thought, as he turned into the service tunnel towards the accommodation block, he was good at assuming roles. It wouldn't be the first time he had faked it.

*

Clay picked up the phone in the Med Centre. "Nancy?" he said, with a heavy voice. "I'm sorry, we did everything we could…"

*

In the blue haze of the subbasement, the elevator doors slid open.

"I'm so sorry," said Nancy. She was wringing her hands, her face chalk white. "They just called."

Elijah walked towards her, his eyes on the empty bed space. His voice was thinner and higher than usual. "Why didn't you inform me before? I left strict instructions that *no one* was to leave this facility without my authorisation!"

"I'm know, sir, I know, but the medic couldn't wait – she was seizing and he couldn't stop it—"

Elijah leaned towards her. "Who was the medic?"

*

The doors to the Med Centre burst open and Clay looked up from his desk.

"Where is she?" barked Elijah.

Clay paused, then said, "They took her away."

Elijah's pale face drained further. "Who did?"

"Staff from Sector 4," said Clay.

"What staff?"

"I don't know," said Clay, bemused. "We did the paperwork and they took her away. I assumed they were taking her for a post mortem." He stood up. "Look I need to check the other subjects, to make sure that it's not—"

Elijah leaned across the desk, so that his face was inches from Clay's. "*What. Staff?*" Clay pulled back and opened his hands. "I don't know! They didn't leave their names and numbers!" He picked up the sheaf of papers from the desk and thrust it at Lazaro. "They had the paperwork!"

Surprised by the strength of Clay's conviction, Elijah took the forms and leafed through them, slowly.

"Now," said Clay. "How about we go back and make sure the same thing doesn't happen to all your other subjects?"

*

Ron looked up from his desk in the glass office, the list of his INTP participants on the screen before him. As Jack walked in, Ron shook his head.

"I've tried them all, texts and calls," said Ron. "None of them are answering."

"Shit," breathed Jack. "Send out another email, and keep trying."

Ron sighed and picked up the phone again.

*

In a darkened room, in another place, a screen flashed with the words *Call Diverted*. And the number to which the call was directed just rang out.

CHAPTER FIFTEEN

R obert tumbled onto a rooftop and rolled to a stop, as stars seeded his vision, his fist gripping Ben's toy car. He waited until the wave of nausea passed then glanced around, finding himself fully formed and alone. Placing the car in his pocket, next to the stone, he rose to all fours and gingerly got to his feet.

Pigeons cooed and fluttered off in a united decision to abandon their perch. The edge of the roof loomed before him as he swayed and tried to make peace with his balance. When he mastered it, he saw a doorway with a CND sign spray-painted in purple across it. He reached for the door as a voice came from behind.

"You alright?" Sattva was standing behind him.

He nodded, although he wasn't sure. "Is he here?"

*

They descended into the dark stairwell. On the next level down, a door with a broken pane of glass led off to the right. Robert looked over the bannister into the hollow of the stairwell below, listening. A clink came from behind the door. He peered in over the shards of spiked glass to a large open room with pillars sprayed in graffiti: an abandoned warehouse. Rubble lay in clumps around the floor and grey light seeped in through the broken windows. The noise came again, from the far end of the room. Robert followed Sattva's lead as he closed his eyes, allowing the light to drain from him, becoming unseen. He passed through the substance of the door and into the cavernous room.

Something was at the far end, shuffling and sniffing in the shadows behind the pile of rubble. They stopped, Robert breathing hard, waiting for it to emerge. When it didn't, they crept closer. The shuffling stopped suddenly as if it had heard them and for a moment it felt like both they and whatever was making the sound, were straining to hear through the silence. Slowly, the Eidolon advanced until they were level with the mound of broken concrete. They inched forwards to see what lay behind.

Ben was sitting on the floor, his deep hazel eyes looking directly at Robert from under a spray of long lashes. Robert's gaze flicked down to check — he was definitely unseen. Only the faintest suggestion of his presence persisted, a presence that no ordinary person should see. The boy did not blink nor did he smile, but just looked at him. Beside him sat a plant pot, a hairbrush, a mobile phone case, a stuffed owl and a collection of other things. He rubbed his snub nose as his eyes moved from Sattva to Robert.

"Can you see us?" whispered Robert.

Ben nodded solemnly.

Robert and Sattva crouched down beside him. "What do you see?" asked Robert.

Ben stared back at them. "You look a bit... funny. Like you're only there a bit."

"Does that scare you?" said Sattva.

Ben shook his head. The substance began to fade from his small frame. "I can do it too, sometimes."

Robert pulled back. He stared at Sattva. "He's one of us?" he breathed.

"So it would seem," said Sattva.

"I didn't think children could..." Robert stopped, unsure how to finish the sentence.

"Why not?" asked Sattva. "Adults have lived longer, so they think they know more. The truth is children have had less time to live, so they have forgotten less." He smiled and extended a hand as Ben reformed to his normal self. "Nice to meet you, Ben."

Ben giggled when his own hand slipped through the space where Sattva's should have been, until Sattva focused himself fully into his physical form. They shook hands properly and Ben stared at up him with large wide eyes.

"You've got a lot of interesting stuff here, Ben," said Sattva, as Robert regained his material self. He picked up a paper plane. "What's this for?"

"For flying in," said Ben.

"Like this?" asked Sattva. Ben giggled as Sattva swooped the plane around in the air between them, then handed it to him. Ben folded it and placed it carefully in his pocket.

"What about this?" asked Robert, lifting the plant pot.

"For putting things in," said Ben. He picked up a bicycle bell, pinged it and placed it in the pot to demonstrate.

"Where do you get it all?" asked Robert.

"I find it," said Ben.

Ben eyed the car in Robert's hand. "Ah," said Robert. "I think this belongs to you too." He handed Ben his toy.

Ben took it, smiling as he ran the car over the bumpy ground.

"And so does this," said Robert.

The car slowed to a stop as Ben's eyes fell on the stone in Robert's hand. He was completely still for a long moment before he shuffled towards Robert and reached out, his gaze absorbed in the stone's black surfaces. Lifting it from Robert's palm, he turned it over in his small hands, studying its contours, feeling its smoothness beneath his fingers, as his chest rose and fell faster than it should.

"I got it from a friend of yours," said Robert. "His name was Tenzin."

Ben looked up. The ghost of a smile touched his lips.

"He said to tell you," continued Robert, "'it's your turn... Sonam.'"

"Sonam," breathed Ben. The smile spread across his face as his hand enclosed his stone. He closed his eyes.

A moment later, his grin faded. He got up and padded to the broken window, looking out over the wasteland to the fog that was thickening and gathering across the ruins. He turned to them and whispered, "They're coming."

*

Katie Crookshank took her phone from the pocket of her ripped jeans as she listened to the message again. She tutted. Why did they change it to this time of night? Still, it got her out of the house, away from her parents, she thought. She ran her fingers through her short, dark, messy hair and popped another piece of gum in her mouth as she followed the map on her phone towards the Gosford Building. Not that she would have been getting any sleep, anyway, she thought. Part of her was glad – she couldn't face another sleepless night without knowing what the fuck was going on inside her head. She snorted at their disorganisation. The woman who had left the message had sounded apologetic. *So she should be, silly bitch*, thought Katie. First a change in venue and then a change in timing… At least she sounded hopeful – like Dr Locke had actually found a cure – and any inconvenience was worth that.

She rounded a corner as the dusk settled in, stopping in front of a large building built in the sixties, wondering why Dr Locke had decided to move things here, to this new place. She stood at the entrance and read the blue plaque on the wall, then checked the address again. This was the right place. She went inside.

A woman Katie did not recognise stood at a desk with some information leaflets spread out on it. "Hi," smiled the woman as she checked her clipboard. "Katie, is it?"

"Yeah," said Katie as the woman ticked her name off the list.

"Just go through," said the woman, still smiling. "First door on your left. Help yourself to something to drink."

Katie slid her sullen gaze from the woman as she pushed open the door. What was there to smile about? She hated fake cheeriness, and her lack of sleep meant her tolerance for it was at an all-time low.

Inside was a large windowless room with a small platform at one end. Another smiler – a man this time – directed her to the group of a hundred or so people sitting in the waiting area. Chairs were arranged around small tables with magazines, a water cooler, some large plants in pots. Drinks and nibbles were laid out on a table in the corner. She recognised a guy in his early twenties with a mop of ginger hair and a beard, from one of her sessions in the study. Like everyone else in the group he looked worn, like he hadn't slept in days. Behind her, the door closed.

"Hey," she said, sitting down next to him, propping her clumpy boot on the table to tie its lace.

"Hey," he said. "Katie, isn't it?"

"Yeah," she replied. "I'm sorry, I don't remember your name. I don't remember much these days."

"Oliver," he said. "Don't worry about it – I'm the same."

"Well, you *did* remember me," she said.

"Only because you kicked up a stink in the lab that time," he said.

She lowered her gaze, grinning, then looked him in the eye. "I was just stating my opinion."

"Whatever," said Oliver.

"I hope we get this over with soon," said Katie. "I can't face another onslaught from my parents when they find out I left the house again. They're so paranoid." She blew a gum bubble and watched it pop, then took out her phone. "Huh. No reception."

"Is that your dog?" asked Oliver, nodding to her phone.

For the first time, her face radiated warmth as she turned it round for him to see. The photo showed bright eyes staring out from under a shaggy brown coat. "Yeah," she said. "Rocco. Isn't he beautiful?"

"Totally."

She glanced around the room. "You know what's going on?" she asked.

He shook his head, then straightened up. "Looks like we're about to find out."

A door opened at the far end of the room and another smartly dressed woman Katie did not know, walked onto the platform. Her voice projected over the babble of quiet chatter, which fell to silence as all eyes turned to her.

"Good evening, ladies and gentlemen. Thank you for your

patience. I'm pleased to announce that Dr Locke has made an exciting breakthrough with regards to understanding the nightmares you have all been experiencing lately." A murmur rippled round the group. "He is keen to share this with you as he believes it will help resolve them. Again, apologies for the change in timing, but as we explained when we called you, he felt that it makes more sense to investigate what happens during sleep at night time. He has teamed up with another research group, based at a facility just across the city. It's a little tricky to find, so we thought it best to have everyone meet here. We have transport waiting to take you, so I would ask you to follow me." She turned, walking out through the far door. The crowd, uncertain to begin with, gradually began to follow.

Katie eyed her suspiciously. "What do you reckon?" she whispered.

"I'm past caring," said Oliver. "As long as they fix these feckin' nightmares, anything's worth a try."

Katie frowned, but followed him towards the door.

It was difficult to make out the details in the fading light, but they were in a backstreet lined by a high stone wall. Three shiny black coaches were parked up and the woman smiled as she stood by the door and ushered them on board. "Watch your step," she said sweetly. Katie glowered at her as she boarded, walking past the driver who was enclosed behind a glass panel, then took a seat at the back of the bus next to Oliver.

When the bus was full, the engines growled to life and the doors hissed closed. But the sound of hissing continued even after the doors clunked shut and the wheels rolled across the cobbles – a soft, persistent sound like a pipe leaking gas.

Katie turned to him, panic rising in her chest. "Oliver, something's wrong…"

She yawned, suddenly unable to keep her eyes open as the coach pulled onto the street. Her head slumped onto his shoulder, her eyes closing. Like the others, she did not see the black shutters glide down to obscure the windows, shutting them in from the outside world.

She did not see the masked man who watched from the shadows as the coaches pulled away, before he stole back inside the building. Carefully pressing the charges with their protruding wires into the soft putty bed of C-4, he placed them on the platform of the meeting room and set the timer, its red digits counting backwards as they peeled away the moments he had left to retreat. He pulled out a radio and said, "We're live."

*

The lights glowed from the seventh floor of the Innovatics Institute. The atrium was quiet as they took the elevator, Ben between Robert and Sattva, holding their hands. When they reached the mezzanine, they saw Cora pacing at the other side of the office, glancing through the glass window to the dark street below. Ron was typing on a computer next to Jack, while Locke sat with Zoe against the solid walls that divided the rooms. Zoe did not seem to register their arrival.

As Cora caught sight of Robert, she froze. He read her wariness as he approached, like she was coming face-to-face with a new kind of animal, one that might turn on her at any moment.

"It's alright," he said quietly, so that only she could hear. "I'm still me."

"What's going on, Robert?" she breathed.

"Hello, Cora." Sattva joined them and extended a handshake. As their hands touched and he held her eye, Cora hesitated. "I know you," she whispered.

Sattva just smiled then turned to meet Jack, Ron and Locke.

Ben appeared behind them and padded across to Zoe. "Mummy?" he said, quietly. Her eyes were on him but she showed no sign of recognition. "Mummy, this is my stone." He placed the stone in her palm. "The real one," he added. Her fingers ran over it, but she did not speak.

"Ben," said Locke as he leaned closer. "Your mummy's very tired."

"They got her, didn't they?" Ben said, squeezing her hand.

"Who?" said Locke.

"The nightmares. They only came at night, before. I think they want the stone."

Locke glanced at the others then turned back to Ben. "What does your stone do, Ben?" he asked.

Ben took it from his mother's limp hand. "It makes your thoughts bigger," he said. "And then they happen."

"Jack?" said Robert as he plugged Seth's flash-drive into the computer. "There's something you need to see." The image of a lumpy globe began to upload. "The CERN collisions?" he said as Jack watched Switzerland erupting its turquoise gravity wave that spread out across the landmasses. "They didn't just create new particles." He glanced at Jack. "You're looking at the spread of newly formed consciousness. That's why your team was getting such good results."

Jack and Ron stared at the screen as Cora and Locke joined them.

"Is this real?" breathed Jack, leaning closer, his eyes absorbing every detail of the image.

"New consciousness brings fresh thinking," said Sattva. "It hangs on the air like dew, waiting to condense on open minds."

Robert watched Jack's face. "Gravity attracts, electromagnetism binds and communicates, the strong and the weak forces bind and change. Thought," said Robert, "creates."

Jack looked like he was witnessing the birth of a new star; something of unspeakable majesty.

"The Fifth Force," said Robert. "The Universal Network. You were right, Jack. You were right."

Sattva nodded. "We interact with it through Thought and Consciousness, just as we interact with light through our eyes."

"Thought is our connection to the Field," said Robert. "It's how we communicate with it. But that fog out there?" he said, as he moved to the window that looked onto the outside world. "It's carrying something that scrambles the signal."

"Splitting our focus, weakening our intentions," added Sattva.

Jack was silent. He seemed vindicated and at the same time appalled.

"It's why your results suddenly dived," said Robert.

Approaching the window, Jack stared down at the grey soup swirling below. "What's in the fog?" he said.

"You don't want to know," said Robert. "But it's alive."

"It brings the nightmares," said Ben.

They turned to him. He was holding his mother's hand as she looked at him like he was a distant memory.

"And the stone...?" said Jack.

"The stone amplifies intention," said Robert. "Which is why we need to look after it."

The adults watched Ben as he placed the stone back in his mother's limp hand and turned it this way and that, but Jack's attention was drawn to the window again. He stepped back, his eyes fixed beyond it. "Robert..." he breathed.

Robert turned to the glass wall that separated them from the outside world. In the distance, the fog was rising over the rooftops and spires of the city, darkening too fast for dusk's surrender to nightfall.

One by one, the others turned to the window then began to back away.

"Get behind us," ordered Sattva. "Robert?"

Robert stepped up next to him, as the light seeped away from the world outside. A dankness crept into the air that seemed to shroud any sense of hope. It was suddenly cold.

"Clear your head," said Sattva. He turned to Ben. "Ben, we're going to need your help."

Ben lifted his stone from his mother's hand as he padded towards Sattva. The Eidolon crouched down beside him, his eyes gentle. Behind him the windows were darkening and beginning to tremble. "Ben, I want you to think with your stone. I want you to imagine you can see the sky outside, with all its stars. The moon is shining. Can you do that?"

Ben looked down at the stone in his hand and nodded.

Standing up, Sattva turned to others. "We need your focus too, all of you. Keep it pure. Focus your thoughts only on a clear sky. Nothing else, understand?"

Ben, flanked by Cora and Ron on one side and Jack and Locke on the other, held his stone in his small hands. Locke was eyeing the approaching storm. "Maybe we should go to a lower level," he said.

"No," said Robert. "We can't outrun this, Locke. Concentrate."

Ron glanced along the line of people facing the windows and let out a nervous laugh, as though someone, at any minute, was going to tell him this was all some sick joke. But as dark shapes glanced off the windows, glimpses of things more substantial, Ron's anxious smile faded. "What the fuck is that...?" he breathed.

A sudden shattering splintered the silence and he jumped as the spotlights in the ceiling fizzled and exploded, one by one, plunging the room into darkness. Locke let out a yell as he ducked, shielding his eyes from the showering shards of glass.

Blackness pressed in against the windows, and with it the sound of the wind and the feeling of despair. Robert felt his spirit plunge.

"Keep your focus!" shouted Sattva.

They stood, eyes closed, as the rattling on the windows crescendoed and oppression squeezed their minds. Robert felt the conflict in his very cells as they wavered on the edge of resignation; of giving in to a force that felt too powerful to contradict.

You think you can win this? That you're strong enough?

He dragged his mind back to the clear night sky.

What makes you think you're special?

Clear sky...

Why should you resist?

Clear sky... clear sky... it was fading... he couldn't remember what it looked like as blackness pressed in on his mind...

That's it. Give in, let us in...

A stuttering, barely formed memory of the moon appeared inside him...

It was still possible.

No.

Imperceptibly at first, a glow emerged in the darkness. Bluish-white and pure, it began to spread across the room, brightening in a slow, deliberate wave. Ben opened his eyes as it intensified and looked down to see his stone radiant like the heart of a star. Emerging from it were strands of light that connected everyone in the room. He smiled – it made thinking about the sky easier.

"It's working…" breathed Jack. Locke stumbled to his feet again, his eyes on the stone. The glow brightened into a fierce light. On the other side of the glass the mist seemed to hesitate, the things within it pulling back. Between them, a hint of moonlight appeared through the fog.

"That's it!" said Robert. "Keep it going…"

They closed their eyes again, swelled with the glimpse of their own power. The oppression of the room began to lift and their hearts expanded as the rattling windows stilled to silence.

And then, while the others stood with eyes closed, facing the receding mist, Zoe stood up. Slowly, she walked towards the windows. On the other side of the glass was one remaining Revenant, its head undulating gently as it watched her approach. It pressed a hand against the glass as she drew level with it. She reached out, folding her fingers around the handle, turning it…

"NO!" shouted Cora.

The window shot open and Zoe was thrown across the room, shattering the glass wall opposite as she struck it with the side of her head. Robert turned to see her slump to the floor, blood oozing from her temple and her ear, as the mist outside began reforming, billowing up like boiling tar.

A deafening repetitive shattering punched the air, as the windows along the side of the building blew out one by one and a fierce wind howled in.

"Keep your focus!" bellowed Sattva, he and Robert both still facing the dark tower of fog that had become a hurricane beyond the shells of the windows. Their bodies shook with the force of it, as they fought to stay upright. Cora crumpled to her knees, but still faced the storm.

As Ben turned to see Zoe unmoving on the floor, the stone fell from his hand. It lay there, its white brilliance dimming, as he abandoned it and scrambled on his hands and knees towards his mother. "Ben!" Cora opened her eyes and bolted after him.

Zoe's chest did not move and she stared with unseeing eyes as he sat on the floor, holding her limp hand in his, tears running down his cheeks as the wind tore around them and the light in the room drained away. Behind them, the stone's glow faded and faltered then went out. Blackness engulfed the room.

Cora reached for Ben in the darkness and he wrapped his arms around her neck. She shielded him as much as she could from the things that ripped and howled around them, as the ferocity of the storm reached new heights. As they huddled together with their eyes squeezed shut, Cora cradling Ben's head, the wind screamed in their ears and the building groaned and shook, straining to stay upright.

Fumbling, Robert's hands searched the floor for the stone's smooth surfaces as the hurricane screeched round the room. A vice gripped his chest and he could not tell if it was the panic inside or the squeeze of the storm around him. A glint of something – the last embers of a tiny dying star – caught his eye. He lunged for it as something dark foreboding swept towards him, like an eel diving for prey.

Repelled by a sudden unseen force, Robert felt himself thrown across the room as something else intervened. Looking up, he saw Sattva's shadow illuminated almost imperceptibly at the boundary between his body and the air by a translucent blue haze, the static between worlds. Sattva picked up the stone as the Revenants encircled him, their shifting forms undulating, poised; waiting.

Jack, Ron and Locke lay face-down, shielding themselves from the terror as Cora and Ben clung to one another, trembling, Cora's eyes still shut, tears spilling down Ben's cheeks. "She won't remember me," he sobbed softly. Cora squeezed him harder.

Robert's eyes were on Sattva. A glow rose from the heart of the stone, spreading to blend with Sattva's being and the Revenants halted their advance. Robert turned to the night. Against the clouds, the mist was brewing, seething again…

Something else was coming.

A sudden flash of red heat – an explosion from outside – the building shook and chunks of concrete flew through the streets, ammunition for the storm…

"Get down!"

Through the whirlwind of darkness and flying debris, Robert found his face to the floor. When he looked up, he glimpsed armed men in black webbing, their faces and hands behind dark balaclavas and gloves, as they jumped through the broken glass frames from the mezzanine. Black boots pounded through the room as the storm raged, but he lost sight of them as the darkness thickened. A scream pierced the tempest and Robert's blood chilled.

Cora...

Frantically scrambling towards her, Robert felt his way in the blackness, his palms bleeding on the shards of glass that littered the floor, his chest constricted in panic as he was met by nothing but emptiness.

Behind him a blue light swelled, radiating out in a charged haze across the room. He turned to Sattva as the circle of Revenants closed in on him. The light from Sattva's being was beginning to fade but the old Eidolon's gaze was on Robert. They locked eyes. Displaced by an ominous silence, the wind dropped. Time stood still and all sounds fell away in the tenderness of his gaze.

No, breathed Robert.

In his eyes and the ghost of his smile, Robert saw Sattva's eternity.

"Disappear," ordered Sattva. As the circle of Revenants consumed him, he lifted his arm and the faint light of a fading star arced across the room. Robert reached for the stone as it landed, absorbing it in his fading substance.

*

In the deep silence that remained, the storm's dark tentacle withdrew, snaking back to the mother-cloud. It rumbled as it receded to the northwest, trailing the darkness in its wake. As the dusk-sky edged in and the moon and the city glow cast enough light to see, Robert's substance flooded back into him. He looked around the shattered room. Broken furniture and splintered glass lay strewn in the aftermath under a shroud of deathly stillness. Locke was helping Ron to his feet. In the distance, sirens approached, blaring their out-of-sync warnings.

Only Robert, Locke and Ron were left.

*

A single light bulb hung from a long wire in the ceiling and did little to dispel the dimness of the large damp room. Its ceiling and walls were metal, but the dampness was in the fabric of the air, not the structure of the frame. Dust and the smell of something dead hovered in the ether. A shaft of moonlight peeped through the crack in the open door, uncertain if it should proceed.

Sitting in a chair beneath the light bulb in the middle of the empty space, was a monk. His hands were tied on his lap, his eye bruised and swollen, the stain of his blood blending with his red robes.

Victor Amos sat opposite, his legs crossed, his hands loosely clasped on his lap. To him, it was like meeting an old friend.

"It has been a long time, Tenzin Chodron," he said. "How were your lives?"

Tenzin watched him, but said nothing.

"I have something of yours," said Amos. "At least it was, once." He reached into his pocket and removed the mandala. He turned it over, his fingers caressing its surfaces. It did nothing to his touch but sat old and silent in his palm. Tenzin's eyes stayed on him.

"You know what I want," said Amos. "And you're going to help me get it."

Tenzin studied him, his expression like a calm pool of water. Eventually he spoke. "I have no attachments. Not to this body, not to the stone, not even to my mind." He smiled at Amos through bloodshot eyes. "I know the eternity of things."

Amos sighed. He stood up and walked to the door, looking out beyond the warehouse to the dusty barren land beyond. He closed his eyes and breathed in. A part of him felt pity, but that was always the way, and it never lasted long. He reached for the handle and the door swung shut, snapping out the moonlight.

*

Robert stood trembling, his face and hands scratched from shards of glass, his beard blood-soaked. He staggered to the frame of the window that opened over the street, steadying himself on the twisted metal. Red and blue lights scored the air in flashes from somewhere below and the sound of sirens wailed and crescendoed, competing with the high-pitched trill of alarms. It all faded into insignificance.

All he heard was Cora's scream; all he saw was Sattva's sacrifice.

Locke laid a hand on his shoulder. "We'll find them," he said.

As Robert's fist closed round the stone, he looked down at it. When his voice cleared the ache in his chest, he breathed, "I know we will."

*

The phone beeped. Max picked it up, listening with his eyes shut, reassembling his thoughts as he stirred from his sleep.

"What the hell do you think you're doing?" Emily's voice – pissed off.

"What?"

"How dare you go public."

"What are you talking about?"

"Publishing? When we're this close? What were you thinking?"

"Emily, stop. Send me whatever you're talking about then phone me back."

He hung up and swung his legs over the side of the bed, pinching the bridge of his nose. Opening his laptop, he rubbed his eyes and yawned as he waited for it to boot up.

A ping alerted him to her message, and he clicked on the attachment – a newspaper article:

Physicist Linked to Espionage Racket – by Max Guthrie, Freelance Journalist

Former British physicist, Robert Strong, has been identified as one of the leading members of Sipherghast, an underground organisation which trades scientific information. Strong, who goes by the alias Damien Volker, is suspected of trafficking sensitive information for large sums of money in collaboration with General Jason de Vrise, a former military commander. Several high-profile incidents have been linked to the organisation whose whereabouts remain unknown...

Max was on his feet as the phone rang and Emily's voice said,

"Three international newspapers, Max? Do you realise what you've done?"

"I didn't write this," he said.

There was a pause. "Well, who did then?"

"I don't know," said Max. His phone beeped as another call came through. "Hold on, let me take this..." he said, changing lines. "Josh?" He listened, absorbing the words. "When?" He hung up. Throwing on some clothes, he set off into the night.

Sirens wailed in the distance and the closer he drew, the more aware he became of the sinking sensation in his gut. The street ahead was closed. He abandoned his car as close as he could and walked. Emergency vehicles clogged up the road, their lights casting red and blue pulses into the darkness. Ahead of him on a street corner, a news crew were filming under bright lights, as smoke from the street behind rose into the air. The reporter faced the camera, her expression grave, as flashes of neon lit up her hair.

"A police spokesperson confirms that no live casualties have been found. The Synthetic Telepathy program was hosting a meeting here this evening at the Gosford Building, where it is thought that a gas leak sparked the explosion. Over a hundred people may have been involved in the incident, which occurred just as a freak storm hit Edinburgh, damaging several buildings, including the Innovatics Institute. Emergency services have begun working to control..."

Max stole past the crew and edged closer to the scene. His eyes were not on the decimated building but on the alleyway next to it where three figures made their way through the shadows.

*

The large van rumbled over the uneven ground and Cora winced as the back of her head hit the cold metal frame of the inside of the vehicle. "Ben?" she said. "Are you okay?" She could not see for the black hood over her head. Her wrists were scored by the handcuffs which bound them behind her back and her ankles ached from being shackled together. She had lost track of time, but the sounds of the city were long gone. There were no windows in the back of the van, only a feeble glow which emanated from the flat light in the ceiling.

"My wrists hurt," said Ben. He was sitting on the bench opposite, his arms tied in front of him by a rope. The two men on either side of him were masked behind balaclavas, dark clothes and black gloves; pistols strapped to their sides.

"It's okay, Ben," she said. "We're going to be okay."

"His name is Ben." The guard's voice had the quality of gravel. There was no warmth in the words, rather the sense that he now possessed something of value.

"Don't you touch him," hissed Cora.

"Or?" asked the guard.

"I swear, I'll kill you." Her voice was quiet and low.

He reached to the side of the seat, pulled out an iron bar and jabbed her in the gut. She groaned and doubled forward as the smaller guard looked on in silence.

"Don't!" shouted Ben. "Leave her alone!"

"It's a long journey," said the smaller guard. His voice was a flat monotone, like he had deliberately ironed the emotion out of it. "Save your breath." As the road rumbled on beneath them, his eyes stayed on Cora.

"I need to pee," said Ben in a small voice.

"Hold it in a bit longer," said the larger guard. "We'll be stopping soon."

"I can't," said Ben. "I need to pee."

"For Christ's sake, let him go," said Cora.

The smaller of the two guards got up and banged a closed fist on the metal partition which separated them from the driver. As the vehicle lurched to a stop, he leaned across Cora, his hand on the metal wall of the van behind her, his mouth inches from her ear. "I told you to be quiet," he whispered. He removed her hood and she blinked in the limp light. His gaze took in her face and her body. "Take him outside," he said quietly, his eyes still on her. "This won't take long."

The larger guard grabbed Ben's arm and pulled him onto his feet.

"Cora?" said Ben, his voice trembling.

Cora steadied her breathing. "It's okay Ben. You go and pee. It's okay."

The larger guard opened the rear door and moonlight spilled in as he stepped onto the road. "Move," he said.

Ben stood rooted to the spot. A damp patch spread down his trouser leg.

"It's okay, Ben, you go on," said Cora. "I'll be okay."

Ben shuffled towards the door, his head hung low, then jumped down from the van.

Behind him, the guard watched Cora as he took off his gloves and loosened his belt. His eyes – one green, one brown – held hers. She didn't need more of his masked face to see the look of a man who had decided, with merciless intent, the course of time's next few moments. She looked back, unblinking, staring through his outer shell, past the violence and isolation into what lay within.

In that instant, everything changed. It was as though she was no longer herself; that she was detaching from her body, or that something greater than her small existence was moving her aside. The part of her that was afraid fell away, dissolving into immense stillness. She saw that she was beyond fear, beyond anything that could happen to her. It was not who she was. Whatever happened to her now, she was not that.

When he was close enough for her to smell his sweat, still she did not look away. Blinking, he dropped his gaze like he had stared too long at the sun. He shifted his focus onto the metal behind her, fumbling with his button. What happened then, she could not rationalise, but the world faded as she felt a surge of energy course through her, like she had been picked up by a tidal wave that held her completely still. She became the space for it, the vessel through which it flowed, its iridescence a shimmering current that was every colour and no colour in one, blending with him until there were no boundaries, just its vibrant, alive stillness. The wave of her small existence, as she had always thought it to be, was only a surface ripple to the ocean that was all. That ocean resonated within her, as her, beyond her, and she felt it extend to him, as compassion. Whether it was she who spoke or the stillness that had taken residence inside her, she did not know. "You're afraid."

He met her gaze, the aggression in his eyes faltering as though someone else looked out through them. He staggered, backing away until he hit the opposite side of the van.

"What the... Jones?" The other guard's voice, from outside. "*Jones!* Get out here!"

Breathing hard, unable to look at her now, Jones stuffed away his limp dick and zipped up. He swung open the door, clattering it off the back of the van and stumbled onto the road. Cora's breath shuddered from her and with it the stillness. Fear flooded in, in its place, trembling through every nerve fibre into every cell. She sat shaking uncontrollably.

*

Jones stood on the tarmac, tense, his fists clenching and unclenching. The larger guard was standing a few feet from the van, which was parked up on the empty unlit road. Moonlight bathed the field of wheat to one side which undulated in a soft breeze, beneath strands of fog drifting on the air, echoes of the strangled city.

"He was right here," said the larger guard, staring at the tarmac as he paced. "I swear, right in front of me. Then he just... he just—" He picked up the rope that lay on the road as the driver appeared from the front of the vehicle.

"What?" Jones spat. "You *lost* him?"

"No! I... he vanished. He literally disappeared—"

"Bullshit, Ripley. You lost him you *fucking* idiot..." Jones grabbed the front of Ripley's shirt and twisted it hard, then pushed him away as he released his grip.

Ripley staggered backwards. "Jesus, Jones! I swear I didn't lose him..."

Jones turned sharply and jumped into the back of the van. A moment later he reappeared, dragging Cora down the step onto the road. "Kneel down," he said. She dropped to her knees.

"Ben?" called Jones. "Ben! If you come back now, I won't hurt her."

Silence. The soft breeze rippled through the field.

"Don't come back, Ben!" shouted Cora. "Run away, you hear me? Run away!"

Jones struck her face with the back of his fist and she fell sideways onto the tarmac. He grabbed her shirt, dragging her upright again, then pulled out his pistol and dug it into her temple. She swallowed her breath in gasps, choking on her fear.

"Ben!" shouted Jones, scanning the field. "I will kill her, Ben. Do you want me to kill her? Do you?" His hand was trembling.

Ripley shot a sideways glance at him. "Easy, Jones," he breathed.

A rustling came from the long blades of grass a few feet away, their stalks bending to an unseen presence.

"There," breathed the driver.

Jones nodded to him and then to Ripley. *Go.*

They stepped slowly into the field, their pistols drawn, closing in on the origin of the sound. Gently, Ripley teased back the blades with his free hand revealing a patch of flattened grass. Nothing else was there. His eyes scanned the swaying stalks beyond and he nodded to the driver who pulled out a flashlight and stole deeper into the field, the beam sweeping across the dark crop like a tentacle of light feeling for prey.

*

Ben stood very still. He had watched them approach – they were hard to miss, lighting up like beacons in the darkness. The driver's colour was a harsh red, solid and impenetrable, and Ben felt it push him away even when he was still on the road. Ripley's, however, was softer – the amber hue the sky turns in the dusk. He waited for Ripley to come close enough then, when he looked away across the field, Ben seized his chance and stepped inside him.

It was like walking through space, but underwater. Muffled breathing echoed in his ears, like it wasn't his own. It wasn't, he remembered. He watched as Ripley's mind thrashed around like shark robbed of water, observing it with detachment and waiting for it to succumb. All he had to do was keep his attention on his own self, and eventually Ripley's mind would lie down. It was easy – his self had a sound. It was a clear steady sound, like a singing bowl that held the same eternal tone of silence, a sound he could feel more than hear. Its resonance was always there, but inside another, he could hear it as the backdrop against which the other's noisy static played out. Whilst he felt the fight in every fibre of Ripley's body, he stayed detached, tuned only to his sound. When the shark suffocated in air and stilled, Sonam Dorje looked out through Ripley's eyes.

"*RIPLEY!*" Jones was bawling at him from the road. "Are you deaf? Where is he?"

Ripley stood motionless, observing Jones' ranting, then turned and walked slowly, deliberately, towards him.

*

Cora glanced up and saw Ripley approach, but saw no sign of Ben. Ripley pulled his mask from his head, revealing cropped fair hair, a crooked nose and a set jaw. He dropped the mask on the ground as he advanced. In the distance, the driver's flashlight carved up the darkness of the field, back and forth.

"What the hell are you—" began Jones. His words fell to silence just as Cora registered the change. *His aura...* Rather than the haze of a burning ember, she saw it was green; sharp and more defined. Then there were his eyes. Not the dull brown they had been moments before, they now shone with an iridescence that seemed unearthly, as though they focused light from a distant place.

Without breaking stride, Ripley held up his pistol, stopping only when it rested between Jones' eyes. "Let her go," he said quietly. His voice was layered, as though it echoed or harmonised with itself, as though two voices spoke, their unison displaced by only the slightest fraction of time.

Jones didn't move.

Ripley's index finger curled round the trigger and Jones lowered his weapon. "Drop it," said Ripley.

The pistol clattered onto the road.

"Unshackle her."

"Ripley..." began Jones.

Ripley pushed the pistol deeper into Jones' forehead, blanching the skin. Fumbling, Jones unhooked the clip from his belt and lifted the keys in front of him as he tried to select the right one. Ripley repositioned the pistol onto Jones' temple as they moved behind Cora, Jones' fingers slipping as he forced the key into the handcuffs.

They burst open and her arms fell to her sides, then she felt the rush of blood to her feet as he released her ankle shackles.

Catching Cora's eye, Ripley said, "Pick up the weapon. And stand up. You," he said, turning to Jones. "Stay on your knees."

Cora did as he said. Instinctively, she levelled the weapon at Jones' heart.

"If he moves, shoot him." With a swift movement, Ripley cuffed Jones' arms behind his back and shackled his feet, leaving him bound on his knees on the cold road. "Can you drive?" he said to Cora. She nodded. "Check the vehicle for keys."

"Where's Ben?" she asked.

"Do it," said Ripley.

Cora walked hastily to the driver's window, seeing the bunch of keys dangling from the ignition. Her heart was hammering inside her chest, her mind not daring to think. She glanced at the field as she returned, where the distant flashlight still swept back and forth. When she reached the back of the van, Ripley's eyes were on Jones. "How well do you remember your lives?" he asked.

"What?" breathed Jones.

"Remember this one, because I will remember you."

Jones was shaking, beginning to cry, as Cora stared at Ripley. "The keys?" he asked.

"In the ignition. Where's Ben?" she said again.

"He's with me," said Ripley. "Get in the driver's seat."

"What?" she said.

Ripley turned, staring deep into her, and she drew breath as though her mind had been slapped. In that moment nothing made sense, and she could not have explained it to anyone, but she knew. "What was the first thing I said to you?" she breathed.

"We don't have time for—" began Ripley.

"The first thing!"

"'That's a nice owl'," said Ripley.

She pulled back, digesting the distortion in reality.

"Now can we go?" said Ripley.

"Almost," she whispered. She drew her gaze from Ripley and turned to face Jones. He looked up at her, his chest heaving silent sobs, but at that moment, compassion for him was a distant memory. She snapped a boot deep into his groin. He groaned and folded, his face smacking the tarmac. The pistol trembled in her hand as she aimed it at his crotch.

Ripley's hand came to rest on her arm. "Who is the one doing this?" he asked quietly. "And who will have to live with it?"

As though he had turned on a light inside her mind, she saw Jones for what he was, as he quivered at her feet. She lowered the weapon in silence.

Jones blurted out a sob, like he had been holding his breath for a lifetime, and it echoed in the night.

The flashlight in the field snapped towards them and froze.

Grabbing Cora's arm, Ripley steered her behind the vehicle to the driver's door. "Get in," he said. She scrambled inside, glimpsing the beam through the passenger window as it shook across the field, coming for the van. Ripley jumped in behind her.

A shot rang out. "Start up!" she shouted.

Ripley stared at the wheel in front of him. "I don't know how!"

"What?" she said. "Move over!" She scrambled across his knee as they swapped seats. "And lock the door!" Ripley punched the lock and jumped as a *thud* landed on the passenger window and a fist and the driver's masked face appeared. The door handle rattled.

Jones was shouting instructions from behind the van. The flashlight pulled back and the silhouette of a pistol replaced it, pointing at Cora.

Time slowed down as she crouched for cover. "*Please...*" she breathed, turning the key. The engine growled and she stamped on the accelerator, as a shot rang out and the window shattered. The tyres screeched on the gravel and the van swerved wildly along the darkened road. From the side mirror, she watched the chasing figure become smaller as the van gained speed.

*

Cora stole a glance at Ripley who was staring ahead to where the headlights bored holes in the blackness. Branches loomed up on either side of the van like skeletal fingers grasping for them as they raced past.

"Is this real?" she said. "I mean, you're really… Ben?"

He breathed out slowly, then said. "I'm the essential nature that you know as Ben, yes."

"How did you… you know…"

He shrugged. "It's just something I can do. As long as there's not too much resistance."

"What about Ripley?"

"He's still here, but it's like he's asleep."

She paused, listening to the hum of the van on the road, then said, "Can you read his mind?"

"It's easier if I don't," he replied. "It risks waking him. I'll have to leave him soon, though. There's only so long you can dwell in another body uninvited."

"Oh." She didn't want to think about that too closely. "How do you know he won't come after us?"

"I don't," he said. "But I hope that something in him will understand. Once you blend with someone, a part of you never really leaves – you're always entangled, more or less."

"Right."

She sat in a surreal silence. Then, like flipping a light-switch, her mind came to its senses – here she was, driving a stolen van down a dark road in the middle of nowhere, in the middle of the night with an armed man who claimed to be possessed by the essence of a six-year-old boy. She came closer to murdering another human than she had ever done before (although he had almost raped her, her mind reminded her), and Ben was nowhere to be seen. Whatever thought processes had bought her into all this abandoned her now – her mind was frozen. *Jesus Christ, am I crazy? What the hell was I thinking?* Panic rattled up inside her and she gripped the wheel, afraid to look at him.

From the corner of her eye, she became aware that he kept reaching for his head. He pulled at his collar, like he was finding it difficult to breathe. "He's beginning to fight," said Ripley. "I have to get out of him. Quickly."

She slammed on the brakes and lifted the pistol, pointing it with a shaking hand at his head. "Get out," she breathed.

"Cora…" Ripley reached for his temple, wincing. "Please what are you…"

"I'm going back for Ben," she said. "Get out!"

"Cora, I am—"

"*Now!*"

He fumbled for the handle and stepped out onto the road beside a dark clump of trees and fallen trunks. Still pointing the shaking pistol at him she reached over and yanked the door shut, then, fumbling with the gearstick, rammed it into reverse and stamped on the accelerator. The tyres screeched and smoked as the van sped backwards. She spun it round, facing back the way they had come, and centred it in the middle of the road, her foot poised over the accelerator. Had she not glanced in the side mirror, she may have missed it, but what she saw when she took one last look, stopped her. A swell of light was coming from the clump of trees, as though a million emerald fireflies emerged at once from the amber glow of a man. They hovered on the air before coalescing into space – forming the shape of a small boy.

"Oh my god," she breathed. She sat rooted to the spot, watching his small frame inside his hoodie, next to the man who towered over him.

Slowly, Cora opened the door. Stumbling onto the tarmac, she stood motionless. She felt like she was entering into a dream, only the dream was real. *This is real.*

Ben walked towards her, his pace slow, his steps faltering, as though his body was weakened; that these were its last steps. He stopped then slumped to the ground.

"Ben," she breathed as she ran towards him. Ripley raised his eyes to her as he raised his pistol. She stopped dead.

The world was suspended. There was no panic this time. There was no thought. There was only the road and Ben and the man. She found herself taking a step, then another, her eyes fixed on Ripley's. She was aware of her own breathing, too fast, and the clamminess of her skin, but she attached no meaning to it. It simply was. Observing Ripley raise his left hand to support his grip on the pistol, it meant nothing to her as she moved forward in the void of space, steady and sure. Whatever happened now, it would be the right thing; it was a certainty, or absence of doubt. When she reached Ben, and crouched down to pick up his limp body, Ripley adjusted his stance and his aim. She stood up, facing him in the moonlight, unmoving. If he was going to shoot her, he could shoot her face-on. She waited.

He lowered his pistol in silence and she turned and carried Ben back to the van. As she reached the door, he blinked, squinting at the world, and wrapped his arms around her neck. She placed him carefully on the passenger seat as he mumbled something unintelligible, then she swung the van round, passing Ripley, his eyes to the ground, his pistol by his side, as they drove off into the night.

*

Amos sat at his desk, Max Guthrie's press report laid out in front of him. He was motionless apart from the rapid rise and fall of his chest, and the clenching of his right fist. He reached for the intercom. "Bring me Mr Y."

Lifting his gaze from the words on the page to the image which dominated the wall, he stood up and walked towards it – a flock of starlings swooping and diving in silent accord on a red sky. They moved as one being, as though each responded to the same thought at the same instant; murmuration.

A voice from the intercom broke the silence. "Sir? Mr Y is not in his quarters. His things are gone."

Amos stared ahead, his eyes no longer seeing his surroundings, as cold fury dissolved the tranquillity of the sunset, like acid dissolving living tissue. "Find him and bring him to me."

*

Three men made their way from the debris of the smoking building and the chaos of the storm's aftermath. Moving like ghosts through the dank stillness of the fog that submerged the world, they kept to the shadows and the alleyways. As they turned into an arched stone passageway, their footsteps echoing on the cobbles, a figure limped out ahead of them, blocking the way. Silhouetted against the haze of grey light beyond the arch, its burly form was wrapped in an oversized coat which flapped almost to the cobbles. The three men froze.

Robert peered into the dimness. "Crowley?"

"You look like you could use some help, if you're not too pigheaded to admit it," said Crowley. The growl of his voice echoed in the dank tunnel.

"He probably is," said another voice. Robert squinted into the shadows. There, propped on one shoulder, arms folded, against the stone wall of the passageway, was another figure. Robert did not need to see his face to feel his presence. As the figure moved to stand next to Crowley and Robert's eyes adjusted to the dimness, he recognised the leather bands around his wrists and the markings on his neck – a spider's web tattoo.

"*Balaquai?*" breathed Robert.

Ron and Locke glanced at Robert, uncertain; waiting. As Robert turned to hold Crowley's eye, a faint smile touched his lips. He nodded.

"Right then," said Crowley. "You'd better come with us."

ABOUT THE AUTHOR

Libby McGugan has had a lifelong fascination with the boundary between science and the human spirit - working as an emergency medicine doctor gave her a grounding in science, and witnessing the strength of the human spirit in the face of seemingly insurmountable challenges made her question what else might be going on. She was nominated Best Newcomer in the 2014 British Fantasy Awards for her first novel, *The Eidolon,* which came to her following the death of her father, Tom, in 2007. Her short story, *The Game Changer,* was published in Jonathan Oliver's anthology, *Dangerous Games.* She is a student and teacher of understanding the inside-out nature of human experience and is constantly surprised by how life seems to know what it's doing.

Facebook - libbymcgugan

For her work around wellbeing, see – io-wellbeing.com

Printed in Great Britain
by Amazon